CRAZY
in LOVE *at*
THE LONELY HEARTS
BOOKSHOP

Annie Darling lives in London in a tiny flat, which is bursting at the seams with teetering piles of books.

Her two greatest passions in life are romance novels and Mr Mackenzie, her British Shorthair cat.

Also by Annie Darling:

The Little Bookshop of Lonely Hearts
True Love at the Lonely Hearts Bookshop

CRAZY *in* LOVE *at* THE LONELY HEARTS BOOKSHOP

ANNIE DARLING

HarperCollins*Publishers*

HarperCollins*Publishers*
1 London Bridge Street
London SE1 9GF

www.harpercollins.co.uk

Published by HarperCollins*Publishers* 2018
1

A catalogue record for this book
is available from the British Library

ISBN: 978-0-00-827564-8

Typeset in Bembo by Palimpsest Book Production Ltd, Falkirk, Stirlingshire

Printed and bound by CPI Group (UK) Ltd, Croydon CR0 4YY

Dedicated to Mr Mackenzie,
the smooshiest cat in all the world.

CHAPTER

'She was a wild, wicked slip of a girl.'

It was morning. Apparently. Weak shafts of sunlight were doing their best to penetrate the gloom of the little flat above the Happy Ever After bookshop.

Nina O'Kelly cursed the sun streaming feebly in through her bedroom windows then cursed herself for not closing the curtains the night before. In fact, she was amazed that she was in her own bed, because she had absolutely no memory of how she'd got home.

She wasn't hungover. Not exactly. Fragile, sleep deprived, and the sound of her flatmate, Verity, walking from her bedroom to the kitchen sounded like an elephant had been let loose, though generally Verity was quite light-footed.

With an unhappy whimper Nina turned over. Another ten minutes couldn't hurt. Maybe fifteen. Perhaps she should open one eye very slowly just to check the time, or perhaps she should keep both eyes closed and just doze ever so lightly . . .

There was a gentle knock on the door. 'Nina? It's nine o'clock. It takes you an hour to do your make-up alone,' Verity cooed softly. 'I'm coming in. I want feet on the floor.'

Nina wasn't fooled by the gentle cooing; Verity was not a woman to be messed with. One morning when it had been much later than this and Nina was still in bed, Verity had shocked her awake with a glass of water. It had played havoc with Nina's hair.

Though every muscle in her body protested, Nina levered herself to a sitting position and swung her legs round so that when Verity opened the door, all ten of Nina's toes, adorned with a nail polish in a jaunty aqua green, were touching the floor.

The inevitably pained expression on Verity's face was a blur to Nina who still couldn't fully open her eyes. 'I'm up,' she grunted, taking the mug of coffee that Verity handed her and opening her mouth so Verity could shove a piece of toast in it, because she was actually the best flatmate ever.

Then, because she was a skilled multi-tasker, Nina drank her coffee while having a shower and not getting her hair wet. Her hair was currently baby pink and arranged in Marilyn Monroe-style pin-curled waves. Each Monday and Friday lunchtime Nina went to the old-fashioned nana hairdresser around the corner to have a shampoo and set under a hood drier that was twice as old as she was. Very little could wither her hair between visits. All it needed was a little teasing at the roots and a generous spritz of Elnett, and Nina was good to go.

Well, not quite good to go. She hadn't taken her make-up off before she'd collapsed into her bed and because time was marching on – Verity had already gone downstairs to the shop to start her working day, though technically they weren't on the clock until ten and it was only nine fifty-seven – Nina decided to use yesterday's make-up as her base.

A generous dollop of foundation, primer and ungodly amounts of concealer, then she got to work with liquid eyeliner, mascara and then more liquid eyeliner. A sweep of blusher and then several coats of deep-red lipstick, and Nina had done all she could do with her face. Not that it was a bad face. Nina had all the regular features – eyes, nose, mouth, chin arranged in the usual order – and now she had transformed herself into a vision of retro glamour.

There was just time to don her hated grey work T-shirt with 'Happy Ever After' scrawled across her chest in a pink cursive script. It was very hard to dress around the T-shirt: frocks were a no-no, Nina rarely did jeans, but she wriggled into a tight pencil skirt, slipped on her day heels and by the time she tripped down the stairs into the shop, she was only . . .

'Fifteen minutes late!' complained Posy, the owner of Happy Ever After, in an unnecessarily loud voice. 'You live *above* the shop. You have a ten-second commute, so how come you're *still* fifteen minutes late?'

'Obviously, my body clock runs fifteen minutes later

than yours,' Nina pointed out. 'I can't be responsible for my biological needs. Talking of which . . . coffee!' It was a plaintive moan. 'Be a love and nip to the tearooms and bring me back the largest mug of coffee possible.'

'I am a love but I'm also your boss,' Posy said sternly, but she never could pull off stern. Her softly pretty face just wasn't made that way. 'Just the one sugar?'

'Better make it two,' Nina decided. 'As it is, I wouldn't expect too much from me until after lunch, Pose.'

Posy shook her head in despair as she headed through the arch that led to a series of anterooms, which in turn led to the tearooms from where the heavenly scent of freshly brewed coffee and cakes just out of the oven wafted through the shop.

And what a lovely shop it was. Happy Ever After was the only bookshop in Britain, maybe even the world, dedicated to books about love. 'Your one-stop shop for all your romantic fiction needs' as it said on the bookmarks Nina tucked into every book she sold.

Even before she lived above the premises, Happy Ever After had always felt like home to Nina, and from where she was perched on a stool behind the counter, she surveyed her domain. In the centre of the main room were three sofas in varying stages of sagging decay arranged around a table heaped with books. There was a wall of new releases and bestsellers, the top shelves accessed by a rolling ladder, while the opposite wall had yet more books and a series of vintage display cabinets full of romantic fiction-related gifts, from mugs to cards, T-shirts and jewellery.

Then on either side were the arches which led to a series of smaller rooms, all stuffed from floor to ceiling with yet more books. It was the kind of shop where you could spend an hour browsing contentedly – although at that moment, Nina was far from content.

'That coffee you made me this morning, not that I'm complaining, was as weak as a kitten's fart,' she shouted to Verity, who was at her desk in the office at the back of the shop, behind the counter. The door was only slightly ajar, hence the need to shout. 'Is Tom in today?'

'It sounds quite a lot like complaining to me, and no Tom today, he phoned to say he was having a footnotes emergency with his dissertation,' Verity called out. 'And Posy has a meeting with her accountant this morning, so you'll have to hold the fort single-handed.'

'Yeah, well, if it gets really busy, you'll just have to help in the shop.' Nina was going to be very firm about that. Verity couldn't skulk in the office and leave Nina to completely fend for herself if they were suddenly overrun by customers. Though – she squinted out of the shop's bow-fronted windows – it was a damp, grey Tuesday morning and so Nina hoped they'd be quiet until after she got her second wind.

From experience, when she was this fragile, her second wind didn't usually make an appearance until she'd consumed at least three baked goods and had a kill-or-cure fry-up for lunch. And there was Posy, back with Nina's coffee and a muffin the size of her head.

'Is that muffin for me?' Nina asked hopefully.

It was and it was studded with blueberries, which any fool knew were a superfood, so it was a very healthy muffin, Nina thought to herself as she stuffed huge chunks of it in her mouth and started to tackle the teetering pile of books waiting to be shelved that were on the counter in front of her.

'Don't get muffin fingers on them,' Posy warned but Nina had been eating cake and handling new books in a professional capacity for three years, so she ignored her employer.

It wasn't as if she were turning the pages. All she was doing was reading the back-cover blurbs so that when a customer came in and said that she was looking for a paranormal romance featuring a time-travelling, shape-shifting duke/werewolf and that it probably had a blue cover, then Nina would be able to point her in the right direction.

Once digested (the blurbs rather than the muffin), Nina separated them into different piles for easier shelving. Historical, Regency, which had its own section, Erotic, YA . . .

'What exactly are you doing?' asked a voice to Nina's left. It was a male voice. They didn't get many male voices at Happy Ever After and this wasn't Tom's world-weary tones or Posy's husband, Sebastian's haughty posh-boy drawl. It was a soft voice; polite, curious and yet it had a steely undertone that instantly made Nina bristle.

She turned to see a man *behind her counter*. He had red hair, an auburn-y, russet-y, Rita Hayworth shade of red that Nina had tried and failed to replicate on her own hair a few months before. To go with the hair he had pale skin liberally dotted with freckles, and green eyes, which admittedly were quite nice, but that wasn't important. What was important was that he was standing *behind her counter*.

'What am I doing?' Nina asked incredulously. 'What are *you* doing?'

'Observing,' the man said, glancing over at the small pile of erotic-romance novels that Nina had been looking at (she was pretty sure that at one point she'd said, 'Oooh! I love a threesome scene' out loud) and making a note on his iPad. 'Just pretend that I'm not here. You've done a pretty good job of it so far. I've been standing here for the last half hour.'

'You should have said something,' Nina protested. She felt . . . *violated*. She'd been sitting there stuffing her face with muffin, maybe even chewing with her mouth open, slurping her coffee, making lascivious comments about the books, and the whole time this random man had been standing there. 'Observing what? Observing *me*? There are laws about this sort of thing.'

'Actually, this is a public space and . . .'

Nina couldn't stand people who began a sentence with 'Actually . . .' when challenged. It meant that their argument was weak and that they were about to drop some more multi-syllable words at her.

'It's private property,' she snapped. 'You're here at the owner's invitation, and talking of which . . . POSY!' Bellowing like a Billingsgate fishwife wasn't enough. Nina was forced to jump down from her stool, always a tricky manoeuvre in a tight pencil skirt, to push open the office door as the flame-haired *usurper* made another note on his iPad. 'POSY! Some strange bloke is trespassing.'

The strange bloke muttered something under his breath, the pale skin beneath his freckles pinking up. 'I have every right to be here,' he said stiffly, and Nina was sure that he reminded her of someone but she couldn't think, for the life of her, who. Maybe that ginger bloke from last year's *Great British Bake Off*?

'Yeah, he does,' said Posy, sticking her head round the office door. 'This is Noah. Didn't I introduce you?'

'No, you didn't.' Nina swept another glance over this Noah. He was wearing a suit − a navy-blue suit, a white shirt and a narrow navy-blue tie. Honestly, who wore a suit *and* tie in this day and age? Apart from Posy's husband Sebastian, but at least he accessorised his suits with polka-dot hand-kerchiefs or brightly coloured socks. Not like this guy, who coordinated his suit with his tie. Why would anyone do that?

'Well, I'm pretty sure I did. I definitely introduced him to Very and it serves you right for being fifteen minutes late,' Posy said implacably. 'Noah's a business analyst. He's here to analyse the business. We did cover this in the staff meeting yesterday.'

'That was yesterday. Have you any idea how much vodka I've drunk since then? Anyway, you know the business side of the business isn't any of my business.'

Nina was genetically designed to tune out certain words like 'business' and 'analyst'. And also 'index-linked pension', 'slippers' and 'early night'.

'Nina!' Posy said with a sigh. 'You knew we were looking at ways to grow the business. Working smarter. Digital whatnots. All that jazz.'

Noah, the business analyst, that Nina was still pretty sure she hadn't been told about, had been silent during this exchange, but now he took a step forward.

'I'm just here to observe your best business practices,' he said, though Nina wasn't sure she had any of them. She just turned up, clocked in, sold some books then trooped upstairs to get ready to go out and blow her wages on boys, booze and um, something else beginning with b.

'It's very creepy to just stand there and watch someone when they obviously don't know you're there,' Nina persisted.

'I did say hello, but you were shouting about coffee so perhaps you didn't hear me,' Noah said. 'Anyway, it's been established that I'm Noah and you're Nina. Posy filled me in on the rest.'

'I did,' Posy said blandly, which could mean anything. It wasn't as if Nina had led a blameless life. Far from it. 'Nina, I've really got to go to the accountant's now. He gets very stroppy if I'm even a minute late.'

Nina was feeling very stroppy herself and maybe Noah got the message because when Posy left in a panicked scramble, he decided to relocate to the office. Verity, though quiet herself, was sure to take a very dim view of being quietly observed, but as Nina perched on a stool and waited for the first customer of the day, she could hear unsettling noises from behind her.

Verity was chattering away. Laughing. Once, even snorting with mirth. It was very unlike Verity, who rarely chattered, or laughed, or snorted with mirth in the presence of strangers. 'Can you believe that we still input stock into a ledger?' she giggled.

'You mean you write it down in a book?' Noah, the so-called business expert, asked incredulously.

'Yes, and then when we sell a book, we tick it off in the ledger.'

'I didn't notice a barcode scanner on the counter and your till . . . it belongs in a museum, doesn't it?'

Nina patted the old-fashioned till affectionately. Bertha was at least forty years old and a little temperamental. Her drawer tended to stick but there was a particular spot you had to thump when she did, and then she was right as rain.

'Lavinia – who owned Bookends, and left the shop to Posy, who turned it into Happy Ever After – was quite set in her ways,' Verity was explaining earnestly. 'Especially after her husband Perry died. She didn't like things that beeped, and I like that the shop is quite quaint and charming but . . . but . . .'

'But what?' Noah prompted. 'You can tell me. I'm just an observer. No judgement, no consequences.'

'Don't trust him!' Nina wanted to yell but at that moment the door opened, the bell tinkled and two women came into the shop, so she was forced to stop earwigging and pin a smile on her face. 'Welcome to Happy Ever After. Let me know if there's anything in particular you were looking for.'

The women were middle-aged and in sensible shoes, slacks and pac-a-macs, but Nina knew not to try and second guess any customer's reading preferences from their outward appearance.

'Vampire erotica?' One of the women queried, proving Nina's theory right.

'Erotica section is the end room on the right. Paranormal erotica on your left as you go in, then the vampire fiction will be on the top two shelves,' Nina told her. 'We've had a new book in last week by a woman called Julietta Jacobs about a vampire mafia boss. It's pure filth.'

'Oooh, sounds just my thing,' the woman said, and she and her friend went through the arch on the right.

Meanwhile Verity was still happily complaining to Noah about how rubbish the shop was. '. . . it all has to be inputted manually so everything takes three times as long as it should. Stocktaking, inventory, cashing up; it's a bit of a nightmare really.'

'Yeah, it doesn't sound very time-effective,' Noah said in a sympathetic voice even though he wasn't meant to be offering opinions.

Already Nina didn't like him and she had famously low standards when it came to men. Her scowl was interrupted by another customer; Lucy, a pretty woman who worked at the council offices round the corner, came through the door. She read a romance novel a day, three on the weekend. Nina worried that there might come a day when Lucy had read every romance novel ever published.

Not today though. 'Are those the new releases?' Lucy

asked, her eyes gleaming at the sight of the pile of books on the counter.

'They are,' Nina agreed. 'Have at 'em!'

Verity was giggling again – she hadn't been right since she fell in love a few months back – and Noah was murmuring again, but the bell was tinkling, more customers piling in, and Nina's hangover had abated enough that she felt well enough to leave her stool and actually venture onto the shop floor to help them.

CHAPTER

'She burned too brightly for this world.'

Noah and his infernal iPad left the shop before lunch, not to return. Nina hoped that he was done with his creepy, silent observing but when she got back from the accountants, Posy said that Noah would return the next day.

'He seems nice though, doesn't he?' she insisted. 'He's a friend of Sebastian's.'

'Really? Sebastian has friends?' Nina shook her head. Sebastian Thorndyke was many things: a digital entrepreneur, Posy's childhood nemesis and now recently wed husband, but he was also the Rudest Man in London and completely lacking any filter. The last time Nina had run into him, when she'd been debuting her new pink hair, Sebastian had taken one look at her neatly set, sherbet waves and sniggered.

'Torrid night of passion with a candyfloss machine, was it?' he'd asked.

As a result of that and many other insults, Nina couldn't imagine that Sebastian had many friends, but here was Posy, insisting that he did and that apparently this Noah was one of them. Maybe that was why Nina still had a nagging thought that she knew Noah from somewhere, even though she'd rather poke her eye out than hang out at boring techy things with Posy's husband. He certainly hadn't been at Posy and Sebastian's wedding, which had been a very small affair thrown together at three weeks' notice. 'They met at Oxford,' Posy said, her face going all melty as it did when she was thinking about Sebastian. 'Been friends ever since. Noah doesn't put up with any of Sebastian's nonsense. Don't you think he's a little bit sexy, in a nerdy way?'

'Ugh! No! He was wearing a tie!' Nina exclaimed with a shudder. 'And a suit. So not my type. I do bad boys. I don't do nerds.'

'Have you ever thought of going against type?' Verity asked out of the corner of her mouth because she was cashing up and if she got too distracted, she lost count.

'Why would I want to do that?' Nina asked. 'It would be like asking me to have brown eyes instead of blue. Or to stop being five foot six. I can't change the way I am.'

'Change is good,' Posy insisted as she picked up the books that had been discarded on the three sofas that dominated the centre of the main room and began to reshelve them. 'There's been lots of changes round here in the last few months and they've all been pretty positive.'

There was truth in this. Last summer, the old and ailing Bookends had become Happy Ever After with a new romance remit and colour scheme, and a reopened tearoom. Nina was much happier selling romance novels to mostly ladies than she had been not really selling anything much to the occasional punter who had infrequently visited the shop.

But in order for Bookends to become Happy Ever After, lovely Lavinia, their boss and mentor, had died and Nina missed her as much now as she did that awful morning a few months ago when she'd first heard the news. It was why their central display table was a little shrine to their much-loved friend. Each time Nina caught sight of Lavinia's favourite books stacked on it or caught the heady scent of Lavinia's favourite pink roses in the glass vase she'd bought from Woolworths in the sixties, she felt the same sweet piercing ache.

Also, Posy had gone from never dating (unless Nina bullied her into it) to marrying Lavinia's grandson, Sebastian, in the space of what felt like five minutes. Posy said that it had been building for years, but as far as Nina could tell, one minute Posy and Sebastian were shouting at each other as they usually did, the next they were plighting their troth at Camden Town Hall.

But in some ways that, too, had been a good change. Evidently Sebastian made Posy very happy. The frown that she'd always worn had been replaced by a slightly dazed smile and even better, she, and her younger brother Sam, had vacated the flat above the shop to live with Sebastian in Lavinia's house in a pretty garden square on the other side of Bloomsbury. Though Nina missed Sam dreadfully – he could always be persuaded to go on a chocolate run or fix her iPhone when the screen froze – Posy had offered her old flat to Nina and Verity rent-free.

Nina hadn't waited to be asked twice. Paying rent had taken up a huge chunk of her not-very-big bookseller's wages. Not to mention that Nina had been stuck out in Southfields in a houseshare with five other people, no lounge, and an infestation of silverfish in the kitchen that would not quit. It had been a hell of a commute, especially when the District Line was malfunctioning, which it did frequently. There had also been an awful lot of sleeping on friends' sofas after missing the last tube home.

So, the good changes and the bad changes just about balanced each other out. And some things never changed, like Nina waiting for Posy to finish reshelving and Verity to complete the cashing up, before she asked hopefully, 'Pub?'

Going to the pub after work was a time-honoured tradition, except that was another thing that had changed – and not for the better.

'I would . . .' Posy began then shook her head. 'But I really should get home. Sebastian's been away on a business trip and I haven't seen him for three whole days. We are still practically on our honeymoon.'

Nina didn't think that it was still a honeymoon if you'd married last June and it was now fricking February, but she decided it was wiser not to mention it. Instead she turned pleading eyes to Verity. 'Pub, Very?'

'I can't. I need a half-hour decompression lie-down then Johnny and I are going to a lecture about art deco at the Courtauld Institute,' Verity said, because one of the other changes was that Verity, *Verity*, a self-professed introvert, was besotted with her newish boyfriend, a posh architect called Johnny, and Nina hardly saw her. She'd much preferred it when Verity had been seeing an oceanographer called Peter Hardy who'd mostly been away oceanographing so Verity could often be persuaded to go to the pub.

'What's that? What's that I hear?' Nina cupped a hand to her ear. 'Oh yes. It's the sound of wedding bells breaking up my old gang.'

'I went to the pub with you yesterday,' Posy pointed out.

'And, I'm not married and have no plans to,' Verity added.

'Alcohol?' said a heavily-accented voice from the archway on the right and Nina turned gratefully towards Paloma, the tearoom's barista who was standing there with a hopeful expression on her face. 'Alcohol? Nina? Alcohol?'

'Alcohol!' Nina gratefully confirmed. '*Si!* Alcohol!'

Paloma was Spanish, from Barcelona, and hadn't been in London for long. Her English was rather basic, though she said that coffee was pretty much a universal language, and she had more piercings than Nina (who had seven holes in one ear, eight in the other and a metal bolt through her tongue) or even Nina's friend Claude, and he pierced people for a living. Paloma also had an on/off Cuban boyfriend called Jesus, who wasn't as godly as his name suggested. It often sounded to Nina like they were having the most tempestuous rows, as it did ten minutes later, once they were settled round the table in a tapas bar just off the Grays Inn Road.

As usual, Paloma and Jesus were shouting at each other and gesticulating wildly as Nina sat there nursing a vodka and tonic to chase away the last dregs of her hangover. 'Guys,' she said eventually when there was a pause in the argument. 'Really guys, I'm a big believer in passion, but can we just dial it down a notch?'

'*Que?*' Jesus shrugged.

'We just talk about if we need the . . . the *papel de baño* . . .'

'The papel de whato?' Nina asked.

'How do you say . . .' Paloma swiped her hand in the region of her crotch where she apparently had quite a few piercings too. 'For after when you pee.'

'Oh, you mean loo roll.'

'*Si!* Loo roll.'

Just as Nina was starting to despair of her Wednesday night, the door opened, letting in a gust of wind and a group of Paloma and Jesus's friends. There was much hugging and kissing and shouting and gesticulating. It was a sea of unfamiliar, though smiling, faces.

The friends commandeered two extra tables, ordered what seemed like hundreds of tiny plates of delicious food and shouted at each other in Spanish. They tried to include Nina, to pull her into the conversation with halting English, but in the end she was left to her own devices and a bowl of *patatas bravas*. This was how Paloma must feel a lot of the time; everyone chattering away in another language, so

Nina took it as her due. She also took the lingering looks from one of Jesus's friends, Javier, and returned them with interest.

Javier had tousled black hair, the kind of hair that was designed solely to be rumpled by a lover's hand. He had dark eyes that a girl could lose herself in. He also had a smile that was pure sex and seated as he was across the table from Nina, she was pretty sure that it was Javier's leg that was rubbing against hers.

Nina glanced at Javier from under her lashes, her fingers trailing provocatively along her neckline to highlight her cleavage displayed to best advantage in the tight black vintage dress she'd quickly changed into before they left the shop.

But when Javier's tongue did something quite obscene with his bottle of lager, Nina began to wonder how they were going progress things when she only spoke five words of Spanish. And when he did it again, this time with added and very unsexy slurping at the bottle neck, she found herself go suddenly cold.

Nina knew precisely nothing about Javier, except that he was from Spain (though she wasn't completely sure about that, he could just be from a Spanish-speaking country), he was Paloma's friend and, judging from what he was doing to his poor lager bottle, he was angling for a hook-up.

Oh God, she was so tired of this merry-go-round. It was time for Nina to make her excuses and leave because she had a three-date minimum before hooking up. And how could you have three dates with someone when you only understood a few words they were saying? Also, if she and Javier did get past three dates, got intimate with each other, only for things to fizzle out (after all, intimacy was no guarantee of a happy ever after), then things could get awkward between Nina and Paloma. Paloma did make a stellar cup of coffee and Nina would hate it if Paloma started spitting in hers or worse, withholding coffee altogether. This was why dear, beloved Lavinia had been fond of saying, 'Don't get your bread from the same place that you get your eggs,' or as Nina's father would say more brusquely, 'Don't shit where you sleep.'

What Javier was doing *now* with his tongue was actually starting to make her feel a bit nauseous and weary with it all. Since when had hooking up become so . . . boring? If there was one thing that Nina didn't do, it was boring. 'Boring' wasn't the reason why she'd upgraded her daytime make-up to an evening look, which involved yet another lorryload of eyeliner, a more strongly defined brow and industrial amounts of red lipstick. 'Boring' wasn't why Nina had poured herself into a black satin wiggle dress and teetered to the tapas bar in five-inch heels.

Nina had gone to all this effort because she wanted to bewitch and beguile the man of her dreams and she had a very clear idea of just who that man was. Some ten years before, Nina had read Emily Brontë's *Wuthering Heights* and it had changed her life forever. Heathcliff and Cathy were star-crossed lovers who couldn't live with each other and couldn't live without each other. It was all passion and angst and rugged Yorkshire moorland. And though in his worst moments, Heathcliff was one hundred per cent toxic masculinity, in his best moments, Nina had glimpsed the kind of man who would make her happy. A man who was her soulmate. Her one true love. A restless heart to match her own. A man who'd try to beat her at her own game but would only succeed on Tuesdays, Thursdays, Saturdays and alternate Sundays. A man who'd share all the highs and lows of a love that was too great to be contained. A man who loved with everything he was and wouldn't settle for second best, so why should Nina? And that was why she was holding out for a Heathcliff and would accept no substitutes.

But it turned out that in real life, Heathcliffs were pretty thin on the ground and Nina knew without a shadow of a doubt that a Heathcliff would *not* be passionately tonguing a cheap bottle of euro-lager on a Tuesday night.

Nina smiled regretfully, tucked her legs under her chair before Javier gave her friction burns, and pulled out her phone.

The night was still young, she thought as she logged into HookUpp – maybe her romantic hero would be lurking in its algorithms tonight. HookUpp was a dating app designed and owned by Sebastian's company ZingerMedia, so Nina was always slightly terrified that he had access to her login details and might share classified information with Posy over dinner.

'Wouldn't expect Tattoo Girl to be on time tomorrow,' he'd say, poring over Nina's metadata. 'She's just up-swiped on a graphic designer who up-swipes a different woman every evening and never gets less than a four-star rating from any of them.'

Still, Nina wasn't fearful enough to delete the app. Not when there was every chance of love lurking around the next corner. Or rather Steven, 31, writer, who was apparently 0.3 km away and had already up-swiped Nina and sent her a message: Fancy a drink?

It was quite dimly lit in the tapas bar and Nina had to peer quite closely at her screen to get a good look at Steven's picture. Not that she was shallow, but she didn't want to go for a drink with someone who looked like they'd buried their last four HookUpps in shallow graves.

Steven looked all right. He was posed with a Labrador, who was absolutely gorgeous. How bad could Steven be if he was friendly with a dog? Dogs were great judges of character.

Nina up-swiped Steve and sent a message back. Thornton Arms, ten minutes?

Steven messaged back. I'll be waiting outside.

It wasn't very romantic, but looking for love, even looking for a Heathcliff, was a numbers game. A girl had to manoeuvre around a lot of frogs to find her prince. In Nina's experience, which was vast, it was best to get the meet and greet out of the way ASAP and then, hopefully, she and Steven, 31, could get on with the falling in love.

With a renewed sense of optimism, Nina scraped her chair back and stood up. 'Guys! I have to go now,' she said. There was a gratifying chorus of 'No's and many hand-wringing gestures. Javier, though, just shrugged and stopped making love to his lager bottle, so Nina knew she'd been right to trust her instincts. If Javier had the Heathcliff gene, he'd have thrown himself to the ground to prevent Nina from leaving or at the very least, he'd have offered to buy her a drink if she agreed to stay.

There was just time for a quick primp and spritz in the bathroom to ensure her hair was still immaculately set and that her lipstick was still where it should be.

All was well. Watch out, Steven, 31, writer, get ready to fall madly in love.

Nina left the bar and walked round the corner, took a left, and even now, after years of blind dates and meeting men whose picture was a little avatar on her phone screen, she still got the same feeling in her stomach. A churny, tingly feeling of expectation, excitement and yes, a little bit of dread. It didn't matter how many times Nina took a walk to meet a man, she never failed to have that colony of butterflies fluttering deep inside her, because she might be about to meet her destiny. This. Could. Be. The. One.

'You Nina, then?' asked the man in the suit stood outside the Thornton Arms. 'You looked thinner in your picture.'

He'd looked at least ten years younger, five inches taller and had definitely had more hair. 'Steven,' Nina confirmed with a bright smile, even as the butterflies stopped fluttering and she wondered why she'd bothered to reapply her lipstick for *this*.

'Shall we?' Steven opened the door not for Nina but so he could enter the pub first, which was just bad manners.

At least he didn't let the door shut in Nina's face, but he was already on one strike.

'So, let's find somewhere to sit,' Nina suggested, but Steven was too busy giving her the once over to reply.

His eyes lingered on what Nina lovingly called her three b's: boobs, belly, booty. Not with admiration or longing or lust, but with obvious distaste.

'You know,' he said, 'you really should include a full-body shot on your HookUpp profile. Saves a lot of time. I don't normally contact women who only have a headshot.'

Nina refrained from pointing out that he'd uploaded a picture from the dim and distant days when he'd had a full head of hair. 'I'm sorry that my curves are too much for you to handle,' she said icily, drawing herself up so those curves were displayed to their best advantage.

She was a size fourteen. Size sixteen. Size fourteen. OK, she was somewhere between a fourteen and sixteen depending on the time of the month, which shop she was in and how many of the tearoom's delicious baked goods she'd scoffed that week. And Nina was OK with that. She liked her body. It looked good in her beloved vintage dresses. It looked good with no clothes on at all. It could walk great distances in high heels. It could walk even greater distances on the very rare occasions when she wore flats. If she wanted to feel bad about her body, then she could go and visit her mother. She certainly wasn't going to let this Steven, with his cheap suit and sweaty upper lip, try to make her feel that she should be something less.

'You know what, let's call it quits,' she said, which was very reasonable of her.

'Why should we do that? I'll get you a drink,' Steven offered but it sounded very ungracious, like he was doing Nina a huge favour. 'Then you can make it up to me.'

Make *what* up to him? For failing to have the words I'M NOT A SIZE EIGHT emblazoned on her profile? And how exactly did Steven think she was going to make amends for this dreadful oversight? Well, his eyes had barely left her boobs for the last five minutes so Nina had a pretty clear idea.

'I'm very good at making up,' she purred, fluttering her eyelashes at Steven, whose upper lip glistened even more. 'You go and get me a vodka tonic, a large one, while I powder my nose.'

Steven had the nerve – the sheer nerve! – to pat Nina on the bottom and that was maybe his fifth strike, she'd lost count of just how many strikes, which was why she didn't go through the door marked Ladies but carried on down the hall until she came to a door marked Private, which she knocked on.

It was opened by a burly, middle-aged man in a One Direction T-shirt who didn't look surprised to see Nina. 'Operation Frog?' he asked.

'Operation Frog,' Nina confirmed. 'I could kiss him from now until the end of eternity and he'd never be anything but a total arsehole.'

'Say no more, my love,' said Chris, landlord of the Thornton Arms and self-styled saviour of any customer on a bad date. 'Follow me.'

He led Nina further down the hall to a door, which he unlocked so Nina could sneak out the back while Steven was still waiting to order her very large vodka and tonic.

'You're a real gent, Chris,' she said gratefully, because this wasn't the first time, and it probably wouldn't be the last, that Chris had come to her rescue. 'I owe you one.'

'You owe me more than one,' Chris said with a grin. 'Time you settled down with a nice bloke.'

Nina pulled a face. 'I don't want to settle down with a nice bloke. I want nothing less than mad, passionate love with a man who'd give me the moon and stars if I asked for them.'

'Good luck with that, sweetheart.' Chris shook his head then pulled the door shut behind her.

Nina took her phone out of her coat pocket so she could block Steven. She was still logged into HookUpp, the app pinging to let her know there were matches close by, and for a moment, Nina was tempted. The night was still young, after all, and it wasn't as if *she* was getting any younger. Or she could go back to the tapas bar and maybe have another crack at Javier. Perhaps she'd written him off too quickly.

Or she could just go home. She was only around the corner from Happy Ever After and, as if they had a mind of their own, her feet were swinging left and down Rochester Street then into Rochester Mews. Nina sighed as she tapped the security code into the panel of the electric gate that prevented undesirables from gaining access to the mews after hours.

Then it was an unsteady, vertiginous wobble across the cobblestones towards Happy Ever After. The shop was in darkness and Nina didn't bother to turn on the lights as she locked the door behind her then gratefully eased off her shoes.

She padded across the main room, past the shop counter to the door that led to the stairs. There were no lights on upstairs but that didn't necessarily mean that Verity was staying over at Johnny's *again*. She could be home and doing yoga, which she preferred to do by candlelight. Or she could be reading, which was another quiet activity and one she could easily abandon to listen to Nina spin an amusing yarn about her adventures this evening.

'Very? Are you in?' Nina called out as she climbed the stairs. 'Had a lucky escape from a total loser tonight. He had the worst hair plugs of anyone I've ever seen.'

'Roooowwwwwwrrrrrrrr!' came the plaintive reply, not from Verity, but Strumpet, Verity's obese, needy cat who waited for Nina to get to the top of the stairs then hurled himself at her shins.

'Mr Strumpet! Did she leave you home alone?' Nina hefted Strumpet into her arms, nearly giving herself a hernia in the process, and padded down the hall to the kitchen wearing Strumpet like he was a fur stole.

There was a note pinned to the fridge. 'Hey Nina, probably going to stay at Johnny's tonight. Strumpet has already been fed, despite what he might tell you. Be good. See you tomorrow. Very xxx'

It was only a short time ago that Verity and Posy, with

a bit of nagging, could be persuaded to go out with Nina. And now it wasn't even nine o'clock on a Wednesday evening and Posy was snuggled up with her husband, and Verity was sharing sofa space (she really wasn't the snuggling sort) with her extremely eligible handsome architect boyfriend. And where did that leave Nina?

While she would rather die than become a smug married, it would be wonderful to have someone to come home to. And God, a passion-filled all-nighter with her Heathcliff-alike would absolutely hit the spot right now. Instead, Nina's companion for the night was a chubby, demanding cat, like she was a spinstery crazy cat lady, with nothing to do but put on her pyjamas, ferret in the fridge for some leftovers and catch up on the latest episode of *Tattoo Fixers*.

It was less *Wuthering Heights* and more the absolute pits.

CHAPTER 3

'But I begin to fancy you don't like me.'

Though Nina was very fond of saying 'I can sleep when I'm dead' every time any of her friends, especially Verity who was evangelical about eight hours of shut-eye, remonstrated with her about burning the candle at both ends, there was a lot to be said for an early night.

She'd been in bed by an unprecedented half past ten and woke up the next morning *before* her alarm. It was quite a revelation that getting showered, dressed and made-up could be done in a leisurely fashion, and when Verity finally came home from staying the night at Johnny's, she did a double-take to see Nina sitting in the kitchen, lingering over toast and jam and her first cup of coffee of the day.

'Morning, Very!' Nina picked up the cafetière. 'Do you want a cup?'

Verity goggled at her. 'What is going on here?' she asked in a bewildered fashion. 'Did you stay out all night?'

'I beg your pardon!' Nina gasped, like she was affronted at the notion that the only reason she was up was because she hadn't gone to bed. 'The very idea! Not like you, you dirty stop-out!'

It was Verity's turn to gasp in outrage. 'I'm not a dirty stop-out. I'm in a loving, committed relationship, thank you very much.'

Half an hour later when Posy arrived for work, Nina took great delight in opening the shop door for her with much ceremony and a chirpy, 'Posy! You're five minutes late! No need to worry though, I've already signed for a couple of deliveries and done the till float.'

Posy put a hand to her forehead and pretended to swoon. 'Oh God, I must be hallucinating. Are you really Nina?'

Nina nodded. 'I'm a new, improved Nina who had an early night.'

'I always knew this day would come,' Posy said with a grin, nudging Nina. 'If you continue to be new and improved, I might have to promote you to deputy manager, then you could open the shop every day and I could have a bit of a lie-in.'

'I'm pretty sure that come tomorrow, I'll revert back to Nina version one,' Nina decided and then Posy pretended to cry and it set a jokey mood for the morning, which was just as well, because the day was grey and drizzly, yet again, and the shop was very quiet. Nina hoped that it was just because of the weather and not because they'd run out of customers. Verity still seemed to have a lot of orders coming in through the website and Posy insisted that it was just a lull and 'things will pick up nearer to Valentine's Day.'

But Valentine's Day was only a week away and Nina couldn't see that people would want to buy more romantic fiction if they had the real thing. And if they were single, why buy a romantic novel as a special Valentine's Day treat, when it would only remind you of the fact that no one loved you?

Anyway, Valentine's Day or not, the shop had become awfully quiet now that Christmas was long gone.

When they'd reopened as Happy Ever After last summer, they'd planned all sorts of exciting things. Author events, blogger evenings, a book-of-the-month club, but as yet none of these exciting things had happened.

No one even bothered to update the shop's Twitter or Instagram feeds any more. Sam, Posy's sixteen-year-old brother, and Little Sophie, their Saturday girl, had promised to take responsibility for them, but their good intentions had lasted a maximum of two weeks. Nina wouldn't have minded taking them over, or the Instagram at least, so she could take pictures of the new releases, but no one seemed to know the login details for each account. When Nina had asked Sam, he'd gone full teenage strop on her, so she suspected that he couldn't actually remember what the passwords were.

Still, there was something to be said for a slow morning. Nina painted her nails then read a very sexy workplace romance called *Billionaire In The Boardroom, Gigolo In The*

Bedroom in between texting back and forth with her friend Marianne about her new-found resolve to stop taking a chance on losers and really focus on finding her own true love, so despite the lack of customers, the morning sped by.

As the shop was quiet and she had actually started work early that morning, Nina reasoned that no one would mind if she was a little late back from lunch. She had planned to grab a quick bite with lovely Annika, girlfriend of lovely Stefan who ran the Swedish deli on Rochester Street, but Annika and Stefan had had a massive argument, which sounded far from lovely, so Nina had to listen to an entire repeat of said massive argument and then offer advice.

Usually when her women friends were fighting with their significant others, Nina would argue that passion made a relationship stronger as long as the reason for the fight didn't involve cheating or skidmarks, but Annika wasn't convinced.

'He cares more about his smokehouse than he cares about me,' she said sadly of the little wooden shed in the backyard of the deli where Stefan cured his own salmon.

So, Nina was late back from lunch. Only by fifteen minutes, which was nothing. She'd been back from lunch much later than that before. Much, *much* later.

Unfortunately the sun had come out since Nina had left the shop and when she returned, Happy Ever After was full of customers, as if the romance novel-reading public only ventured outside for blue skies.

'Sorry!' Nina said in a jaunty voice as she approached

the counter where Posy was manning the till and a very reluctant Verity had been press-ganged into helping. 'I got held up.'

'There's a reason why it's called a lunch *hour*,' Posy snapped in a very un-Posy-like manner. 'That's because it's only meant to last sixty minutes.'

'I said I was sorry. Keep your hair on,' Nina said, nudging Posy out of the way with her hip, so she could serve the next customer. 'Hello! Shall I take those from you?'

'I'm going back to the office now,' Verity announced in martyred tones, because she hated interacting with the general public in any way, shape or form. She'd only answer the phone under extreme duress, whereas Nina was happy to answer the phone every time it rang *and* chat to every customer, which even Posy got a bit bored with, so Verity and Posy could just get over themselves.

Her timekeeping might be a little free-form but Nina was excellent at customer service. She said as much to Posy, who was now taking the books that Nina rang up, and bagging them along with a complimentary Happy Ever After bookmark, but Posy just muttered darkly that she already missed the new and improved Nina.

The queue seemed never ending but it did end eventually, and Nina could take off her coat, stash her bag under the counter and come face to face with . . .

'Not you again! How long have you been standing there?' Nina demanded of Noah, who was indeed standing at the other end of the counter in his stupid suit with his stupid handheld device. No doubt he'd been writing copious notes about the amount of backchat Nina gave to Posy and was recommending that she be fired immediately.

'Quite a while actually,' Noah replied mildly. 'You see, *I* wasn't back late from lunch.'

Nina gave him a hard stare – she didn't appreciate his sarcasm. Not one little bit. He had a clever, kind-looking face but when he smiled blandly at Nina, as he was doing now, it just stoked the flames of her dislike.

'Noah's here for the afternoon,' Posy said. 'Which you'd have known if you'd got back from lunch in time.'

'God, Posy, will you let it go?' Nina groaned and Noah made another mark on his iPad, which Nina was going to spill a hot drink on first chance she got, and Posy sniffed and said that she had work to do and that she wasn't to be disturbed, and disappeared into the back office.

She even shut the door so Nina couldn't eavesdrop on her and Verity, which meant they were sure to be talking about her. She glanced around the main room of the shop then craned her neck to see what was going on in the anterooms on her right and her left. The browsers had thinned out. The shop was almost empty again. Just like the old days when they'd been Bookends and the only thing stopping them from closing down was the fact that Lavinia had a private income to keep the shop afloat. Nina sighed.

Back then, she had half-expected to be made redundant. And now, if these last few weeks of not many customers in the shop was the new normal or the new old normal, was she going to live in fear of losing her job again? She'd been the last member of staff to be taken on, after all, and everyone knew that the last one through the door was the first to pick up their P45 when cuts were being made. Even though Verity refused to serve any customers, she was the only staff member who knew how the stock system worked. And Posy had been left the shop by Lavinia because she was practically family (her father had been the shop manager and her mother had run the tearooms until they'd been killed in a motorway crash), and anyway, she could hardly sack herself.

Tom was only part-time and refused to wear the official Happy Ever After staff T-shirt, but he had a way with their older customer base that defied belief. Also, Nina could imagine that if Posy did fire him, Tom would just tell Posy very crossly that he wasn't fired and that would be the end of it.

Before she'd come to work at Bookends, Nina had as much success in keeping her jobs as she did in keeping her boyfriends. Both employment and relationships usually lasted between three days and three months. She'd been let go from pretty much every position she'd ever had for a variety of reasons ranging from poor timekeeping and a bad attitude to daydreaming. But it wasn't really Nina's fault – she'd become so bored with her old profession. She'd been on her feet all day, the chemicals had played havoc with her manicure and she got into trouble if she didn't convince her customers to buy overpriced products that they didn't really need.

Then that miraculous moment, three years ago, when

Nina had bumped into Lavinia at a David Bowie exhibition at the Victoria and Albert Museum. It had been a hot July day, Nina had been wearing a sleeveless fifties dress and had been staring at a display case featuring outfits from the Ziggy Stardust years, when someone had tapped her on the shoulder.

'Excuse me, my dear,' a very posh female voice had said. 'Is that an *Alice in Wonderland* tattoo on your arm?'

Nina had turned round to see an elderly woman standing there, though there was nothing decrepit about the curious, warm look on her face.

'It is,' Nina had replied, holding her arm out so that the woman could get a better look at the intricate, inked artwork depicting the Mad Hatter's Tea Party, and the words weaving through it: 'You're mad, bonkers, completely off your head. But I'll tell you a secret; all the best people are.'

They'd read out the quotation in unison, both of them laughing, and then Lavinia had introduced herself and asked Nina if she could tempt her to a pot of tea and a cake. She'd offered Nina a job at Bookends about ten minutes after that.

But Lavinia was gone and so was Bookends. It was a new era of Posy and Happy Ever After, and Posy had been so convinced that becoming a 'one-stop shop for all your romantic fiction needs' would bring in new customers in huge numbers, but what if Posy had been wrong?

'Don't mind me, I am just meant to be observing, but are you all right?'

'You what?'

Nina's doom-laden reverie was interrupted by Noah who'd felt moved enough to put down his iPad as he gazed at her with some concern. If only she could remember where she knew him from. 'It's just you've been standing there for the last six minutes and forty-three seconds without moving. Do you suffer from low blood sugar?'

'Hardly! Not with the amount of cakes I eat,' Nina said honestly. She shook her head and blinked. 'I'm fine. Don't stare at me like that. It's weird.'

She was a fine one to talk. She was being very weird herself. Noah obviously thought so because he muttered to himself as he picked his iPad up again and made a note. Of course he did. Nina could just imagine what he was writing about her.

Nina is a terrible employee. She has no work ethic. She doesn't even attempt to look busy when the shop's quiet but stands there like she's about to go into hypoglycaemic shock. Also, I think she was dribbling.

'Enough of this!' Nina said, though she wasn't sure if she was talking to Noah or putting herself on a warning. Either way, she needed to do some work. Or else, look like she was doing some work. The bell above the door tinkled as a couple of people came into the shop.

'Hello! Welcome to Happy Ever After. Just ask if you need any help,' Nina called out as she so often did and not just because she was being steadily and creepily observed.

Thankfully, there was a constant flow of customers for the rest of the afternoon and Nina didn't have to pretend to look busy. She was run ragged dealing with one woman who stayed for over an hour because she was in the mood for 'a multi-book series set in a country house a bit like *The Cazalet Chronicles*' but had read everything that Nina pulled from the shelves. Or if she hadn't read them, then she didn't like the look of them.

In the end, Nina persuaded her to reread *The Cazalet Chronicles* and sent her off with all five books, as the woman had lent her copies to her sister-in-law who she hadn't spoken to for eighteen months, since they'd had words at a family christening about some Tupperware that hadn't been washed and returned after a barbecue.

In between it was the usual routine of ringing up and bagging books, sharing recommendations and asking customers to leave their email addresses so they could be added to the Happy Ever After mailing list and get sent a monthly newsletter. (Though that was something else that everyone had been very excited about pre-relaunch and still hadn't happened post-relaunch.)

All the while, Nina was aware of Noah, always in her eyeline. Lurking. Making notes. Not being the least bit helpful even though he could see that she was rushed off her feet, and would it kill him to put down his sodding iPad and slot a complimentary bookmark into a book, put the book in a bag and hand it to its new owner?

But, apart from dropping the f-bomb when she had to put in a new till roll (always a tricky manoeuvre), Nina had been an exemplary member of the Happy Ever After team.

Not that Noah said anything to Posy when she finally

emerged from the office. He just said, 'Well, I'll be off, then. See you tomorrow.'

Then he couldn't leave the shop quick enough, probably so he could collate his gazillion notes on Nina's lacklustre work ethic. Nina waited for the door to shut behind him, then rounded on Posy. 'Three times I asked you to help me on the till! Three times! Have you any idea how busy it's been this afternoon?'

Posy put her hands up as if she could hold back Nina's wrath. 'Don't, Nina,' she said plaintively. 'Very and I were going through the accounts. If I'd paused then I'd never have been able to find my place again. It will be better tomorrow. Tom said that he's finished with his footnotes emergency and he'll be in.'

Nina would also be having words with Tom tomorrow for abandoning her for what sounded like the flimsiest excuse ever. Just wait until he found out about Noah. Talking of which!

'And as for *that* Noah! I won't have it any more, Posy! He is literally stalking me with my employer's permission . . .'

'Come on! He's hardly doing that.' Posy patted Nina on the arm in what was meant to be a placating manner but simply annoyed Nina even more.

'He is. I can't even catch a breath without him making a note of it. I shouldn't have to put up with this.' Nina was on a roll now. 'I have rights! Workers' rights!'

'Actually you don't,' said a haughty voice from the door. It was Sebastian Thorndyke, of course it was, because he always popped up when Posy was in trouble, as if he had a sixth sense that let him know when his beloved was under attack.

Nina whirled around to jab her finger at Sebastian. Normally she had a lot of time for Sebastian because he understood that passion and drama were the foundations of true love, and also he made Posy wildly happy, but today she had no time for him at all. 'I do have rights,' she insisted. 'Any employment tribunal would tell you exactly the same.'

'Oh my God, no one's talking about employment tribunals,' Posy said desperately. 'Honestly, Nina, you're completely overreacting about this.'

'Overreacting or reacting just enough?' Nina demanded. 'How can you let that Noah invade my privacy with his electronic spy pad? I bet it's against the Data Protection Act too. Like I said, I have rights.'

'It's all right, Morland, I've got this,' Sebastian said, which was the other thing that really annoyed Nina – when he acted as if Posy was helpless without him, which she wasn't. 'Like *I* said, you don't have that many rights because the other thing you don't have is a contract of employment.'

Nina opened her mouth but all that came out was a shocked gasp because Sebastian, God damn him, was right. Lavinia had been lovely, the best of all the bosses, but things like contracts and job descriptions hadn't been too much of a priority for her.

At least that made things easier for everyone. Nina opened her mouth again to *what*? Was she about to quit in a fit of pique? Was she really that stupid? Then the injustice, the unfairness, the Noahness, of the current situation swept over her in a wave of fury. 'Right, fine, then I qu—'

'Shut. Up!' Posy snapped, her eyes flashing, because unlike Nina, Posy was slow to get angry but once she did, it was best to stand well back, preferably behind some kind of protective barrier. Though why Posy was angry with Nina was one more unfair thing in a whole week of unfair things. 'Just shut up, Sebastian! Talking of contracts, how I wish I hadn't signed a marriage contract! Nina, Very: pub! That's an order.'

'But we haven't done the cashing up,' Verity pointed out timidly.

'DON'T UNDERMINE MY AUTHORITY! WE ARE GOING TO THE PUB!'

CHAPTER

4

*'I'm not going to act the lady among you,
for fear I should starve.'*

Half an hour later, they were sitting in The Midnight Bell, an empty bottle of Shiraz and the debris of three bags of crisps on the table, as Posy reassured Nina for the umpteenth time, 'Nobody is being dismissed, unless it's my husband. Noah isn't there to create problems; he's there to give us solutions. OK?'

'OK,' Nina agreed, though she was still a little sulky, even after Posy had explained that since the relaunch, apart from a surge over Christmas, footfall was down, which meant that sales were down and they couldn't make a profit on website orders alone. Nina had wanted to remind Posy of all the brilliant ideas they'd had to bring in more customers when they were planning the relaunch but Posy had a stress rash all over her neck so Nina decided it was best to leave it for the time being.

'Honestly, being married is really hard work,' Posy was now complaining. 'Don't get me wrong, like seventy-five per cent of the time, Sebastian is lovely and makes *me* feel lovely too but the other twenty-five per cent of the time, he's an absolute pain in the arse. Also, I have hardly any time to read any more.'

Verity sighed long and low. 'I know what you mean. I never thought that I could bear to have a full-time boyfriend . . .'

'What about Peter Hardy, oceanographer?' Nina interrupted. Peter Hardy who'd been Verity's boyfriend before posh architect, Johnny.

Verity blushed as she always did when her ex was mentioned. 'He was hardly full-time, what with him being away so much graphing oceans!' She shook her head as if she could hardly bear to talk about him. 'Anyway, as I was saying, I can't believe that Johnny fits into my life with the ease that he does – you know how much I need my own space – but my reading time has really suffered.'

'World's smallest violin, ladies,' Nina said, rubbing her thumb and forefinger together. 'I thought we'd come to the pub to reassure me that I wasn't about to be sacked, and then we'd order another bottle and bitch about Tom and it would be just like the old days before you two "settled down", so will you stop banging on about your relationships?'

'You say "settled down" the same way that someone else

would say "venereal disease",' Verity noted with a small smile.

'Or "terrible personal hygiene",' Posy added and Nina didn't even mind that they were ragging on her because she'd missed *this*, missed them. No one was more supportive of her friends' love lives than Nina but God, it was so boring when they all safely and sedately paired up.

'I would rather have a venereal disease than ever settle down!' Nina said, which wasn't at all true but it had the desired reaction. Verity gasped in shock and Posy pretended to choke on her wine. 'Although . . . I have been thinking that it's maybe time to give HookUpp a rest.'

Very and Posy gawped at her.

'Close your mouths, for God's sake. It's not that surprising that I'm sick of it, is it?'

Very and Posy glanced at each other and then began to howl with laughter.

'It's not at all funny.' Nina was actually quite offended now. 'Do you know how many evenings I've wasted with men from HookUpp, who always turn out to be complete losers? I told Sebastian that he needed a better dickhead filter on that app. I just know that I'm not going to find my soulmate, the other half of my heart, with the help of a dating-app algorithm invented by some spoddy geek on Sebastian's payroll, who's probably never even had sex.'

Posy wasn't laughing any more. 'I'll be sure to mention your ringing endorsement to the other half of *my* heart,' she said dryly.

Very wiped her eyes. 'When you say soulmate, do you

mean someone who's covered in tattoos and doesn't return your phone calls because they're "too cool"? You know you love a bad boy, Nina, but part of the deal with bad boys is that they don't like to be tied down either.'

'Yes,' argued Nina, 'but just look at Cathy and Heathcliff. They were full of passion and romance and—'

'Yeah,' scoffed Posy, 'and their love story ended *really* well.'

'—yes, but it's not the eighteen hundreds so I'm not going to die in childbirth mourning my lost love. And anyway, Cathy and Heathcliff *were* soulmates,' Nina persisted, 'and I want one of them for my very own. God, it shouldn't be this hard to find a man who's fiendishly good-looking, has a devil-may-care attitude and an adventurous spirit. A guy who wants to stay up all night dancing and drinking and generally being spontaneous but in the morning, he'll get out of bed first so he can make me a decent cup of coffee.' Nina fanned her face. 'And you don't even want to know what we were doing in that bed.'

Verity fanned her own face. 'You got that right.'

'Anyway, that's what I want in a man and I'm not going to settle for anything less any more. But I certainly won't be settling down with him, because settling down is for boring people with no romantic vision, and I would rather be alone than be boring.'

Very raised her eyebrows. 'Are you saying that Posy and I are boring? Because if you are, that would be incredibly rude and hurtful.'

'*And* untrue,' Posy continued. 'Very and I aren't boring. We have layers and you, Nina, have no will power. Your

HookUpp-ban won't last more than two weeks, and then you'll be back to up-swiping on any man with a tattoo.'

'Well,' sniffed Nina, 'that's very rude too. I'm serious, Posy – no more HookUpp, I'm on a serious hunt for my very own romantic hero and I'm going to delete your husband's stupid dating app off my phone.'

They glared at each other for a moment, until Verity smacked the table with both hands, jolting them out of their glare-off.

'Time out! Honestly, this is like a night out with my sisters. Let's stop arguing and start bitching about Tom instead. Are we really buying this footnotes emergency?'

They weren't buying it. Tom had been working on his PhD dissertation for *years*. That wasn't even Nina exaggerating – it had taken four years for Tom to write what was basically a really long essay on who knows what? Tom wasn't very forthcoming about his other life around the corner at UCL, where he also did some undergraduate teaching. Some of his students had turned up to help paint the shop just before they'd relaunched and even they knew very little about Tom's PhD.

It wasn't just Tom's academic world that was the source of much debate. Nina interacted with him the most and knew that he lived in Finsbury Park, because she'd practically dragged the information out of him by threatening to pin him down and read out the dirty bits in the filthiest books they stocked in their erotica section. But everything else was a mystery. Girlfriends? Boyfriends? Family? Pets? Who knew, but it was fun to speculate.

'Tom is deep undercover, *deep*, waiting for his handlers in Moscow to activate him,' Verity, who was currently reading a spy romance novel set during the Cold War, decided as there was a commotion at the door of The Midnight Bell.

The three of them looked over to see someone entirely obscured by hundreds upon hundreds of flowers stumble into the saloon bar. Then this unknown person staggered to their little corner, their usual table in fact, and a familiar voice said, 'Morland, I'm in anguish. Don't be angry with me. You know I hate it when you're angry with me. Also, I think there's every chance that I have late-onset hay fever.' Sebastian finished up with an extravagant sneeze that dislodged a few freesias.

'I'm still very cross with you,' Posy said calmly. 'And you need to apologise to Nina, who is getting an employment contract first thing tomorrow morning.'

There was a pause. Nina wasn't going to hold her breath. Sebastian Thorndyke apologise to someone who wasn't Posy? Hell would freeze over first.

'Tattoo Girl, accept these as a token of my esteem and abject shame, blah blah blah,' said Sebastian and he managed to thrust several bunches of roses in the general direction of Nina.

'Crap attempt at an apology accepted,' Nina decided, because the roses were beautiful; a deep blood red, their petals velvety soft, their scent heady and deep enough to mask the smell of chlorine from the pool of the Health Club a couple of doors down.

'Vicar's daughter, you can have some flowers too.'

Verity was gifted a few bouquets of gerbera daisies, Carol, the landlady of The Midnight Bell, was very happy with a selection of stocks, imported tulips and lilies, and Posy said that they'd take the rest home with them, even though they'd only just finished their first bottle of wine.

As soon as Posy and Sebastian left, Verity was on her feet with an apologetic smile. 'I'm not seeing Johnny tonight,' she announced as Nina opened her mouth to accuse Verity of doing just that. 'I really need to spend some quality time with Strumpet and I have a ton of washing to do.'

'Just this once, I'll forgive you for cruelly abandoning me,' Nina said, standing up too. 'But only because I'm meeting Marianne and Claude in Camden in half an hour. Don't wait up.'

'I won't but don't get so drunk that you can't remember the code to the gate and end up ringing my mobile,' Verity said as they left the pub together.

'That happened once!'

'Once this month, you mean,' Verity said. '"You take delight in vexing me."'

When Verity felt the need to quote from *Pride And Prejudice*, it meant that she was actually quite cross.

There was only one thing for it. '"It is for God to punish wicked people; we should learn to forgive,"' Nina quoted from *Wuthering Heights*, which made Verity hoot with delight because that girl had never met a literary quote that she didn't like. Plus, Verity was a vicar's daughter so Nina got extra points for mentioning God.

★

God was nowhere to be found in The Dublin Castle on Camden's Parkway, but Nina's two best friends were. It was easy to spot them; they both had jet-black hair (the couple that dyed together stayed together, apparently), though Claude favoured a gravity-defying quiff and Marianne preferred a Bettie Page-style pageboy. Tonight Claude was wearing a bright-red teddy boy-style suit and white brothel creepers while Marianne was poured into a leopard-print catsuit and had accessorised it with her bitchiest resting face. In short, they looked terrifying. Imposing. Intimidating. Then they caught sight of Nina coming through the door and they both smiled like loons and jumped up to hug her.

Nina and Marianne had met at a burlesque class years ago, and as well as being her bestie, Marianne was Nina's main supplier of vintage clothing and Claude was her personal tattooist and piercer. They were also both avid readers (Claude perhaps slightly less interested in Nina's stock these days than he was pre-Happy Ever After) so it was a very expensive, very enabley dual friendship. No sooner had Nina sat down after getting her round in, than Marianne was handing over a bulging Happy Ever After tote bag. When Nina had last seen the bag, it had been bulging with a carefully curated collection of romance novels for Marianne and now it bulged with . . .

'A cherry-print wiggle dress, two pencil skirts for work and a leopard-print cardie with diamante buttons,' Marianne said, as Nina pulled out each item. 'They should fit, shall I add them to your tab?'

Marianne had Nina's measurements on file though Nina

really had to stop eating so much cake, otherwise those measurements might be subject to change – or she'd have to start double Spanx-ing. 'You know me, I never say no to anything leopard print,' Nina said as Claude pulled out a sharpie and his phone and took hold of Nina's left arm, which was a work in progress.

Eventually it would be an entire sleeve dedicated to *Wuthering Heights*. They were currently halfway through; Nina's forearm had the silhouettes of Cathy and Heathcliff embracing by a gnarled, barren tree and the quote, 'Whatever our souls are made of, his and mine are the same.' The tree's branches, bowed by the wind, would continue up her arm, along with swallows flying in a stormy, bruised sky.

Nina's mother hated it. She'd also hated the rose-and-thorn design, which Claude was covering up, and she wasn't too keen on Nina's other arm, which had the full *Alice in Wonderland* sleeve that had so enamoured Lavinia. 'Just you wait and see what I have planned for my legs,' Nina was fond of saying, which just made her mother crosser.

'I have the sketch you sent over. Shall I freestyle it for you so we can see how it looks?' Claude asked, gesturing at Nina's upper arm, which was adorned with the barest outline of gnarled tree branches.

'Be my guest,' Nina said. She drank her vodka tonic one-handed, chatting to Marianne about the vintage fair her friend was attending at the weekend, then filled her in on the latest trials and tribulations of working in Happy Ever After.

'I wouldn't stand for having some business-studies geek stalking me,' Marianne said. 'How creepy!'

'Isn't it, though?' Nina was relieved to *finally* be with people who saw her point of view.

'Who knows where your personal details will end up?' Claude mused as he drew delicate black swallows swooping on Nina's upper arm. 'Probably in a filing cabinet in Vladimir Putin's office.'

Claude was a bit of a conspiracy theorist – Nina had once made the three-hour mistake of mentioning in his hearing how sad it was that Hillary Clinton hadn't won the US election – so Nina and Marianne ignored him. It was best that way.

'I could come into the shop and pester you with queries, which you could help me with in a charming way,' Marianne suggested. 'Then he could report back that you're an excellent employee.'

'Might be worth a shot,' Nina thought, then held her glass up. 'Talking of shots, I think it's your round, Claude.'

Two more vodka tonics and Nina's whole world was in lovely soft focus. They trooped into the little backroom of the pub to see a band play whiny moperock, and they sounded like every other whiny moperock band that Nina had had the misfortune of seeing in and around the backrooms of Camden pubs.

This particular bunch of moperockers, The Noble Rots, were clients of Claude, so Nina made enthusiastic noises ('I thought you were *very* good! So much emotional depth!') when they came to find Claude after their set.

They were with a little entourage, which consisted of a taciturn, dumpy roadie, an even more taciturn guy (who steered clear of Nina and Marianne like he might get girl cooties) who was their manager and two Japanese girls who didn't say a word but stared at the four boys in the band in a creepy way that would have Noah suing for copyright. The girls had come all the way from Osaka to see The Noble Rots play second on the bill at The Dublin Castle. Nina couldn't help but think that it was a terrible waste of airfare.

With pickings that slim, it wasn't surprising that all four members of The Noble Rots made a beeline for Nina, after it had been quickly established that Marianne was with Claude. 'Don't even think about it,' Marianne had advised the singer when he asked what starsign she was. 'I've been with Claude for eleven years and you really don't want to get on the wrong side of a man who regularly applies needles to your skin.'

After vowing that she was quitting HookUpp, it was extremely pleasing to have four able, real-life men jostling each other out of the way to get closer to Nina as they headed towards Camden High Street to get something to eat.

Nina had been spurned so many times by men like Steven, 31, writer, that she'd forgotten that she was actually considered to be quite attractive, pretty even. Or as Noel, The Noble Rots' singer, purred in her ear, 'You look like a nineteen fifties pin-up girl. I'd love you to be my Miss February.'

It was quite a good line but Nina didn't do lead singers.

Far too much ego. She didn't do drummers either. *Everyone* knew that drummers suffered from haemorrhoids and it was impossible to put a sexy spin on haemorrhoids.

Which left the bassist and the guitarist, one on each arm. The bassist, Nick, had dirty blond hair and a dirty smile to match and bought Nina a bag of chips. The guitarist, Rob, didn't buy Nina anything, but stared at her broodingly as she lasciviously licked ketchup off a chip.

Oh, be still her heart! Nina did have a weakness for men who stared at her broodingly. This was why you needed to meet men in a real-world setting rather than an app. So you could lock eyes with a stranger on a street, feel that tingle in your fingers and toes, get that good, lowdown ache in your belly. There wasn't an app in the world that could make you feel like that.

'So, you're coming home with me,' he said.

Nina also had an undeniable attraction for men who took charge. However . . .

'I'm not coming home with you,' Nina said firmly because Rob was going to have to work much harder than just staring broodingly and saying things in a purry, author-itative voice. Also there was the third-date rule and this didn't even count as a first date. Despite the tingling, Nina couldn't be certain that Rob was her soulmate, so she'd have to take him out for a couple of test runs. Though surely if he were her Heathcliff, wouldn't she know as soon as they'd first clapped eyes on each other? Maybe this was a slow-simmer kind of deal. 'But you can walk me to the bus stop.'

'I suppose I could,' Rob agreed and he walked Nina to the number 168 bus stop and leaned in closer and closer until she could smell leather and cigarettes and lager, a heady combination of scents as far as Nina was concerned, and then he was kissing her.

There was nothing brooding about Rob's kisses. They were a little sloppy but eager, enthusiastic and her MAC Ruby Woo lipstick's famous staying power wasn't able to survive the onslaught.

'I'll message you,' Rob said when they came up for air and the LED board above the bus stop promised that a 168 was only two minutes away.

They swapped numbers, had another brief snog, then Nina boarded her bus.

She was a little bit drunk, which meant she was also a bit more introspective than usual. Maybe that was why a little voice in her head was saying, 'God, you're nearly thirty and you're *still* snogging at bus stops like a teenager.' It was a very judgemental little voice. Sounded quite a lot like her mother.

'Another boy in a band, Nina? Ugh, you're *so* predictable.'

That wasn't a judgemental little voice inside her head but a judgemental voice *outside* her head. Nina turned around and her heart sank even as her lips curled into a dismissive smile.

'Gervaise,' she said tightly, because her absolute *pig* of an ex-boyfriend was sitting behind her. He was with . . . a person of indeterminate gender wearing all black with slicked-back, bleached blonde hair, thick black pencil around each eye and a smirk. In short, Gervaise had managed to find a double, a doppelganger, a mini-me, which wasn't surprising as he was the most egotistical person Nina had ever met. 'Still sexually fluid, are you?'

'Oh Nina, I'd ask if you were still hopelessly plebeian but you've already let me know that you are,' Gervaise said sweetly.

Gervaise was a performance artist who Nina had met at a tattoo convention. He had come striding up to Nina in a leopard-print coat that she'd instantly coveted, told her that she was the most beautiful woman he'd ever seen and that it would never work because he could never have a meaningful relationship with someone more beautiful than himself.

Nina had been instantly smitten, flattered and keen to take up the challenge. 'How about a meaningless relationship then?' she'd husked and Gervaise had grinned.

'My favourite kind of relationship.'

They'd had a heady week of going to see French films, Polish art and drinking Russian vodka, then Gervaise had told her that he was sexually fluid.

'Eh?' Nina had asked, pushing Gervaise away because it was the third date and they were getting hot and heavy on his futon. 'Bisexual?'

'Oh, Nina, you're such an innocent,' he'd said, which no one had ever said to Nina before. 'I mean, that I don't believe that my sexuality is a fixed point on a graph.' And just as Nina was about to question him further, his eyes had lit up. 'My God, you really do have incredible breasts,' and the moment had been lost.

Verity had said that it sounded like Gervaise planned to cheat on her with other women *and* men, but Nina had dismissed that because Verity was a vicar's daughter so really, what did she know?

Quite a lot actually. Because it turned out that their relationship mostly consisted of Gervaise being unfaithful and, as Verity had predicted, he cheated on Nina with other women, other men, and once with one each at the same time. Then they'd fight about him being unfaithful because he never bothered to hide it, then Gervaise would claim that he was bereft without Nina in his life. It had all been very dramatic but also not that much fun. In the end, Verity had threatened to set up an all-night prayer vigil if Nina didn't kick Gervaise to the kerb once and for all, which she had finally done just over six months ago.

And now here he was, on the 168 bus, looking very pleased with himself even though the last time Nina had seen him, Gervaise swore that he'd never get over her. Also, she just *knew* that her red lipstick was smeared across the lower half of her face.

As she repaired the damage to her face, she heard Gervaise say to his mini-me, as she was clearly meant to, 'She's so provincial, parochial even.'

'Provincial?' Nina queried sharply, refusing to turn around. 'That's rich from someone born and bred in the Home Counties.'

There was a sharp intake of breath from behind her. 'Stevenage is a very depressed area. It's practically a ghetto.'

'Yeah, but you don't come from Stevenage, you come

from Welwyn Garden City.' Nina pressed the bell for the next stop and clicked her compact shut, put it in her bag and stood up. She felt more confident now that her face was restored to its former glory. It was also clear that although Gervaise had treated her terribly, he still wasn't over her, otherwise he wouldn't feel the need to bad-mouth Nina to her replacement. Still, she wasn't done with Gervaise yet. 'Oh, and by the way,' she added to said replacement, 'his name isn't even Gervaise. It's *Jeremy.*'

She didn't even care that Gervaise called her a 'bitch' as she ran down the stairs. The only thing on Nina's mind, as she scurried down a now-deserted Rochester Street and into the Mews, was making it home safely. It was nearly midnight and who knew what might be lurking in the shadows. She held her breath as she tapped in the security code on the gate.

It wasn't until she was creeping through the silent shop that she felt her stomach twist in the way it did when she got a letter from her bank or her mother called. Tonight, she'd met a good-looking, brooding man who'd snogged her face off and given her his number. Even counting the unpleasant encounter with Gervaise, there should be no reason for dread and doom to have settled in the pit of her stomach.

'*You're* so *predictable.*' Gervaise's words echoed in Nina's head as she tiptoed up the stairs, even though she was anything but. She aimed to be, in the words of Emily Brontë, 'half-savage and hardy, and free.'

So, why did this night out feel like a hundred, a thousand

other nights? She was nearing thirty and yet – that nagging voice was back again – there she was, still snogging at bus stops.

She was meant to be living fast, on the edge, convention be damned, with her very own Heathcliff by her side.

And yet here Nina was, standing in her kitchen eating peanut butter straight from the jar while her flatmate's cat wound around her ankles, after an evening spent with friends who were all happily settled down while she was still auditioning frogs.

If this was her best life, then she wanted a refund.

CHAPTER

5

*'He might as well plant an oak in a flowerpot,
and expect it to thrive, as imagine
he can restore her to vigour.'*

The next day, Tom was back. Nina could have hugged him but she didn't because Tom would threaten to write her up in the sexual harassment book. The sexual harassment book was the stuff of Happy Ever After legend but it didn't actually exist. Also, Tom didn't deserve a hug.

'I'm furious with you,' Nina told him before he'd even had a chance to take off his coat or unwrap his breakfast panini. 'Footnotes emergency? Yeah, right!'

'I really did have a footnotes emergency,' Tom said earnestly. He tended to have two settings: earnest or stern, though Nina liked Tom's third, lesser-spotted setting, absolute piss taker, the most. 'I realised they were formatted wrong, then when I tried to correct them, it reformatted my entire thesis and I lost all my italics. Honestly, Nina, my entire life flashed before my eyes.'

'Still doesn't sound much like an emergency,' Nina grumbled. She opened her eyes particularly wide. 'You'll have to do a chocolate run to make it up to me and get me coffee from the tearooms whenever I'm flagging.'

'You make me do that even when you're not furious with me,' Tom reminded Nina, then he held up his hand. 'Not another word until I've eaten my panini.'

Tom's five minutes with his breakfast panini were sacrosanct. Nina shot him a fond look as he stuffed bacon and egg wrapped in toasted Italian bread into his mouth. Though he couldn't be more than thirty, even Tom's exact age was a mystery, not helped by the fact he dressed like an elderly academic. Today he was wearing a pair of grey trousers that looked like they'd started life in the nineteen thirties, a white shirt with frayed cuffs and collars, a knitted blue tie and, dear God, no, instead of his usual tweed jacket, Tom was wearing a cardigan with leather patches on the elbows.

His dark-blonde hair was swept up in a quiff and his hazel eyes peered out at the world from behind dark-rimmed glasses, though Nina often suspected that Tom could see perfectly well without them. The whole effect was a hapless, bookish manchild who needed looking after. Certainly Tom had a huge fanbase among their customers, 'every single one of them post-menopausal', as Nina had remarked to Posy once, who'd promptly spat out a mouthful of tea. One of Tom's most devoted admirers, who had to be knocking on for eighty, had once come in with a tie that she'd knitted especially for him.

Nina couldn't see Tom's charms herself, which was just as well. She was easily distracted as it was, without lusting after one of her co-workers.

'So, where's Posy and Very this morning?' Tom asked, after he'd swallowed the last of his panini. 'I expected one of them to pop their head around the office door to reprimand me about my poor timekeeping.'

As well as his so-called footnotes emergency, Tom had been twenty minutes late. Though the only reason Nina had been on time was that Verity had let an unfed Strumpet into her bedroom and he'd sat on her head and yowled until Nina got up to feed him.

'They've gone to a trade show at Olympia to look at gifts and stationery. Posy wanted to check out ideas for next Christmas,' Nina told Tom. 'And Verity decided to go with her to make sure that . . .'

'Posy didn't come back with five hundred tote bags,' Tom supplied.

'That was pretty much how the conversation went.' Nina folded her arms. 'So, you put out new stock and I'll serve.'

'We'll both put out new stock until such time as a customer comes in and needs serving.' Tom folded his arms too and looked at Nina from over his glasses, which had slid down his nose as they were wont to do.

'You owe me. Footnotes emergency, my arse! You don't know what it's been like with you away! Just wait until you hear about—'

Nina was all set to bring Tom up to speed on the latest and most unwelcome development at Happy Ever After when the door opened, the bell tinkled and the latest and most unwelcome development walked into the shop, bringing in a rush of cold air in his wake.

'—Noah,' Nina said. Her tone was neither friendly nor unfriendly. It was as neutral as Switzerland.

'Nina,' Noah replied evenly. 'Hello,' he added to Tom as he walked past him, around to the counter and into the back office, then returned minus his coat in navy suit and with iPad held aloft. It was a bitterly cold day and Noah's cheeks were scoured pink by the wind, his hair tousled by the breeze so he seemed to practically glow with vitality.

'Noah?' Tom queried, pushing his glasses back up his nose. 'And you are?'

'He's just observing,' Nina said and before Tom could say anything else, she took hold of his tie and pulled him through the first arch on the left. 'We have some urgent stocking to do in the erotica room. You don't need to observe this,' she added to Noah, who raised his eyebrows at the mention of erotica.

Then, in fierce whispers, she filled Tom in on the spy in their midst. 'A fox in the henhouse,' as Tom put it once Nina had finished. 'This is an absolute infringement of our civil liberties.'

'Posy said that no one was getting sacked. Or at least she said *I* wasn't getting sacked,' Nina said helpfully. She loved Tom like a brother but on the open job market, he was eminently more employable than she was. 'Anyway, you always tell Posy when she's trying to make you wear the T-shirt that Waterstones would have you like a shot.'

'I don't want to work at Waterstones,' Tom hissed. 'They wouldn't have been half so understanding about my footnotes emergency.'

They heard a distant tinkle then Noah called out, 'I think you have a customer.'

It would have been a rare treat for Nina and Tom to have the shop to themselves. Nina loved Posy and Verity unfailingly, unquestioningly, but Tom was her wingman. Her co-pilot. Together they worked the coalface of customer service; Tom charming the customers with his grave but sincere manners then Nina sealing the deal with a bit of heavy-handed persuasion. 'Go on, treat yourself,' she would say to any customer dithering over their selection of books. 'Take them all. It's nearly payday.'

But with Noah on the premises, *observing*, it really cramped their style. Also, Tom was working really diligently. Restocking the shelves in half the time it usually took him. Primly castigating Nina when she texted Paloma to bring her coffee, *like she did every morning*, because she could just as easily get it herself. Laying on the charm so thick with one customer that the poor woman went into a spontaneous hot flush. And there was Noah lurking behind the counter or peering around one side of the rolling ladder and even skulking in the Regency section to make notes on how Tom was a total boss at shifting books.

It was almost as if Tom was playing the part of an industrious and conscientious bookseller, so that anyone *observing*

63

him would think that he was a model employee. Which he absolutely wasn't. He always talked back to Posy, refused to go into the erotica room unchaperoned, tried to avoid the more enthusiastic romance novel-buying public and, most importantly of all, knew very little about any of the books they had for sale unless they were in the classics section.

Nina had expected more from Tom. 'I've nurtured a viper in my bosom,' she told Mattie when she had to walk *all* the way through the shop to get to the tearooms instead of texting for a delivery. 'Who would have thought that Tom would be such a suck-up?'

'That's men for you,' Mattie said darkly. Saying things darkly didn't really suit Mattie's gamine demeanour – she was a dead ringer for Audrey Hepburn in *Funny Face*. But she'd recently returned from Paris where she'd learned the art of patisserie and had her heart broken and the whole experience had left her very unenthusiastic about the male species. 'You can't trust a single one of them.'

Posy and Verity still weren't back at lunchtime. Posy texted to say that they'd barely scratched the surface of their stationery needs.

'Well, I'm only going to pop out for a sandwich,' Tom said sanctimoniously. 'As it's just the two of us.'

'I'm not going to pop out at all then,' Nina said, because two could play at that game. 'I'll just get something from the tearooms and eat it behind the till. But it's all right, Tom, off you go. I can hold the fort for ten minutes.'

Tom hissed as he got his coat and shut the door behind

him in what was practically a flounce. Nina heard a soft chuckle behind her and whirled around to see Noah, as if it could be anyone else, leaning against the office door jamb.

'Is he always that keen?' he asked.

'Hardly ever,' Nina said tartly. 'No, don't write that down!'

'I don't write down everything,' Noah protested, his brows furrowed at the suggestion.

Most of the time Nina avoided looking at Noah. Just the mere suggestion of his presence was enough to irritate her but now when she glanced over at him, she was struck once again by the sensation that she'd seen him before.

She still couldn't think where. She didn't tend to hang out with business people and she'd certainly remember Noah, what with the hair – it was really a glorious colour when Noah was caught in a patch of sunlight as he was now – and the freckles; he wasn't the type of person you forgot. Especially when he smiled at Nina as he was doing now. The smile transformed his face so he stopped being a geeky business analyst in a navy-blue suit and became quite an attractive man. He had good cheekbones too.

It seemed that Noah was softening so it would be a pity not to take advantage of it. 'You write down most things.' She came around the counter so she could sidle closer to him. 'Go on, let me have a little look.'

Noah clasped his iPad to his chest. 'At what I've written? That would be a violation of ethics, don't you think?' This close, his eyes weren't just green but had a ring of hazel around each pupil. 'Though if you come any closer, I *will* have to write that down.'

Was that a threat or a joke? Nina couldn't tell.

'I'll make it worth your while,' Nina said in her huskiest voice. She batted her eyelashes and quivered her bottom lip. If she hadn't been wearing her hated Happy Ever After T-shirt, which sadly hid her cleavage, she'd even have used her breasts as part of her deadly arsenal.

Noah, however, was unmoved. Though he did smile again. 'Where's the famous sexual harassment book?' he asked. 'I think what I'm about to write down would be more appropriate there.'

'We don't actually have a sexual harassment book,' Nina said. 'The only person that Posy, Very and I could possibly sexually harass is Tom and he's not worth the effort.'

'Or Tom could sexually harass you?'

'He wouldn't *dare*,' Nina laughed delightedly at the thought of Tom sexually harassing anyone, and Noah must have thought she was smiling at him because he smiled at her. Again.

Nina smiled back, it seemed the polite thing to do, which meant that she and Noah were locked into a whole smiling back and forth thing like they were having a moment.

Which they weren't. No moments were being had here.

'Look, if you're nipping over to the tearoom for lunch, then I could come with you?' Noah suggested because this was what smiling at people got you. 'I'm still working my way through the savoury selection. Is there anything you'd recommend?'

'Well, Mattie makes this amazing pork-and-apple sausage roll flavoured with harissa,' Nina replied, because Noah was a sort-of-colleague and it was just idle lunch chat. It wasn't like she was being friendly or anything. 'It's not for the faint-hearted.'

'Sounds great,' Noah said enthusiastically. 'I love spicy food.'

'Except I can't leave the shop until Tom gets back,' Nina pointed out because there was no way she wanted to be lunch buddies with Noah. Not if he wasn't even going to let her sneak a peek at his iPad. Although if she could get on his good side, he was sure to give her a glowing performance review and that would serve Tom right.

Talking of which, the shop door opened with great force and Tom stood there in the doorway. 'Nina! What are you doing?' he said.

'Nothing!' Nina protested, side-stepping away from Noah. How had she got so close?

'Didn't look like it,' grumbled Tom. 'Anyway, I need a word with you.'

It was a blessed relief to step away from Noah and stop smiling. 'Are you finally going to admit that there was no footnotes emergency, then?'

'What? No! Let it go already.' Tom shut the door. 'That's not what we need to talk about.'

Suddenly there was a hand on Nina's arm. Warm fingers covering Cathy and Heathcliff as they embraced against the gnarled old tree. 'Should I wait for you? Or do you want me to get you one of those sausage rolls for your lunch?'

'I've already got Nina lunch,' Tom said with a little edge to his voice, like he doubted Noah's intentions. 'A smoked-salmon bagel from Stefan and a cinnamon bun for afters. Now, if we could have that talk . . . *alone*,' he added pointedly.

Noah looked a little put out as he walked around the counter. 'Actually I could do with some fresh air before that sausage roll,' he said and Nina found herself smiling again.

'It does get a bit stuffy in here,' she commented as Tom glared at her.

He waited until the door had shut behind Noah then seized Nina's hands in a very unTom-like way. 'Am I going to have to write you up in the sexual harassment book?' Nina asked, tugging her hands free.

'No fraternising with the enemy,' Tom said and Nina was about to point out that Noah wasn't an enemy so much as an unregistered alien, when Tom took her hands again.

'I wanted to say sorry about before,' he said. 'I don't know what came over me.'

Nina shook herself free *again*. 'You mean your "employee of the month" routine? Honestly, Tom, I didn't know you had it in you to be such a little bitch.'

'Neither did I,' Tom agreed. 'I'm quite ashamed of myself. I say united we stand, together we fall, right? Shall we just do what we normally do when *that* Noah is around?'

'God, yes! But maybe not quite as normally as usual,' Nina suggested. 'Probably less backchat when Posy and Verity are being particularly bossy.'

'Sounds like a plan.' Tom handed over a brown paper bag from Stefan's Deli as if he'd been planning to withhold lunch if Nina had refused to stand in solidarity with him.

'Also it was *exhausting* being so efficient. I can't keep the act going for another minute longer.'

'I am surprised you managed to last a whole morning,' Nina said with a grin.

'Although you and Noah looked quite cosy when I interrupted you,' Tom remarked as he unwrapped his own bagel.

'Interrupted implies we were in the middle of something and believe me, we weren't in the middle of anything.'

'I just wondered if . . . no . . . forget I brought it up . . .' Tom shook his head.

Tom often did this. Started saying something tantalising and then clammed up so that Nina had to work really hard to ferret out a piece of juicy gossip or a spectacular example of bitchery.

'What?' she asked. 'Don't leave me hanging.'

Tom took his sweet time chewing a mouthful of bagel before he answered. 'Really, it's nothing.'

'Tom!' Nina growled.

'I was just wondering, if you were cosying up to that Noah anyway . . .'

'Hardly cosying up,' Nina said indignantly.

'Well, it certainly looked as if you were employing your feminine wiles,' Tom said because he did like to sound like a nineteenth-century novel.

'I would never do that,' Nina said, although she had just been doing that. 'I'm shocked at your low opinion of me, Tom.'

'Of course you wouldn't do that,' Tom hastily agreed.

'But if you were flirting to find out more information, going behind enemy lines, on behalf of the both of us, Verity too, then it would be for the greater good.'

Nina couldn't believe what she was hearing. From Tom. Of all people. 'You want to pimp me out to Noah? When he's absolutely not my type. In his suit. With his business solutions. Ugh!'

'I'm not suggesting that you have sex with him, but you are very attractive,' Tom said quickly, fluttering a hand in Nina's direction. 'Just a little bit of flattery and sticking your breasts in his face. You know, that kind of thing.'

'Tom!' Nina was genuinely shocked. 'What kind of girl do you think I am?'

Tom's face was so red that it looked like he had third-degree burns. 'I think you're a lovely, altruistic woman who loves to stick her breasts in people's faces anyway, so you might as well have a good reason for it.'

Well, when Tom put it like that . . . Nina always found it hard to resist a challenge. But Noah?

'Bit too close to home for my liking. You do know that he's friends with Sebastian, right?'

'Just some light flirting,' Tom persisted. 'I mean, you nearly got down and dirty with that awful Piers. Taking one for the team, you called it. Verity told me.'

Piers had been a dastardly but quite hot property developer who'd come sniffing round Nina but only because it was all part of his nefarious plan to buy Bookends and turn it into a luxury block of flats. It hadn't ended well. In fact, it had ended with Piers locking Posy in the coal hole under the shop and flinging grey paint around the shop two days before they reopened, then Sebastian turning up to rescue Posy and beat Piers to a pulp.

It had all been quite thrilling actually but also a timely reminder, not that she really needed one, that Nina had terrible taste in men. 'That whole Piers thing was very complicated,' she offered weakly. 'Anyway, I've decided that I'm not going to waste any more of my precious time flirting with randoms. I want a soulmate, not a—'

'Soulmates only exist in the pages of the books we sell. Anyway, Piers was evil and this Noah doesn't seem evil at all, but how will we know for sure unless we have someone on the inside?' Tom asked plaintively. 'For instance, he might recommend that we become a solely online business and you know how impressionable Posy is. We'll definitely be let go if that happens.'

Tom had a point. They could be very annoying but Nina enjoyed dealing with the general public in a face-to-face kind of way and if they became an online business, then Verity and Posy could easily manage between them.

'Just a little light flirting, you say?'

'Exactly,' Tom said, patting her arm. 'You know it makes sense. And it'll give you some practice for when you find the right chap. Your "soulmate",' he added with airquotes and a smirk.

When Noah got back to the shop half an hour later, it was to find Nina creating a Valentine's-themed window display, which featured a hell of a lot of red paper hearts and should have been done weeks ago. As it was, Nina stared down at the red card she was carefully cutting as she could hardly bring herself to look at Noah, much less shove her breasts in his face.

Tom was sitting behind the till reading *Bridget Jones's Baby* and barely looked up as Noah came through the door. 'Research,' he muttered.

But Noah was not alone; two women followed him into the shop. 'Yoo hoo! Tommy, dear! Have you missed us?'

Nina looked up just in time to see Tom's face drain of all colour. He jumped down from his stool, opened his mouth, shut it again then dived for the safety of the office, door slamming shut behind him.

'Does that mean that Tommy won't climb up the ladder to get books down for us?' the older lady asked, eyes gleaming behind a pair of diamanté-studded spectacles. 'I particularly wanted something from the top shelf.'

'I bet you did,' Nina said, rising up from her kneeling position and shaking out her skirt so that tiny red-sequinned hearts rained down on the floor like confetti. 'Wanted to perv at our Tom's bottom, more like.'

'Us? But we're God-fearing ladies on our way back from church,' the second lady said, and with her tight grey curls and sensible beige anorak, slacks and lace-up shoes, she did look as if she was more likely to be communing with the Lord than exhorting Tom to stretch a little further than was decent. 'We would never perv.'

'I'm glad to hear it,' Nina said fervently, not that she believed them. 'But Tom's very busy so I'm afraid you'll have to make do with me.'

Their faces fell, but only for a moment. Then they caught sight of Noah who'd been watching this exchange with a look of horrified amusement.

'Nina, you naughty girl! You didn't tell us you had a new man on the staff!'

'We do still need a book getting down from the top shelf!'

Nina was tempted to throw Noah, who was clutching his iPad with white-knuckled hands, on their not-so-tender mercies but that would be unfair. Hilarious, but unfair, and not even a little bit like light flirting.

'He's not on staff and he's terrified of heights,' Nina said. She didn't know if Noah was scared of heights but he looked the type who'd be scared of any activity that might crease his suit. 'Anyway, you don't need a man because I've already put some books aside for you. Janet, you said you were after medical romances and Hilda, I ordered some inspirational romance in just for you.'

'Oh!'

'Praise be!'

Noah was forgotten as the two ladies hurried to the counter and Nina produced the small pile of books she'd weeded out for them.

Janet had spent forty years working in Patient Services for the NHS and yet still had an appetite for medical romances that featured chisel-jawed surgeons and sassy nurses, whereas Hilda loved 'clean' Christian romance novels, which seemed to feature an awful lot of mail-order brides, not that Nina liked to judge.

As Noah did his usual observing, Nina good-naturedly answered the two ladies' questions about her tattoos, stuck out her tongue piercing and waggled it while they shrieked in delight, and admitted that she had yet to accept Jesus Christ as her Lord and Saviour. Then she finally rang up their purchases so they could leave and Tom could emerge from his self-imposed exile.

It was an average afternoon that followed, despite Posy and Verity being MIA. Nina worked on her window display, Tom rearranged the new-releases shelves and in between, they took it in turns to serve any customers who ventured in on what had become a blustery, wet day and all the while, Noah took notes. Nina marvelled at how quickly she'd got used to his presence, like a reality TV show contestant forgetting that there were cameras filming their every move. That was probably why she treated Tom to an interpretative dance to 'My Funny Valentine' when he said that the big heart in the centre of her window display was wonky.

Posy and Verity didn't get back from their trade show until Nina was flipping the shop sign from open to closed. They barrelled through the door, nearly knocking Nina down in the process, both of them pursed of lip and red of cheek in a way that had nothing to do with the chilly evening air.

'Pub!' Posy growled, flinging her handbag at the sofa, and didn't even make it a hopeful question like Nina did. 'Pub. I need so much alcohol.' She turned to Verity, who'd shrugged out of her coat and had thrown it on the sofa opposite, an act which went against Verity's whole brand ethos. 'You've driven me to drink!'

'Well, I need a lot more alcohol than you do,' Verity snapped back. 'Honestly, someone should send you to tote-bag rehab.'

'How many new tote bags did you order, Pose?' Nina asked with a grin. Ever since they'd first started planning the transformation of Bookends into Happy Ever After, Posy had been obsessed with tote bags. They currently had five exclusive designs on sale and Verity had banned Nina and Tom from saying anything in Posy's hearing that might work well as a cute literary slogan on a tote bag. 'I was thinking only the other day that the first line from Shirley Conran's *Lace* – you know, "Which one of you bitches is my mother?" – would look amazing on a tote bag.'

Posy failed to take the bait. 'Never mind tote bags. I can't even buy a book of stamps because Very refuses to hand over the shop credit card. Even though it's *my* shop, so really it's *my* credit card.'

'Yes, and it will be *your* bankruptcy hearing that we'll all have to attend,' Verity snapped. 'Pub! For the love of God, let's go to the pub so I can drink my body weight in cheap red wine and repress all the traumas of the day.'

'It wasn't *that* bad,' Posy grumbled. 'Traumas! I find that very offensive.'

Usually Posy and Verity were such good friends that Nina felt like the third wheel. Still, it wasn't nice to see them bickering.

'Pub,' Nina echoed. 'And it's quiz night so if you two

must argue, which I wish you wouldn't, then you can argue in a productive way. Tom? You coming? Or are your footnotes beckoning?'

Tom had been cashing up while all the tote bag *sturm und drang* had been going on. He had looked quite chipper when Nina mentioned that it was quiz night but his face fell at the mention of the f-word.

'I really shouldn't. My bibliography needs tweaking.' He looked at Nina imploringly. 'Tell me to go home and tweak my bibliography.'

'Don't be so dull, Tom! And you know we need you in case any boring sci-fi questions come up. I'll be furious if you try and bail on us,' Nina said because she and Tom both knew that he wanted nothing more than to ditch his bibliography and get quizzing, but he had to pretend that it was Nina's bullying that put his bottom on a bar stool and not his own free will. 'Right, come on, people. I'm not getting any younger and there's a bottle of Pinot Noir and a bag of pork scratchings with my name on them.'

There was a flurry of activity. Posy and Verity retrieving bags and coats from where they'd been flung in temper, Tom switching off the printer and turning out the lights in the back office, while Nina put the cover over Bertha and patted her goodnight.

'Pub!'

'Pub!'

'Pub!'

It was like the word 'pub' had ceased to have any real meaning, it had been uttered so many times.

They all turned to Posy because it was her turn to say it. 'Pub!' she said obligingly. Then, 'You'll come too won't you, Noah?'

As Noah stepped out from the archway where he'd been watching their antics, Nina realised she hadn't even done the lightest bit of flirting with him yet. Somehow it just felt *wrong*. Still, there was always tomorrow. Obviously he wouldn't come to the pub, as it was clear that Posy was only asking to be polite and that actually coming to the pub with them would be violating Noah's 'observe only and take lots of notes' principles. God forbid, because if he did come to the pub with them, then Nina would have to engage in mild sexual banter with him or Tom would get in a strop, and sometimes Nina quite fancied a night off from mild sexual banter.

'I'd love to. Can't resist a pub quiz,' Noah said enthusiastically and because she had her back to him, he was unable to observe Nina rolling her eyes and pulling faces at Posy.

'What?' Posy asked because she was about as subtle as a male stripper at a hen do.

'What? What yourself?' Nina asked innocently, but not innocently enough because there was a hurt expression on Noah's face as he walked past her to the door. His bottom lip quivered and his brows were pulled together in a way that looked painful so Nina immediately felt like the worst kind of person.

There was nothing else for it. She was going to have to welcome Noah into the pub-quiz fold then flirt with him like she meant it. Or rather, just enough to reel him in but not enough to make Posy or Verity suspicious.

'I hope you're bringing your A-game,' she said to Noah as they slipped out of the door together. 'We play to win.'

'Well, I hope I don't let the side down,' Noah said with another of his amused side-glances at Nina.

'Death before dishonour, that's our team motto,' Tom said, coming up on Nina's other side. 'There's this bunch of guys who work at the computer-repair place round the corner who are the worst winners . . .'

'They do a victory lap of the bar, it's really sad,' Nina explained, her lips curling because every week, their team captain, an Australian called Big Trevor, came up to their table so he could shout 'Losers!' at them. 'We can't let them beat us.'

'So you have a pretty good success rate, do you?' Noah asked, as they came out of the Mews onto Rochester Street. 'It must be working in a bookshop . . .'

'What Nina means is that we can't let them beat us *again* like they've done every week for as long as I can remember,' Tom said sourly. 'If every round was about romance novels and cake, we'd be undefeated.'

'Yeah, much as it pains me to admit it, we're going down,' Posy said. Then she brightened. 'But it's the taking part that counts, isn't it?' She pulled open the heavy door of The Midnight Bell. 'And it's the drinking that counts even more.'

CHAPTER 6

*'You know that I could as soon
forget you as my existence!'*

T he Midnight Bell was a beautifully preserved art deco pub, its wooden panelling intact, the sunburst tiling in the loos often Instagrammed, a plaque on the wall outside boasting of its Grade 2 listed status.

But it was also cosy enough that it was a second home to the Happy Ever After staff. They congregated in their usual corner of the saloon bar, annexing banquettes and stools and arguing over what to drink and how many portions of cheesy chips to order.

Tom and Noah were despatched to the bar to procure a bottle of red wine and whatever the two of them were drinking, Posy texted her younger brother Sam to come down (even though it was a school night and his all-important GCSE year) because he was their only hope in the sports round, and Verity and Nina paid their quiz subs to Clive, landlord of The Midnight Bell, who told them that he expected a good, clean game.

'Tell that to Big Trevor,' Nina muttered because Big Trevor had just arrived with his posse of computer-repair colleagues, all of them wearing orange T-shirts with the name of their team, The Battering RAMs, emblazoned across their chests. 'They look like a gigantic bunch of Wotsits in those T-shirts.'

'Now, now, young lady, let's have a friendly quiz,' Clive said, as he handed over the envelope with the quiz sheets in it. Opening them before Clive gave permission, at exactly seven thirty sharp when the quiz officially began, meant instant disqualification. 'Now give me your mobile phones.'

When Clive said it was a nice, friendly quiz what he actually meant was that The Midnight Bell Thursday Night Pub Quiz was an event with so many rules and regulations that, by comparison, it made the Brexit negotiations look like a sweet little cake sale.

Tom and Noah returned with the drinks, Sam arrived with a put-upon expression on his face, which disappeared as soon as Posy said he could have a very weak shandy as long as he had a bowlful of cheesy chips to soak up the negligible amounts of alcohol.

Nina sat happily on the banquette, Sam next to her, cheesy chips in front of her, humungous glass of red wine in her hand and, for a moment, she felt that all was right in her world.

'Is there room for me?' Noah asked and before Nina could force herself to purr, 'There's always room for a little one,' he squeezed in on her other side so Nina no longer had room to spread out.

She wriggled until Sam shifted down a little bit but she was still aware of Noah's leg brushing against hers as he reached forward for his pint of lager. 'Hi Sam,' he said easily. 'How's the Hackintosh project coming along?'

'You two know each other?' Nina asked a little stiffly, because there had been a time a few months ago, before Posy got married and she and Sam moved out, when she knew everything that went on in Sam's life. She had seen him every day when he got home from school, usually accompanied by his friend Pants, who had an out-of-control crush on her. Now, she hadn't seen Pants in *weeks* and Sam, like everyone else, it seemed, was moving on, and Nina was stuck in exactly the same place.

'Well, Noah's mates with Sebastian,' Sam said diffidently, though he adored his new brother-in-law. He shook his fringe out of his eyes. 'So, we hang sometimes.'

'And what's a Hackintosh?' Nina persevered.

'Sebastian and I are building an Apple Mac on a regular PC,' Sam replied, though Sebastian was rich enough that he could go to the Apple store and buy a hundred MacBooks without breaking a sweat. 'You get the parts online, depending on the modifications you want, and then you put it together . . .'

Nina smiled and nodded but she was sure that her eyes were glazing over. Across the table, Posy and Verity were now arguing about what their team name would be, while Tom sipped his wine and looked as if he'd much rather be at home, wherever that was, wrestling with his bibliography.

'. . . then we were going to turbo-boost the processor,' Sam was explaining to Noah, who seemed riveted by this blow-by-blow account of extreme nerdiness. Go figure.

'Oh really? I reckon you could get up to two point nine gigahertz,' he said. 'Providing that you're modifying a standard Intel Core M processor.'

'Sounds fascinating, boys,' Nina said, even though it sounded the exact opposite. 'Talking of computers, Sam, have you managed to remember the shop Instagram and Twitter login details yet?'

Immediately Sam shook his head so his face was obscured by his fringe once more. 'I haven't had time. This is a very important year for me academically,' he said sanctimoniously even though he was in a pub drinking shandy on a school night talking about his Hackintosh project, which seemed to be taking up an awful lot of his waking hours.

'Sam, what is the point of you being in charge of the shop's social media if you never update any of our accounts?' Nina demanded.

'Sophie's meant to update the Twitter account,' Sam said in a small voice. 'But . . .' his voice got even quieter, 'she can't log in because I used this random program to generate passwords for all our accounts, and it turned out it was infected with a virus and I managed to sort that out – don't tell Posy, she'll freak – but now we're locked out of Twitter and Instagram.'

'Oh Sam, you muppet!' moaned Nina. 'Isn't there a way to reset it?'

'Shut up,' Sam hissed. 'Posy'll hear you.'

'Aren't the accounts linked to a mobile phone number for verification?' Noah asked. 'Or an email address?'

'Probably.' Sam frowned. 'Maybe. Perhaps.'

'Why don't we sit down tomorrow and figure it out?' Noah suggested. 'I bet we can find a way in and then Nina can take over the accounts for you.'

'So I can post pictures of new stock and quote from books and stuff,' Nina said.

'Boring! Who wants to look at that?' Sam sneered.

Nina poked him in the ribs until he squealed. 'You do realise that I work in a bookshop owned and run by your sister? And that people who visit the shop's Instagram account might want to look at pictures of pretty books?'

'And you could post a picture of your Valentine's window display?' Noah said as Sam made a big deal of rubbing his side though Nina had barely touched him.

'I could,' Nina agreed. 'That reminds me, I think there are some heart-shaped fairy lights in a box in the coal hole.'

Noah smiled at her and she smiled back and oh God, she hoped they weren't going to get into that whole smiling thing again: she really didn't want Noah to get the wrong idea.

In the soft, very flattering light of The Midnight Bell, Noah's hair made Nina think of marmalade and autumn leaves. And his green eyes were very twinkly, though that could just be the reflected glint of the candles that landlady Carol dotted about the place.

But mood lighting or not, Noah's smile was the same as it always was: friendly, warm, inviting. A bit like a hug.

Nina shook her head. She wasn't a hugger. She'd just have to tell Tom that Operation Pimp Nina Out was aborted.

She stopped smiling and Noah's smile fell off his face too, and not smiling at each other was even more awkward than smiling. So awkward that even Sam, who was a teenage boy and oblivious to emotions and feelings and similar things, felt moved to say, 'Why are you two being weird?'

'Nobody's being weird,' Nina said crisply and she'd never been so relieved to see Mattie who'd also been summoned for quiz duties but had had to finish doing her prep for the next morning first. 'Mattie! There you are!'

'Yes, Nina, here I am,' Mattie agreed with a slightly perturbed expression at Nina's enthusiastic greeting. 'Everyone all right for drinks?'

'I'll help you,' Nina offered, anything to get away from Noah and smiling or not smiling at him.

'No, you're all right.' Mattie flapped a vague hand at Nina then wafted over to the bar in the languid way that she did everything, even dealing with the lunchtime rush.

'What's the matter?' Noah asked Nina quietly. 'Sam's right. You are acting weird. It's OK, we're off the clock, I can be an active participant rather than just an observer, so things needn't be awkward.'

'Nothing's awkward. Everything's cool,' Nina said, and Posy and Verity were *still* going on about the bloody tote bags and Tom was now talking to Sam about Sam's revision techniques and Sam was looking as if he wanted to die and Mattie was taking forever at the bar and Nina was racking her brains for something to talk about with Noah that was non-controversial and she'd never been so relieved to hear a little squeal of feedback as Clive switched on his microphone so he could start the quiz.

'Ladies and gentlemen, you know the rules, I know you know the rules, but I'm going to go over them anyway,' he began and everyone in The Midnight Bell gave a collective groan and Nina could relax, knowing that they were about to get their quiz on.

Although The Midnight Bell Thursday Night Quiz wasn't often that relaxing. Posy always insisted on being in charge of the pen and writing down the answers, but she always got side-tracked and would lose her place and Verity would have to keep a keen eye on her to make sure that she didn't write down the answers for the previous round in the wrong place.

Then Tom would get cross when they all looked to him to supply the answers in the sports round because Sam only knew about football and only from 2012 onwards. 'So heteronormative to insist I know about sport just because I'm a man,' Tom would hiss if anyone dared to ask him who the captain of the England rugby squad was.

To make matters worse, there would be the smug hoots of glee from The Battering RAMs in the opposite corner as they made short work of each round, when there were very few questions on literature or baked goods for Team

Tote Bag to excel at. (Though being a vicar's daughter, Verity really came into her own if there were any questions about saints or religious holidays.)

So, the quiz was not usually an enjoyable experience and as Clive led them into the first round, Inventors, Nina feared the worst.

'One for all the ladies,' Clive declared. 'Who invented the first bra?'

'Oh, I actually know this,' Nina exclaimed excitedly. 'Wasn't it Jane Russell, the actress? She was in a film called *The Outlaw* and . . .'

'Actually, it was a New York socialite called Mary Phelps Jacobs, who was granted a patent in 1914 for what we now know as the modern bra,' Noah interrupted. 'She used two handkerchiefs and a pink ribbon to create what she called The Backless Brassiere.'

'My hand's cramping and it's only the first answer,' Posy complained while everyone stared at Noah, who blushed a fiery red for knowing so much about the history of women's underwear.

'Second question, who invented the first flush toilet?'

Team Tote Bag looked at each other. 'Thomas Crapper?' Verity ventured, as The Battering RAMs high-fived each other and Big Trevor wrote the answer down on their quiz sheet. 'I'm pretty sure it was Thomas Crapper sometime in the nineteenth century.'

'I think it was a bit earlier than that,' Noah said apologetically. 'Between 1584 and 1591, Elizabethan poet John Harrington designed and installed a flushing toilet in his new house, The Ajax. Queen Elizabeth was so impressed that she ordered him to make one for her too.'

'Oh my goodness. How do you know this stuff?' Posy asked in amazement.

Noah shrugged. 'I just have one of those memories. Every single thing I read or hear stays in my brain. Quite useful when I'm doing a crossword.'

It was also very useful when doing The Midnight Bell pub quiz. There was no question that fazed Noah. No answer that managed to elude him. Whether it was classic British sitcoms, political dissidents or the infamous cheese round, Noah came through for Team Tote Bag again and again and again.

When the last question had been answered ('Beaufort. It's a French Alpine cheese, quite similar to Gruyère, very good in a fondue.') and the quiz sheets collected, the Happy Ever After gang turned to Noah with matching expressions of awe.

'You're like the god of pub quizzes,' Posy sighed dreamily in a way that would have had Sebastian challenging Noah to a duel if he hadn't been in San Francisco doing techy entrepreneurial things. 'This is what you're doing on your Thursday evenings from now on until the end of time.'

'We don't know that all of my answers are correct,' Noah said modestly and he bashfully smiled into his pint glass, which even Nina was forced to admit to herself made him look cute. Mattie and Verity seemed to think so because they both made silent 'ah's in appreciation. 'The political dissidents round was very hard. All those foreign names!

You don't really expect to find a political dissidents round in a pub quiz.'

'Ever since Clive was on *Fifteen To One*, he's had delusions,' Nina explained. She dropped her voice to a whisper because it was still a sensitive subject. 'He fumbled a really easy question about ABBA winning the Eurovision Song Contest and ever since then, he's had a point to prove.'

'1974 with "Waterloo",' Noah said immediately, then slapped his forehead. 'Sorry, I'm in full quiz mode now.'

Nina was keen to rise to the challenge. 'OK, name all of the *Strictly Come Dancing* winners in chronological order.'

Noah thought about it for a second, green eyes almost crossing with the effort. 'Right, um, Natasha Kaplinsky, Jill Halfpenny, Darren Gough . . .'

Sam muttered something about how they shouldn't treat Noah like a freakshow, but Noah wasn't a freakshow. He was Wikipedia in human form. Google made flesh. Ask Jeeves but not a butler. So, it wasn't much of a surprise when Clive came over to them with their answer sheet and made them promise on their collective mothers' lives that they hadn't sneaked a rogue mobile phone past him.

'You got one hundred and seven out of a hundred,' Clive admitted at last. 'Had to give you some extra points for additional information supplied.' He shook his head in disbelief then stared at Noah with a slightly bitter expression. 'You should think about going on *Mastermind*. You'd clean up.'

'Oh, I was just having a good night,' Noah muttered.

Noah was very respectful of other people's feelings. Not

once had he made any of his teammates feel bad about their own general-knowledge shortcomings. Nina mentally scrolled through her list of exes to see if any of them would have behaved in a similar fashion. Not that a single one of them would have been able to correctly answer a question about political dissidents or cheeses of the world and if they had, they wouldn't have been very gracious about it either.

And if they had single-handedly led their team to victory as Noah had, none of them would have ducked their heads and insisted that everyone had contributed as Clive announced Team Tote Bag as the winners, to stunned disbelief then a smattering of applause.

'We couldn't have done it without you,' Nina told Noah, having to raise her voice over a commotion in the corner where The Battering RAMs were not taking the news of their defeat quietly. 'Honestly, we usually manage second from last. This is all down to you.'

'It is,' Posy agreed fervently, waving the envelope with their winnings in it. 'And now we're rich! Rich beyond the dreams of avarice!'

They'd won the princely sum of ninety-eight pounds and seventy-six pence, some of which they immediately spent on more alcohol and cheesy chips. Nina liked to think they were good winners, calm and composed, unlike The Battering RAMs.

Big Trevor stormed over to demand a recount, then he pored over their quiz sheet to query each answer and finally demanded that Clive disqualify them for bringing in a ringer.

Clive was having none of it. 'The quizmaster's decision is final and abiding,' he insisted and Nina could take it no more.

'Hey! Big Trev! Nobody likes a sore loser!' she called out. 'Now, stop bellyaching and show a bit of dignity.'

It wasn't often that Nina got to lecture people on their lack of dignity. Usually it was the other way round, she thought as Trevor slunk back to his corner.

'My God, I thought it was a pub quiz but it seems to have turned into some kind of blood vengeance,' Noah said. 'Is it always like this?'

'No, because The Battering RAMs always win.' Tom shuddered. 'We'll have to leave together in case they're waiting outside to jump us.'

'Talking of leaving, it is very late for a school night.' Posy looked flinty-eyed at her younger brother. 'And just how many shandies have you had?'

'This is my second,' Sam replied with a slightly hurt intonation to his voice, like he couldn't believe that his sister was implying that he'd broken her 'two shandies on a school night and any other night, come to that' rule. It might even have been convincing if Nina didn't know for a fact that it was actually Sam's fourth shandy, which was why he'd been getting increasingly giggly. 'I'm not even a little bit drunk. Anyway, it's only nine. It's still early. Let's stay for a bit.'

It seemed a pity to break up the party but Nina had an elsewhere to be. 'Actually, I have to bail,' she said with genuine regret because it was very comfy on the banquette, even though she was still thigh to thigh with Noah, and she could easily go another bowl of cheesy chips. 'Got a hot date with that guitarist I met the other night.'

There were blank looks.

'Come on! I told you all about him. His name's Rob, he plays guitar in some whiny rock band and he broods beautifully,' Nina told her colleagues *again*.

Tom shook his head. 'No, doesn't ring any bells. But there have been a lot of brooding guitarists in your life.'

'Well, I'm sure he's lovely,' Posy said supportively and Nina pulled a face. She didn't want lovely. Lovely brought to mind the kind of men who gave you teddy bears with 'to the world's best girlfriend' printed on their stomachs and wanted you to meet their parents before you'd even had sex with them.

'I don't want lovely,' she insisted, as she got to her feet and began to gather her belongings together. 'But I do want my very own Heathcliff and, like I said, Rob is very good at brooding.'

To her slight horror, Noah was on his feet too. 'I'll walk you out if that's all right. Time I was going home anyway.'

Nina shrugged like she wasn't bothered one way or another and tried to ignore Tom's pointed look, which implied that he was very disappointed at her failure to flirt with Noah.

Noah held the door open for her and adjusted his quick stride to a slower pace to accommodate Nina who could only hobble over the cobbles of Rochester Street if she was wearing anything with a heel.

'Which way you heading?' he asked.

'Camden, so just to the nearest bus stop,' Nina said and as they turned the corner into Theobalds Road, the bus stop was in sight.

'I'll wait with you,' Noah said even though it wasn't even nine thirty and it was perfectly safe. 'See you on the bus.'

Noah was as lovely as Posy wished Nina's suitors to be. Even Nina's mother would love him and she was a tough crowd. But not my type, Nina reassured herself, as they lapsed into an awkward silence. Still, she'd been on enough dates to know what to do with an awkward silence and it wouldn't hurt to indulge in a little light flirtation. If nothing else, it would limber her up for her date.

'So, you really do have some amazing pub-quiz skills,' Nina said, because everyone liked getting compliments. 'When you're short of cash do you hunt around for a pub with a general-knowledge quiz machine so you can win a few quid?'

'It never crossed my mind but now that you mention it, it could be a lucrative side gig.' Noah smiled. 'Although there are whole areas that I'm patchy on.'

'Like, what?' Nina challenged. 'Seemed to me like you knew everything.'

'Hardly everything. I'm not good on all sorts of things. Insects. I always get my Greek and Roman gods mixed up. And ice-skating. I know nothing about ice-skating.'

Damn it! Nina was smiling. At Noah. Again. 'I don't believe you. I bet you have tons of facts about ice-skating stored away up there.' She almost but not quite touched his forehead.

'I don't. I really don't,' Noah assured her.

'I've seen you in action now. You know everything. You know it all.'

Know it all. Noah. Know it all.

Oh God, that was it! Of course she knew him! How could she ever have forgotten? He was Know It All Noah!

Nina had the look of a cartoon character a split second before something heavy fell on them from a great height. Her eyes bugged out, mouth hung open as she continued to stare at Noah in utter disbelief, so it was no wonder that the smile gradually faded from his face.

He took a step back from Nina, his expression slightly bewildered.

'I can't believe . . . Ow!' Nina had to bite down *hard* on her tongue to stop herself blurting out her unexpected revelation because now she also remembered why being called Know It All Noah wouldn't hold many happy memories for him.

'Sorry, I was, um, you know, er, first-date nerves.' Nina grimaced – as excuses for acting like a total loon went, it was a pretty weak one. She tried out a sheepish smile that Noah did not return. 'Normally I don't get nervous before a date, but this guitarist, he's a feisty one! Grrrr!' And yes, she had just fashioned her hands into claws and growled. What was wrong with her?

'I see,' Noah said, his eyes fixed at a point somewhere beyond Nina's shoulder. 'Look! There's your bus. Wouldn't want to miss it and be late for your hot date.' Nina turned to see the 168 trundling towards her.

She turned back to Noah to say goodbye, maybe apologise again, crack some lame joke, but he was gone. Striding away from her as if he couldn't wait to put as much distance between them as possible.

CHAPTER

7

*'I hate him for himself, but despise him
for the memories he revives.'*

Know It All Noah. Although in all the years that Noah had attended Orange Hill Secondary School, people had just called him Know It All.

Not because he was always getting in people's faces with his huge intellect, far from it. Now that Nina had finally answered that nagging voice asking her where she knew him from, she found that she could picture adolescent Noah quite clearly.

Back then his hair had been really orange; the kind of orange hair that glowed so brightly it was as if it had its very own power source. He wore a pair of glasses with thick lenses that magnified the size of his green eyes to manga-like proportions. More often than not, those glasses were held together by Sellotape because they were frequently knocked to the ground.

He'd been gangly too, all elbows and knees, and walked with an odd loping gait like a newborn giraffe only recently upright, so he always looked as if he was waiting to grow into his school blazer, even when he'd been in sixth form. Probably because, by that point, Noah had skipped several years ahead. He'd been a couple of years older than Nina, the same age as her brother, Paul. But he'd been moved up a year for maths and all the science subjects. Then another year. Then yet another year. Had even been in the local paper for doing his GCSEs and A-levels early, which had earned him nothing but derision from his classmates.

Paul and his friends, but mostly Paul, a fact which made Nina go hot and cold thinking about it, had made Noah's life a misery for daring to be better than them. Then the older kids had made Noah's life a misery too for daring to be better than *them*.

Whichever way you looked at it, Noah's adolescence had been a misery. Lots of shoving him in corridors and shouts of 'F★★★ off, Know It All!' whenever he appeared. Nina didn't even want to think about what horrors might have happened in the boys' cloakroom as they changed into their football kit.

It was bad enough that nobody ever called Noah by his real name unless they were singing an infantile version of 'Who Built The Ark?' when he scuttled past. 'Who did the fart? Noah! Noah! Who did the fart? Know It All Noah did the fart!'

Nina couldn't remember if she'd ever joined in with the singing. She hoped not. Really hoped not. But she'd been one of the sheep back then. Had looked like all the other girls. Walked like them. Talked like them. Hadn't wanted to stand out . . .

'What's the matter, Nina? Goose walk over your grave?' Verity asked and Nina shivered again, returned, blinking, to the present – Friday morning in the tiny kitchen off the back office where she was meant to be making tea.

'Just thinking about stuff,' she mumbled, her face flushing.

Verity stared at her keenly because mumbling and blushing weren't usually Nina's thing. Usually they were more Verity's thing.

'Thinking about your date last night? How did it go?' Verity asked. 'Do you think he might be a long-haul type of guy?'

After recognising Noah, Nina had been off her game for her date with brooding guitarist Rob. Also, she'd quickly realised that he wasn't so much brooding as a bit thick. Boring, even. Had no decent chat in him, just kept wittering on about effects pedals. 'Definitely not my Heathcliff. Not even a third-date kind of guy, Very,' Nina confessed sadly. 'Though I will say that when you have to decide if you really want to have sexy fun times with the person you've already been on two dates with, the third-date rule really does sort the men from the boys.'

'Though you don't *have* to have sex with someone on the third date,' Verity reminded Nina.

'You don't *have* to, but if you *want* to then the third date is the green light,' Nina said firmly. Before Verity and Posy had gone and settled down, they'd treated Nina as the oracle on all things relating to men, dating and sex. Some of it, well, actually, quite a bit of it, she just made up on the spot, but she still missed being her friends' go-to girl on relationship advice.

'And if you really *wanted* to, like, if you'd fallen head over heels in love with someone, then maybe even the first date,' Verity mused. '*Un coup de foudre.* Love like a thunderbolt, the French call it.'

'Sex on a *first* date,' Nina echoed in her most outraged voice. 'And you a vicar's daughter too, Very.' Verity pretended to huff at the same time that the kettle came to the boil. 'Tea, then? Shall I make for Posy? Tom's not in today. Noah?'

Her voice actually cracked on the two syllables that were his name though Verity didn't seem to notice. 'Noah's not in today either. Sent an email late last night saying that he was going to work off-site for the foreseeable future.'

'Oh?'

'Not sure he's going to be able to report back on everything we say and do if he's not on-site to observe,' Verity said tartly as if she wasn't quite on board with the scheme to make Happy Ever After work smarter if not harder, which was news to Nina.

'Oh?' Nina said yet again.

'I love Posy. We all love Posy but she doesn't need a Noah.' Verity rolled her eyes. 'She just needs to find the flipchart that has all the ideas from the brainstorm we had before the relaunch.'

'That's so true. My idea for a book group was pure genius and yet we still have no book group. We don't even have a proper social media presence.' Nina thought mournfully about the locked Instagram account – damn Sam! 'Although maybe Noah might come up with some good ideas that we'd never think of,' Nina said, because she was never ever going to have another uncharitable thought about Noah ever again. He'd had enough uncharitable thoughts aimed his way at Orange Hill to last a lifetime. 'Fresh pair of eyes and all that.'

'Noah's very nice, I'm not saying he isn't,' Verity insisted, because thinking uncharitable thoughts was probably covered in the Ten Commandments. 'I'm just saying that Noah isn't the answer to all our problems.'

'When you say problems, it makes me worried. Is the shop really doing that badly?' Nina asked.

'You don't need to worry about that,' Verity said but she said it in a pretty anxious way. 'And you don't need to worry about Noah either. Though I would worry that I heard the shop bell three minutes ago and we've probably got customers waiting.'

Nina wished that she could take Verity's advice and not worry about Noah, but Noah was all that she could think about for a lot of Friday, most of Saturday and especially Sunday when instead of spending it sleeping off the excesses of the week, she was going home for Sunday lunch.

Or rather she was going to her parents' house in Worcester Park, Surrey. Nina hadn't lived there for years but instead had shared flats as near to the centre of town as she could afford. The last one had been in Southfields, which Posy had always described as 'being as far out of London as you could get while still being in London.'

It was just as well that Posy had never been to Worcester Park, Nina thought glumly. The tube didn't go this far south-west so Nina had to get the tube to Waterloo, then change onto a proper train to travel deep into the suburbs of Surrey and street after street of identical nineteen-thirties semis, broken up by the odd parade of shops, a pub, a park.

The train chugged through Earlsfield, Wimbledon, Raynes Park, Motspur Park and finally Worcester Park. By now a gloom had settled on Nina's shoulders like a fine coating of dandruff. As she exited the station a gang of teenage boys were doing wheelies on their bikes in the almost-deserted car park but they stopped to gawp at Nina as she strode past them, eyes forward, trying not to thrust her chest out.

'Freak,' one of them shouted at her.

'But nice tits!'

Oh, she wasn't in Kansas any more. Certainly she wasn't in Bloomsbury where no one batted an eye at Nina, unless it was another woman giving her an approving glance or someone looking at her in a way that suggested they found her very attractive.

Nina had even toned it down today. She was wearing a little black dress, a vintage nineteen-forties number in rayon, fishnets, black suede shoes with a block heel and her leopard faux fur. Even her make-up was a little less today. She'd decided against the false eyelashes, her eyeliner was a discreet flick, and she'd gone for a tasteful rosy-pink lip when usually she applied several coats of her trusty MAC Ruby Woo.

Though she returned to her ancestral homelands on the second Sunday of every month, every single time Nina forgot that even her most subtle daytime look was still too much for the mean streets of Worcester Park.

She pulled her coat tighter around her and resisted the urge to say, 'I know your mother, young man,' to the one who'd shouted out 'Nice tits.' She *was* pretty sure that she'd been to school with his mum, he had the same pugnacious look as Tanya Hampton who'd been in the year above her, but it was such a Nana-ish thing to say and what if Tanya Hampton turned up on her parents' doorstep to have it out with Nina? It was the kind of thing Tanya Hampton used to do.

No, it was best to ignore the boys who were losing interest anyway and cycling off to do wheelies through a large puddle. Nina was going to go home, see her family, eat Sunday lunch, not rise to the bait of her mother's most passive-aggressive barbs and be back on the train in three hours tops. That was the plan and Nina was sticking to it.

CHAPTER

8

'*Your presence is a moral poison that would contaminate the most virtuous.*'

It was a ten-minute walk from the station through identical streets of identical houses until Nina was turning into the cul-de-sac where her parents had lived for the last thirty-three years.

Number nineteen looked the same as it ever did. Front garden completely paved over to make room for her dad's black cab and her mother's nippy Mazda convertible. As Nina stood on the doorstep and fished for her keys in her handbag, she could see her reflection in the gleaming gold doorplate.

She nearly jumped out of her skin at the rapping on the window next to her. She turned to see her two nieces, Rosie and Ellie, jumping up and down and waving at her.

Nina waved back, grabbed her keys as she heard shouts

of 'Auntie Nina has *pink* hair now!' and got the door open wide enough that Rosie and Ellie could hurl themselves at her so hard, she rocked back on her heels.

'Hello! Hello! Hello!' They both shouted at an ear-perforating volume, hugging Nina so enthusiastically, she was amazed that she didn't snap a rib.

'Steady on, ladies!' Nina panted. 'Let me put down my bags.' Rosie and Ellie loosened their grip by a fraction so Nina could drop her bags on the floor then held out her arms. 'OK. Now you can give me some loving.'

Nina had forgotten that there were some good things about her contractually obligated once-a-month trip home and she had her arms full of them. Two curly blonde heads nestled against her chest, fists clutched around the material of her dress in a way that would definitely leave wrinkles, but Nina didn't care.

'I have to breathe now,' Nina said softly and her nieces relinquished their Vulcan-like hold on her so they could gaze up at her.

'Your hair makes you look like a mermaid,' eight-year-old Rosie said gravely.

'Or a princess,' her five-year-old sister Ellie added.

'Mermaid princess was the look I was going for,' Nina agreed. 'Where is everyone?'

It was no surprise that 'Nana and Mum' were in the kitchen cooking lunch and that Nina's father and her brother Paul were performing some acts of DIY upstairs. It was all about the traditional divisions of labour in KT10, Nina thought, her lip curling.

'Did you bring us presents?' Ellie wanted to know. 'We have both been very good.'

'We've been excellent,' Rosie said.

'Well, in that case, I might have a small gift for both of you,' Nina said because she always had presents for them whether they'd been excellent or not. Books, usually.

This time she had a book called *Bad Girls Through History*, a collection of stories about everyone from Cleopatra to Rosa Parks for Rosie, and a lovely picture book called *Ada Twist, Scientist* for Ellie. Nina didn't doubt that her mother was filling her granddaughters' heads with all sorts of nonsense so it was up to her to redress the balance. Besides, she and her nieces had agreed that while it was perfectly all right to want to be a mermaid or a princess when they grew up, it was good to have other options.

Nina left both girls settled on the sofa with their new books and headed down the hall towards the kitchen where her mother, Alison, and sister-in-law, Chloe, had finished their lunch prep and were perched on stools with a big glass of white wine each.

That was the one other good thing about coming for Sunday lunch – there was alcohol. Chloe looked up as Nina came into the room.

'Hope the girls haven't been driving you mad,' she said by way of a greeting. 'They both had sleepovers last night but I don't think either of them did much sleeping.'

'No, they were lovely as usual,' Nina murmured as she got close enough to brush her cheek against Chloe's. 'Did you and Paul go out for a date night with the girls away?'

Chloe shook her head and grinned. 'No. We were in bed by half past eight. Solid twelve hours' sleep. It was the best thing ever.'

'Oh, Nina, what *have* you done to your hair now?'

Nina exchanged a long, long, *long*-suffering glance with Chloe then turned to her mother.

'It's a pink rinse,' Nina said evenly and this time she didn't make skin-to-skin contact but kissed the air somewhere near her mother's cheek. 'You look nice.'

It wasn't a word of a lie. Alison O'Kelly was a youthful fifty-three. On the very rare occasions that she and Nina were seen in public together, somebody *always* remarked, 'Oh, but I thought you two were sisters!' She was blonde, blue-eyed, went to great lengths to maintain her size-eight figure and was never anything less than impeccably put together.

For a family Sunday lunch she was wearing a blue-and-white striped Breton top, smart, slim-cut black trousers, discreet gold jewellery and a pair of patent black ballet pumps, no slippers for her.

Not that Alison was pleased that Nina was wearing a dress and heels, her own version of Sunday best. 'You look like you've put on weight again,' she commented, ignoring Nina's compliment.

Nina *had* put on weight *again*. That was an unfortunate side-effect of having Mattie foist baked goods on the shop staff at regular intervals. *I am not going to react*, Nina reminded herself and she even managed to dredge up a smile. 'Actually, talking of which, I've brought you cake. I told you about Mattie and the tearooms, didn't I? You really should come for a visit.' Nina pulled out a Tupperware box containing the best part of Mattie's famous Raspberry Meringue Layer Cake. 'Anyway, we're shut on Sunday so on Saturdays we get to divvy up all the cakes and pastries that are left over. Thought we could have this for pudding.'

Alison shied away from the Tupperware that Nina was holding out as if it were covered in some kind of radioactive ooze. 'You know I don't eat cake!' she hissed.

'Well, everyone else can try a piece,' Nina said through gritted teeth. Although she was meant to be not rising to the bait, her blood pressure was certainly climbing. 'Dad can have some cake. Dad loves cakes.'

'Meant to be watching my cholesterol,' said a cheery voice behind her and then Nina smelt Davidoff Cool Water and a faint whiff of wood shavings and engine oil, and a pair of arms wrapped around her.

Nina was almost thirty, but when her dad put his arms around her, she felt the same as she did when she was almost five or almost ten or almost fifteen. That she was safe and she was loved and she was protected.

'The cake has raspberries in it,' she said, as Patrick O'Kelly kissed her cheek. 'It's practically a health food.'

'Maybe just a little slice then,' Patrick agreed and Alison's lips tightened and Nina thought she was going to say something, but then the oven timer beeped at the same time as the doorbell rang.

'The roast,' she said over the sounds of squealing in the hall as Rosie and Ellie ran to the front door. 'Somebody let Mum and Dad and Granny in.'

Then it was a flurry of activity. Nina's grandmother, Marilyn and Nina's great-grandmother, Hilda, came into the kitchen to supervise the last stages of the Sunday roast. Nina knew to stay well out of the usual heated debate over steamed veggies vs. boiling them for so long that they resembled sludge, so instead she poured herself a generous helping of Chardonnay then went to waggle her tongue piercing at Rosie and Ellie to make them shriek with horrified glee.

On the dot of one, Sunday lunch was served. Nina sat between her mother, so Alison could watch and comment on every piece of food that Nina put on her plate, and her great-grandmother, who had already been the grateful recipient of two large-print romance novels.

Of course, Nina's grandparents wanted to know if she was seeing someone special. To which the answer was no. It was always no, even when Nina was seeing someone special because the thought of having to bring a man home to Worcester Park to meet the family was too terrifying to contemplate. Gervaise had been Nina's last someone special and his bleached blond hair and unisex black clothing (often a black kilt over leggings) would have gone down like a 'whore at a christening', as her grandfather would have said once he'd had a couple more lagers.

It was the same old Sunday lunch chatter. Both her dad and her grandfather, Teddy, were black cabbies so they had a good old moan about how slow trade was. Paul was a plumber so he had a good old moan about the water company trying to get the local residents to fit smart meters. Chloe was a childminder so she had a good old moan about the parents of one of the children she looked after who were in the middle of an acrimonious break-up and were using the poor kid as a pawn.

Nina didn't really have that much to moan about. She had a sweet, rent-free flat in Central London and although things were quiet on the finding-her-one-true-love front, they had to pick up soon and she liked her job. Except she was still worried about how long she'd keep her job, which led her thoughts swinging back to Noah.

'Paul, you'll never guess who I've been working with,' she said in the break between the roast and pudding. 'Do you remember Noah Harewood from school?'

Her brother shuddered so hard that the dining table shook. 'That's a blast from the past,' he said slowly. 'Christ, I've gone clammy just thinking about what we used to do to that poor sod. How is he?'

Back in the day, Paul had been the scourge of Worcester Park. He'd run with a gang who styled themselves as gangsters, when actually they'd been a bunch of white kids from Surrey in tracksuits and Gazza haircuts. They frequently bunked off school to shoplift, hang around outside the dodgy off-licence where they could buy single cigarettes or loiter outside the station on their bikes probably telling passing women that they had nice tits. And when they were at school, they were rude to the teachers, disrupted lessons and made Noah's days a living hell.

Paul had left school with hardly a qualification to his name and then two life-changing things had happened to him. Firstly, he'd been involved in an accident on a stolen moped and he'd collided with a lorry and wrapped himself around a lamppost. He ended up in hospital with a broken neck and a full-body cast and no one had known for a week or so if he'd be paralysed for life. It had frightened the bad right out of him and then, to make sure that it stayed gone, he'd met Chloe at Cheam Leisure Centre, where he was swimming to improve his mobility, and had fallen head over heels in love with her.

'Never underestimate the love of a good woman,' Hilda had said sagely when Paul, determined to be the man that Chloe deserved, had got an apprenticeship with a local plumber and gone back to college to get his qualifications. Now, ten years later, he was a loving husband, a devoted father and had his own business. It was quite the turnaround. Paul was a completely different person to the boy he'd been back then and Nina could hear the guilt in her brother's voice, see it in his eyes as he enquired after his adolescent whipping boy.

'He's all right,' Nina said. 'He looks quite different now, it took me a whole week to recognise him.' She frowned. 'He didn't seem to recognise me at all.'

'Why would he though? I mean, you look completely different to how you were at school.' Paul waved a hand at his sister to encompass the hair, tattoos, piercings and all the other facets of Nina version 2.0.

'Well, you're at least four st—'

'Anyway,' Nina hurriedly cut her mother off from speculating on how much weight she'd put on since she was at school, when her main goal in life was to get into a pair of size-six skinny jeans. 'I only just managed to stop myself from shrieking, "Oh my God, you're Know It All Noah!" Can you imagine? How traumatic for him. As it is, I bet he's had some hardcore therapy so he could get over his school days.'

'Don't! That bloody song we used to sing. We were so cruel,' Paul moaned, head in his hands. 'But what the *hell* is he doing working in a soppy bookshop?'

There was no point in arguing that selling only romantic fiction didn't mean that the shop was soppy. Nina had tried countless times. 'He's not actually serving on the till or ordering stock. He's come in as a business consultant to see how we can improve our working practices.'

'Business consultant. Sounds fancy,' Great-Granny Hilda decided. 'Doesn't sound like a proper job though.'

'Don't let his grandmother hear you say that,' Alison sniffed. 'Comes into the salon for her weekly set on a Friday and all she talks about is her wonderful grandson Noah and how he went to Oxford and then Harvard after that, which apparently is in America and doesn't let in any riff-raff, and how he's worked for Google, and your Aunt Mandy said, "Well, our Nina reads a lot *and* she works in a book-shop." That shut her up.'

'I don't see why it would,' Nina said, because reading a lot and working in a shop hardly compared to Noah's achievements. 'Noah was always really clever. I don't even know what he was doing at our school.'

'Well, his parents had very funny ideas about state schooling,' Alison said. 'The amount of times I had to go down to the school for a meeting with the head and that Noah's parents when Paul had got a little too high-spirited . . .'

'Mum, I was a thug in a Kappa tracksuit . . .'

'He really was, Ally,' Nina's dad interjected.

Alison shook her head like it was all untrue. 'Paul just got in with a bad crowd. As I was saying, Noah's parents, they were very left-wing. Hippies.' She said the last word in a shocked whisper. 'The headmaster, Mr Hedren, he *begged* them to take Noah out of Orange Hill. Said the local grammar would be delighted to have him but his mum said that they didn't believe in selective schooling and Noah would find his own path in life.'

'I think finding his own path in life was why he took his A-levels two years early,' Paul said. His head was still in his hands. 'So he could get away from all us lot. Look, next time you see him, will you tell him I'm sorry? I'd love to take him out for a drink, install a new power shower in his gaff, do something to make it up to him.'

Nina grimaced at the thought of it. That was one conversation that she never wanted to have. 'To be honest Paul, I've got no intention of telling him that I knew him from school. What's the point? It would just be dragging up memories that he'd rather stay buried.' She paused, rewound the conversation. 'Anyway, Mum, what were *you* doing in Aunt Mandy's salon on a Friday? You always go to get your hair done on the second and fourth Wednesday of every month.' And had done for the entire time that Nina had been on the planet. 'Isn't Friday your Pilates day?'

There was an uncomfortable silence around the table,

quite unlike the uncomfortable silence when Alison was needling Nina about just how many roast potatoes she was going to eat.

'What? What's going on? What are you not telling me?' Nina demanded, eyes sweeping around the guilty faces of her nearest and dearest.

'Oh, nothing you'd be interested in,' Marilyn said quickly. 'Really, you don't want to know about all our comings and goings.'

'Of course I want to know about your comings and goings,' Nina protested. 'Maybe not all of them. I really don't need a blow-by-blow account of Granddad's visit to the urology consultant, but of course I'm interested in what you're up to.' That wasn't strictly true and besides, none of her family were wildly interested in what Nina got up to, which was just how she liked it. A phone call every couple of weeks, a once-a-month family lunch and a lot of sending amusing gifs back and forth on Twitter with Chloe. She wasn't even included in the family WhatsUpp group, but still . . . 'Mum, you changing your hair date is *huge*.'

'It's not *that* interesting and . . .'

'GRANNY'S GOT A JOB BUT NOBODY'S ALLOWED TO TELL YOU!' Ellie shouted as if she couldn't bear the lies and deceit any longer. 'She answers the telephone at Great Aunt Mandy's hair salon and says "Can I take your coat and do you want a cup of coffee?"'

Nina had to steady herself by clutching on to the table edge for dear life. 'You've got a job?' she asked her mother in a tremulous voice because this went against her entire belief system. In fact, it went against her mother's entire belief system.

Alison believed that a woman's place was in the home. Especially when that woman liked to clean that home from top to bottom every day. Nina looked around the dining room to confirm that everything was still in sparkling, gleaming form. Not a single speck of dust or smear. Not a single ornament on the sideboard out of place.

Her mother was the only person Nina had ever met who vacuumed twice a day. Once after dinner (and woe betide the person who made a mess after seven p.m.) and then again in the morning, in case the carpet had managed to cover itself in crumbs during the night.

It wasn't just the hours of daily housekeeping. There was Zumba on Mondays, Pilates on Tuesday and Friday mornings and Aquacise on Thursdays.

And yet, somehow Alison O'Kelly had decided to take up the position of receptionist at her older sister Mandy's salon, Hair (and Nails) By Mandy on the High Street.

'This is why I didn't want you to know. I knew you'd make a big fuss about it,' Alison said in a strained voice.

'I'm just a bit surprised,' Nina said, which was the understatement of the year. '*Why?*'

'Because things have been a bit tight recently so I'm doing my bit.'

'Trade isn't what it was, not with that bloody Uber,' Patrick grumbled. 'And that bloody Lyft mob too. I was going to work longer hours but we hardly got to see each other as it was, so when Mandy needed a new receptionist for a couple of days a week, your mum said she'd do it.'

Alison tilted her chin defiantly as if she expected Nina to make some disparaging remark, much as she would have done if their positions had been reversed. Still, Nina was struggling to think of something neutral to say about this staggering turn of events.

'Are you enjoying it?' she managed to ask at last.

'I've only been doing it for a couple of weeks. There's a lot of new things to take on board: the computer, the bookings software, but it's all right.'

'That's good. I always think the idea of computers is scarier than actually using one,' Nina said encouragingly because really she was a saint; the saint of unappreciated daughters. 'They're just like ginormous smartphones, right?'

'Right! Yes, exactly,' Alison agreed then she smiled shyly. 'Mandy's getting all sorts of ideas. Says she wants to train me up to do nails. Can you even imagine it?'

'That would be great,' Chloe chimed in. 'You always do a good job on mine.'

Nina had a crystal-clear memory of Sunday evenings long ago: Spa Sundays, they'd called them. Nina and her mother would put on face masks and intensive conditioning treatments on their hair and do each other's nails. To this day, Nina always used toothpaste and a toothbrush to clean her nails and get rid of any yellowing when she was doing her own manicure, just as Alison had taught her.

'You should do it, Mum,' she said enthusiastically. 'It could be the start of a whole new career.'

'Well, Mandy says she's fed up with taking on these young girls who only last a few months before they decide they'd rather work in a posh salon in Earlsfield. She just can't keep the staff.' Now that Nina had got over the initial shock, she was genuinely pleased that Alison was expanding her horizons, even if it was only as far as Aunt Mandy's salon five minutes' walk away. But Alison's face suddenly assumed a mournful expression. 'Oh, Nina,' she said sorrowfully. 'Mandy still says that you were the best colourist she ever had.'

'Don't start!' Nina groaned. 'I love Auntie Mandy but I was *stifled* in there. The most exciting thing that ever happened was when someone wanted a full head of highlights.'

Posy and Verity thought that Nina had always worked in retail and Nina had never disabused them of this fact. But actually ever since she'd left school at sixteen, Nina had worked in hair. Namely, the dressing, cutting and mostly colouring of it. She'd started at her aunt's salon while she studied for her NVQ and when Nina had finally left Hair (and Nails) By Mandy for a job in a fancy West End hairdressing salon, neither Mandy nor Alison had taken it very well. Short of Nina taking a job with Mandy's arch rival, Derek of Hair to Eternity at the other end of the High Street, they couldn't have acted more betrayed.

Now Nina's mother straightened her shoulders. 'We've moved with the times you know,' she said as stiffly as her spine. 'We even do balayage now.' She folded her arms. 'But you think you're too good to do people's hair.'

'I don't think I'm too good to work as a hairdresser.'

Nina could only spit the words out. 'It just wasn't what I wanted to do with the rest of my life.'

Her mother snorted in derision even as Patrick said, 'Come on, you two. Do we have to have the same row every time Nina comes over?'

'It gives me the most dreadful heartburn,' Hilda added, reaching for her handbag and her Rennies.

Alison wasn't done. 'Well, when you finally figure out what you want to do with your life, then please let us know because you're thirty . . .'

'I'm not thirty. I'm *nearly* thirty . . .'

'. . . and you're working as a cashier in a shop and you're not even married.'

'I'm not a cashier! I'm a bookseller and getting married isn't the be all and end all of everything. I'd rather fall madly in love with someone and even if it only lasted a week, at least I'd have known passion and excitement,' Nina proclaimed so loudly that she was practically shouting. 'There's nothing passionate or exciting about getting married before you've had a chance to figure out who you are, then a few years down the line you realise that you have nothing to talk about but endowment plans and whether the washing machine will last another month.'

'There is a bit more to being married than that,' Paul said with a hurt look at his sister because by the time Nina left the house, she would have managed to offend every single member of her family present. It was like a very useless superpower.

'Yeah, we go on date nights,' Chloe insisted. 'And anyway,

we've never once talked about taking out an endowment plan.'

'I just want something different out of life,' Nina said, in the same way she'd been saying for years, in the same way her family always took as a personal attack. What had been right for Hilda, then Marilyn and finally Alison — to be married with a baby on the way before they'd blown out twenty candles on their birthday cake — wasn't right for Nina.

Though she was *nearly* thirty and still didn't know what exact form the something different she wanted out of life would take.

'There's nothing wrong with being married,' Alison said forcefully.

'But you don't have to get married to be happy,' Nina said equally forcefully, whereupon eight-year-old Rosie burst into tears.

'I want to get married so I can wear a pretty dress and eat cake,' she sobbed, because Nina could even alienate the prepubescent members of the O'Kelly clan.

'Rosie, sweetheart, you can get married if you want to,' Nina said, getting up so she could hurry over to Rosie and put her arm around her. 'And you can also wear a pretty dress and eat cake without getting married if you want to.'

'Although no one will want to marry you if you eat too much cake and get fat,' Alison said firmly and though she swore that she wasn't talking about Nina and her non-married size fourteen to sixteen depending on where she was in her menstrual cycle, it sure felt like she was.

Nina left quite soon after that; refusing pudding, coffee

or a lift to the station and taking her raspberry meringue layer cake with her. When she got home, she'd change straight into her pyjamas and eat the whole damn cake while she caught up on her reading or watched a trashy film.

She gave an angry snort as she got to the station, realised that the Waterloo train was pulling in and then had to run, in heels, in a tight dress, carrying a collapsible meringue cake in a Tupperware container.

She made it with seconds to spare. The doors slid shut behind her and Nina leaned against them to get her breath back and cast her eye around the carriage.

It was early Sunday afternoon, that strange lull when most people were still lingering over lunch, so there were lots of empty seats. Nina could have a whole four-seater to herself if she wanted and she did want. Didn't want to have to look, or worse, talk to another human being for a good few hours. This must be how introverted Verity felt when she was overloaded at the end of a busy day.

Nina levered herself upright and tottered along to the middle of the carriage and the cluster of four-seaters. There was a man just sitting down in one of them. Nina hoped he wouldn't tell her off for putting her feet up but God help him if he did.

Then she got nearer and she saw his face and he raised his eyes from his iPad screen as if he could sense Nina's scrutiny and they both gazed blankly at each other for a very long moment.

It was Noah. Of course it was Noah because this was the day from hell.

CHAPTER 9

I am now quite cured of seeking pleasure in society, be it country or town. A sensible man ought to find sufficient company in himself.'

N oah lifted his hand in a half-hearted gesture and Nina could absolutely style this out. Wave back and carry on walking to the end of the carriage.

Or she could just act like a grown-up and sit down opposite Noah. 'Well, this is a coincidence!' Of course it wasn't a coincidence when his parents lived five streets away from hers; God would smite her for all the lying she was about to do. 'So anyway this is already awkward enough without us ignoring each other all the way to Waterloo, but if you want some quiet time, I can just shove off?'

He shook his head. 'No, you're all right.'

Noah really knew how to make a girl feel special. 'So, where do you live anyway?' Nina asked.

'Bermondsey.' He seemed a little awkward, but Nina was used to working a tough crowd. She had *just* survived a family dinner, after all.

'Cool. By the Tate Modern?' she asked and this feigned interest in the face of zero encouragement was actually a lot like being on a bad date.

'Nearer to Borough Market.'

'There's a stall in Borough Market that sells this salted caramel chocolate tart that makes me want to cry even thinking about it.' Nina closed her eyes at the memory of said salted caramel chocolate tart, then opened them again to see Noah looking at her. He quickly averted his gaze. 'Mattie must never know that I'm having impure thoughts about someone else's French patisserie,' she added and she wasn't even joking, though Hallelujah! Was that the tiniest of smiles breaking through the stormy look on Noah's face?

'I'll take your secret to the grave,' he promised solemnly, then gestured at the Tupperware container on Nina's lap. 'Where've you been then?'

'My parents' house. Sunday lunch once a month is a bit of a ritual slash torment now that I live up town.' Nina sighed. 'At least, it was meant to be for Sunday lunch but then World War Three broke out between me and my mother.'

Noah raised his eyebrows. 'That bad, eh?'

'Yeah, but we'll leave it a week then she'll phone, it's her turn to phone after we've had a row, I did it last time, and neither of us will mention it. It's our way.' Nina shook her head at the utter trainwreck that was her relationship with her mother. 'What about you?' She just about stopped herself from asking if he'd seen his folks too – after all, they were strangers and she couldn't know that his family were from Worcester Park too.

Noah had a small collection of Tupperware next to him on the seat. He gave it a look of repulsion. 'Yeah, same as you, visiting the parents. No World War Three but a few minor skirmishes,' he confessed in a tired voice. Then he rubbed his eyes like his own trip to the bosom of his loving family had exhausted him.

Nina could empathise. 'Well, at least you got leftovers out of it,' she pointed out, because she wanted to turn Noah's frown upside down. And though she hadn't been directly involved, she still felt guilty about the rotten time he'd had as a kid. 'Who doesn't love a cold roast potato?'

'I love cold roast potatoes,' Noah said dreamily then fixed grave green eyes on Nina. 'There are no cold roast potatoes in any of these containers though. It's all high-fibre vegan food.'

Her mother had said something about Noah's parents being hippies with funny ideas, but then as far as Alison was concerned anyone who wore Birkenstocks or didn't eat meat was a hippy with funny ideas. Nina didn't share her mother's viewpoint. In fact, she even willingly went meat-free a few days each week because she cared about the planet and yeah, admittedly, sometimes dinner was just a bowl of cheesy chips from The Midnight Bell. 'Yum.

Some of my happiest moments have involved stuffing my face with a black-lentil dal.'

'I hear you,' Noah said morosely. 'Unfortunately, my parents' vegan cooking hasn't moved beyond the nut roasts they learned to make when they were students, though they have got with the times and added chia seeds to them now.' He rubbed his eyes again. 'Today's nut roast was so dry that it's sucked every last drop of moisture out of my body. Or maybe it was the mung-bean bake.'

Nina had once lived with a militant vegan who'd left bowls of soaking mung beans everywhere so she could empathise.

'I'm getting cotton mouth just thinking about it,' she said. And she didn't realise she'd been tensing her muscles until she settled back in her seat and felt the tension leave her. 'Was that what the skirmishing was about? Did you try to sneak a Scotch egg past your mum?'

'I could murder a Scotch egg. I might have to go home via Tesco Express to get one,' Noah said with the same dreamy expression as before. When he'd first rocked up at Happy Ever After in his suit and with his iPad, Nina would never have imagined that he'd have so many layers. He wasn't wearing a suit today. There were jeans and underneath his navy-blue peacoat, a navy-blue jumper peeked out. God, he really did love a navy-blue ensemble. 'But no, I know much better than to try and sneak any animal products past my parents. We skirmished over my lifestyle choices.'

'You too? I never imagined we'd have so much in common,' Nina said, and Noah laughed, and Nina didn't think she'd seen him laugh before. The laughter was like an instant Instagram filter, wiping away the tired, tight look from his face and bringing his features to life again.

'You mean that your parents are also very disappointed that their own flesh and blood has sold their soul out. Then they harped on about sucking on the corporate teat for a while but I tuned out,' Noah said with an exasperated edge to his voice. 'As soon as they start talking about "The Man", I know what's coming and I switch off.'

'They're not proud of you? But, why not? I mean, you've been to Oxford and Harvard,' Nina reminded him, though Noah was hardly likely to forget.

'Did I tell you about that at the pub?' He looked confused and Nina found herself coughing wildly to distract him – no he hadn't bloody well mentioned it, dammit, that had been Alison.

'Do you need a sip of water?' Noah sat up, patting his pockets as though a water bottle would miraculously appear. Nina managed to get control of her 'coughing fit', and waved a hand at him weakly.

'I'm fine,' she croaked.

'It's a bit of a coincidence that you're from Worcester Park too,' Noah said as she wiped her watering eyes. 'And you're about the same age as me.' His brow furrowed and Nina closed her eyes in silent agony in anticipation of the next question he was definitely going to ask. 'What school did you go to?'

'I've pretty much repressed all memory of school,' she said desperately. 'Absolutely not the best days of my life.

Whoever came up with that expression didn't know what they were talking about.'

'Ha, yes! To be honest, I don't think about school that much either. It was pretty shitty for me too, but do you know what? I learned some life lessons from it and then I moved on,' Noah said calmly as if his dark days at Orange Hill weren't that big a deal. 'I wouldn't be very good at my job if I couldn't compartmentalise.'

Was it possible that she was going to get away with dodging his question? After all, Noah didn't seem to recognise Nina at all from their Orange Hill days, let alone realise that she was Paul's sister: good thing they didn't really look alike. But should Nina tell Noah about the connection? Would it be the right thing to do?

How would she even begin to bring it up? *Actually my older brother Paul used to beat you up on a regular basis.* Nina winced. 'Yeah, I've moved on too. Thank God!'

'It's best to leave all that stuff in the past,' Noah agreed. 'And right now, all I can think about are Scotch eggs. I'm starving,' he said plaintively, casting a baleful look at his Tupperware.

Nina stared down at the Tupperware on her own lap. She gave the container a cautious shake. Its contents felt a lot less intact than they had done before she'd run for the train. She prised open the lid to confirm her suspicions. Mattie's peerless raspberry meringue wasn't quite smashed to smithereens but it had certainly been broken into large lumps.

'Will this do?' Nina offered the box to Noah who peered

inside, then an expression of sheer joy came over him, which was much more pleasing to look at than his stony face of before.

He selected a large piece of very crumbly cake and then looked around. 'I need a plate and also a bib.'

Nina was already delving into her bag. 'When you wear as much make-up as I do, you never go anywhere without a packet of wetwipes. I also have tissues, cotton buds and some anti-bacterial hand gel.' She handed Noah a couple of tissues and watched as he took a happy bite of cake.

The smell wafting up from the container was heavenly: the soft, sweet cloud from the meringue and the sharp tang of the raspberries, but Nina wasn't going to eat cake in public. Not after spending two hours with her mother, meaning all she'd be thinking about was how many calories, carbs and grams of sugar she was consuming.

Hopefully, by the time she'd got home, these feelings would pass and she could eat cake and any other thing she damn well wanted without hearing Alison carping in her ear, 'A moment on the lips, a lifetime on the hips' or 'Nothing tastes as good as skinny feels' and her very favourite fat-shaming mantra, 'Little pickers wear enormous knickers.'

She didn't want to keep staring at Noah as he munched away – there was every possibility that she might start drooling, which was what happened when you denied yourself cake. And what if Noah thought she was slavering over him?

She shuddered and busied herself with her phone. There was a text from Chloe (Hope you're OK. We left just after

you once I'd told your mum not to give Ellie and Rosie complexes about their bodies. That went down well. Not! Speak soon. xxx) and a couple of messages on HookUpp from men she'd up-swiped but hadn't HookUpped with yet before she'd sworn off it. Checking it absolutely didn't count, because she wasn't going to reply, unless either of them categorically stated that they were looking for the Cathy to their Heathcliff. But neither of them had. They'd just sent her dick pics.

Had any woman ever formed a meaningful relationship with a man who didn't bother with any of the niceties, not even a 'how are you doing?' but went straight to sending her a photo of his tumescent yet still very unimpressive penis? Nina doubted it.

'I can't eat any more of this,' Noah declared and Nina looked up from her phone to see him putting the lid on her Tupperware. 'I want to leave room for my Scotch egg and I'm starting to go a little trippy from so much sugar.'

They were pulling into Earlsfield station, a few people waiting on the platform to board, and in a few minutes they'd be at Waterloo. Nina was just debating the merits of getting the Northern Line to Tottenham Court Road and then walking the rest of the way or whether she should get an Uber, though maybe she should delete the Uber app off her phone in solidarity with her father, when she realised that Noah had been speaking to her, because all of a sudden he reached across and gently tapped her on the knee.

'But don't you think it's weird?' he asked.

Nina blinked at him. 'What's weird?'

'That we've never met before.' Noah gestured at Nina with a slightly meringue-y hand. 'We grew up in the same place, we're about the same age and you're not the sort of person to fade into the background.'

At the thought of her days at Orange Hill, even though those days hadn't been the terror ride that Noah's had been, Nina got the same twinge in her stomach that she always got. A slightly panicky, sicky feeling. She willed it away. But also Noah had just confirmed that he didn't know that Nina had attended his school, let alone was related to his chief tormentor, and it seemed a pity to tell him now when they were getting on so well. She'd wait until they were in the shop, in a professional setting, and take him to one side to deliver the news, but for now it could wait.

'Well, I suppose technically we lived nearer to Cheam than Worcester Park,' she hastily amended. 'And I didn't look like *this* back then.'

Noah gave Nina a sweeping, assessing glance that started with her suede open-toe shoes and travelled upwards, lingering in the places that Nina wouldn't have expected him to linger, then settling on her face. He smiled as if her face was especially pleasing though Nina was pretty sure she'd chewed off her lipstick – she'd been planning on doing a quick repair job on the train before she'd bumped into him.

'I'd definitely have remembered you if you looked like *this*,' he said and his tone was appreciative and entirely male in a way that threw Nina off-course. Was he flirting with her? No. She surely wasn't his type; he certainly wasn't hers, though at this very moment, Tom's idea that Nina should do a little light flirting with Noah was quite appealing. Not to discover Noah's agenda but because Nina liked to be both giving and receiving of flirtation.

'Well, back then I had buck teeth, braces and bee-sting boobs. Then when the braces came off and puberty finally kicked in, I spent most of my waking hours straightening my hair and making sure that I had plenty of midriff on show, thanks to my huge collection of cropped T-shirts and hipster jeans. Even in winter.'

'And how did you go from that to this?' Noah asked with another long look at Nina, his eyes heavy-lidded, so she felt another twinge in her stomach, though this twinge didn't make her feel panicky or sick. It was the good kind of twinge.

Obviously the scene at her parents' house had unsettled her. And now Nina was dragged back to the past. To Worcester Park. And the girl she'd once been. 'Like I said, a lot of things have changed.' It was time to switch it up. Forget about that girl, be the woman she'd become. 'What about you? Any teen fashion no-nos lurking in your closet?'

'Oh, too many to mention. I was a late bloomer.' Noah shrugged modestly. 'Also, I eventually realised that pocket protectors and the huge glasses I used to wear weren't doing me any favours. It was quite a revelation.'

'I can imagine,' Nina said carefully, because she didn't want to blurt out anything tactless about Noah's former look and the bottle-top glasses and give the game away.

'Once you get past the pimples and all the hormones, puberty is a wonderful thing, isn't it?'

'Yeah, though the acne was hard. You couldn't tell where it ended and where my freckles began,' Noah said and Nina's eyes were drawn to his face, which was blemish free, though he still had freckles, mostly over his nose and forehead.

'I like freckles,' she declared truthfully. 'Sun kisses, aren't they? When I was going through my Doris Day phase, I even drew some on with brown eyebrow pencil.'

'Don't take this the wrong way, but I don't really see you as a Doris Day,' Noah remarked as the train began to slow down as they approached Waterloo.

'This is why my Doris Day phase barely lasted a week,' Nina said over the announcement that they should check that they had all their belongings with them before they left the train. She gestured at Noah's collection of Tupperware. 'I was going to suggest that you leave those behind but I guess they might get blown up as a suspicious package.'

'So true,' Noah sighed, standing up and gathering his Tupperwared vegan fare. 'Also, if I don't return the Tupperware, I'll *wish* that I'd been blown up.'

It was perfectly natural to fall into step with Noah once they got off the train to walk towards the ticket barriers. 'Well, I hope you've still got room for that Scotch egg,' Nina said and actually she was feeling quite peckish herself.

Although they'd only been living together for a few months, Verity always made sure she was home from Johnny's to spend the evening with Nina after she got back from her trip to the family home. Not that Nina liked to share much about her Worcester Park life, but Verity seemed to sense that all was not well and that Nina needed company and a takeaway as she watched something trashy on TV.

'I always have room for a Scotch egg,' Noah said happily. He patiently waited as Nina hunted for her ticket. 'Though now I think I fancy a steak.'

'God, you're really desperate to purge the memory of that nut roast,' Nina said with a laugh.

They were on the concourse of Waterloo station. Unbelievably it was only three thirty but it felt later, though Nina could see the weak afternoon sun streaming in from one of the street entrances.

'I'm going to walk home along the South Bank and stop off for *steak-frites* on the way. There's a really good French restaurant on Bermondsey Street if you fancy it?' Noah asked so casually that Nina barely registered what he was saying as she began the hunt for her Oyster card.

Then it registered. 'Oh! *Steak-frites* sounds nice but . . . Very and I have this whole girls' night in thing on a Sunday after I've been to my folks,' Nina said.

'Right,' Noah said and his face set in a sudden and determined expression. 'Just to be clear, that was me asking you out. On a date.'

'Oh!' Nina exclaimed again. 'OK.' Was it OK? They were worlds apart . . . and he was her employer's husband's bestie . . . and the navy-blue wardrobe left a lot to be desired . . . and there was the UTTER DISTASTER of the secret she was keeping from him . . . but sharing a four-seater with

Noah hadn't been an ordeal. In fact, it had been a welcome distraction, otherwise she'd have sat there stewing and seething about the argument she'd just had with Alison, so that her mother would have managed to ruin Nina's entire Sunday.

Also, now Nina felt an obligation to genuinely be nice and charming to Noah, if only to make up for the vile way her own brother had treated him. It was a way to redress the balance, to pay penance, show Noah how to have some fun because he'd certainly never had any when he was at school.

'So, that is OK, then?' Noah prompted, his face quite pink though he still looked quite resolute. Nina did actually like a certain steely quality to her men.

'Yeah, it is OK,' Nina decided.

'Dinner then, this week coming. Is Wednesday evening good for you?' Noah persisted and Nina realised she'd been half expecting/half hoping that they'd swap phone numbers and play a little text tennis and nothing would ever come of it. But no. Noah was going to lock this date down. Again, she had to give him props for being so to the point. She was heartily sick of men who wouldn't even commit to a vague plan to meet for a drink, as if Nina was going to get the wrong idea and start picking out engagement rings. 'I'm working on another project this week so I won't be at Happy Ever After,' he clarified.

Nina opened the calendar on her phone, though she knew that she was free on Wednesday. If she really wanted to bail, she could invent some longstanding other engagement for Wednesday. 'No, Wednesday's fine,' she heard herself say, because apparently she didn't want to bail. She'd ponder that later tonight.

'Great. I'm working in Soho . . .'

'I'll come to you,' Nina said quickly, because this was just *one* date, a sympathy date, and she didn't need any of her friends to know about it. 'Shall we say eight o'clock outside the Cambridge Theatre?'

'Perfect.'

And then it was back to being awkward so that Nina died a little inside at the thought that she'd just committed to a date with Noah.

'Well, I'll see you Wednesday, then,' she said brightly as if Wednesday couldn't come soon enough. She was already backing away while Noah stood there, his face still pink and now frowning as if he was having second thoughts too. 'Enjoy your *steak-frites*!'

'I will,' he said and Nina couldn't bear it a second longer. She was now several paces away from Noah and with a farewell salute, she turned around and hurried away so she could be swallowed up in the crowd of travellers back from weekends out of town.

CHAPTER

10

'It's no company at all, when people
know nothing and say nothing.'

Wednesday was Valentine's Day and the shop was
madly busy with people buying romantic novels,
completely disproving Nina's theories that the loved-up
wouldn't need to and the lovelorn couldn't bear to. Though
the bulk of their customers were panic-stricken men who
descended in their droves at lunchtime and just before
closing to buy cards and romantic gifts and 'I don't suppose
you sell flowers, do you?'

Happily, Nina had customers to serve and books to pimp
and not that much time to dwell on her date that evening
but the important question was WHY had Noah asked her
out for a date on Valentine's Day? What was *that* about?

She had decided to keep it on the down low. Hadn't

told Verity or Posy because they'd make something of it and Tom would sneakily convince Nina to ferret out vital information about their job security. Anyway, Nina had already decided that she'd put Noah straight right from the start. Before they'd even ordered a round. They weren't on a date date; they were on a non-date; they were just two people having a drink together.

Because although she had a rule that she never turned down a date, on the way back to Happy Ever After on Sunday afternoon, Nina had remembered one of her other rules: not to mix business with pleasure.

For someone who tried to live her life as passionately and spontaneously as she could, she seemed to have a lot of rules, Nina thought to herself with a small sigh as she turned the shop sign to closed. A quick tidy up of the main room, then she had about an hour and a half to get ready.

'Nina! Are you ill?' Posy asked in a concerned voice, putting her hands on her hips as she stood behind the counter.

Nina frowned. 'No, I'm fine. Why would you think I was ill?'

'Because you haven't asked if we're going to the pub,' Posy replied. 'You *always* try to rustle up a pub posse. Are you sure you're not sickening for something?'

'I don't *always* go to the pub after work,' Nina insisted, because she didn't. At least, she didn't think she did. Not *every* night. 'Way to make me sound like a complete alkie.'

'Not an alcoholic, you're just sociable,' Verity called out

from the back office. She made being sociable sound like a fate worse than death.

By now Nina was at the office door so she could stick her tongue out at Verity, who stuck her own tongue out in riposte. 'Anyway,' Nina said, as she retrieved broom and dustpan and brush from the tiny kitchen off the office. 'Anyway, I have a date tonight.' She muttered the last bit and even though she didn't drag her colleagues to the pub *every* night, she did have dates most evenings so it wasn't that much of a revelation. Not even worthy of comment.

'Oooh! Who? Where did you meet him?' Posy asked. 'On HookUpp?'

Nina began to sweep the floor. 'No, not on HookUpp, you know I've sworn off it. Just some bloke I met on the train home on Sunday. You absolutely don't know him.' She could only hope that Noah hadn't mentioned it to his good friend Sebastian either. There'd be endless questions, teasing, speculation and it was only one date. Not even a date – a non-date.

'So, come on, tell us more. Is he in a band?' Verity had left the office and was now standing in front of the till, fingers entwined as she stretched her arms in preparation for cashing up. 'What does he look like? How many tattoos does he have?'

'What is it with all the questions?' Nina demanded, as she viciously attacked the bottom of one of the display units with the broom. 'Do I interrogate you about your love lives?'

'Yes! All the time! Even when I didn't have a love life,'

Posy scoffed. She was meant to be reshelving the books that browsing customers had unshelved but had given that up in favour of sprawling on one of the sofas in the centre of the room, her legs dangling over the arm. 'You are the queen of unsolicited dating advice. When Very had her third date with Johnny, you pretty much demanded that she have sex with him.'

'I didn't demand. And we agreed that she could have sex with him on a fifth date on account of her being a vicar's daughter, didn't we, Very?'

'Yes, there have been many times we've discussed my previously non-existent sex life,' Verity said in a deadpan fashion. 'Usually in front of a shopful of customers and now you're being strangely coy about a first date when you must have been on a thousand first dates.'

'Not a thousand,' Nina said automatically, crouching down to sweep up a day's worth of crumbs, receipts and other detritus into the dustpan. Then she thought about the last ten years of her life. In that space of time she'd had two semi-serious relationships that had lasted roughly six months each. A handful of not-serious relationships that hadn't made it to the three-month mark. So, that took care of about two and a half years, which left seven and a half years of dating.

Nina did some rapid mental arithmetic, which made her head hurt. Three hundred and sixty-five days in a year. So in seven years that was er, let's call it two thousand and five hundred days. Two thousand and five hundred days of internet dates and HookUpp dates and friend of a friend dates and meeting eyes with a stranger on the other side of the bar dates and yeah, God, she probably had been on, at the very least, a thousand first dates.

'What am I even doing with my life?' Nina muttered under her breath as the futility of trying to find love – passionate, fulfilling, the-beat-of-his-heart-matches-mine love – when you'd already been on at least a thousand first dates, suddenly struck her.

'Well, you do always say that you have to snog the face off a hell of a lot of frogs before you find your prince,' Posy said. She held up her hand so her wedding ring and the huge sapphire-and-diamond engagement ring Sebastian had bought her caught the light. 'God, I'm so glad I didn't have to snog hardly any frogs at all.'

'You're a dear friend, Posy, and that's why I have to tell you that you're starting to sound like a smug married,' Very said sternly, wagging the pencil she was holding in Posy's direction.

'We're only pointing that out because we care,' Nina added, but she was a little cheered at Posy's reminder of her own advice.

Yes, there had been a lot of frogs in Nina's life but all it took was one date, one man, one kiss to turn the tide; to be a prince and not some kind of low-life amphibian. And it was too bad that Nina was wasting a date on Noah when he was never going to be her 'heart's darling' as Emily Brontë put it, but once she'd established that they could never be anything other than friends, he might have some good-looking mates he could set her up with.

★

Ninety-three minutes later, Nina hurried down Shaftesbury Avenue. She was late, she was always late, but the nerves were a brand-new experience and Nina didn't like them at all.

Because there was nothing to be nervous about; it was Noah. She'd spent two weeks being silently observed by him. Had been to the pub with him. Had sat on a train with him. In fact, she'd been at school with him and witnessed various incidents involving Noah that probably still gave him nightmares, not that he was ever going to know that.

So, Noah was far from an unknown quantity and yet on all those other first dates with men she hardly knew, a lot of them just a tiny pic on a phone screen and a couple of messages, she hadn't been nervous. There'd just been that delicious champagne tingle of excitement, of what if-ness, but now as she crossed over to Charing Cross Road, fighting her way through the crowd of people spilling in and out of Leicester Square station, Nina felt quite sick with apprehension and despite the chill of the February night she was sweaty in places she didn't want to be sweaty: her hands, her armpits, and, despite the fact that she'd spritzed her make-up with fixing spray, there was a tell-tale clamminess on her forehead and upper lip.

'It's only Noah,' she told herself, as she waited at another set of lights. Their meeting point was just across the road and like a teenager on her very first date, Nina was too scared to look to see if Noah was already waiting for her.

But as soon as she crossed the road, before she had time

to scan the faces of other people waiting for their dates to arrive, she felt a hand on her arm.

'Nina,' said a voice, Noah's voice, and she sucked in a breath before she turned round with a smile that was completely faked.

'Hi,' she said in a peppy voice that was faked too. 'Hope you haven't been waiting . . . long.'

'I only just got here,' Noah said and he leaned across so he could kiss her cheek, which quickly became awkward when Nina offered Noah the other cheek, because didn't everyone do two kisses?

Apparently Noah didn't because he was already stepping back. 'Look, when I asked you out, I didn't realise that today was Valentine's Day,' he said with genuine distaste so that Nina immediately felt embarrassed that she'd ever suspected otherwise. 'But anyway, hi. Hello. You look nice.'

Nina pulled a face. 'Well, I don't but thanks anyway.' To go along with the nerves, she'd also had a wardrobe crisis. Most of her first-date outfits involved tight dresses with plunging necklines but she didn't want to give Noah the wrong idea or false hope and so she'd had to scrap that and go with a plan B. Plan B was jeans though Nina rarely did jeans; a high-waisted, dark-denim, fifties-cut jean with a wide turn-up, which she was wearing with a leopard-print twinset and motorcycle boots. No wonder she was hot and sweaty and felt as covered up as a nun, so nice didn't even come close. 'You look good though.'

It was Noah's turn to pull a face. 'Oh, this old thing!' he said tugging at his navy peacoat. 'So . . . ?'

'So . . . ?' Nina echoed and wondered whether she should launch into her 'this is not a date' speech. It couldn't make things any more awkward than they already were. But where to start? 'So, look . . . Noah. You seem like a—'

'So, I was thinking—'

Oh God, now they were both talking at the same time. Noah pinked up and Nina was sure that her make-up, despite the very expensive fixing spray, was now completely sliding off her face.

'Sorry.'

'No, I'm sorry.'

'You were saying—'

'What were you saying—'

They were talking over each other again. Nina held up her hand. 'You go first,' she said a little desperately.

'Are you sure?' Noah asked.

Nina shut her eyes because she couldn't look at the doubt on Noah's face a moment longer. Like, he was regretting his decision to ask her out in the first place. Which was fine, she felt the same way, but he didn't need to make it so obvious. 'Yes,' she gritted. 'What were you going to say?'

She opened her eyes to see Noah swallow hard and mutter something she couldn't catch. 'Right,' he said more decisively. 'What I was going to say was that I don't know about you but I really need a drink. To clarify, a drink that contains alcohol. Does that sound like a good idea?'

Nina had never heard of a better idea. 'Yes,' she said fervently. 'For the love of God, yes.'

CHAPTER 11

*'If I had caused the cloud, it was
my duty to make an effort to dispel it.'*

Nina would have sworn that she knew her way around Soho blindfolded, but as they walked along Old Compton Street, Noah guided her left then right then down a tiny alley she'd never noticed before.

Very soon they were seated opposite each other in a booth in a burger joint called Mother's Ruin. The jukebox was playing Elvis, the burgers were dirty and piled high and they each had an Old Fashioned in front of them.

'This might be my new favourite place in the world,' Nina told Noah and he raised his glass and clinked it against the side of hers.

'I passed this place a couple of weeks ago and I remember thinking then that it would probably be your kind of thing,' he said, making sure to look Nina in the eye so she couldn't mistake the intent of his words. 'Because I've been thinking about you a lot these past couple of weeks.'

Nina blushed, which was starting to become a nasty habit, even though she'd had many similar compliments. Not once before had she blushed.

'So, my awesome sales technique has been keeping you up at night?' Never before had Nina had to try so hard to come up with cheeky banter.

Noah's eyebrows shot up. 'Not that your sales technique isn't awesome but that's not what was keeping me up all night.' He screwed his eyes tight shut like he was in pain. 'I mean, I haven't been *up* all night thinking about you. Just . . .' He shook his head. 'Let's look at the menu. Are you hungry?'

If this were a proper date then Nina would probably have said lasciviously, 'I'm starving and not for food,' but it wasn't a proper date so she settled for a truthful, 'I could eat.'

It was much better with their menus open so they could talk about the merits of a dirty burger versus buttermilk fried chicken and if they should get a mac and cheese on the side to share along with their rosemary-and-thyme fries and deep-fried onion rings. 'And a side salad,' Nina decided. 'Just to show willing.'

'Yeah, we should probably have something green and leafy on the table,' Noah agreed. 'And what do you want to drink? Another Old Fashioned or do you want to get a bottle of something?'

'I never mix grape and grain, it makes for the worst hangovers.' Nina shuddered at the memory of all the terrible hangovers she'd suffered. 'I think I'll stick to the Old Fashioneds.'

She felt more at ease now, and boiling enough to slip off her leopard-print cardigan and push up the sleeves of her matching leopard-print jumper. Noah mirrored her movements, unbuttoning the cuffs of the navy-blue (big surprise) shirt he was wearing so he could roll up his sleeves, and that was when Nina saw it: the large, elegant, black type, a series of numbers and letters marching up the soft skin of his left forearm.

'What's that?' Nina demanded. 'What's that on your arm?'

Noah grinned. 'It's a tattoo, Nina,' he said evenly. 'Have you never seen one before?'

'Of course I have!' Nina held up her inked arms as proof. 'You! *You* have a tattoo?'

'I do.' He grinned again. 'Is there going to be a copyright problem?'

'What? No! I just . . . I just can't believe that you have a tattoo. You don't seem the sort.'

Noah wagged a finger at her. 'You work in a bookshop, you must know all about not judging books by their covers.'

'True. Sorry. So,' Nina gestured at Noah's arm. 'What is it?'

Noah held out his arm so Nina could have a proper look at the letters, which made no sense. In fact, they were giving Nina alarming flashbacks to GCSE maths.

'Is that . . . is that *algebra*?' she asked.

'It is,' Noah admitted cheerfully. 'It's my favourite equation. Bayes' theorem.'

'Bayes' what 'em? Can you explain it to me in words of less than three syllables?'

'I'm sure I could.' Noah wrinkled his brow in thought. 'So, Bayes' theorem describes the probability of an event, based on prior knowledge of conditions that might be related to the event.'

'OK,' Nina said slowly. 'Right.'

'For instance, I knew that you liked vintage clothes and whatnot and I knew you ate meat because we talked about it on the train, so based on this knowledge, I picked this place for our date because it's a retro burger joint.' Noah tapped his tattoo with a longer finger. 'Bayes' theorem in practice.'

'I'm impressed!' Nina was. 'If my physics teacher had bothered to explain things so clearly at school then perhaps I wouldn't have abandoned physics at the first opportunity.'

'My physics teacher was never the same after he had an affair with the B-stream French teacher,' Noah said as their second round of drinks arrived.

Nina smothered a gasp of genuine shock – not Mr Clark and Mrs Usher, whose French lessons mostly involved anecdotes about what she got up to on holiday in France with Monsieur Usher? 'Scandalous! How did you find out that juicy morsel of gossip about these two people I've never even met?'

Noah quirked his eyebrow at her. 'One Saturday I went to an exhibition at the Wellcome Collection and I saw them holding hands in the coffee shop.' He paused to take a sip of his drink. 'Thought it was best not to say anything.'

With a guilty start, Nina knew that if she'd seen her two teachers canoodling it would have been all around school by lunchtime the next day. Back then, even though he'd had no reason to, and who would have blamed him for lashing out, Noah had been more kind and thoughtful than any teenage boy had the right to be.

Nina rewarded that kindness and thoughtfulness with a smile. She was here, after all, because Noah deserved a good date, dammit, and Nina was a veteran of a good date. The one surefire way she knew to a man's heart wasn't through his stomach, though the heaving platters of food that were coming their way should see to that. Oh no, if Nina had learned anything on those thousand or so first dates that she'd been on, it was that no man could resist talking about himself.

'Your tattoo,' she prompted as Noah's chicken and Nina's burger were placed in front of them. 'Did you study physics at Oxford?'

'Well, I'd categorise Bayes' theorem as more probability than physics and that's what I studied at Oxford – probability and statistics. How do you feel about condiments?' he added as the waiter put down a small tray groaning with mustards and ketchups.

'Love condiments,' Nina said. 'One of the major food groups as far as I'm concerned. So, probability and statistics? Why did you want to do a degree in them?'

'I like solving puzzles and I like to think that things

happen for a reason rather than just sheer random luck,' Noah said, though Nina liked to think just the opposite. That life was about fate and destiny, though there were times you could give fate a little nudge. There was nothing romantic about reason and living your life guided by probability and statistics. What with that and the exclusively navy-blue wardrobe, Nina didn't think she'd ever met a man who was less likely to be her one true love. Still, she was here, on a non-date with Noah for altruistic reasons, so she'd give it her all.

'How was Oxford then?' she asked, as Noah helped himself to an onion ring.

'It was scary,' he said. 'I was two years younger than everyone else because I skipped a couple of years at school, but once I settled in, it was fine. Better than fine really, because I was surrounded by people who wanted to learn. It was an uphill struggle to learn anything at my school: even in the top stream, there was always someone or something kicking off.' He took another onion ring. 'And Oxford wasn't like a normal university. The porters in my college were like over-protective parents and Sebastian, of all people, decided to take me under his wing pretty quickly. Then once I realised that I was studying with people who didn't want to beat the crap out of me, I started to make friends.'

Nina nodded along, even though every time he mentioned school, her stomach would clench and she'd have to put down her burger and take a large gulp of her drink.

She so desperately wanted to say she was sorry, apologise for what Paul had done, but it was a first date, their only date, a non-date, and it was best to keep the mood light and fun.

'Did you go to Harvard straight after Oxford?' she asked and hoped that the change of subject would mean no more oblique references to her brother and the horrible things he'd done to Noah.

'Not straight after. I was still only nineteen so I decided to take a couple of years out, do some travelling, paying my way as I went. Started off in Thailand . . .'

Noah had been everywhere. Thailand, Vietnam, Singapore, all over South-East Asia, then Goa and India before getting on a long-haul flight to explore South America. He'd trekked through the jungle in Peru, narrowly avoided being kidnapped in Colombia, had inadvertently taken psychotropic drugs in Bolivia and had got to Rio just in time for Carnival.

'You have had some adventures,' Nina breathed. She was a creature of passion and spontaneity but to be honest, the furthest she'd ever travelled and the biggest adventure she'd ever had was the time she went to Mykonos for a hen weekend and had ended up in hospital with two broken ribs and a broken toe from falling off a podium in a nightclub after too many shots.

'I was young and completely wet behind the ears, so the adventures found me, but I did discover that I was a bit of an adrenalin junkie. White-water rafting, bungee jumping, being suspended from a great height with a zipline. I never feel more alive than when I'm facing certain death, I suppose,' Noah said with a wry smile. He pushed away the bowl of chips that he'd been dipping into. 'Talking of certain death, if I eat anything else then I'm a goner.'

'Tell me about it.' The waistband of her jeans felt as tight as a tourniquet. Nina had been mindlessly eating the onion rings and laughing as Noah had kept her entertained with tales of his many near-death experiences while travelling. 'Could go another cocktail though.'

'Me too,' Noah agreed. Once the waiter had taken their drinks order and cleared the table, Noah, after a little prompting, brought Nina up to speed with the last ten years of his life.

After Brazil, he'd met up with a friend from Oxford who was living in San Francisco and had helped him with his tech start-up, then he'd been headhunted by Google who'd paid for him to do his MBA at Harvard. Then after six years at Google, he'd decided to go it alone.

'I'm not a big fan of routine. I much prefer being my own boss,' he told Nina, who, if Posy was anything to go by, didn't think being your own boss was that great. It seemed to involve a lot of responsibility and having to fill in VAT returns every three months or so.

'But what is it that you actually do?' she asked as yet more Old Fashioneds arrived. 'Apart from harassing hard-working employees with your iPad?'

'If I were you I'd take me to a tribunal,' Noah said again with another smile because both of them had that glow that came from a lot of good food, four whisky cocktails each and a conversation that had managed to remain almost free of any awkward moments. 'Specifically, I work with businesses to find a solution to a particular problem, whether it's not being able to retain staff or how to sell more romantic novels. It's much easier as an outsider to come in and see the bigger picture.'

'That makes sense, I suppose,' Nina said and she was all good to go with some more questions but Noah held up a hand.

'Anyway, that's quite enough about me,' he said firmly. 'I don't want to be that guy on a date who only talks about himself. I want to know what you've been doing since you left the mean streets of Worcester Park.'

Working a series of unsatisfying jobs and dating a series of unsatisfying men – compared to what Noah had packed into the fifteen years since their paths had crossed, it didn't seem that impressive.

Oh God, what am I even doing with my life? It wasn't a new thought. On the contrary it was a very old, much-visited thought that Nina usually had after binning or being binned off by either employer or boyfriend. And she usually had it when she was on her own, in the dead of night, unable to sleep, not in public, not when she was on a date. She really needed to find a direction in life, if only not to have more of these excruciating conversations on first dates.

'There's not much to tell,' she said breezily, because now was not the time to give in to her angst. 'Got some tattoos, a couple of piercings, endured a few hangovers – that's about it.'

Noah was not to be put off. 'I'm sure that's not it,' he

said. 'Posy said that you'd always worked in retail. What was your last job before Happy Ever After?'

Nina couldn't help but pull a face at the thought of where she'd worked before she worked at Happy Ever After. And where she'd worked before that and so on and so on.

'God, was it that bad?' Noah asked in response to Nina's facial contortions.

'Yeah,' Nina sighed. 'It wasn't retail – Posy just assumed it was and I never denied it – it was more . . . um, service industry, I think?'

'My mind is racing with the possibilities . . .' Noah widened his eyes. 'Service industry could mean anything. Were you an arms dealer? Did you run an illegal drinking den? Cat burglar?'

'I was a hairdresser!' Nina admitted grudgingly. 'Colourist mostly, some cutting and styling.'

'That's probably why your own hair looks so good,' Noah said, with a nod at Nina whose hair was still a very sherbet pink and currently arranged in a French twist, the front section quiffed and pinned back. 'What made you decide to swap hairdressing for bookselling?'

There was no judgement in Noah's voice. He sounded as if he were genuinely interested to hear what had prompted Nina's career change, and it was rather a leap: to swap her scissors and her foils for books and bookmarks.

'Well, like I said, I left school after my GCSEs, which I aced by the way,' she added a little defensively. 'Then it was a done deal that I'd go and work for my aunt who has a salon in Worcester Park, Hair by Mandy – maybe you know it?' she said, knowing full well he would.

'My gran goes there. I think you'll find it's Hair *and Nails* by Mandy,' Noah corrected her and Nina smiled.

'You must never forget the "and Nails",' Nina said gravely because Mandy went ballistic if any of her staff did.

'I still can't believe we've never crossed paths before,' Noah said, shaking his head. 'You must have done my gran's wash and set at least once while you were there.'

Nina tried to smile breezily. 'Maybe. But there were so many wash and sets, with so many old ladies, you know what I mean?' Noah nodded, even as he looked slightly disappointed.

'Anyway, I started there as a trainee and also went to college to do my NVQ. I mean, I have qualifications.' That same defensive note crept into her voice. 'I worked there for four years but I didn't want to spend my whole life in Worcester Park doing the same cut and colour on the same customers week in and week out, so I got a job in town . . .' Nina tailed off and shook her head.

'How did that go down with Aunt Mandy?' Noah asked.

'Like a lead balloon,' Nina said baldly. 'I'm amazed that I wasn't officially excommunicated. I got a job in a salon in the West End, which was a bit more happening and I moved around, worked in some quite edgy places, I did balayage, ombré, dip-dyeing, colour melding, so it wasn't as if I was always doing the same thing.'

'I have no idea what any of those things are,' Noah said. 'Ombré? Isn't that a painting technique?'

Nina nodded but she was too far down memory lane to stop and explain how she achieved an ombré effect on someone's hair. 'My last salon even specialised in vintage and retro styles but I'd been doing people's hair for the last twelve years and it just . . . I just . . . I wasn't enjoying it and I kept getting the sack because of my attitude – there was this whole incident in my last-but-one salon where I ended up having a barney with the mother of the bride about a wedding package. I won't bore you with all the details.' Nina sighed again. 'Then I met Lavinia. She owned Bookends . . . that's what Happy Ever After was called before the relaunch.'

'I know about Bookends and I knew Lavinia. She and Perry would come up to Oxford to take Sebastian out for lunch and he'd drag me along in the hope that they wouldn't give him a telling off in front of company.' Noah laughed. 'It was a case of hope over expectation. I witnessed some pretty epic bollockings.'

Nina laughed too at the thought of Sebastian, the Rudest Man in London, getting a dressing down from his grand-parents.

'I forgot that you and Sebastian go way back,' she said.

'Way, way back, but we were talking about you, not me,' Noah said quietly but in a way that made it clear that he wasn't to be deterred from his goal of learning more about Nina's chequered path through life. She imagined that the same quiet determination was a very effective way of dealing with Sebastian too. 'The thing about Lavinia was, she could immediately see right through to the heart and soul of someone, couldn't she?'

'Oh, yes! She absolutely could. I met her by accident and after ten minutes I felt as if I'd known her forever and, more than that, she knew me. Saw a side to me that nobody else ever could.' Nina raised her glass in a silent toast to her late mentor. 'I miss her so much.'

'Yeah, so do I.' Noah raised his glass too. 'To Lavinia. So, she saw the secret bookseller in you?'

'Kind of. Or rather she saw my tattoos. Was very taken with them.' It was Nina's turn to hold her arms out for Noah's inspection. 'My *Alice in Wonderland* sleeve was complete though I'd barely got started on the *Wuthering Heights* design on the other arm, but she offered me a job on the spot, and I loved reading but I'd never have dreamed that I could work in a bookshop.'

'Why not? If you love reading then it seems like the perfect job?' Noah enquired, and Nina wanted to tell him that she wasn't a problem to be solved, but she didn't want to harsh their whisky-induced mellow. Besides, Noah was one of those rare people, like Lavinia, that you wanted to say stuff to. Your deep, personal, inside stuff because it seemed impossible that he'd take your words and use them against you. Or judge you for them.

'Yes but . . . I'm not clever enough to work in a bookshop,' Nina blurted out, before she lost her nerve. 'It's why the others don't know that I used to be a hairdresser. They all have degrees. Like, Tom is working on his *third* degree and all I have are seven GCSEs and an NVQ. Listen to me! I think I've had too much to drink. You'd better cut me off.'

'One for the road?' Noah suggested with a smile. 'I will if you will. And you can tell me more about those tattoos while we do.'

Nina could never turn down one for the road. 'Oh, go on then, twist my arm.' She did twist her own arm then, so Noah could see her tattoo, Cathy and Heathcliff, leaning against the gnarled tree. '*Wuthering Heights* is my favourite novel.' Was she going to? She barely knew him. But Noah was leaning forward, his eyes intent on Nina, his expression bright and alert, as if everything she said was endlessly fascinating. Nina couldn't remember the last time someone had looked at her like that. She was pretty sure that it had probably been one of the last times she'd seen Lavinia, so yes, she was going to share the secret of what made her tick.

'In fact, *Wuthering Heights* has been my inspiration for the last ten years of my life. It's why I quit Hair (and Nails) By Mandy, why I left Worcester Park, why I do most of the things I do.'

'Why's that then?' Noah asked.

'Passion. Cathy and Heathcliff were ruled by their passions. They didn't settle for safe or mediocre.'

Noah didn't respond at first but took a sip of his drink. 'I'm all for following one's passions, but I have to say that there are happier books to be inspired by.' He shrank back a little as Nina stiffened. 'I mean, things didn't turn out so well for Cathy and Heathcliff, did they?'

'Of course they didn't and I know that Cathy and Heathcliff were both high maintenance and that if you knew them in real life, they'd absolutely do your head in, but if I've learned anything from *Wuthering Heights* it's that a life without passion is a life half-lived,' Nina said with all the passion that she could muster, which was quite a lot of passion.

'So, you're passionate about working at Happy Ever After then?' Noah asked reasonably enough.

'Well . . .' Nina dithered slightly. 'I like working there. A lot. Like, really a lot,' she insisted, picking up her glass and glaring at it. 'God, these cocktails are like a truth serum. I'm happy enough, I just thought that at nearly thirty I'd be *happier.*'

'I hear you,' Noah said with great feeling. 'I really don't want to be that guy who quotes U2 . . .'

'Please, don't be that guy,' Nina said but Noah shook his head. He wasn't to be deterred.

'I've literally been halfway round the world and I still don't know what I'm looking for. Sometimes I wish I'd followed my childhood dreams and become a fighter pilot.' He tapped a finger to the corner of his eye. 'I'd probably fail the sight test.'

'I did wonder,' Nina said as delicately as she could for someone who'd drunk five whisky-based cocktails. ''Cause at school you wore really thick glasses.'

She froze, face hidden by her whisky glass. Would he pick up on her slip? Thankfully, it seemed five whisky-based cocktails were enough to make Noah a little fuzzy around the edges too.

'Contact lenses. Bifocal contact lenses. But could you

even imagine how horrific military training might be? At least at school, I got to go home each afternoon.' Noah swatted his own words away as if he couldn't bear to dwell on them. 'What about you? What did you really want to grow up to be when you were a kid?'

Nina couldn't help the shudder that rippled through her. 'Honestly? I wanted to be married by the time I was twenty because that's what my mum and my gran and my great-gran all did, like it was this grand family tradition.' She shuddered again at the thought of her lucky escape. 'But I loved art. Maybe even more than I loved reading. I had such a crush on my GCSE art teacher.'

'I didn't do art,' Noah said. 'I got special permission to take an extra maths class instead.'

'You freak,' Nina said without thinking but Noah laughed.

'Haven't got one artistic bone in my body. Maybe half a bone.' He held up his little finger. 'Half of this bone here. So, this art teacher, was she a goth? All the ones at my school wore way too much black.'

Ms Casson had been a bit of a goth. She had long black hair and wore long floaty black dresses and to stop her students throwing paint and X-Acto knives at each other, she'd kept them enthralled with tales of art college. But more than that, she'd seen something different in Nina, even though Nina had dressed the same and acted the same and behaved the same as all the other girls in her year. Ms Casson had told Nina that she had real talent and that she should stay on to do her A-levels, maybe even go to art college, but by then Nina was already working Saturdays in Hair (and Nails) By Mandy and going steady with Dan Moffat from the year above who'd already left Orange Hill and was studying engineering at the local college, and her future was set.

'Yeah, she was a bit of a goth,' Nina said to Noah. 'But she'd gone to the Royal College of Art and she painted when she wasn't teaching. One time she had an exhibition in a gallery up in town and our class went and that made me think that I'd love to be an artist. To create things that made people feel something. That's quite an amazing thing to do, isn't it?'

'It is,' Noah agreed. 'There's no reason you couldn't go to art class now. Life drawing or something?'

'Everyone in the class would be so much better than me,' Nina stated with absolute certainty. Also, there was nothing more tragic than someone constantly harking back to their school glory days. 'I haven't picked up a paintbrush in years. Wouldn't have the first clue what to do with a stick of charcoal. Anyway, I get to do my window displays at the shop and I've designed all of my own tattoos so I still get to be creative.' Nina caught their server's eye. 'Shall we get the bill then?'

Noah must have got the message that Nina wasn't up for any more self-improvement because he changed the topic to the company he was working with that week. They had a room you could only reach by rope ladder, called The Birdhouse, designed to encourage 'blue sky' thinking. And another room painted yellow called The Egg but no one could remember why.

'Maybe it's where they hatch new ideas,' Nina suggested with a smile because somehow Noah had managed to turn the non-date around again. 'Or crack a few yolks.'

Noah groaned as if he was in pain. 'Egg puns? I expected better from a chick like you.'

The bill arrived on a saucer that was placed in the dead centre of the table because this was a modern establishment that had no truck with outmoded conventions of dating. Much like Nina herself. She reached for the bill, about to suggest they go Dutch, but Noah's reflexes were much quicker.

'My treat,' he said firmly, barely glancing down at the total.

'We'll go halves,' Nina said just as firmly. 'You'll be bankrupt with the amount of cocktails we've just drunk.'

Noah clutched the bill to his chest. 'Hardly. Look, I asked you out, so I get the bill. That's how it works. It's common courtesy.'

Nina had been to this rodeo before. Quite a few times. You let the man get the bill and he expected something by way of return. There had even been a few charmers that Nina had met on HookUpp, who'd demanded that Nina reimburse them for the one measly drink they'd bought her after she'd messaged them to say that it had been lovely to meet up but she didn't want to take it any further.

'I always pay my way,' she said tightly. 'My look might be 1950s but my outlook certainly isn't.'

'This is my way of thanking you for a lovely evening,' Noah said, as he produced his credit card. 'Tell you what, why don't you put in the tip?'

Nina grudgingly agreed and put in a generous cash tip for their server and when she and Noah staggered outside, almost knocked sideways by the sudden cold wind that greeted them, she touched his arm hesitantly.

'I did, actually. Have a lovely evening,' she said, because it had hardly been the ordeal she'd expected. In fact, she'd enjoyed herself for a good seventy-five per cent of the non-date. Which reminded her that she still hadn't mentioned the non-date status of the time they'd spent together. It seemed churlish to bring it up now when Noah had just paid for their meal. She'd send him her tried and tested 'great to meet up' message in a couple of days.

'Me too,' Noah said with a note of surprise as if he hadn't been expecting to. 'So, did you want to maybe arr—?'

'How are you getting home?' Nina quickly asked because it sounded a lot like Noah wanted to lock down a second date. 'I'm going to jump on a bus at Charing Cross Road. Great thing about living in the centre of town – most buses pretty much take you from door to door.'

'But it's quite late. You're not getting an Uber?' Her plan to distract Noah had worked.

'My dad's a cabbie. The guilt I feel when I get an Uber outweighs the convenience,' Nina said. By now, they'd emerged from the tiny alley where the burger joint was situated onto Dean Street.

'Oh dear, maybe I should stop taking so many Ubers.' Noah took Nina's arm as they crossed the road, but then removed his hand from her elbow as soon as they reached the safety of the pavement. 'I'll see you onto the bus, shall I?'

'You don't need to do that,' Nina said a little desperately because Noah was intent on being a perfect gentleman, the perfect first date, and yet Nina was already planning how she'd bin him off.

'I don't need to but I want to,' Noah insisted as they went down the narrow alley next to The Pillars Of Hercules pub on Greek Street. 'There could be all sorts of ne'er-do-wells lurking between here and the bus stop.'

'You quite good in hand-to-hand combat, then?' Nina asked and for about the fifteenth time that night, she instantly and inwardly berated herself. If Noah had been any good in a fight, then his school days would have been very different.

'I am quite good in hand-to-hand combat these days. I have a black belt in Krav Maga . . .'

'You've got a black belt in *what*?'

'Krav Maga! It's a self-defence system developed for the Israeli Defence Forces and includes everything from judo to kickboxing. It was the big thing when I lived in San Francisco,' Noah explained.

'Show me some moves then,' she demanded as they reached the corner of Charing Cross Road. 'Do a kicky thing.'

Noah laughed and shook his head. 'I have to have been on at least three dates before I pull out the kicky thing. Talking of which . . .'

'My bus!' Nina had never been so pleased to see a 38 bus, even though, if she let it go, another one would appear in less than five minutes. 'I've got to go. Thanks for dinner.'

She ran towards the stop but Noah easily matched her pace. 'It was my pleasure. So, shall we do this again?'

'I'll text you,' Nina panted because she wasn't used to this kind of exertion and then she was at the stop just as the bus pulled in.

'I don't think we've swapped numbers,' Noah said as the small crowd of people already waiting got on board. 'Shall I call you at the shop?'

'Look, I really have to go,' Nina said. Normally she absolutely smashed it when it came to end-of-date proceedings. But this was a non-date and she didn't know whether to kiss Noah on the cheek or hug him; either one seemed appropriate.

In the end, as Noah leaned towards her, she settled for a mash-up of both, patting him on the cheek, then jumped on board the bus.

'I had fun,' Noah said, standing there with his hands in the pockets of his navy peacoat, his hair a riotous colour in the glow of the streetlights, a smile on his face like he really had had the best of times. 'See you soon.'

Nina was saved from having to reply by the bus driver shutting the door, so all she could do was wave then give Noah a thumbs up, like she was a contestant on a cheesy quiz show.

For a girl with all the moves, Nina couldn't remember a single one of them.

CHAPTER 12

'Nonsense, do you imagine he has thought as much of you as you have of him?'

Despite the five whisky cocktails of the night before, Nina emerged from her bedroom the next morning relatively unscathed. But then she'd been home at a decent hour: no late-night carousing around the fleshpots of Soho because Noah wasn't the carousing type and Nina knew that the heart which matched her own would beat to a drum which didn't stop until dawn.

'What is this madness? Usually you put your alarm on snooze at least three times,' Verity wanted to know when Nina walked into the kitchen. 'And I heard you come in last night.'

'Oh, sorry, I thought I was being quiet,' Nina said as she debated whether to make toast or to wait and see what Mattie had in the way of breakfast pastries.

'You were, for you. I was just surprised you were home so early. Bad date, was it?' Verity asked sympathetically.

'Very, stop being so chatty first thing,' Nina admonished. 'It's completely out of character and you're freaking me out.'

As distractions went, this one proved a winner. Immediately, Verity forgot about Nina's date because she had to insist in the strongest possible terms that she wasn't chatty first thing in the morning. 'I was only enquiring after your emotional well-being. That's what good friends and flatmates do,' she said then expanded on that theme for the next half hour.

Verity might be an extrovert who relished her own company and forbade Nina from even speaking for half an hour after work because she needed time to decompress but my God, she could ramble on. Not that Nina minded the rambling. All three of them – Nina, Posy and Verity – loved a good ramble and this morning, Verity was still pleading her non-chatty case as they went down the stairs to start the working day.

'Nina's accused me of being too talkative!' she informed Posy and Tom as they arrived together. 'Me! "You expect me to account for opinions which you choose to call mine, but which I have never acknowledged."'

'It's not even ten and you're already quoting *Pride and Prejudice*,' Posy protested.

'I thought we agreed that you wouldn't start quoting Austen until after lunch; this is far too early,' Nina said, then she narrowed her eyes at Tom. 'Far too early for you too, Tom. Did you not stop to get your breakfast panini this morning?'

'I didn't,' Tom said and his voice cracked on the last syllable as if he were under undue amounts of stress. 'In fact, I'm only here this early to tell you that I have to start work late today.'

Posy had been taking off her coat but she paused. 'I think this is what Sebastian means when he says that you all take advantage of my good nature,' she said. She assumed a stern expression. 'No, Tom. You're not starting late. I absolutely forbid it.'

Nina, Verity and Tom, who all served at Posy's pleasure, looked at her for one shocked moment then looked at each other and burst out laughing. Nina suspected that she might still be a little bit drunk because she laughed so hard that breathing became a bit of an issue. 'Say that again, Pose,' she wheezed. 'And don't forget to do the face.'

'You have no respect for my authority,' Posy grumbled. She folded her arms and settled for a baleful look this time. 'OK, I'll bite. Tom, why are you going to be late when you're already here?'

Tom held up the carrier bag he had with him. 'Because I have to go to a place in Russell Square to get two copies of my thesis bound, at great personal expense, so I can hand it in.'

'That sounds fair enough,' Verity decided and Posy and Nina nodded.

Nina looked at the carrier bag again. 'Hang on a sec.

You've finished your thesis?' she asked. 'You've checked all your references and sources? Even your bibliography?'

'I have,' Tom said and again his voice caught on the last syllable. 'I mean, it's no big deal.'

'It's a huge deal,' Posy said, her voice catching too because she really was the softest of touches.

'It's, like, three whole years of your life in that bag,' Nina said and she couldn't imagine working on just one thing for one tenth of your entire life. Well, apart from having a full sleeve tattooed but that was hardly the same thing.

'Four years actually,' Tom pointed out.

'Four years! Well done, you!' Verity gently punched Tom on the arm, which was hardly an appropriate way to celebrate this monumental event.

'I'm going to have to hug you,' Nina announced and though Tom tried to wriggle away, Nina quickly had him pinned against the counter so she could put her arms around him and squeeze.

It was like nestling up to reinforced concrete. 'Nina, please, I can feel your breasts,' Tom moaned faintly. 'I'm sure this counts as sexual harassment.'

'I'm pretty sure it doesn't,' Nina said but she released Tom from the prison of her embrace and tried to make a grab for his carrier bag, but this time he was too quick for her. 'Come on! Let us have a peek! At least show us the title.'

'Pffffttt! You don't need to see it. Really, it's too boring for words,' Tom demurred. He straightened up. 'And not to be rude or anything, but unless you know anything about critical theory, with particular reference to Lacan, it will probably go right over your heads.'

Nina felt that familiar pang at her lack of education but even Posy and Verity, with their degree apiece, flinched at the mention of critical theory.

'I hope that you're not going to be so pompous when you actually get awarded your doctorate,' Posy snapped. Then she made a shooing motion. 'Go! Get bound, before I change my mind!'

Of course, even though he could be very annoying, they couldn't let the fact that Tom had finished his four-year-long thesis pass without a celebration. Not that they knew any of Tom's other friends, or indeed if he had any, but later that afternoon Mattie baked a cake and Posy nipped out for a couple of bottles of something sparkling and Nina made a card. It was the least they could do and everyone was so busy making a fuss of Tom that nobody asked any questions about Nina's date the night before. Or even thought to wonder why Nina wasn't oversharing all the gruesome details like she usually did.

Creating a 3D card, which featured a pop-up Tom in scholar's gown and mortarboard, in between serving customers, was a great distraction for Nina too so she didn't have to think about last night's date.

Scratch that. Last night's non-date.

It meant she didn't have to think about Noah either. About her last sight of him: shoulders hunched against the chill of the night, his joyful grin, hair aflame. It wasn't an image that repulsed her. It was so far away from her memories of gangly, gawky Know It All Noah with his spots and his Coke-bottle glasses and pocket protector. Now, Noah was actually quite *pleasing* to look at, though he really needed to leave his navy-blue comfort zone.

Nina shook her head to dispel all thoughts of Noah. They'd had one non-date and now they were done. She'd worked off her guilt so it was time to move on and go on a date with a guy who lived next door to Stefan and Annika from the Swedish deli.

Stefan swore Nina would love him but it turned out that Stefan had even worse taste in men than Nina did. Josh addressed all his remarks to Nina's cleavage and as he did nothing but talk about himself for the forty-seven minutes that Nina sat there, she was sure he'd be able to pick out her boobs in a police line-up.

He didn't ask Nina one single question about herself and said nothing to make her laugh or want to stay for a second drink to find out more about him.

He was also wearing tight jeans (which normally she liked) rolled up to show his hairy ankles because he was also wearing loafers with no socks (which Nina always hated, always). In fact, it was such a lacklustre date compared to the high points of the non-date the night before that Nina didn't even bother with her usual subterfuge. Instead of excusing herself to powder her nose then escaping into the night through a side door, she just stood up and put her coat on. 'This is never going to happen again,' she told Josh. It was the first thing she'd said in thirty minutes.

'So you don't fancy coming back to mine for a quick bang?' he asked hopefully.

'Not while I have breath in my body,' Nina said grandly before she swept out and went back home to not think about Noah and the non-date. And to text Stefan and tell him that he owed her at least a week of free lunches.

Nina was still not thinking about Noah the next day, enough that she asked Posy casually when he might be in the shop again.

'I don't know. Maybe next week. Maybe the week after,' Posy said vaguely. Her keenness that they all start working smarter thanks to Noah's business solutions had fizzled out in the way that it so often did after Posy's initial burst of enthusiasm. 'Why? Do you need him for something?'

'Just curious,' Nina said and they had a peculiar ten seconds of staring at each other as Nina wondered if Noah had mentioned to Posy, his good friend's wife, that he'd been on a date with her employee. And Posy was probably wondering why Nina was staring at her without blinking. Nina forced herself to look down at the Post-it she was holding. 'Anyway, we don't really need a business analyst, do we? I was thinking . . . all that stuff we talked about before we relaunched, the special events and a book group and things, when are we going to crack on with it all?'

'I haven't forgotten about any of that,' Posy said, her eyes wide, her brow creased. 'It's just that it's all I can do to keep on top of the day-to-day things. Ordering stock, talking to reps, managing my staff.'

'Still seems a shame to let it all slide,' Nina said casually. She had no experience in organising *things*, but it would be something new, something challenging. It might not be creative but she'd be dealing with creative people: authors, bloggers . . .

'Of course, now that Tom's finally finished his thesis, and I still don't understand how it takes four years to write a really long essay, then he might be up for taking more of an active role in the shop,' Posy mused. 'I mean, he's been teaching while he's been doing his PhD so he has experience in telling people what to do . . . though I guess he might become a full-time academic now.'

'Yeah, Tom would probably be pretty good at that side of things though he knows sod all about romantic novels,' Nina pointed out. 'Or—'

'Ha, not that our customers of a certain age care about that,' Posy interrupted. 'They just treat Tom like a tweedy book god.' She shook her head in disbelief then went into the office and shut the door behind her so she couldn't see Nina's shoulders slump. Normally Nina had no trouble asserting herself but then she so rarely expected anyone to take her seriously. Especially not Posy, who tended to treat Nina as comic relief from the stresses of being a small-business owner rather than as a valued employee. But then it was hardly Posy's fault when Nina spent so much time playing the fool.

'Excuse me, do you work here?'

Nina's unhappy train of thought was derailed by a customer who wanted a book brought down from a high shelf and another lady who wanted a recommendation for her mother-in-law's birthday and many people after that, all wanting to buy books and Nina chatted to them all. She did love chatting to people about books; it was her favourite part of her job. Made every day different.

And she was only preoccupied with the lack of creativity in her day job because of the non-date with Noah. Nina glanced down at her outfit; the hated Happy Ever After T-shirt, which she'd paired with a tight black pencil skirt and green snakeskin mary janes with a punishingly high heel. She held out her arms to check that they were still covered in tattoos. Checked her tongue, nose and several ear piercings, then admired her face with its perfectly arched brows and red lips in the little mirror she kept under the counter.

She *was* creative. You couldn't look the way Nina did if you were uncreative. Each morning when she stood in front of her wardrobe and decided what she'd wear, or rather what would go with that horrid grey thing Posy made them wear, Nina was choosing who she wanted to be that day. That was creativity right there, she thought as the bell tinkled above the door and a bike courier came in.

'I can sign for it,' Nina called out because when the office door was closed it meant that Posy and Verity were hard at work and didn't want to be disturbed.

The courier held up a bag from the London Graphic Centre in Covent Garden. 'For a Nina O'Kelly?'

Nina frowned. 'That's me.' She knew for an absolute fact

that she hadn't ordered anything from the London Graphic Centre, which was like Selfridges for stationery lovers and artists alike. 'But that can't be for me.'

'That's your name, innit though.' The courier didn't care, he just wanted Nina's signature so he could move on to his next job.

He was out of the door before she'd even opened the bag. Inside were two beautiful, black, soft-bound sketchpads, the paper inside as smooth as velvet, a tin of really fancy Faber Castell coloured pencils and a smaller tin of stubby charcoals. 'What the hell?' Nina wondered out loud. Was there another Nina O'Kelly in a parallel universe who'd actually stayed on to do her A-levels and had then gone to art college and become a successful graphic artist?

It was a mystery until Nina peered into the bag again and drew out an envelope. Her name was written on it in an almost illegible scrawl. She opened it to find a single sheet of paper with the same spider's-web writing on it. It took a little while to decipher it.

Dear Nina

You said that you wouldn't know what to do with a stick of charcoal so here's your chance to find out.

Noah

Underneath his name, he'd written his email address in block capitals so it was at least more legible than the rest of the short note.

Nina looked at the sketchbooks, the coloured pencils, the sticks of charcoal. Two nights ago she'd confessed her secret dreams to Noah, even though she hadn't even shared the same aspirations with her closest friends. And because her secret dreams were also her secret resentments, Nina had got defensive and dismissive when Noah had suggested she take a life-drawing class.

Now, she felt something inside her give, like a flower slowly unfurling its petals. Noah had listened to her, really listened to her, and stored all that information away so he could buy her this thoughtful gift. It was the nicest thing that anyone had done for Nina in a long, long time.

I don't want nice, said the voice in her head (as it so often did). But she was definitely going to have to commit to a second date now, she thought, as all the complicated feelings that Noah roused in her – amusement, annoyance, bewilderment but mostly guilt – rose up in her again. This time, Nina would absolutely confirm its non-date status before they'd finished their first drink. Maybe even draw Noah a diagram of the friendzone that she was going to put him in. Give him a whole speech about how they should just be mates because he wasn't her type and God knows, she couldn't be his type. She only had seven GCSEs, after all.

Perhaps another drunken non-date was the wrong message. Nina could be just as thoughtful as Noah. Or at least, she could *try*. As she served customers and discussed new releases on autopilot she came up with and discarded half a dozen possible non-date scenarios with the help of *Time Out* and Google.

Noah would probably enjoy going to a lecture at the Royal Geographical Society about climate change or to the Institute of Contemporary Art on The Mall to listen to a 'theorist and media activist' talk about 'futureability' but Nina would rather have root-canal treatment without an anaesthetic.

He'd mentioned wanting to do the Gumball Rally, a transcontinental car race, but no way could Nina afford a day at Brands Hatch and as for his other high-adrenalin pursuits, Nina wasn't going to do anything that involved having to wear figure-hugging Lycra. She liked to play to her strengths and having every lump and bump showcased was not playing to her strengths.

Nina was still mulling it over when Sam popped into the shop after school. 'Oh! Hello stranger,' Nina exclaimed in delight because a Sam visit was sadly a rare occurrence these days.

Before Sam and Posy had moved in with Sebastian, Sam had always been cluttering up the place. Arguing with Posy about whether he'd done his homework or if he needed new school trousers. Asphyxiating them all with the noxious body spray he'd douse himself in so that he might attract the attention of Little Sophie, the Happy Ever After Saturday girl, who he'd known since they were both at primary school together and who seemed likely to return Sam's affection though he was too dense to realise it.

Sam extricated himself from his school bag, which was almost strangling him, dumped it on the floor and collapsed onto one of the sofas. 'Posy and I are going to look around a sixth form college this evening,' he said wearily as if even the thought of it was exhausting. 'Is there any cake going?'

'You could go and ask Mattie yourself,' Nina said. The shop was fairly quiet, just a couple of browsers, so she came out from behind the counter to perch on the arm of Sam's sofa and prod him on the shoulder. 'She might even have forgiven you for helping yourself to those Maltesers she needed to decorate a special-order birthday cake.'

From under his long fringe (Nina made a note to remind Posy that Sam really needed a haircut) Sam grimaced. 'How was I to know she was planning on using Maltesers as cake decoration?'

'Sam! You ate three whole family-sized bags.'

He groaned like he was in pain. 'This is a very stressful year for me, I have my GCSEs. That should give me a free pass.'

Nina poked his shoulder again. 'Nice try.'

With great effort, Sam levered himself up to an upright position. 'If you go and get me cake, I'll give you all the shop's social media passwords,' he countered with a sly smile. 'Sebastian was going to hack into my hard disk to try and retrieve them but then Noah came round and he asked me a few questions and then I remembered the password for the program that generated all the passwords for Happy Ever After.' Sam shook his head. 'It was like witchcraft.'

'Noah,' Nina echoed in what she hoped was a casual voice. 'Did he mention anything about what he's been up to the last couple of days?'

'Why would he?' Sam folded his arms. 'Chop, chop, Nina, that cake isn't going to get itself.'

Much as she missed him, Nina wasn't going to let Sam get away with such barefaced cheek. It set a dangerous precedent. 'Or I could just tell Posy that you lost the passwords and that now you're blackmailing me over them.'

'You wouldn't,' Sam groused. 'I never thought you'd go darkside.'

'At least say please,' Nina insisted.

Fifteen minutes later, Sam was happily rooting his way through a plate of pastries, and Nina had the passwords to Happy Ever After's Twitter, Instagram and Facebook accounts. Sam had handed them over with great ceremony like he was passing on the nuclear codes and made a vague promise that he'd show Nina how to upload content to the shop's website. She immediately logged into the Instagram account, which consisted of one blurry picture of the shop sign, which only two people had liked. With the bar set *that* low, even Nina should be able to raise it a little.

Then Posy poked her head around the office door to say that she and Verity were *still* doing the quarterly VAT return and she was longing for a quick and painless death but she should be done in half an hour tops. In the meantime, it had started to rain, which had scared off any customers.

Soon it would be time to close up the shop and usually Nina would spend this time on HookUpp to try and scare up a date for the evening. But the thought of going on a date, yet another bloody date, with some random guy, made Nina feel so tired and even a little sick to her stomach that she wondered if she was going down with something.

Maybe it was best to figure out her next non-date with Noah. She plonked herself down next to Sam so she could pinch a pistachio macaron and decided to Google a few more non-date options.

Googling 'high adrenalin date options' wasn't really that helpful. As far as Nina knew there were no rollercoasters in the Greater London area. She also quickly ruled out white-water rafting, sky-diving and something called zorbing and poked Sam again.

'I'm planning a date with a guy, you absolutely positively don't know him, and he's into all sorts of daredevil stuff. Like bungee jumping and extreme hiking and whatnot. Any ideas of something I can do with him?'

Sam contorted his face like he was in agony. 'Like sex stuff?' he spluttered.

Nina didn't poke Sam this time but punched him hard enough that he spluttered again. 'No! As if I would ever ask your advice about sex stuff. Never! Not in a million years!'

It took both of them a little while to recover from this miscommunication. Then Sam stirred. 'You mean extreme-action sporty stuff that you can do on a date?' he asked carefully.

'I guess, but not super sporty,' Nina replied. 'Nothing that involves handling balls.'

Sam choked on a profiterole.

'Get your mind out of the gutter, young man.'

'Last summer one of my friends had his birthday party at a zipwire place in Battersea Park. They called it a treetop adventure. You all right with heights?'

'They're not my absolute favourite thing in the world but I can cope with the rolling ladder if someone stands underneath it,' Nina said. 'So I should be all right, shouldn't I? And this random guy that you totally don't know would be well up for a treetop adventure.'

'Oh, Nina, this is not the answer.' Sam swept his fringe out of his eyes all the better to give Nina a disappointed look. It was quite unnerving to see the face that Sam would wear twenty years from now if he had children and he was disapproving of their lifestyle choices. 'Posy and Sophie and both my grandmothers say that women shouldn't change themselves just to please a man. It's like Feminism 101!'

'I'm not changing myself,' Nina protested. 'I'm just ready to endure an hour or so of discomfort to do something that I know this random guy will enjoy. It's called being selfless. You should try it, Malteser thief!'

Sam settled back on the sofa with a little sigh. 'Harsh, Nina.'

'Dude, you just tried to mansplain feminism to me, you deserved it,' Nina said and she'd missed this, winding Sam up, so much. She was tempted to try and hug him but he'd probably suffered enough what with all the poking and punching. 'So, Battersea Park, you say?'

Alas, further investigation uncovered the fact that the place was closed over winter so there would be no zipwire shenanigans among the treetops. She couldn't help but feel as if she'd dodged a bullet or saved herself from breaking several bones.

'Any other ideas, then?' she asked Sam.

He munched ruminatively on a Viennese whirl. 'I went to a laser tag party in Whitechapel once.'

Lasers. East London. High adrenalin *and* fashionable. 'That could work.' Nina nudged Sam. 'How come you don't go to normal teenage parties where you sneak in alcohol and get off with girls?'

'Because I have a lot of friends with helicopter parents,' Sam said sadly. He looked sideways at Nina. 'Actually, I think I've got a voucher for the laser tag place – I'm on their mailing list. I could reserve you the tickets, if you like. Just tell me when you want to go.'

'Oh, that's very sweet of you.' Nina narrowed her eyes. 'Very sweet. Why are you being so sweet?'

'I'm being selfless.' Sam echoed her own words back at Nina. 'Just like you told me to. And also, if you are going to play laser tag then you're going to have to wear trainers.' He looked down at Nina's four-inch heels. 'Do you even own a pair of trainers?'

'I have a pair of leopard-print Converse. Will they do?'

Sam closed his eyes. 'Just promise me that you'll film it. Please . . .'

Before Nina could ask him why, Posy poked her head round the office door again, a plaintive look on her face. 'Do we have to go to this open evening tonight? Because I have officially lost the will to live now.'

'We don't have to go,' Sam agreed. 'Although my entire future depends upon good A-level results, then getting into the university of my choice, but if you'd rather go home and watch *Don't Tell The Bride* then that's your call.'

Posy groaned and retreated back into the office.

'You're really quite evil, Sam,' Nina noted with grudging respect.

Sam shrugged. 'You don't know the half of it.'

CHAPTER

13

*'It is for God to punish wicked people;
we should learn to forgive.'*

'I am going to kill Sam,' Nina told Noah five nights later as they stood outside Ye Olde Laser Tag Experience on Whitechapel Road. 'I am going to flay him alive with my PedEgg while he begs for mercy.'

'"The latest laser technology and SFX lighting combined with all the fun of a Renaissance Faire"', Noah read from the poster. 'Wow. I'd like to have been in the meeting when they came up with that concept.'

'I'm so sorry,' Nina said. 'So very sorry. I should have researched it properly and I should have been way more suspicious when Sam offered to reserve two tickets with a voucher he had.'

Noah nodded. 'You must have done something to really piss him off.'

'I fetched him cakes,' Nina remembered. 'And the next thing I will serve him is vengeance.' She looked at Noah who was still staring at the poster, which featured two men in cheap-looking chainmail holding some very unmedieval laser guns bedecked with flashing green lights, with an air of bemusement. 'Shall we just move on to the second part of the evening and go to this bar I found in an old discount-suit shop?'

Bemusement turned to amusement. Noah put a hand to his heart and furrowed his brow like Nina had done him ten kinds of wrong. 'No way! You promised me laser tag and we are going to play laser tag.' He tapped the poster. 'Do you think we'll have to talk in Olde Worlde English, my comely wench?'

As compliments went, Nina had had much worse. She'd also had much better. 'If you say anything else in Olde Worlde English, then I'm going home. I'm not even joking,' she said.

This was already going down in the annals as one of Nina's Worst Dates Ever. Not as bad as the date watching a nine-hour Japanese film with only two intervals; or the date that had involved a funeral then a wake, though at least there'd been alcohol.

Also, the nerves she'd had before their first non-date were nothing compared to her heart-thudding, sweaty-palms, churny-stomach nerves as she'd taken the Central Line to Bethnal Green tube station.

Her heart-thudding had upgraded to a full-on slam dunk when she'd heard someone call her name and had turned round to see Noah standing on the platform, a still point in a sea of people rushing home from work. He'd smiled at her and she couldn't help but smile back.

Nina had waited for him to reach her and there was no time for their usual awkward meet and greet because, as if he'd given the matter some thought and had prepared for the moment, Noah took her by the elbows so he could lean forward and kiss Nina on her right cheek and then her left cheek. Then he'd pulled away, smiled again and said, 'You always look like you've stepped out of a film.'

Nina had been feeling frumpy and stumpy. No tight hobble skirt today but a black-and-white polka-dot dress with a full-circle skirt, under a voluminous net petticoat, so she'd have freedom of movement while she was laser tagging. And she was wearing trainers. She couldn't find her leopard-print Converse so she was wearing a pair of three-stripe Adidas shell-toes, which she'd borrowed from lovely Annika who'd assured Nina they were very in, but they left Nina feeling like she was wearing a pair of ortho-paedic shoes.

He added, 'You're like Ava Gardner but with pink hair.'

'People usually say Marilyn Monroe,' Nina said.

'No, not Marilyn,' Noah said firmly, tucking Nina's arm into his so they could start walking to the exit. 'I think you're too complex to be a Marilyn.'

His words had secretly thrilled Nina, that someone else could see that she was a creature of hidden depths and grand passions. She'd also felt an unexpected thrill course through her as Noah had pulled her in to kiss her cheeks; something to do with suddenly being pressed so close to him that not even a whisper could come between them. Close enough that she could smell his aftershave, which was subtle, not at all overpowering, like Noah himself, and reminded Nina of posh soap and clean sheets. But more than that, Nina could tell from the way that Noah had pulled her into his brief embrace that despite his unassuming, navy-clad appearance, he was strong. Obviously all the hanging from zipwires and hiking through rainforests had given him muscles. Wait . . . *what*? Nina couldn't possibly be having lustful thoughts about a man who wore so much navy. Her Heathcliff would never be a man so buttoned up, so 'compartmentalised', so . . . so tied to her own past in the worst possible way.

Still, as they'd caught the bus for the short ride to the venue, Nina had been heart-thuddy and palm-sweaty all over again, not in dread of the ordeal ahead, but rather because of a delicious mix of nerves and excitement and oh God, that usually meant that she was attracted to a man who would inevitably turn out to be a wrong 'un.

Not that Noah was a wrong 'un, but he wasn't a right 'un either and Nina had spent the bus journey agonising over exactly what Noah was and if this really was another non-date, until they got to the address of the laser tag place and then other matters took precedence. Mainly, if she'd be able to kill Sam and not have Posy hold it against her.

But she'd worry about that later. Right now, she was

going to worry about how she could get out of an hour playing a mash-up of Quasar and Dungeons and Dragons. 'It's not too late to turn back,' Nina said, trying to drag her heels, but Noah was having none of it.

'I never back down from a challenge,' he insisted, pulling her along with his superior strength. 'Do you think they'll make us dress up in chainmail?'

'Chainmail is my absolute deal breaker,' Nina said grimly.

There wasn't chainmail, but there was a horrible garment called a laser utility vest, which was a vinyl tabard decked out with green lights and not designed to be worn by anyone with breasts.

They were given their vests by one of the instructors, or laser marshals, an officious, beardy man in his late thirties called Peter, who kept staring at Nina in disbelief as he led them to a holding area to meet the rest of their team.

'Team? Can't we play just the two of us?' Nina demanded. The word 'team' never led to anything good. She'd once worked for a big chain of hairdressers and had been forced to attend an excruciating team-building away day, which involved enough trust-building exercises and role-playing to put her off the word 'team' for good.

'It's an interactive group activity.' Peter addressed all his remarks to Noah, whose lips were twitching like he was trying really hard not to laugh. 'You'll join up with the other guests booked for the same session and I'll split you into two teams. All this information was on your confirmation email, you know.'

Nina stuck her tongue out at Peter when he strode on ahead down a long, dark tunnel and Noah's lips twitched again. 'I live for an interactive group activity,' he said, though his smile dimmed when he saw the other 'guests'.

Twenty boys ranging in age from ten to fifteen were gathered to celebrate twelve-year-old Sunil's birthday. They knew this because Peter gave Sunil a special glowing badge to pin on his tabard, while Sunil stared at the floor as if he was in his own special hell. Nina could empathise.

Then there was a long talk about the rules of laser tag, prefaced with the predictable joke: Rule number one, you don't talk about laser tag. As far as Nina could tell, because Peter had a very droney voice and so she'd tuned out quite early on, the aim was to laser tag the hell out of the opposing team. Why it took ten minutes to tell them that, she didn't know.

'After this is over, I'm going to need a cocktail bigger than my head,' she whispered to Noah, who was listening intently to the rules and studying a map of Ye Olde Medieval Village in a leaflet he'd picked up in the foyer.

'I must admit that being in close proximity to so many adolescent boys is giving me unpleasant flashbacks to my schooldays,' he whispered back and Nina felt the familiar flash of guilt, which was why she'd agreed to go on that first non-date in the first place. 'Let's make that a cocktail each.'

'We could still bail . . .' Nina started to say until Peter glared at her.

'Why are you talking?' he demanded. 'If you're talking then you can't be listening to the very important things I'm saying about Health and Safety, can you?'

'Sir! Yes, sir!' Nina said and when she clicked her heels and saluted some of the boys laughed and Peter looked at her like he wished he were allowed to shoot real guns at people and not just laser tag guns.

He got his revenge two minutes later when he divided them into teams. He picked off the nine youngest and smallest boys and told Noah and Nina to join that team, helmed by a spotty, nervous-looking Ye Olde Laser Tag employee called Jamie, while he took the older and bigger boys off with him to talk tactics. 'I have never lost a game of laser tag yet,' they heard him say loudly as he led his troops into the bowels of the building. 'We're going to slaughter them and it's not going to be pretty.'

'Gin cocktail, bigger than my head,' Nina chanted her mantra. 'Gin cocktail, bigger than my head.'

'So, yeah, I think defence is, like, our best form of attack,' Jamie said, scratching at a particularly painful-looking spot on his chin, so Nina longed to perform an intervention on him. 'I'd pick a hiding place, hope they don't find you and if they do, pray that it's quick.' He looked around furtively. 'Peter is an absolute beast.'

This rousing pep talk was met with groans. 'So unfair,' Sunil muttered. 'I didn't want to invite all my brother's friends and my cousins but Mum said I had to and now they're going to gang up on me like they usually do but with laser guns and on my birthday.'

'Sucks, man.'

'Your brother's a dick, innit.'

'When we going to Nando's then?'

'Gin cocktail, bigger than my head,' Nina chanted again and Noah smiled sympathetically and Nina thought he might be coming round to her point of view but then he stepped forward.

'Come on, guys!' he said jauntily, which earned him ten evil looks. Eleven if you counted Jamie too. 'Are you going to admit defeat that easily?'

'Yes.' And 'What's even the point?' was the general consensus. Nina wondered aloud where Sunil's parents were and why they were letting their son's birthday party get derailed along with his dreams.

Apparently they were in a nearby Nando's where Sunil and his guests would reassemble, and were under the mistaken belief that Sunil's older brother, Sanjay, would look after him.

'I don't need looking after and anyway I hate him,' Sunil said woefully. 'This is, like, the worst birthday ever.'

'No! We can still turn things round,' Noah said, crouching down so he was on Sunil's level rather than looming over him. 'We've just got to have a plan and I am the man with the plan.'

Nina edged away as Noah started talking about 'an element of surprise', 'pincer-like formations' and 'attacking them on the flanks'. Maybe if she kept edging away, she'd eventually find herself back at the entrance and could flee. Except, she was on a date, or a non-date, whatever, and

Noah appeared to be in his element and wasn't going to be leaving anytime soon.

He now had all the kids and Jamie gathered round him in a semi-circle, looking much cheerier than they had done, as they formulated their battle strategy.

'The only thing is that we need to use someone as bait,' Noah was saying regretfully. 'So I'm afraid they're going to have a pretty short game. Any volunteers?'

Nina practically mowed down her pint-sized laser-gun-toting compadres in her rush to step into Noah's eyeline and put her hand up. 'I'll do it!' she yelped. 'Got to be a team player!'

'Peter is going to be so mad,' Jamie said gleefully. 'I can't wait to see defeat written all over him.'

'And he's definitely going to launch his attack from the church?' Noah queried.

'Always. If we win, he'll put me on loo-cleaning duties for the rest of the year but it will be worth it,' Jamie gloated. Nina hoped, really hoped, that Noah knew what he was doing and that he could rescue Sunil's birthday from disaster and let Jamie take revenge on his despotic co-worker. But Peter had worked here for years and Noah had only been here for fifteen minutes, even if they were some of the longest fifteen minutes of Nina's life.

'Right, troops, let's march out.' Noah was *really* getting into character, but as Nina walked past him (no way was she marching) he winked at her.

When they reached the lame replica of a medieval village, Noah quickly and quietly dispersed his army, who split in two and belly crawled in opposite directions so their flashing lights wouldn't be seen as they mounted their offensive positions.

'OK, you know what to do?' Noah asked Nina. 'The success of this entire operation depends on your sacrifice.'

He'd gone method and though it pained Nina to admit it, Noah's zeal, his eyes shining in the dim light, a huge grin on his face, was actually quite adorable.

'Always happy to take one for the team,' she drawled and she touched her hand to the side of her head in what was meant to be an ironic salute but Noah solemnly saluted back and then disappeared into the shadows.

Nina wasn't belly crawling anywhere. Instead she ambled further into the medieval village, gun held in front of her, though every now and again she'd swing it around wildly as if she was genuinely staking out the place just to show willing. She headed for Ye Olde Red Bulle, a mock-tavern which sadly didn't seem to serve any alcohol, when there was a large, lusty roar behind her and the other team ran out of the church and quickly had her surrounded.

'Kill her!' Peter shouted and Nina stood there while she was pelted by lasers. After a few seconds of being shot at, the lights on her vest, which had chafed something rotten, went out and she was dead. Metaphorically speaking.

'You're meant to die!' Peter shouted at her. 'On the floor.'

'Dude, I'm wearing vintage, no way am I getting on the floor,' Nina protested and as Peter argued back and his teammates stood around and watched, their guns hanging limply in their hands, Nina saw her own team quickly surround them and open fire.

They never knew what had hit them. One by one the lights went off on Team Peter's vests until it was just Peter left, ducking and diving and contorting his body to try and deflect the laser tagging, until he was writhing on the ground, firing his gun into mid-air as all his lights went off one by one until there was just one forlorn light on his belt, blinking on and off.

'Sunil, do the honours!' Noah shouted. 'Team, cover him!'

'You won't get away with this!' Peter shouted back as Sunil stood over him and shot out his last light.

'Oh, grow up!' Nina hissed at him, as Sunil was swamped by his teammates and some excited and noisy high-fiving. 'You just lost a stupid laser game. Deal with it!'

Peter struggled to his feet as even the dreaded Sanjay and his friends offered congratulations to Sunil who was smiling so hard, Nina feared that his face might snap in two.

'I counted at least five illegal moves,' Peter blustered and the grin on Sunil's face faltered. 'You'll have to forfeit the game and I'm taking all of your names because you're banned for life from . . .'

He stopped when Noah put a hand on his shoulder. 'A word, please.' It wasn't a question, or even a suggestion but an order, which went with the grim expression on Noah's face so that even Nina, who for once was wholly innocent, gave a guilty twitch.

As the lights came on, Noah led Peter over to a secluded corner and with arms folded, delivered a short speech.

Noah didn't put his hands on Peter and as far as Nina could tell over the excited chatter of the boys, he didn't raise his voice, or even wag a finger or point. But whatever Noah was saying, it wiped the belligerent expression from Peter's face, made his shoulders drop and he took a step back. Noah continued talking until finally Peter nodded.

The two of them walked back to where the boys were still congregated. Peter headed straight for Sunil, who tried to hide behind his older brother though Sanjay adroitly side-stepped away, leaving Sunil to face the wrath of the angry man in the boiler suit.

'Well, yes, congratulations, young man,' Peter said as if every word was choking him. 'And happy birthday. I'd like to offer you and three friends a complimentary session at Ye Olde Laser Tag Experience anytime in the next six months.'

To his credit, Sunil didn't gloat until they were all standing outside. 'Yeah, I got him good! No one messes with the mighty Sunil!'

'Shut up, Sunil,' Sanjay said witheringly. 'And thank the nice man and lady.'

Sunil solemnly shook hands with Noah and Nina like they were visiting dignitaries. 'Thank you,' he said. 'Do you want to come to Nando's with us?'

'It's very tempting,' Nina said. She turned to Noah. 'Isn't it?'

'Very tempting,' he agreed, with another of those almost imperceptible winks, unless you knew to look out for them.

'But you don't want us spoiling your cheeky Nando's,' Nina pointed out.

'True dat,' said Sanjay, the little beast, but Sunil shook his head.

'Well, my parents will be there. So you'll have other old people to talk to,' he explained earnestly as Nina tried not to look too destroyed because she wasn't even thirty and that wasn't old, although, yes, she could easily have a ten-year-old son, even a twelve-year-old son like Sanjay, but she didn't and anyway she was a *fun* grown-up.

'I really need a gin cocktail bigger than my head,' she explained to Sunil who blinked at her in confusion.

'Another time,' Noah said, putting his arm around Nina to guide her away. Then he paused. 'How are you all getting to Nando's anyway?'

'We're walking, bruh,' someone called out. 'Is only a minute away.'

'We just have to ask a friendly-looking person which way the Mile End Road is,' Sanjay said. He nodded decisively. 'I think we go right.'

Nina sighed and pulled out her phone to call up Google Maps. They needed to go left. 'Not a step!' she barked. 'We're taking you to Nando's.'

'You'd better do what she says,' Noah advised. He gave a theatrical shudder. 'She's frightening when she gets cross.'

'Terrifying,' Nina said in her scariest voice. 'OK, get into pairs 'cause we are going to make like a crocodile and I don't want any bitching about it.'

There was no bitching but quite a lot of groaning and then with Nina at the head and Noah bringing up the rear, they delivered twenty boys to Nando's and the neglectful parents of Sunil and Sanjay.

CHAPTER

'Why am I so changed? Why does my blood rush into a hell of tumult at a few words?'

It was a good half hour later that Nina finally had a gin cocktail bigger than her head on the table in front of her. Unfortunately, she'd only managed one sip because she was currently crying with laughter.

'And . . . every . . . time . . . he . . . got . . . shot . . . he . . . acted . . . like . . . he'd . . . just . . . been . . . elec . . . tro . . . cuted,' she wheezed as she recounted Peter's last stand. 'Really, he's wasted at Ye Olde Laser Experience . . . he should be . . . on the stage . . . Oh God, don't make me laugh any more. My ribs are killing me.'

'I haven't . . . said . . . a . . . word.' Noah shook his head; he was laughing so hard that he had to stop speaking and cling to the edge of the table to keep himself upright. His face was pink, the freckles standing out in stark relief, as he dabbed at his eyes with a napkin. 'Can't speak.'

Nina had recovered enough that she could now take an appreciative sip of her spiced-pear martini. 'Talking of which, what exactly did you say to Peter? He went quite pale.'

Noah waved a feeble hand, the laughter dying down to a few stray chuckles. 'I told him you were an undercover trading standards officer sent in by the council to make sure they were complying with all aspects of Health and Safety after several customer complaints. And once that had softened him up, I told him that he was being a dick to a ten-year-old boy who was there to celebrate his birthday.' Noah took a sip of his negroni. 'I hate bullies and now that I'm in a position where I can stand up to them, I do.'

And there it was again: the reason why this could only ever be a non-date. Why would Noah ever want to willingly spend time with the sister of the boy who'd bullied him mercilessly when he hadn't been able to stand up for himself? It was probably time to confess. Maybe she should start with mentioning how sorry Paul was – he'd texted Nina earlier that week reminding her of his offer to do free plumbing for Noah.

'You're *very* good with the pre-teen male demographic,' was what Nina heard herself say. She rarely shied away from a confrontation, except, apparently, tonight. 'Is this where you tell me that you have a couple of sons tucked away at home?'

'Not that I know of.' Noah shook his head again. 'Actually, I can categorically state for the record that I have no children. Though I'm racking up an alarming number of godchildren and nephews and nieces. How about you?'

'No godchildren,' Nina said, because none of her friends had got around to reproducing yet, though she'd bet even odds that Posy would be pregnant before the end of next year. Sebastian was already talking about adding another wing to their already huge townhouse to accommodate the brood and though Posy usually rolled her eyes and told him to shut up, she didn't seem averse to the idea of having children. 'Nieces in the plural. My two favourite people in the world.'

Again, this was a perfect opportunity to bring up the father of those nieces but instead Nina pulled out her phone so Noah could admire Ellie and Rosie in a selection of princess and superhero outfits.

Then Noah showed Nina his nephews and one niece, who were still quite pint-sized and ranged in age from two to eighteen months to just hatched.

'Kids don't really give you a lot to work with until they're at least a year old,' he said. He flashed up another picture of two-year-old Archie. 'This one didn't start speaking until a few months ago though now he never stops. Mostly about trains. We took him to an adventure park with a Thomas the Tank Engine ride and he just about exploded.' He picked up his almost empty glass. 'Now, you, you were very good with our new best friends. Very indulgent when it came to the selfies.'

Before they'd parted company at Nando's, Nina had agreed to numerous selfies with Sanjay's friends and cousins.

She'd refused the requests for kisses, but had gamely draped an arm around each of their shoulders so they'd have bragging rights back at school for having their picture taken with 'a fit bird'.

'My twelve-year-old fanbase are pretty easy to please,' she said modestly. 'It's the grown-up boys that are real hard work. Present company excepted.'

'I'll take that as a compliment,' Noah said lazily and he clinked their now empty glasses, and it *was* a compliment because being with Noah, in a non-work scenario, felt like the easiest thing in the world.

They'd been on two non-dates and Noah hadn't even seen Nina in actual date mode, when her dresses were skin-tight and she was cleavage as far as the eye could see, but she still caught him giving her these appraising side glances, when he thought she wasn't paying attention, like he was properly checking her out. And from the way his eyes darkened and he caught his bottom lip between his teeth, Noah liked what he saw.

Nina really should have brought up the non-date thing by now but actually this was all starting to feel quite date-like. Noah's legs were brushing against hers under the table, not in a lecherous way, but because he had long legs and it felt as if they were both comfortable with each other now and yet it also felt thrilling, giddy, *sexy*.

'You should take it as a compliment,' Nina said slowly. 'You *are* really nice.'

But I don't think we should be anything more than friends.
But you do realise that this is a non-date.

197

But there's something I have to tell you.

But I don't have feelings for you. Not in that way.

But the buts never came. And Noah pulled a face. 'Nice? Nice is a bit lukewarm, isn't it?'

It was. Especially when your type could be filed under B for bad boy . . . 'Nice is a bit of a welcome relief after some of the horror shows I've dated,' Nina said truthfully. And then because this was going off-message fast and their glasses were empty, she stood up. 'My round. Same again?'

Noah nodded and looked at her, thoughtfully this time, as Nina picked up her purse. She smiled at him a little warily and yes, she was a little regretful that she was wearing a big twirly skirt so that he couldn't check out her hips as she walked away.

When Nina got back from the bar with their cocktails and with an order of nachos to come, her mind was made up. They'd talk of innocent, innocuous subjects like their assorted nieces and nephews, maybe even a bit of business analysis, but Noah didn't even give her a chance to take the first sip of her drink.

'So, you said that your dating hasn't been entirely successful,' he prompted.

Nina sighed. 'It's been an absolute disaster lately. Nothing but creeps and chancers. What about you? Are you on HookUpp?'

She was pretty sure Noah wasn't because he would have come up in her matches when they were both at the shop together, unless Sebastian's dating algorithms had decided that they were spectacularly incompatible.

But Noah was shaking his head. 'I wouldn't trust Sebastian not to hack into my account and either pair me up with some right shockers or completely rewrite my profile.'

Nina grinned. 'I worry about that too. Worse! That he and Posy discuss my matches and dates over breakfast. "Nina's not going to be fit for anything this morning. She was up-swiping past midnight."'

'So, you're on HookUpp a lot?' Noah asked carefully then fixed his eyes on his drink.

'Well, *yeah.*' Nina felt as if she was confessing to some terrible crime or a disgusting habit like one of her old flatmates who used to pick at her toenails while she watched TV. 'It's the twenty-first century, it's what people do. Not so many opportunities to lock eyes with someone across a crowded ballroom these days, is there?' There was really no need to mention her new resolve to quit HookUpp and really redouble her efforts to find her one true love; it might give entirely the wrong message . . .

'But it is pretty much for hooking up, not so much for relationships,' Noah mused. He was still staring down at his glass like it was the most fascinating receptacle for liquid that he'd seen in a long while. 'I mean, casual dating can be fun but sometimes it feels a bit like being on a hamster wheel. Going round and round in circles without achieving anything. You know what I mean?'

'I've been on that hamster wheel for *ages,*' Nina said with great feeling. 'Stop the wheel, I want to get off!' Then she realised how that sounded. 'Not the rude kind of getting off . . .'

'Though the rude kind of getting off can be fun,' Noah said and he was looking up from his drink now, directly into Nina's eyes, so she squirmed in her seat, stretching out her legs so she bumped knees with Noah under the table and just that incidental touch seemed to light a fire deep in her belly and made Nina squirm again. Now it was her turn to stare down at her glass because she knew that if she looked at Noah, she might do something silly. Giggle or blush or reach across the table to yank him closer so she could kiss him.

'I don't agree to any kind of funny business until the third date,' she muttered with only five per cent of her usual sass.

Noah picked up his phone from the table. 'I must make a note of that,' he said in such a dark, drawly voice that Nina had to steel every muscle she possessed so she wouldn't squirm for an unprecedented third time.

'So, past relationships, have you had any?' Nina asked baldly as she told herself sternly to calm the hell down. The only reason she felt so *giddy* every time Noah's leg brushed against hers was because this was an actual second date after months of first dates that never went anywhere. The thought lifted her heart – a man! Not a Heathcliff, not by any stretch of the imagination, but a rare breed of man who didn't think that getting the first round in counted as foreplay!

'Yes, Nina, I have managed to persuade a few women to see me on a regular basis,' Noah said gravely. 'It was quite hard at Oxford, because all the girls were at least two years older than me and I still had acne and my beloved pocket protector but Sebastian gave me some tips on personal grooming and an introduction to a girl in his tutor group, a maths prodigy, who was also two years younger than anyone else.'

'Sebastian is actually quite the nurturing sort,' Nina said because Sebastian had taken Sam under his wing too and now Sam would only wear jumpers made of cashmere and no longer asphyxiated them all with the noxious smell of Lynx because he'd upgraded to asphyxiating them all with a Tom Ford cologne that he was only meant to use sparingly. 'Did he tell you all about the birds and the bees too?'

'Thankfully no, I don't think either of us would ever have recovered. Anyway, I was with Laura for my last two years at Oxford, then I went travelling and she went off to do her masters degree at Durham and we agreed that the long-distance thing wasn't practical. We're still friends,' Noah said and it sounded *nice* that his first relationship had been so cordial but it was hardly a story to stir the passions.

Noah went on to describe a couple of very casual relationships from his travelling days, then he'd moved to San Francisco and become part of the tech scene and a very work-heavy culture, and dated until he met 'Patricia, who I was with for nearly four years. We broke up last summer before I came back to London,' Noah said, but his attention was distracted by his empty glass. 'Shall we get some more drinks and find out what's happened to our nachos?' So it was impossible to know how he felt about Patricia and the break-up.

201

Still, Nina was determined to find out. To see what lurked behind Noah's mostly affable, occasionally sarcastic, exterior, so as soon as he came back from the bar with their drinks and with the news that apparently their nachos were on the way, she asked maybe a little too eagerly, 'Did Patricia break your heart? Or did you break hers? Was it very painful?'

'Well, during the big fight that led to our parting of the ways, she threw a Microsoft-branded stress ball at my head, which was painful,' Noah said and he rubbed his right temple as if he could still feel the phantom pain. 'But she was more cross with me than heartbroken.'

'She sounds pretty heartbroken to me. You don't throw stuff at the person you're splitting up with if you don't care,' Nina said, because if something didn't get broken (usually crockery or glassware, and once an iPhone) along with her heart then the relationship had hardly been worth it – and if Noah could rouse this kind of passion in his ex, then perhaps he might have hidden, Heathcliff-like depths.

'Nope, definitely cross.' Noah took a sip of his fresh G&T and wrinkled his nose. 'See, Patricia was a planner. She had a one-year plan and a five-year plan, even a ten-year plan, and live-in boyfriend transitioning to husband then to father of her babies was an important part of the plan, but it felt like any spare man would do. Like, ticking the boxes was more important than being in love.'

Nina leaned closer. 'So, you believe in love?'

'I think so.' Noah raised his glass to the elusive spirit of love. 'But love doesn't come with a five-year plan. It either happens or it doesn't, right?'

'So, I'm told,' Nina said with a wistful sigh because she was also a huge believer in love but it always seemed to happen to other people.

'And what about you? What's been your longest relationship?' Noah asked as he had every right to because Nina had been grilling him about his love life.

Five years, seven months, three weeks and six days, Nina could have replied because she used to be the sort of girl who would measure out a relationship in really specific terms. Like she deserved some sort of long-service medal when actually what made up a relationship was kisses and longing looks and staying up all night talking about everything and nothing, and rowing then storming off but running back into each other's arms in the rain, and still getting that feeling that made you tingle when you'd been apart and were about to be reunited. That kind of thing.

'It was a childhood sweetheart deal,' she said breezily. 'Started dating when we were practically children and then of course by the time we were all grown up we realised we had nothing in common.'

Noah sat up a little straighter. 'Oh. Was he from Worcester Park too?'

Nina slumped in her seat as if she could shrink back into the leather-look red vinyl. 'Yeah,' she admitted unwillingly. 'But I'm pretty sure you wouldn't have known him. He didn't . . . he went . . . he kept himself to himself.'

Both of them flinched. Noah because the mention of

their hometown must conjure up all sorts of barely repressed memories and Nina, because she knew that her brother had been the root cause of the agonies that Noah had suffered.

And as for Dan, Nina really didn't remember him being involved in the bullying but then again, so few boys in their year were innocent bystanders.

Nina could hardly bear to think about how much pain, both physical and emotional, Noah would have been in while she walked the same corridors and playgrounds completely oblivious. God knows, she couldn't bear to think about Dan either, not after their terrible break-up, and so it was easier to distract, divert, deflect.

Her usual tirade would do. 'Anyway, that was then and this is now, and now I don't want to settle down or settle for some all-right guy just so I can be in a "relationship".' Nina made scathing quote marks around the word. 'I want more than that. It's like I told you when we went out last week: I want passion. Life without passion is just existing.'

Noah blinked a few times like he had something in his eye. 'I'm not sure I agree with you. You can still settle down and have the passion too, can't you?'

'Well, yes, but—'

'I mean, you can be madly and passionately in love but the two of you still need to pay your Council Tax and do a supermarket shop every now and again.'

'I hear what you're saying,' Nina said in the time-honoured way of someone who violently disagreed with what was being said but didn't want to cause a scene. 'But that doesn't sound very passionate to me.'

Noah grinned like he was enjoying playing devil's advocate. Or maybe he wasn't playing at all and was simply enjoying winding Nina up. 'You could have passionate rows in the cereal aisle over whether to get cornflakes or Rice Krispies.'

It was very hard not to grin back, but Nina didn't want to encourage Noah and also the subject of passion was something that she felt very serious about. Still, she did mutter, 'Cheerios. Always Cheerios.'

Noah took pity on her. 'You can't have passion 24/7. You need more solid foundations to build love on. Unless you'd rather have passion than love.'

'I want love too. Of course I do, doesn't everyone?' Nina asked with a sigh. 'But then I don't want to be in a relationship for two years, five years, ten years and it just becomes safe, dull, routine. That's why *Wuthering Heights* resonated so much with me.' Nina wasn't going to say anything but the lingering adrenalin from their laser tag victory and the kick of her spiced-pear martinis was loosening her lips. 'I was stuck in a safe, dull relationship and my whole life was heading in the same safe, dull direction and around the same time I read *Wuthering Heights* and I realised that I had to jump off before it was too late.'

'Jump off what?'

The matrimonial merry-go-round, Nina almost said but she shook her head. They were only two non-dates, two dates, in and it was too soon to bare her soul and share all of its darkest secrets. 'That relationship I was telling you about. I ended it because I realised that I was twenty and for the first time in my life I needed to listen to what my heart wanted, not what everyone else told me I should want. And my heart wanted passion. God, I'd never been passionate about anything before that, except never eating carbs. It was no way to live.'

'And now you live passionately?'

'Trying to.' And yet, it seemed as if that passionate life still eluded her. It was just out of grasp and instead of passion, Nina had a lot of drama, which wasn't the same thing at all. And then, because they always ended up talking about her, she asked, 'What things are you passionate about?'

'I don't really do passion,' Noah said in an unconcerned manner as if passion was no big deal. 'I'm a pretty middle-of-the-road kind of guy.'

Nina couldn't help the face she pulled. 'You must be passionate about something,' she insisted.

Noah shrugged. 'I'm really not.'

'Do you think it might be a case of still waters running deep?' Nina asked hopefully, though it shouldn't really matter to her if Noah was a passion-free zone.

'I'd say my waters are pretty shallow. Frozen, even.' Noah sounded amused at Nina's persistence. 'Bit of a cold fish, so I've been told; that I don't let people get too close.'

Oh God, it was obvious that what had happened at school had left Noah with serious trust issues and deep emotional scars. Paul had *ruined* him.

'Nina, there's no need to look quite so broken about

my lack of passion. There's all sorts of things I like a lot,' Noah said and it still sounded as if he was half-teasing her. 'I like cocktails and laser tag, obviously. Food. Work, but also life outside of work and going on adventures. And of course I'd like someone to share those adventures with.'

'What kind of adventures?' Nina asked. The closest she ever came to an adventure was trying to blag her way into an after-hours drinking club on a little side street between Oxford Street and Tottenham Court Road, which didn't seem like Noah's kind of adventure. 'I suppose you're looking for a pretty intrepid sort of girlfriend who'd be up for kayaking down the Amazon. Trekking through the Hindu Kush? That sort of thing?'

The sorts of things that Nina would never do in a million years. 'I think my days of doing anything that means I have to have vaccinations for malaria and yellow fever are over. But I do want to take a six-month sabbatical before I move back to the UK for good so I can do a road trip across the States. Stop in every state. Stay in motels, eat in diners, see all the sights from the Grand Canyon to Graceland.'

'That sounds amazing,' Nina breathed, as their nachos finally arrived. 'I've never been to America, but I'd love to go . . .'

'Well, we've only been on two dates, and there hasn't even been any kind of funny business yet, so let's see how things develop,' Noah said dryly and quite rightly, Nina was horrified. And blushing again. She never blushed so much as she did when she was with him. Maybe she was going through an early menopause.

'I wasn't hinting,' she said huffily. 'Like Posy would give me six months off. Haha!' she choked out a laugh to show she was joking too. No wonder Noah was giving her another one of those assessing, analysing looks that always made her nervous. She cast around for something less fraught to talk about.

'So . . . you didn't come back to London with the intention of staying then?'

'I didn't. I was meant to just come back for a Christmas visit but then I found out that my dad's been diagnosed with MS . . .'

'Oh God, I'm sorry . . .'

'It's early stages but he and my mother are convinced that Western medicine will see him into an early grave and that he should treat it with Chinese herbs and meditation, so I want to be around to help out more and, I don't know, Britain just feels like home.' Noah shrugged again. 'Also, since I've been away, I've acquired two nephews and a niece and I'd quite like to see them grow up, be their favourite uncle, that sort of thing.'

Nina had no trouble understanding the ties of blood. 'Truth. My two nieces, Ellie and Rosie, are my absolute favourite people in the world. In fact, I like them so much that I've agreed to go to a soft-play centre for Ellie's birthday party.' She paused with a cheese-laden nacho halfway to her mouth so she could fully contemplate the horror of what she'd agreed to. 'The party starts at ten on Sunday morning. I didn't even know that there was such a thing as Sunday morning. I usually sleep in until lunchtime.'

Noah didn't nod in agreement this time because even though it was past ten on a school night and he was on his third gin and tonic, it was obvious that he was a morning person. 'Early start then?'

'Yes, but I'm actually going to Worcester Park on Saturday evening for a girls' night out with my sister-in-law,' Nina explained heavily. On balance, a Saturday night in Worcester Park had to be better than getting up before eight on Sunday morning. When Nina had told Chloe that she couldn't bear the thought of staying at her parents' and spending Saturday evening with her mother, Chloe had said that if she didn't mind kipping on their sofa, they could have a girls' night out. 'All Bar One has been mentioned,' Nina told Noah with a mournful expression. 'And I can't even get drunk because I have soft play in the morning and then in the afternoon, I'm getting the next part of my tattoo done.'

'So, tattoos and hangovers not good?'

'So not good and I speak from bitter experience.'

'Well, if it's any consolation I'm going back to Worcester Park on Saturday night too,' Noah said. 'Nothing as exciting as All Bar One. My sister and her husband are going to a wedding and their babysitter bailed and I was the only person who could stand in at such short notice.' He sighed.

'Are you worried about being responsible for keeping your nephews and niece alive?'

'Not as worried as I am about having to change a nappy.' Noah grimaced. 'It turns out that there isn't an app that can help with that.'

'There really isn't. I'd practise holding your breath if I were you.'

Noah gave a theatrical shudder, which made Nina laugh. She could have stayed there all night, their legs brushing under the table. But it *was* a school night and they were deep in the wilds of East London. So when Noah asked Nina if she wanted another drink, she regretfully declined.

'We should probably get going,' she said and when they left, Noah placed his hand at the small of her back to guide her and Nina was suddenly glad that she wasn't wearing heels because her legs became alarmingly jelly-like. Whether it was due to the potency of the spiced-pear martinis she'd been drinking or Noah's touch, Nina couldn't – or wouldn't – say.

All she knew was that when they were finally settled in the back of a ruinously expensive black cab (after Noah insisted that Nina was dropped off first even though they were going in completely different directions), they ended up seated so close to each other that another couple of centimetres, and technically Nina would be sitting on Noah's lap.

Normally she'd have something saucy to say about that state of affairs but Nina was starting to feel as if she'd left normal two non-dates ago. 'Sorry,' she said and tried to shift away so Noah had more room but he put his hand on her arm.

'Don't,' he said in a voice that sounded dark and desperate and as sexy as hell and instead of moving away, Nina found herself moving even nearer so that they were almost nose to nose and she could see the ring of hazel around his pupils.

Could also see up close that delicate flush that settled on his skin whenever his emotions were heightened even though he'd said that his emotions were always tightly reined in.

Could count every single one of his freckles but she'd barely counted up to five when Noah lifted his hand to her face to gently tug her even closer, and Nina couldn't say who kissed who first, only that they were kissing.

Oh God, I'm kissing Noah Harewood! Not that Nina needed the headline when she could feel Noah's mouth moving tentatively on hers, his thumb caressing the delicate, hyper-sensitive skin behind her ear.

Nina was powerless to resist the urge to slide even closer still so that their bodies were pressed tightly together and they were kissing without hesitation now. Nina's hands were clasped in Noah's glorious hair and the sinuous movement of his tongue echoed the way his thumb was now rubbing on her pulse point and she couldn't help the greedy moans that leaked from her mouth.

They broke apart so they could both suck in a much-needed breath and then Nina was pulling Noah in for round two and this time there were wandering hands, which led to some low-level fondling and Nina accidentally ripping a button of Noah's shirt until they were interrupted by a cough over the intercom, then the cab driver saying, 'Are you sure I can't do the Bermondsey drop-off first?'

CHAPTER

15

I'm not going to act the lady among you, for fear I should starve.'

Forty-three hours later and Nina was still a bit starry-eyed and kiss-sore from the cab journey as she headed to Worcester Park on Saturday evening with her overnight bag and very low expectations for the evening ahead.

She had strict instructions to go straight to the All Bar One in nearby Sutton to meet Chloe because 'if you swing by the house to dump your stuff and the girls see you we'll never get them to bed.'

Though she'd take the truth to the grave with her, the thought of a quiet Saturday night in with Chloe and Paul and maybe a takeaway curry and a film on Netflix would have been a lot more appealing. Especially as Nina really couldn't drink more than two small glasses of wine if she was spending all of Sunday afternoon and a significant part of Sunday evening being tattooed.

She also wasn't in the mood to spend an evening fending off the attentions of any lone wolves on a Saturday-night prowl. Nina was never going to find her one true love in an All Bar One in Sutton on a Saturday evening. Even if he did make himself known to her, Nina would have to reject him on principle and even though he wasn't her one true love, she couldn't stop thinking about Noah. Specifically, being kissed by Noah and Noah saying with a laugh as the cab dropped her off first, 'I'm so glad that we didn't wait until the third date to get up to a little bit of funny business.'

There *was* going to be a third date. Not even a non-date but a proper date. Or Nina hoped that there was going to be, but it hadn't even been forty-eight hours so it was too soon to make plans. Forty-eight hours was the minimum industry-standard waiting period before contacting someone you'd been on two dates with to enquire about their general well-being and to lock down a third date.

Of course, Noah could have got in touch with her. Nina had hoped he would, but he hadn't. Probably because he was very busy with work or else when he'd replayed their date, from the first sight of the Ye Olde Laser Experience poster to Nina standing on the pavement and waving goodbye as he sped off in the cab, he'd decided that he didn't want the third date.

Maybe the kissing had been substandard compared to

what Noah was used to, although Nina had never had any complaints about the quality of her kissing before.

Nina wasn't used to these doubts. She didn't like them at all. Didn't like that Noah could make her feel like that girl who'd once thought that a Saturday night out in Sutton was the best of times.

It was fair to say that the feelings she had towards Noah were complicated, confusing and so until she worked them out, any Sutton-based Casanovas could do one.

In fact, as Nina changed trains at Waterloo, walking against the tide of the bridge and tunnel crowd heading into the West End from the suburbs for a big night out, she could feel dread swirling about her blood then settling in the pit of her stomach like a dodgy kebab that refused to digest.

By the time she was ushered into the All Bar One on Hill Street by a pair of bouncers, ignoring the catcalls from a gang of lads smoking outside who'd obviously never seen a woman in a figure-hugging cherry-print dress with pink hair before, Nina couldn't wait until Sunday lunchtime when she'd head back to civilisation.

'Blimey! Will you look at that?' she heard a woman mutter to her friend as Nina sidled past them towards the back of the huge space where a text from Chloe promised that she was waiting on a banquette with a bottle of rosé.

You're not in Kansas anymore, Toto, Nina thought to herself then she saw Chloe waving at her and pinned on a smile.

'Ready for our girls' night out?' Nina asked brightly, as she took in the five other women assembled on their two banquettes. 'Shall we see if we can find a quiet table?'

'Oh, sorry. Girls' Night Out has become Mums On The Razz,' Chloe explained with an apologetic little grimace. 'You don't mind, do you? You can be an honorary Mum.'

'Or token aunt! Of course I don't mind,' Nina said, her smile increasing in manic intensity, as she looked around at the other women and caught a little side-eye exchanged between two of them as they took in Nina's tattooed arms as she slipped out of her leather jacket. 'The more the merrier, right?'

Space was made on a banquette for Nina, unfortunately on the other side of the long low table that divided the two sofas so she was on the opposite side to Chloe. She smiled uneasily at the woman next to her, Kara, and was rewarded with an uneasy smile back.

Chloe's friends had all done NCT classes together or Mummy and Me toddler playgroups or were school playground pals so mostly they talked about their children. How little Nathan was still teething and Anjali had been slow to talk but now she never shut up. As one woman complained that her three-year-old twins hadn't got into their first-choice nursery, Nina realised that she'd been in the same year as her at Orange Hill. She stiffened. Glanced around at her drinking companions for the night and was pretty sure that another two of them had been in the year above her at Orange Hill. It wasn't only Noah who had bad recollections about their time at secondary school.

You are more than this, Nina told herself. You live in Bloomsbury and you work in a bookshop and you have lots of interesting friends and tattoos and you've recently been on two non-dates with a man who isn't like any other man you've ever been on a date with.

She did feel a little better to be reminded that you really could take the girl out of the London Borough of Sutton. Then she also reminded herself that it was almost forty-eight hours since she'd last seen Noah and it wouldn't be the worst thing in the world to send him a friendly text. Just thinking about what it would be like if he suddenly walked into All Bar One, relieved from his babysitting duties, was enough to make Nina ride out a little shiver and put a finger to her lips, which still seemed hyper-sensitive since the kissing they'd got the other night.

> How are you getting on? Have you had to change a nappy yet? I'm in All Bar One with a gaggle of 'Mums on the razz'. Do you want to swap places? Nina x

She deliberated over the 'x' for a little bit but after all the 'xxx'-ing on Thursday night, it seemed rude not to. Nina pressed 'send', smiled vaguely at the mums on either side of her who were now discussing baby-led weaning, what-ever the hell that was, and waited for Noah to reply with some anticipation.

And she waited.

And she waited.

And she waited some more.

Even if Noah had actually been changing a nappy, he had to be done now. Had nothing left to do but text Nina back but he hadn't and she didn't want to be *that* woman (though being back on her old stomping grounds always made her feel like *that* woman) but Noah's text silence troubled her deeply.

Did he not like her, even though he was the one who'd asked her out on that first date? Had he only agreed to the second date to be polite? And what about the kissing? Had it really been below par? Nina bristled on her banquette. Well, she'd always had rave reviews before!

Nina stared angrily at her phone, then, just to check that she still had other options, she logged on to HookUpp, which she *still* hadn't got round to deleting. Within seconds, unlike the text function of her phone, it was beeping with matches from guys who'd seen her picture, liked what they saw and had up-swiped her.

'Oh! Is that that dating app?' asked Kara, unashamedly staring at Nina's phone. 'My younger sister is on it all the time. Says she's been matched with some real mingers.'

'Mingers is right,' Nina said. 'Look at this one. He can't be more than twelve!' She clicked on the message he'd just sent her.

'Is that . . . is that a penis?' Kara shrieked and covered her eyes.

'No biggie,' Nina said, holding up her phone. 'Literally. It's just a dick pic.'

There was a chorus of shrieks then Chloe said proudly, 'I live the single-girl life vicariously through Nina. She has the *best* stories. Tell them the one about the bloke that worked in the betting shop.'

Noah might not have texted her back but that was all right because Nina was wild and free. The token single girl mining her rich seam of bad dating stories ('and that's when he decided to rest half a pint of lager on his erect penis and that's when I decided to make my excuses and leave') for the horrified delight of Chloe's friends. She could feel their smug satisfaction that they were already matched up and would never have to log into HookUpp, or worse hook up with someone from HookUpp.

Nina never minded providing the floorshow; often at work, if the shop was quiet, Posy and Verity would beg for a story from her dating repertoire, and now it broke the ice.

It didn't take long for Chloe's friends to realise that underneath the pink hair and the tattoos, Nina was a right laugh. And Nina realised, with a little shame, that Chloe's friends were perfectly lovely and that when it was almost impossible to get a babysitter and you were usually in bed before *News at Ten* because none of their kids would actually sleep through, then Saturday night at All Bar One in Sutton was the equivalent of a week in Las Vegas.

They'd all bonded by the time they were deep into the third bottle of rosé, Nina desperately trying to make her second and final glass last as she and Chloe's best friend, Dawn, chatted about how Nina could optimise Happy Ever After's social media and start racking up followers who would hopefully all want to buy romantic novels. Dawn had set up an Instagram account for her two French bulldogs, Eric and Ernie, and in the space of a year had over fifty thousand followers and companies sent her free stuff, everything from organic dog treats and cotton hoodies to flea treatments. She even had partnership deals so she was more or less getting paid to post pictures. Nina couldn't even imagine how Posy might react if she came up with a new revenue stream for the shop – she'd probably have to have a bit of a lie-down.

'It's all about the hashtags,' Dawn said. 'And follows. I follow pretty much anyone who's ever posted a picture of a dog on Instagram.'

Despite all of Nina's misgivings, it had ended up being a great night. It would have been an even better night if she'd been able to drink more, she thought as she stood at the bar to get her round in and see if they were still serving anything in the way of bar snacks. Chloe was absolutely hammered and she needed something to mop up the alcohol before Nina could even think of getting her in a cab.

Nina had to make do with some sparkling water and a couple of bags of kettle chips and turned round to snake her way through the crowd when she knocked into a man who'd taken a sudden step right onto Nina's foot.

'Ow!' she squealed as she drenched his shirt with sparkling water. 'Watch it!'

'You watch it!' he snarled and turned round and knocked into a group standing behind him who told him to 'watch it' too.

Nina blinked, shook her head then nearly dropped what was left of her sparkling water. There were still echoes of the sixteen-year-old boy who'd first asked her out at a school disco. His hair was starting to recede, his slight frame and face now a little paunchy, and he'd acquired a certain set to his jaw like he was gritting his teeth all the time. It was clear that he didn't recognise her so she could slip away and he'd never be any the wiser but she couldn't stop the high-pitched 'Dan?' that came out of her mouth.

She saw recognition finally dawn on his face. Shock. And finally resignation. 'Nina,' he said flatly. 'It's you.'

'One and the same,' she agreed.

It was almost ten years since they'd broken up; ten years since Nina had given Dan a really garbled explanation as to why she was breaking things off and Dan hadn't listened to a word she'd said. He had kept begging her to change her mind but Nina had been resolute in a way that she hadn't been before . . . or since.

And of course they'd bumped into each other a few times after that until Nina had moved away from Worcester Park. It hadn't taken long for Dan's reproachful sadness to give way to a kind of cocky one-upmanship especially after he got engaged to a girl called Angie, then married, then the two children. Everything that he'd wanted so much.

Now, Nina and Dan moved to one side so they weren't blocking the main route to the bar and Nina could get a proper look at him. He was only thirty-one but the disappointed, bitter air about him made him look older.

But Nina didn't think that the years had been that kind to her either. 'So, how *are* you?' she asked brightly, because she always wanted Dan to be well. 'How are Angie and the kids?'

Dan's face darkened. 'We've split up.'

It was a long story that boiled down to a few unhappy facts. Angie had been seeing someone behind Dan's back. Then she kicked him out of the house that he paid the mortgage on and he'd had to go to court to get access to his children.

'Oh, Dan, I'm so sorry,' Nina told him with genuine sincerity.

'Yeah, well, you should be,' he snapped and yes, she'd done something awful to Dan all those years ago but it was ancient history. It wasn't even like she'd forced Dan into Angie's arms on the rebound. There'd been two years between being dumped by Nina and Dan getting with Angie and while Nina was sorry about how she'd ended it, she was also still relieved that she had ended it. She hadn't felt guilty about it for quite some time now.

'Oh please. I don't know how many more times I can apologise for breaking your heart all those years ago but it *was* years ago,' Nina pointed out reasonably. She deserved a medal for staying calm and not raising her voice. 'This is all water under the bridge. Come on, we both know that if we had stayed together, had gone through with it, we'd have ended up miserable.'

'But you don't know that, do you?' Dan asked sadly without the belligerence or the cocky one-upmanship and a lot like the young man he'd been ten years ago. Her childhood sweetheart. Her fiancé.

Nina put her hand on his arm. 'Yeah, I do know that,' she said firmly.

'Because you're so happy now.'

It was Nina's eternal dilemma: she wasn't happy, but then again, she wasn't unhappy. She was still somewhere bang in the middle but she knew one thing for sure: she'd been right to walk away from Dan all those years ago, walk away from Worcester Park and the safe, dull life that felt like it was choking her. She still had some way to go before she achieved her dreams but standing here in front of Dan made her realise how far she'd come.

'Look, I'm really sorry that it didn't work out with Angie,' she said again and, as she walked off, Dan called something after her but Nina didn't pause, she just wanted to get Chloe upright and leave.

In the few minutes that she'd been at the bar, the last bottle of rosé had caused carnage. The mums had all reached the 'I bloody well *love* you, you're my best mate, you are' stage of drunkenness and they all wanted to hug Nina and tell her that she was an amazing girl and that she needed to find a nice bloke and have kids. 'It will be the making of you.'

Nina didn't point out that she was already made. She was done. Apart from her not-yet-complete *Wuthering Heights* sleeve, she was a finished product. She also hoped that she wasn't this annoying and repetitive when she was drunk.

'Another bottle for the road!' Kara shouted but Nina was having none of it.

'No more,' she said sternly. 'You have to be at a soft-play centre in a few hours.'

There were groans all round and Nina was able to get them all to the Ladies for last wees, then outside where it was a tedious business deciding who was sharing a cab with who. Except Chloe who wasn't sharing a cab with anyone as she was looking so green that no driver wanted to take her.

It was inevitable that during the long, staggery walk back to her house Chloe would throw up at the side of the road. 'There there,' Nina said, rubbing her back in soothing circles. 'Better out than in. No! Don't take off your shoes. You think you want to but you really, really don't.'

Chloe straightened up and wiped her mouth and what was left of her lipstick with the back of her hand. 'I love you, Nina,' she said. 'I bloody well *love* you.'

'Yeah, yeah,' Nina muttered, as she looped her arm round Chloe again and encouraged her to take a few tottering steps. 'I get it. Everybody bloody loves me.'

CHAPTER 16

'Honest people don't hide their deeds.'

It was gone two before Nina finally crawled into bed. Or rather she collapsed on the sofa in Paul and Chloe's front room and pulled a chenille throw around her, which had chocolate smeared on it. Nina prayed that it was chocolate.

It was barely six when she was rudely, and abruptly, jolted awake by her nieces jumping on her. Nothing that Nina said ('I'm telling Santa Claus to put both of you on the naughty list') could convince them to go back to bed.

'Santa Claus doesn't even exist,' eight-year-old Rosie said witheringly. 'And even if he did, Christmas is *ages* away. We've loads of time to get on the good list.'

Meanwhile little Ellie, never one for respecting people's personal space boundaries, shoved her face into Nina's. 'You look weird without your make-up on. I don't like it.'

There was nothing else Nina could do but get up, put on something called *Paw Patrol*, aim cereal in the direction of two bowls then go back to the sofa, bookended by a niece each. Neither of them would stop talking, even though Nina begged them to shut up.

Paul and a grey-looking Chloe didn't come downstairs until eight o'clock. It had been the longest two hours of Nina's life.

'Thanks for the lie-in, sis,' Paul grinned. 'You'll have to wait a bit for a shower. There's no hot water left.'

'I hate you,' Nina said with great feeling, as she slumped across the kitchen island. 'Also, I feel like I've been in a car crash.'

'Yeah, yeah. This is what being a parent feels like every day,' Chloe said, as she poured coffee into a mug so large that it could have doubled up as a soup tureen.

Considering how rotten she felt, she might just as well have got good and drunk, Nina thought to herself a couple of hours later as she entered the living hell that was a soft-play centre.

Everything was neon and fluorescent as far as the eye could see while what seemed like hundreds of little girls, all of them dressed in Disney Princess outfits, ran around shrieking. Their ear-splitting screams competed with a constant soundtrack of tinny pop music, which sounded like it was sung by a group of chipmunks who'd been huffing helium.

And the smell! Fried food, TCP and a base note of vomit. 'They puke all the time,' explained the morose teenager on a vigil to make sure that no one wet themselves in the ball pit.

It can hardly get much worse than this, Nina reasoned, and promptly jinxed herself because in a waft of Chanel No 5 and bad energy, her mother appeared at her side.

There wasn't really much that Alison O'Kelly could complain about this morning. Nina was here, present, mostly conscious, and was being a team player and a good aunt. But this was Nina's mother; she could *always* find something to complain about.

'Oh, Nina, you might have made more of an effort,' she said by way of a greeting. 'It's a birthday party.'

Because she was sleep deprived and also planned to spend a large part of the day having needles stabbed into her skin, Nina had dressed for comfort. She was wearing dungarees from her favourite purveyor of retro denim, Freddies of Pinewood, a vintage silk, dark green and white, polka-dot blouse with a pussy-cat bow and her hair was pinned up and mostly tucked out of sight in a headscarf. Nina liked to think that she was rocking a Rosie The Riveter vibe and besides, she had a full face of make-up, and all the other mums and dads were in jumpers and jeans.

Still, she wasn't going to rise to the bait. 'You look nice, Mum,' she said, nodding at Alison's floral-wrap dress and her immaculately coiffed hair.

Her mother was not to be swayed. 'And you're not even staying for lunch. Poor little Ellie was broken-hearted when she found out.'

Poor little Ellie, in full *Little Mermaid* regalia, was running round after her friends with a cupcake in one hand and a fistful of Wotsits in the other, while screaming at the very top of her vocal register.

'Well, she seems to have made a full recovery,' Nina pointed out but her mother hadn't finished.

'I suppose we're just too boring and suburban for you,' she continued and Nina had never been so pleased to hear the ping of an incoming text message.

'Sorry,' she said, though she wasn't the least bit sorry. 'I need to look at this. It could be about my tattoo appointment.'

It probably wasn't as it was far too early for either Claude or Marianne to be up and compos mentis enough to operate a touchscreen. When Nina pulled her phone out of the bib pocket of her dungarees, it was Noah's name she saw and her heart did a strange fluttering thing like she was going into dfib.

Sorry I didn't reply to your text last night. I fell asleep on the job! Did you know the trains aren't running due to engineering works? Have car, do you want a lift?

Bumping into Dan last night had proved to Nina that she'd been right not to settle for a boy from Worcester Park. That it had been necessary to change everything about her life so she wouldn't end up with a boy from Worcester Park. Noah was a boy from Worcester Park too but . . .

God, yes please! Get me out of here! Am in soft-play centre in Ewell, I think it must be called Hell On Earth.

Because Noah might be a boy from Worcester Park but he'd left the first chance he'd got, too. He'd had adventures. He'd lived and not a half-life either. Also, he was offering to rescue Nina like the proverbial white knight on a dashing steed.

Noah texted her back immediately. Can you send me a location pin?

I totally would if I knew how to.

He texted her the instructions, which she followed as her mother carped on in the background, 'So rude to spend all of Ellie's party on the phone.'

'I think it's time to cut the cake,' Nina said as she saw Chloe approach the buffet area with a huge box. 'We don't want to miss that!'

Then Nina rushed past her mother and not even Alison could fault the way she persuaded the manager to turn off the smoke alarms long enough for them to light the candles on the cake and for Ellie to blow them out. Then Nina led the crowd in a rousing rendition of 'Happy Birthday' and handed out pieces of cake to grubby-handed children and their very hungover mums.

Another ping from her bib pocket. Another text from Noah. I'm two minutes away. Meet you out front.

Oh God! If Nina hadn't been distracted by her mother bitching in her ear, she would have told Noah to meet her around the corner because they still hadn't had the conversation about Paul destroying Noah's life.

What if Noah decided to come into the soft-play centre to find her? It didn't even bear thinking about.

It took Nina one minute and forty-seven seconds to say a hurried goodbye to anyone within shouting distance, hug Ellie, grab her overnight bag and not react to her mother saying, 'You're leaving? Already? But you only just got here.'

There was a car pulling into an empty parking space a few metres away as Nina escaped from the soft-play purgatory. She tilted her head to make sure that yes, the driver had red hair and put up her hand to forestall Noah, but he was already getting out of the car.

'STAY WHERE YOU ARE!' she yelled at Noah who waved at her, a broad smile on his face like he was pleased to see her. 'STAY RIGHT WHERE YOU ARE! DON'T MOVE!'

She was screeching like a hellbeast but it worked because although Noah frowned, he didn't take another step forward so there was little chance of him having an awkward, hideous, world-shattering reunion with Paul who – to Nina's horror – was outside too with Rosie, who was having a mid-level meltdown that Ellie was getting all the attention.

Noah *was* near enough to call out, 'What's the panic? I've come to take you away from all of this!'

Nina flapped her hands at him: she was pretty sure that

Paul was obscured by a blackboard for the moment but surely that wouldn't last. He was squatting down, Rosie balanced precariously on his knee, and he had eyes only for his eldest daughter, thank the Lord.

However, there was no way to avoid saying goodbye to them even with Noah within spitting distance. As Rosie hurled herself at Nina, Paul straightened up and Noah was still by the car and Paul had his back to him and Nina might just get away with this . . .

'Paul,' Nina hissed, yanking him towards the doors of the play centre. 'You're missing your youngest daughter's birthday party and Mum is *furious* with you.'

'Oh Jesus!'

There was nothing more guaranteed to make Paul disappear. He was gone in the blink of an eye, dragging a protesting Rosie with him, and Nina was left to walk over to Noah who was holding the passenger door open for her.

'Hey. Sorry about that,' she said nervously, as she climbed into the car.

Noah walked over to the driver's side and got in.

'That's OK. In a hurry to get away, were you?' he asked as he started the car.

'Yep. It turns out that soft-play centres are even worse than Ye Olde Laser Tag Experience.'

Noah laughed as he caught Nina's eye. 'Well, I'll give you a moment to regroup then.'

She couldn't quite believe that she'd got away with it. Noah hadn't seen Paul, Paul hadn't seen Noah. The Day of Reckoning was still yet to come, though any more close calls and Nina might have died from a heart attack before she had to confess everything.

They drove off in silence and it wasn't until they were on the A3 that Nina broke the ice. 'I didn't know you had a car,' she said because she didn't know how to say any of the other things she needed to say.

'I belong to a car hire club,' Noah said as he changed lanes.

'Oh, right.' Again, Nina wished that she had got drunk last night so right now she'd be hungover and numb of all feeling. Or better yet, still drunk.

She stared out of the window, pulled a despairing face at the houses and gardens that passed by. Maybe The Day of Reckoning was today and it was time to come clean. This *thing* with Noah; the two non-dates and now the rescuing her from the horrors of soft play was turning from a *thing* into a something but how could it be anything when Nina was hiding this secret from him? And yes, it might mean that Noah would want nothing more to do with her, but that was his call. His right to make that decision . . .

'Are you ready for adult conversation yet?' Noah asked.

'I think so.' Nina took a deep breath. 'Look, I have to—'

'It's just, I wonder if you feel the same way about Worcester Park,' Noah blurted out. 'That being back home – not that it feels like home any more – makes me feel like I'm twelve again.' When Nina glanced at him, his cheeks were red and blotchy. 'As if everything I've accomplished since I left that school, all the things I've learned, the new experiences, friends, places, are all gone and I'm back to being a speccy, spotty, swotty nerd who couldn't do anything right. This morning I popped in to see my parents and just walking down our street gave me this absolute sense memory. The same feeling of wanting to be sick that I got each morning when I was walking to school. Y'know, Sundays were the worst, knowing that the weekend was almost over and soon it would be Monday . . .'

'But I thought you said you'd learned to compartmentalise,' Nina said a little desperately because she couldn't bear to listen to another word. She even reached over to put a hand on Noah's arm to comfort him, but mostly to stop him.

She knew then that she could never tell him that it was her brother who'd made those Sunday nights, the anticipation of Monday morning, so hellish.

If she did, it would ruin everything. Instead of seeing Nina, Noah would look at her and only see her brother. Not Paul as he was now; kind, caring, the loveliest father, but as he'd been back then. A thug in a Kappa tracksuit, as Paul himself had said.

'I realise that there are some things I can't lock away,' Noah said. 'Not now I'm back.'

'But it does no good living in the past,' Nina argued in the same desperate voice. Noah had shared something with her and though she couldn't tell him the truth, she wanted to share something personal and painful too. 'Last night, at All Bar One, I bumped into my ex. *The* ex.'

'Oh.' Noah caught her eye again as he changed lanes. 'Your childhood sweetheart?'

'One and the same, Dan Moffat,' Nina said without thinking.

'Dan Moffat? I think the name dimly rings a bell,' Noah said but he didn't say any more than that and there was no telltale flush to his face any more, so at least Dan hadn't made Noah's life a misery too.

'We started going out when I was fifteen. He was my first boyfriend,' Nina said. 'I was obsessed with getting a boyfriend.' Oh God, she had hardly changed at all. 'I was so basic back then. I wanted to look like everyone else, wear the same clothes, hang out at the same places.'

'But most people want to fit in when they're teenagers,' Noah pointed out. 'It's safer that way.'

'Sometimes safe is just another word for boring. Everything about me was boring. Like, all the women in my family were married by the time they were twenty and that was the sum total of my ambition too. So, I went out with Dan and he was perfectly nice and we got engaged on my eighteenth birthday and the wedding date was set, caterers booked, and that was when I read *Wuthering Heights* and realised that I was just sleepwalking. Treading water and it was time that I learned to swim, jump off the really high diving board. You know what I mean?'

'Mostly.' Noah dared to nudge Nina and now he was smiling again. 'Although you're starting to lose me a little with all the swimming metaphors.'

Nina smiled. 'OK, I'll skip the bit about learning how to do butterfly after years of a sedate breaststroke.' Her expression grew more serious, not least because she couldn't tell him that the reason for her epiphany was Paul's accident. 'Anyway, I decided I was done with living the life that my mother had planned out for me. So, I quit my job at my aunt's hair salon so I could work in a place in town that would be more cutting edge and well, I broke up with Dan. Though it was only two weeks before our wedding, so technically it counts as jilting him. That was ten years ago and my mother still hasn't forgiven me.'

'Wow,' Noah said. 'You'd think she'd have let it drop by now.'

'It wasn't just the jilting,' Nina said. 'Everything I did to reclaim myself was a personal affront to her, from dyeing my hair to eating carbs – she'd had me on the Atkins diet since I was twelve.'

'When my parents found out that I wasn't vegan any more – my dad discovered a Ginster's pasty wrapper in my laundry bag when I was home from university – we had a week of family mediation sessions so I could think about what I'd done,' Noah offered.

'I'd rather have a week of mediation than ten years of my mother's passive-aggressive sniping,' Nina said. Then she thought about it. 'Actually it's not even passive-aggressive. It's aggressive-aggressive.' But they were getting sidetracked. 'What I'm saying is that it doesn't matter who we used to be, what's important is the people that we choose to be now,' she said with great force and feeling.

Noah caught her eye again in the windscreen mirror, his expression serious but not sad any longer. 'Amen to that.'

CHAPTER

17

*'If you ever looked at me once with what
I know is in you, I would be your slave.'*

Despite all her protests that he could drop her off at the first tube station they came to, Noah didn't just drive her back into London, but all the way to Marianne and Claude's place in Kentish Town.

En route he introduced her to the *This American Life* podcast and when Nina asked him what he'd meant about falling asleep on the job the night before, he handed her his phone when they were stopped at traffic lights.

'My sister took that when she came home,' he explained. 'Before she woke me up and told me off for being so slack in my babysitting duties.'

In the picture Noah was slumped on a sofa with a baby curled against the crook of his neck and a toddler draped across his chest. All of them fast asleep, with their mouths wide open, same peaceful expression on their three faces.

'Definitely one for the family Christmas card this year,' Nina snorted, as she tried to hold back the urge to tilt her head and make 'aw' noises because the whole scene was unbearably cute. Nina didn't do unbearably cute or ever wonder whether the particular man she was seeing at any one time would make good dad material.

Except she couldn't help but think that Noah would be an excellent dad and then stopped herself right there and purposely asked Noah a question about the podcast ('this Ira Glass – I'm pretty sure he's a character in a J. D. Salinger novel, right?') so she wouldn't start asking him if he'd thought about having kids and did he have a preference for boys or girls and had he picked out any names?

All too soon, even though it had taken them well over an hour, Noah was pulling into the little street off Kentish Town Road where Marianne had her vintage dress shop and Claude had his tattoo parlour upstairs and they lived in the flat on the top floor.

Nina had stayed in text contact with Claude throughout their journey and he was just walking up the road with a carrier bag bulging promisingly with sugary snacks to keep her going through her inking.

She tapped on the window as she took off her seatbelt. 'That's Claude,' she said to Noah. 'He's going to be hurting me with needles for the next few hours.'

'I suppose there are worse ways to spend a Sunday afternoon,' Noah said wryly.

'Come and say hello,' Nina said because she wanted Noah to meet someone that she loved and for it not to be a totally traumatising experience for him.

Claude might look terrifying with his jet-black quiff and sideburns and the tattoos that completely covered every inch of skin visible from the cuffs of his leather jacket right up to his neck, but he was a sweetheart, an absolute teddy bear, and of course he insisted on inviting Noah in when he heard that they'd driven all the way from Surrey without stopping for a coffee.

'Marianne's been baking, which to be fair isn't always the incentive it sounds . . .'

'She often forgets to put in a crucial ingredient,' Nina agreed pantingly as they trooped past the tattoo parlour and carried on up the stairs. 'One time she made these Nigella Lawson Snickers muffins and forgot to add sugar.'

'You still managed to eat three of them!' Marianne reminded her from the top of the stairs where she was waiting for them.

'Well, a lot of Snickers bars had to die to make those muffins,' Nina said as she finally made it to the top and Christ, she was unfit. Noah wasn't even breathing hard as she pulled him forward. 'This is Noah. He gave me a lift from Surrey.'

Marianne gave Noah a quick once over. He was wearing non-ripped, non-skinny jeans, a sensible navy-blue jumper, though this one had a little hint of purple in the ribbing, and a friendly smile. He couldn't look more basic but Marianne's smile was equally friendly. 'Lovely to meet you, Noah. Bet you're gasping for a cuppa?'

'I'd love one,' Noah agreed as Marianne ushered him into the flat. There was a lot to take in, from the tiny hall made tinier by the flamingo-print wallpaper and fairy lights to the living room which was crammed with a mid-century three-piece suite reupholstered in leopard print, a tiki-inspired bamboo mini-bar, and floor-to-ceiling shelves which housed Claude's collection of vinyl records. On every surface there was something to look at, whether it was a lamp in the shape of a pineapple, Marianne's prized collection of Elvis Presley figurines or a plastic hula girl who did a dance when you pressed her belly button.

Noah stood in the centre of the room, even though Marianne had told him to take a seat, and did a slow three-hundred-and-sixty-degree turn so he could take in everything. 'I love the maximalist approach,' he said at last. 'Reminds me of this vintage shop I went to once in Palm Springs.'

'I love Palm Springs!' Marianne called out from the little kitchen just off the lounge. 'Last year Claude and I went to the Viva Las Vegas convention then did a week in Palm Springs. Great vintage shops. Nearly bankrupted myself.'

'Nearly bankrupted me too,' Nina remembered, plonking her overnight bag down. 'She came back with all these dresses she'd handpicked for me.'

'Yeah, but you get mates' rates. Noah, how do you take your tea? And I made peanut-butter cookies and yes, I did put sugar in them.' Marianne made a shooing motion with her hands. 'Go on, sit down! Not you, Nina, take your coffee and go down to the torture chamber. Claude wants to get started straight away.'

'Sorry,' Nina said to Noah, who was seated in one of the bucket armchairs and didn't look too perturbed about Nina abandoning him. Marianne was six foot in heels, with blue-black hair styled in waves and a short fringe under which her impeccably arched brows gave her an imperious look. She was wearing Sunday casual, which consisted of a pair of black cigarette pants and a tight black sweater and the whole effect was quite intimidating. 'She's not as scary as she looks,' Nina added, because Marianne's heart was solid gold. She was a nurturer, a mother hen, and had got Nina through break-ups, evictions, firings: so many crises.

Still, she couldn't help but worry about leaving Noah up there as she arranged herself face-down on Claude's padded black table. But then Claude popped out from behind a screen wielding his tattoo gun and said, 'Let's make sure we're both happy with the design and then I'll get you sterilised,' and Nina remembered why she was there and how much it was going to hurt.

Noah would just have to fend for himself; Nina could only worry about herself.

The first ten minutes were always the worst. The first shock of the first punch of the first needle into her flesh. Then another one. And another one. Like some sharp-toothed bloodsucking insect chowing down. Nina hung her head and tried to breathe around the pain because she knew that she just had to get through the initial agony and acclimatise, while her inner voice declared quite loudly that there was no way she could endure another ten seconds of this, let alone ten minutes, never mind *hours*.

'You all right, Nina?' Claude asked.

'Don't talk to me!' she snapped back. 'Oh God, why do I let you do this to me?'

Claude, wisely, refrained from reminding Nina that she'd asked him to inflict this torture on her, was even paying him for the privilege.

The pain, the stabby stab stab, made her want to scream. How could she have forgotten how much this bloody hurt? Chloe had said that she'd repressed the memory of how pushing out a tiny human being from her vagina had caused her unimaginable agony. If she hadn't repressed it, then no way would she ever have had a second child. Chloe had also said that getting Ellie and Rosie's names tattooed in two hearts on her ankle had hurt much worse than giving birth to them.

'If you ever have kids, Nina, after having all those tattoos, you'll pop them out like you're shelling peas,' Chloe had once said to her in all seriousness and the thought of Chloe's earnest face as she'd said it made Nina smile and if she could smile, then she'd broken through the pain barrier.

It still hurt like a hundred fire ants were eating into her skin but it was a bearable hurt. 'Sorry for being mean,' she said to Claude, untucking her head from where it had been buried in the crook of her shoulder.

'Don't mention it,' Claude said easily as he adjusted the angle of Nina's other arm, the one he was working on, which was resting on the pull-out padded flap of his tattoo chair. 'So, how's life been treating you?'

As Nina told Claude about her Ye Olde Laser Tag adventures, she could just make out the low-level hum of conversation from the flat upstairs and wondered how Noah and Marianne were getting on. Though both of them were the type to get on with anyone – Marianne was particularly beloved of elderly gentlemen in supermarket queues – Nina hoped that Noah wasn't digging for information on her and that Marianne wasn't spilling any of her secrets. More than anyone, Marianne knew where all Nina's bodies were buried and just how many corpses were piled up in her dating graveyard.

There was the sound of footsteps and Nina tensed up in expectation of Noah popping his head round the door to say goodbye, so that Claude's tattoo gun almost bounced off her arm.

'Easy, tiger,' he murmured as the footsteps carried on past the open door of the studio and they could hear Marianne's voice. 'It would be amazing if you could give me some advice as an impartial observer. 'Cause some of my customers want the stock displayed in decades, others in sizes, but I think it looks better to divide it by colour and . . .'

Her voice drifted off and Nina couldn't believe that she'd asked Noah to give her free business advice but then, knowing Marianne, she could believe it only too easily.

It was another hour before they trooped back upstairs, this time stopping at the tattoo parlour and coming inside. 'How you doing, Nina?' Marianne asked in a concerned voice. 'Ready for some sugar?'

'Yes, please,' Nina said because once her energy levels began to dip, the pain started edging towards unbearable again. 'Did you get me some full-fat Lucozade?'

''Course we did,' Marianne said. 'And Noah, another cup of tea or do you fancy something stronger?'

'Tea would be great,' Noah said and Nina raised her head, which had again been buried in the crook of her non-butchered arm to see him standing in the doorway. 'I could go back upstairs if you'd prefer,' he added to Nina.

'No, you're all right,' she muttered, though she wasn't exactly sure that it was all right. She'd wanted to be as comfortable as possible, so she now had bare feet, and had undone the top of her dungarees and taken off her blouse so she was lying on her front in a black vest with the red straps of her bra visible. Nina had been in far more compromising and naked positions with other men, but she was in pain so she felt especially vulnerable. More to the point, it was Noah and she was starting to realise that everything with Noah felt different. She wasn't sure why. Maybe it was because of their past, or their work connection, or that Noah was so not her type that he'd become her type. He was unsuitable for all the right reasons, instead of the wrong reasons. 'Ow! Jesus! Warn me if you're going to hit a muscle,' she added in a snarl to Claude.

'Stop tensing up then,' he told her calmly.

'You're coming at me with a needle gun, how do you expect me *not* to tense up?' Nina demanded.

'Just grab that stool and pull it closer,' Claude said to Noah as he completely ignored Nina's suffering. 'And if this one barks your head off don't take it personally.'

'I hate you,' Nina told him, which just proved Claude's point.

Then Marianne appeared with Nina's Lucozade and the freshly baked cookies and Nina's pain and rage subsided again. Marianne sat down with a pile of mending and Noah scooted his stool right over so he could have a ringside seat for the tattooing.

'Did you draw that?' he asked Nina when he saw the final sketch that Claude was working from.

'I did,' Nina replied and she almost gave a guilty start but stopped herself as she wasn't allowed to make any sudden movements. 'I used those beautiful Faber Castell pencils that I never even thanked you for because I'm an ungrateful wretch.'

'You thanked me in the email inviting me to Ye Olde Laser Tag, which was one of the most fun nights of my life so I think we're even,' Noah said, pulling his stool even closer so he could have a proper look at what Claude was up to. 'You really should think about taking a drawing class, Nina. You've got some serious skills, which are worth developing.' Noah looked again at the pencil sketch Nina had done of the old, weather-beaten tree, swallows flying overhead, Cathy and Heathcliff leaning against its trunk.

Nina tucked her head back into the crook of her arm to hide the delighted smile, which she was sure made her look quite smug. 'Maybe,' she conceded because there was an art school in Bloomsbury, quite near the shop, and it wouldn't hurt to see if they did any evening classes for beginners. 'As long as the life-drawing models are quite fit.'

Noah smiled and shook his head as he often did when Nina was being impossible, then turned his attention back to the needle gun in Claude's steady hands.

'You're doing it freehand,' he noted in surprise. 'When I got mine done, the tattooist used a stencil.'

'I like to go freehand so I can fit the tattoo to her arm better and it makes for a more organic design,' Claude explained.

'And I trust Claude to know what's going to work and what isn't and to put his own stamp on the tattoo.' Nina smiled mischievously. 'I mean, I suppose he's *quite* good at his job.'

'Thanks for the vote of confidence,' Claude said. He was the most chilled person Nina had ever met. It was impossible to rile him, unless Nina had to ask him to see off a persistent and substandard admirer and then Claude could be absolutely terrifying.

'I always wondered how tattooists develop their own style,' Noah mused. 'It's not like you can practise on people, is it?'

'You say that but my brother has a particularly crap tattoo of Bruce Springsteen on his back from when I was an apprentice,' Claude said deadpan as Noah, Nina and even

Marianne looked at him in consternation. 'Nah! Pigskin from the butcher.' He sighed. 'I miss working on pigskin. Didn't bitch half as much as my human customers do.'

'Well, if you weren't so heavy handed,' Nina grumbled and she wanted to ask Claude to stop so she could stretch but she knew that if he stopped then she'd only have to get used to the needle all over again.

'"Whatever souls are made of, his and mine are the same,"' Noah read out the quote from *Wuthering Heights* that curled around the base of the tree trunk on Nina's arm. 'Ah! I didn't get to read this properly on our first date. It was quite dimly lit and I was wearing whisky goggles.'

'Those Old Fashioneds were lethal,' Nina recalled.

Noah peered intently at her arm again. 'So this quote . . . that's your mission statement, is it?'

He didn't sound sarcastic, but genuinely curious, so Nina didn't bristle. Because although it was etched into her arm for all the world to see and although they'd spoken already about what *Wuthering Heights* meant to her, the quote itself was something intensely personal. It wasn't a story many people got to hear. She'd told Claude and Marianne, of course, but even Posy and Verity thought that Nina adored *Wuthering Heights* only for its drama and she'd never bothered to correct them.

'I never read the book when I was at school. Probably wouldn't have paid attention even if we had,' she said falteringly. 'But then someone close to me was in an accident . . .' She prayed that Claude or Marianne wouldn't chime in with 'You mean Paul?' but thankfully they both stayed silent. 'He nearly died. Was on a moped and had a collision with a lorry and ended up wrapping himself round a lamppost. We didn't know if he was going to make it, if he'd ever walk again, so we made sure that there was always one of us at his bedside.'

Nina's voice cracked as she talked. 'I was supposed to be getting married in less than a month and somehow, sitting vigil, listening to the monitors beep and his slow steady breathing . . . it actually felt like a respite from all the wedding prep. When I thought about the wedding, I got the same nauseous feeling of panic as I did when the beeping of one of the monitors in the ICU ward would occasionally become a shrieking and doctors and nurses would run in from all directions . . .' She paused and gulped.

'So, in the end I didn't think about the wedding at all. And anyway, the seating plan was the very last of my worries,' she remembered. 'In the relatives' room was a little bookcase and the only reason I picked up the copy of *Wuthering Heights* was because it was the one book there that wasn't by Len Deighton or Jack Higgins. It was hard to get into to start with and then it stopped being hard and every word resonated with me. All the thoughts and feelings I didn't have words for were there on the page. I was all set to marry my Edgar Linton, even though I didn't love him, I didn't even know what love was.

'And yes, I do know that Heathcliff is like the dictionary definition of toxic but it felt as if I was saying goodbye to ever experiencing that kind of passion. I was sitting there in a hospital only too aware of how short life can be, how it can be snatched away from you in a split second, and so I called off the wedding there and then. By text message.'

'Nina!' Marianne gasped, putting down the sequinned dress she was mending. 'You never said it was by text message.'

'Well, it's not something I'm proud of,' Nina said, 'but it really felt as if there was no time left to lose. I wanted to be a girl again, "half-savage, hardy and free". When I thought about Emily Brontë and her sisters, all trapped in that parsonage, but writing with such wild abandon, I felt that I had to start living instead of just existing. Be more like Cathy, even if I ended up broken-hearted . . .'

'Or dead . . .' Claude pointed out with a tiny sly smile that Nina decided to let go.

'I was going to look how I wanted to look, eat what I wanted to eat, love who I wanted to love – do things because I wanted to do them and not because that was what was expected of me. So this tattoo symbolises all that,' she finished and dared to look at Noah from under her lashes though she'd avoided his gaze until now.

She had his undivided attention. His gaze fixed on hers, his expression thoughtful and serious though a smile softened his features when he caught Nina's eye. 'I get the impression that you don't share that story with many people so thank you for sharing it with me,' he said. 'For trusting me.'

'You've got a very trustworthy face,' Nina said and it seemed as if they were having a moment and all of a sudden she felt stripped bare in a way that had nothing to do with her state of undress or the secrets she'd just spilled. Time to break the spell with a quip. 'If the business analysis thing doesn't pan out, you could always sell life insurance.'

'It's good to have a plan B,' Noah agreed evenly and she couldn't stop looking at him, at the warmth in his green eyes, his smile . . .

'OK, you two, break it up,' Claude said and it was only now that he stopped with his bloody needles that Nina realised that she hadn't even noticed the pain for the last half hour. 'You should have a stretch before I start doing the colour work.'

Nina slowly sat up then gingerly stretched, keeping the arm that was a work in progress pinned to her side. She glanced down to see Claude's handiwork. 'It's perfect. So much better than I ever imagined,' she said.

'It's all right,' Claude decided, as Marianne stood up and stretched herself. 'More tea?' she asked. 'Nina, Noah?'

'I should probably go,' Noah said without much enthusiasm and without moving so much as a millimetre off the stool.

'Don't go,' Nina said softly.

'If you want me to stay . . .'

'Of course she wants you to stay,' Marianne said. 'And as you're not being tattooed or doing the tattooing you could even join me in some alcohol, then afterwards we're going to order a curry from The Tiffin Tin. You don't want to miss that.'

'Well, I'm going to drive Nina home so I won't have any alcohol but I wouldn't say no to more tea.'

So, it was decided that Noah would stay.

For the last two hours of the tattooing session he asked some gentle but probing questions about how Nina and Marianne met. They told people it was at a vintage fair, 'But really it was at a burlesque striptease class,' Marianne admitted.

'Not that we're embarrassed about that,' Nina assured Noah. 'But it does give people the wrong idea.'

'And neither of us could ever master twirling our pasties,' Marianne added and Noah was so pink that it looked painful and even Claude had to set down his tattoo gun and tell them both very sternly to pack it in.

The conversation seemed to flow like the red wine that Marianne opened. It was light and easy, lots of laughing and joking, especially when the tattooing was done and Nina's tattoo was covered up with a sterile gauze pad and clingfilm, and they'd decamped to the living room upstairs to eat their way through an Indian feast.

Even though she skewed heavily towards the bad-boy demographic and a life less ordinary, there had been times when Nina had tried to picture her one true love and she'd always come back to the same image: of this unknown man fitting in with her friends, of him sitting in Marianne and Claude's eclectic, cluttered lounge sharing a takeaway as Nina so often did.

The three of them, Noah, Claude and Marianne, were talking about Palm Springs, how Claude and Marianne had taken a sightseeing tour on an Aerial Tramway only for Claude to realise that he was terrified of heights. Marianne was perched on a pouffe, her long legs stretched out in front of her, as she glanced over at Noah, then caught Nina's eye and winked at her.

It occurred to Nina that as much as Posy and Verity both lamented Nina's many and frequent dating disasters, Marianne and Claude were equally disapproving in their own way.

'Oh *no*, Nina, not him!' Marianne would invariably say if Nina introduced her to a man who'd survived the first three dates so she could loosely describe him as someone she was seeing. And Claude, who often saw fit to act like an overprotective big brother, seemed to like Noah a lot if the way he kept nodding and laughing was anything to go by.

And Nina? She liked Noah very much. So much so that 'like' was an entirely inadequate way to describe how she felt about him as he carefully guided her down the stairs from the top-floor flat. She'd had one glass of red wine, after five hours of being tattooed and with pain endorphins coursing through her blood, so it had gone straight to her head and her very wobbly legs.

Noah's hand curled around her elbow, light but purposeful, as if he enjoyed touching her. As they drove back into the centre of town, Noah's hand brushed Nina's leg as he changed gears because she'd curved her body towards him. She wished that the journey would never end. That they'd stay cocooned in the cosy warmth of a rented car, just the two of them, the silence comfortable.

Since when had she wanted cosy? Or comfortable?

'So, our third date, does this mean that we can officially get down to some funny business now?' Noah suddenly drawled, his voice doing things to Nina's nerve endings that weren't remotely cosy or comfortable.

'This wasn't a third date,' she said sternly, because it wasn't. There were rules about these things. 'This was hanging out.'

'Oh, that's a pity. I was looking forward to more kissing,' Noah said in the same dark voice that made Nina feel quite light-headed while other parts of her felt heavy and languid.

'Good things are worth waiting for,' Nina said as she fluttered her lashes. She really was absolutely hammered just from one glass of Merlot.

'Well, I look forward to it, then,' Noah said. It was almost as if they'd skipped a few steps, and the flirty banter had been discarded in favour of deep discussions, the sharing of intimate secrets, so actually Nina was quite happy to rewind and get her flirt on. 'By the way, I'm back at Happy Ever After this week, but don't you think we should keep *this* under wraps?'

Nina was immediately stung; it hurt even more than the dull throb in her arm. Then she remembered that she didn't even know what *this* was. It changed from minute to minute, hour to hour. One moment as cosy and comfortable as an old cardigan, the next charged with fraught anticipation.

So, yeah, who even know what this thing between them was. But Nina wanted to find out. As Noah pulled the car up at the entrance to Rochester Mews, she said, 'I'm glad we get to hang out this week.'

She turned her head to smile at Noah at the exact same time that he turned his head to smile at her. Then, shockingly, because this was also new territory, he rested his hand on her knee and it was hard to remember why she wasn't going to do anything more with him tonight. 'I'm glad that you're glad.' His voice was low, his eyes heavy-lidded as he looked at Nina. 'How about we seal the deal with a kiss?'

Nina was already unbuckling her seatbelt so she could scoot closer to Noah even if it did mean getting very intimate with the gear lever. 'Sounds like a plan,' she agreed huskily.

CHAPTER 18

'They forgot everything the minute they were together again.'

When Noah arrived at Happy Ever After the next morning, Nina nodded her head vaguely in his direction as he came through the door then went back to informing Posy that she couldn't do any book shelving until her tattoo healed.

'I suppose I could shelve at chest level but anything higher and I have to stretch my arms and stretching my arms hurts too much,' Nina explained.

'Really?' Posy asked sceptically.

'Really,' Verity confirmed from the office. 'I had to help her put her bra on this morning. I'm still traumatised.'

'Can we not talk about my *personal items* when there are men present!' Nina snapped because Tom was on one of the sofas, face first in his usual breakfast panini. But Tom barely counted as a man (Nina had once sent him out to buy cranberry juice when she had a UTI) – she was more concerned about Noah, in the process of hanging up his jacket, who winked at Nina and permitted himself a small smile.

'Sorry!' Verity sing-songed. 'But no heavy lifting for Nina. Honestly, Posy, her arm's all scabby and sore.'

Nina proffered her arm at Posy who shied away from it. 'Urgh! I don't want to see.' She sighed. Posy seemed to sigh a lot lately. 'It's a pity 'cause we do have a lot of new stock that needs shelving.'

'I can do it,' Tom offered, through a mouthful of panini. 'Nina can serve. It's all good.'

'Anyway, I was planning to spend the morning working on the shop Instagram,' Nina said brightly. 'I met a woman on Saturday night who started an Instagram account for her French bulldogs and now she has over fifty thousand followers and people send her free stuff. I know we don't want free stuff but we definitely could do with fifty thousand followers. And also, though I haven't quite worked out how, people can click through and buy the items, which in our case would be books. Lots and lots of books.'

'I don't know . . . selling books from an Instagram post sounds amazing but it also sounds very complicated and techy,' Posy said, her brow furrowed.

'Just as well you're married to someone very complicated and techy,' Nina said as everyone, including Posy, gathered around Nina's phone to coo over photos of Eric and Ernie. Then it was time to go about their respective businesses – Posy popping out for the monthly meeting of the Rochester Street Traders' Association and Noah taking out his iPad and retiring to a quiet corner.

He'd only said two words to Nina: 'Good' and 'morning', but once Verity was back in the office and Tom was sorting through the delivery of new stock, he smiled at her.

'How's the arm? Apart from scabby and sore?' he asked in a whisper.

'Scabby and sore just about covers it,' Nina whispered back. She sidled closer. 'So, now that we've been on two dates *and* hung out, are you going to show me all the mean things you've been writing about us?'

'Never!' Noah put his iPad behind his back. 'And I would never write mean things about you.'

Nina smiled a little coyly. 'I should think not.'

'Maybe some constructive criticism though,' Noah said and Nina sidled even closer so she could pretend to punch him. She was close enough to feel the warmth of his body, which made her feel warm too. Maybe she could lure Noah into an anteroom later on, if the shop was quiet, and they could sneak a few illicit kisses.

'What are you doing for lunch?' she asked.

'I have to go and meet a client.' Noah sounded quite regretful about it. 'Then I'm back in Soho this afternoon.'

'Shame . . .'

'What are you doing, Nina?' Tom was suddenly on the other side of the counter with a huge pile of books in his arms and a quizzical expression on his face. 'Are you harassing Noah?'

Nina broke away from Noah as if she'd just been scalded. 'Of course not!' she scoffed and put as much distance between herself and Noah as she could. 'We were just talking about hashtags, actually. Success on Instagram is all about the hashtags.'

'Is it?' Tom pretended to yawn and Noah made a note on his iPad and it was business as usual, nothing to see here.

Though once Nina started on her mission to improve Happy Ever After's Instagram page, she found it quite engrossing. Under Sam's benign neglect, they'd only posted one picture and gained twenty-seven followers.

Mindful of Dawn's advice, in between a desultory flow of customers, Nina followed anyone who had anything to do with book writing, book blogging and book selling, even a couple of book binders, and as many lovers of romantic fiction as she could find on Instagram, liking their posts and leaving comments. It was a massive two-hour sucking-up session but gratifyingly, it didn't take long for Happy Ever After's Instagram followers to swell in number.

'We're up to a hundred and twenty-three followers!' she announced at one point during the morning.

'If you're going to keep refreshing the page and giving me follower updates every five minutes, then I'm going to hurl myself from the top of the rolling ladder,' Tom snapped, but Noah smiled encouragingly.

'I bet you'll get even more followers once you start

posting pictures,' he said, and that was Nina's cue to go on a picture-posting spree. She posted a picture of a stack of new releases artily propped against Lavinia's chipped cut-glass vase that contained her favourite pink-edged white roses. She posted the Happy Ever After shop sign swinging gaily in the February breeze. She even persuaded a couple of customers to be photographed holding up their purchases and was just cajoling one of them to climb up the rolling ladder when Posy got back from her traders' meeting.

'We have almost two hundred followers on Instagram,' Nina said, once the woman was back on terra firma with her books bagged and paid for. 'One hundred and ninety--three to be exact. I was thinking, can we do a giveaway when we hit five hundred?'

Posy stared at Nina. Then she narrowed her eyes. 'Have you doubled your dose of painkillers?'

'I have not, though now you come to mention it my arm is throbbing like an engine,' Nina noted. The sheer excitement of watching their Instagram numbers increase had completely taken her mind off the nagging pain of her fresh tattoo. 'Why do you ask?'

'You're not normally this enthusiastic about work,' Posy said, which was hurtful though actually now that Nina stopped to think about it, kind of true.

'Actually Posy, I'm enthusiastic about some things,' Nina protested. 'Doing the window displays, for example.'

'And calling first dibs when a new order of erotica comes in and that's about it,' Tom chimed in like the traitor he was. They were standing side by side at the counter and Nina did think about kicking him in the shin but she settled for an exasperated glance at Noah who shook his head like he couldn't believe it either.

'I'm very dedicated to my job,' Nina insisted. 'Look at me on the Instagram. That's taking on new responsibilities, that is.'

'I've already made a note of it,' Noah murmured and Nina beamed at him.

'Talking of taking on new responsibilities . . .' Posy said, then stopped. 'It's a pity that it's past the mid-morning bun break, this is the kind of news that would go better with buns.'

'What is it? Are you sacking one of us?' Tom asked, his voice getting a little shrill. 'Have you any idea how large my student loans are?'

Even Verity felt moved to get up from her desk and stand in the doorway of the office to demand: 'Are the council putting up the rates? Again?'

'Oh, just spit it out, Posy,' Nina advised because Verity and Tom would keep coming up with worst-case scenarios and Posy would keep dithering and they'd be here all day waiting for her to deliver her glum tidings. 'It is bad news, I take it?'

'Well, not necessarily *bad* news,' Posy decided. 'Depends on your definition of bad news, I suppose.'

'Before next Christmas would be great.' Nina made a big show of yawning and stretching her arms over her head. 'Ow! For the love of God!'

Noah was at her side in an instant. He even put down his iPad. 'Are you all right?' He gently touched the elbow of Nina's sore arm, caught the pained expression on her face and snatched his hand away as if Nina were coated in a fine mist of hydrochloric acid. 'I'm only asking because you don't appear to have a first-aid box anywhere, which I'm pretty sure is against Health and Safety reg—'

'All the traders have agreed that we'll do extended summer opening hours,' Posy yelped quickly. 'Starting from May we'll open until seven thirty every night, nine on Thursdays and we're opening on Sundays too. And, FYI, Noah, we do have a first-aid box, it's under the sink in the back kitchen.'

Everyone froze. Nina was the first to recover. 'Are we getting paid to work extra hours?' she asked, because she knew her rights.

'Of course!' Posy looked wounded that Nina would think otherwise. 'Not time and a half or anything fancy, and time off in lieu when we're quieter and we can do the Sundays on a rota, if that's all right. The Traders' Association have all sorts of plans for pop-up shops and food trucks and a street festival for the August Bank Holiday weekend. Sounds like it might be quite good for business.'

There were general murmurs of excited agreement then Posy went off to deliver the news to Mattie and the tearoom staff. 'Mattie is going to be a much harder sell than you lot. She'll want to make sure that none of the food trucks will be selling anything that even resembles cake,' she said morosely before she went.

'I don't really think Posy is enjoying her new-found power,' Tom remarked. 'Now that the novelty's worn off.'

'She thought it was going to be all book-launch parties and author meet-and-greets and it turns out that actually it's filling in VAT forms,' Verity added.

'Not that we've had any book-launch parties, not since our reopening week.' Nina managed to drag her eyes away from her phone screen and the shop's Instagram page where they were now thundering towards two hundred and ten followers. 'I could help with organising book launches and stuff. I've already followed a ton of authors on Instagram and I haven't even got started on Twitter. And then there are editors and publicists, I should probably follow them too and then I can tweet them about what the shop's doing. What do you think, Very?'

'Hmmm, sounds good,' Verity said vaguely, her gazed fixed on Noah, even though she already had a boyfriend. 'Why are you writing down everything we're saying? We weren't *criticising* Posy. We were just commiserating about her new workload.'

Tom turned slowly. 'We would never criticise Posy. We love Posy.'

'I'm just observing,' Noah said mildly. 'I'm not here to pass judgement.'

'Huh! Says the man who's eavesdropping on private conversations,' Verity said and she was getting the tight, pinched look she always got when she was steeling herself to have it out with someone.

'Noah's not eavesdropping,' Nina protested, putting

herself between Noah and Verity. 'He's just doing his job, a job Posy asked him to do. He's working with her, with us, not against us.'

She had her back to Noah while she did a very good impersonation of a human shield so Tom and Verity couldn't see that Noah had placed a warning hand on her shoulder blade. 'We're meant to be stealthy,' he whispered, his breath tickling Nina's ear in a way that wasn't at all unpleasant.

'If you say so,' Verity muttered. 'I don't know how much observing you need to do though. It's a small bookshop with three full-time employees. It shouldn't be taking you *this* long, surely?'

'And one very valuable part-time member of staff,' Tom added urgently.

'He's just crossing the i's and dotting the t's,' Nina insisted and this time Noah's hand pushed her lightly to the side so he could step forward and defend himself.

'You mean dotting the i's and crossing the t's,' he corrected gently. 'And this week is just a follow-up before I present my recommendations.'

'Will there be recommendations about staffing levels?' Tom asked anxiously. 'Again, have I mentioned the size of my student loans?'

'You have,' Noah said and Nina didn't know how he could maintain the same calm, even tone. She'd be getting screechy by now. 'And like I said, I am just following up. In fact, I'm working on another project this afternoon and I really should be going.'

And then he was gone, taking his calmness and his twinkling green eyes with him, so that Nina felt strangely bereft.

Noah was back the next morning though. They exchanged cordial 'good mornings' and polite smiles then Noah retreated to a quiet corner of the main room to do his still-a-bit-creepy silent observer thing and Nina continued with her mission to Instagram every single object in the shop (and it was a bookshop, so there were a hell of a lot of single objects) in between serving customers and sketching a poster with her lovely new pencils to advertise their summer opening hours.

Mattie had completely embraced staying open late and was planning a special after-hours summer menu featuring cakes bursting with exotic fruit flavours and boozy ice-cream floats though Verity kept muttering darkly that they needed a special licence to serve alcohol.

'Let's not get bogged down in minor details like that,' Posy had said and because Posy was quite fired up about their extended opening hours and this morning was emailing editors she knew to see if she could scrounge up some stray authors to come and do signings, Verity had let it go.

Posy also rubber-stamped Nina's first draft of a poster and was obviously in a decision-making frame of mind because she wanted to know if Nina had any ideas for their Easter window display.

'I was thinking of ginormous Easter eggs with books inside them,' Nina said, though she'd been thinking no such thing as Posy had caught her by surprise.

'I'm not entirely sure how that would work,' Posy said tactfully. 'I was hoping for something more along the lines of springy bright colours and lots of books.'

'Though if we did Easter eggs, we could get Strumpet to pose in one of them,' Nina persisted, because Posy's idea was *so* vanilla. 'He'd like nothing better than to sleep in a comfy egg all day if I lined the egg with fleece and bribed him with tuna bites.'

'No, I really don't think so,' Posy said firmly, with just the merest hint of a flashing eye, which meant that Nina shouldn't push her luck any further. 'I want something spring-like and Eastery that also says, "Please buy a shedload of books from our shop." I certainly don't want to have to put up a sign that says "No cats were harmed in the making of this window display."'

'Though Strumpet slumbering in an Easter egg would be cute,' Verity said, as she walked past them on her way to the tearooms with a sheaf of invoices in her hand.

'See, even Very agrees with me . . . Oh! Oh! Oh my God! How could I have been such a fool?' Nina exclaimed. She seized hold of her phone.

'What have you done? Have you run out of credit?' Posy asked in a concerned voice.

'Strumpet! We're sitting on a goldmine with that fat tabby and I haven't taken even a single shot of him for our Instagram. That's a way to grow followers right there.'

'But he's a cat and we sell books so I'm not really seeing the link . . .'

'Instagram loves a cute pet,' Nina said. She waved her phone wildly. 'Look at Eric and Ernie the French bulldogs.'

'Also, I'm pretty sure that there must be a big crossover between cat lovers and readers of romantic fiction,' Noah piped up as if he couldn't bear to be a casual observer any longer. 'I have a friend who works at Buzzfeed. The hits they get on anything to do with cats . . .'

'There isn't a second to lose,' Nina decided, turning a full three hundred and sixty degrees in her agitation.

'What about the window display?' Posy reminded her.

'I'll do something teeth-achingly sweet and spring-like,' Nina said. 'It will be the basic bitch of Easter window displays. But first I need to take some pictures of Strumpet and post them on Instagram.'

'Don't forget the hashtags,' Noah reminded her. 'Shall I run a quick algorithm to see what the most popular cat hashtags are?'

'You can do that?' Nina breathed. 'It sounds very difficult.'

'It's not that difficult. Sebastian runs quick algorithms all the time,' Posy said, because it must have been all of fifteen minutes since she last mentioned her husband.

'Yeah, it's quite simple,' Noah agreed. 'I'll do that, while you come up with some different Strumpet scenarios.'

'I love it when you go all "man with a plan" on me,' Nina said happily, already envisaging Strumpet balancing precariously on a pile of novels. Or maybe Strumpet posing coquettishly on their new 'I love big books and I cannot lie' tote bags.

Of course, Noah had to help with the impromptu photo session because Strumpet was far too rotund and heavy for Nina to lift with her sore arm. Also, Strumpet responded so much better to the touch of a man, even better if the man was armed with some cat treats.

Nina got several shots of Strumpet lolling in gay abandon on shop merchandise and even some video of Strumpet attempting to scale the rolling ladder then getting scared and mewling piteously until Noah rescued him.

Usually Strumpet wasn't allowed downstairs because sooner or later he'd mount an attack on the tearooms. Or more specifically mount an attack on the cakes, sand- wiches and pastries people were trying to eat. But Strumpet loved being snuggled in manly arms even more than he loved stuffing his fat furry face and it seemed that he loved snuggling Noah most of all.

'He's the neediest cat I've ever met,' Noah complained as Strumpet happily draped himself around Noah's neck. 'I'm used to cats who are silent and judgemental.'

'We don't know any cats like that,' Nina said. She put her arms out, wincing a little as her tattoo protested. 'Here, Strumpo, come to Auntie Nina.'

'Is your arm still hurting?' Noah asked, his face creased with concern. 'Have you been remembering to put that special gunk on it?'

Noah never seemed to forget anything pertaining to Nina. Not even the pot of special gunk that Claude had given her to put on her tattoo while it was healing.

'Yes, Dad,' she said with a little eye roll.

'Hardly your dad,' he said and shuddered. 'Please don't say that you see me as a father figure.'

It was Nina's turn to shudder. When Nina thought about kissing Noah, there was no way that she wanted to be thinking of her dad. A world of no.

'Hush your mouth,' she said huskily then she looked at the mouth in question, currently curved into a smile. Noah had a lovely mouth and a full bottom lip that Nina would quite like to nibble on if they ever got round to kissing again.

'I will,' Noah said. 'If you promise that you'll slather on that special tattoo gunk and take some painkillers if it's hurting.'

'I promise,' Nina said and all this promising seemed invested with a deeper meaning than Nina remembering to keep her scabby arm gunkified.

Noah held her gaze and Nina marvelled again that when he looked at her it was as if he saw the real her, beneath the hair and the make-up, the tattoos and the piercings, and that the real her was A-OK with him. Even Strumpet squirming between the two of them couldn't spoil the moment.

'Excuse me, but what *are* you doing with my cat?' asked a strained voice behind them because Verity was much more adept at spoiling moments.

Nina turned and to her surprise saw that the shop was busy and that a very beleaguered-looking Posy was on the till as a long line of customers waited to pay for their books.

How odd! She could have sworn that she and Noah were the only two people in the room.

'We were taking action shots of Strumpet for the shop Instagram,' Nina replied as Verity took custody of her cat. 'Will I have to get his signature on a photo-release form?'

'Or his paw print,' Noah said and Nina giggled while Verity smiled tightly.

'You know Strumpet's not allowed downstairs,' she panted because now that Strumpet was no longer getting snuggles from a man, he was trying to wriggle free of Verity's firm grip on him. 'I'm amazed that he didn't dash out of the door and head straight for the chippy.'

If he couldn't get into the tearooms, Strumpet had been known to hang around outside No Plaice Like Home on Rochester Street and once lovely Stefan had even found him trying to batter down the door of the little smokehouse in the backyard of the deli where he cured his own salmon. Except Strumpet hadn't escaped this time so there was no need for Verity to be standing there with a sour look on her face.

'I don't know what you're getting so snippy about,' Nina said. 'Strumpet was more than happy to be exploited in the name of publicity. Wasn't he?'

'He was,' Noah agreed, but now his smile was tense because of the sudden atmosphere that had descended on the shop: even the customers still queuing shifted uncomfortably and looked down at their feet. Noah glanced at his watch. 'I should go. I was meant to be in Soho half an hour ago.'

He quickly gathered up his belongings and was still

shrugging into his navy peacoat as he hurriedly exited, a muttered goodbye cut off by the door slamming behind him.

Nina watched Noah stride across the mews, a little hurt that he didn't look back once. Then she remembered that it was at least ten minutes since she'd last checked to see how many more Instagram followers they'd added.

'Nina! If you're not too busy a little help would be great,' Posy called out pointedly when she saw Nina looking at her phone because even though she'd married a digital entrepreneur Posy still thought that anything to do with social media was just messing around in work time.

'We're at just over six hundred Instagram followers,' Nina reported as she joined Posy behind the counter. 'And over three hundred followers on Twitter now. But Noah says that Twitter has slowed down a lot lately and that I'd be much better off concentrating on our Instagram and just cross-posting to Twitter instead of . . .'

'Thank you, do come again soon,' Posy said to the customer she was serving. It sounded a lot like she was saying it through gritted teeth.

'Please take a picture of your new books and post them on Instagram with the hashtag FoundAtHappyEverAfter,' Nina called after the lady. 'All one word! Y'know, I love Bertha, but if we had a computerised till and not one dated from before the Industrial Revolution then we could programme it to print messages on all the receipts, including our social media handles and hashtags.'

'There's nothing wrong with Bertha.' Posy gave the

temperamental contraption a loving stroke. 'Anyway, I thought you liked old stuff.'

'There's vintage and then there's just plain knackered,' Nina pointed out and then she was pretty sure that she heard Posy mutter something under her breath.

Uncharacteristically and pleasingly, there continued to be a steady stream of customers intent on stocking up on romantic literature. For twenty unprecedented minutes, even Verity had to come on to the shop floor to do the bagging up while Posy was on the till and Nina helped people look for books.

It was nearly three before the shop briefly emptied out and Nina's stomach was growling in protest at having to postpone lunch until the rush died down.

'I'm starving!' Nina announced. 'Shall I do a deli run for us? I could murder a smoked-salmon and cream-cheese bagel. Are you guys in?'

'Never mind that,' Posy snapped. For someone who'd had a shop full of people spending money she'd spent the last couple of hours extremely snippy. 'I want a word with you, young lady.'

Posy sounded horrifyingly like Nina's mother, enough that Nina gave a guilty start and racked her brains as to what awful thing she might have done. 'Is this about me giving you constant updates on our Instagram followers?'

'No, but now that you mention it, that is beyond annoying,' Posy said. She rested her hip against the counter and folded her arms. 'But it's not about that. It's about you and Noah.'

Nina's previous guilty start became more of a lurch. She managed to right herself because there was no way that Posy could know about her and Noah. There was hardly anything to know. It wasn't as if Posy frequented Soho dirty burger joints or East End gin dens and as for in the shop? She and Noah had been the very definition of stealthy. 'What about me and Noah?' she punctuated the question with a little scoffing noise. 'Aren't you pleased that I'm being nice to him now?'

'Nice? I don't call *that* nice!' Posy cried, which was puzzling. 'You and Noah . . .'

'Yeah. What *is* going on with you and Noah? Honestly, I didn't know where to put myself,' added Verity, who was still lingering at the counter even though she usually had to be prised out of the office to help in the shop.

'I don't know what you two are banging on about,' Nina said, picking up a pile of books that had been dumped on one of the sofas. 'He was helping me with the Instagram stuff. He did use to work for Google, you know.'

'Yes, I do know that but how do *you* know that?' Posy demanded. 'What is going on between you? I mean, what's with all the flirting? Am I right, Very?'

Verity nodded eagerly. 'You were practically eating each other up with your eyes.'

'Yes!' Posy clasped her hands together in agreement. 'Doing things with your eyes that made me go red.'

'Everything makes you go red,' Nina said crisply.

'Nina!' Posy came out from behind the counter so she could stalk towards Nina who quickly moved to the other side of the shop. 'And how did he know that you have special gunk to put on your tattoo?'

'I might have mentioned it in passing,' Nina mumbled.

'And yesterday the office door was open and I could have sworn I saw Noah putting a hand on your back,' Verity said.

'Oh, don't be so Victorian,' Nina said scathingly. 'There could be a hundred reasons for Noah to put his hand on my back . . .'

'OK, then, name three of them . . .'

'The problem with you two is that because you've hooked up and settled down, you expect everyone else to do the same,' Nina said, warming to her theme now. 'But I've told you a million times, I don't want to settle down. Yuck! No offence.'

'None taken, I'm sure,' Posy said a little huffily. 'Anyway, Noah doesn't want to settle down either. He's always off travelling and ziplining through jungles and stuff. Sebastian says it's a wonder that Noah hasn't broken his neck yet or been kidnapped by a Bolivian drug cartel and held for ransom. Not really your type, Nina.'

'I have adventures,' Nina bit out.

'Yeah, but your adventures seem to involve drinking too much vodka and copping off with those *awful* men you meet online,' said Posy crushingly. Nina wouldn't be asking her for a character reference any time soon.

'It's weird though because Merry swore blind that she saw you the other night in this burger place in Soho with a bloke who she said wasn't your usual sort,' Verity mused.

She pulled her phone out of the back pocket of her jeans. 'She took a photo. I said I didn't want to see it because it was an invasion of your privacy but I've changed my mind. I'm texting her right now.'

Nina pretended to put a book back in its rightful place but really she was clutching on to the shelf for support. 'Your sister took a photo of *me*? Well, that's an infringement of my civil liberties!'

'Says the woman who took a photo of Johnny the night she and Posy stalked me to the restaurant where we both were and then showed it to that same sister,' Verity said, which was neither here nor there as far as Nina was concerned. She was actually far more concerned about the ping on Verity's phone signalling that a text message had just arrived. 'Oh my goodness! Yes! That absolutely is you!'

'I bet it absolutely isn't!' Nina hurried closer so she could see the damning evidence for herself. 'It doesn't even look like me!' she insisted, though the pink-haired woman in the photo . . .

'Looks exactly like you!' Posy cried. She snatched the phone from Verity's hand. 'And that looks exactly like Noah! You and Noah! Eating burgers! Drinking alcohol! You were on a date with him! How? How did this happen? When did it happen? Why did it happen? How long has this been going on? Why didn't you tell me?'

Posy was pacing around in little circles as she spat out her endless questions. There was a very real possibility that something in Posy's brain would short circuit. Hopefully. Because try as hard as she could (and she really was trying hard), Nina couldn't think of any innocent reason why she and Noah would be eating dirty burgers and drinking whisky cocktails.

'All right, all right . . . Posy, please stop that, you're making me dizzy,' Nina pleaded and when Posy came to a halt, it was time for the truth. 'Noah and I . . . Yes, OK, we were on a date. But it was a non-date! And then we went on another non-date, except he didn't know it was a non-date but then it turned into a date.'

'WHAT?' Posy was back to walking in circles on the spot again. 'This is big. It's *huge*.'

'Really not that huge,' Nina said a little desperately.

'How would you even know if it was huge or not, you haven't been on your third date yet, have you?' Verity chortled. Nina absolutely did not appreciate the fact that Verity had chosen this moment to crack her first rude joke.

'Haha! Good one, Very! High five!' Posy crowed. 'So, Nina, your third date's looming then? And we all know what happens on a third date!'

How Nina wished that she'd never told Posy or Verity about the third-date rule. 'You know, you *don't* have to shag someone on a third date. It's not the law,' she said.

'Oh really? Because you've always been pretty adamant that it *is* the law, unless there were extenuating circum-stances,' Posy said as Verity nodded her head vigorously in agreement.

'Yes, you said being a vicar's daughter was extenuating circumstances and so it would be all right if I waited until the fifth date but in the meantime, it was only polite to have a bit of oral sex,' Verity recalled, a finger to her chin, which Nina thought was overkill.

'I'm sure I never said that!'

'Yeah, you did,' Verity assured her. The pair of them were enjoying this far too much.

Nina cast a longing look at the shop door, praying that a whole coachload of customers would descend, all with urgent queries that only Nina could help them with. No such luck.

'Oh poor Nina,' Posy cooed, as she saw the stricken look on her friend's face. 'Payback is a bitch, isn't it? But, come on, all those times that you've hounded us about our dating . . .'

'Or lack of dating,' Verity chimed in. 'Or speculated about our sex lives, usually in front of customers. It's quite nice to get our revenge.'

'I'm sure that I've only ever been supportive of your relationships,' Nina grumbled but it was very lacklustre because Posy and Verity were right. God damn them. She was the annoying friend who dragged her single friends out on the pull, even if they didn't want to go anywhere near the pull. And when Verity had been seeing an ocean-ographer called Peter Hardy who'd left her alone for long periods of time while he graphed oceans, Nina had constantly speculated on how Verity was getting her sexual needs fulfilled in the long absences. 'OK, you have five more minutes to rib me about this but then I'm cutting you off.'

'No more ribbing, but I am curious,' Posy admitted as

she flopped onto one of the sofas. The shop was so quiet that Nina decided she might as well flop next to her. 'I mean, *Noah*. I just can't get my head around it.'

'What do you mean, *Noah*?' Nina demanded indignantly. 'He's lovely.'

'Case in point. You don't do lovely. He seems very off-brand for you,' Posy mused. 'You said you were looking for Heathcliff but Noah seems far too nice to be Heathcliff.'

'Although, to be fair, your type hasn't really been working for you,' Verity said gently, perching on the arm of the sofa where Posy and Nina had flopped so that it started to feel a lot like an intervention. 'Heathcliff is the worst possible romantic role model to base your search for a soulmate on – at least Darcy came good in the end. No wonder you end up with all of those so-called bad boys who end up treating you terribly. That can't be much fun, or is it that you just like the thrill of the chase?'

'Pfffffft, don't be silly, Very. I LOVE the thrill of the chase,' Nina said because that was what she was meant to say. It was what she always said. 'You know me, I'm all about the passion and the drama. Without passion and drama, we might just as well be dead. And Noah, lovely though he is, definitely isn't passion and drama.'

'Well, I have to say, Nina, it sounds exhausting,' Posy said with great feeling because she was married to a man who had brought a lot of passion and drama into Posy's life. 'What is the endgame here? Are you still going to be on HookUpp or hanging out in dive bars and dodgy pubs, when you're in your forties, fifties . . .'

'I'm not even thirty yet,' Nina said. 'And anyway, age ain't nothing but a number and the endgame is that I meet my one true love. My soulmate. The one man I can never get enough of: can't live without him, can't live with him.'

'That sounds exhausting too,' Verity noted. 'I know lots of people who are happily coupled up but I don't know anyone who's in that kind of relationship.'

'Because a love like that doesn't come around too often,' Nina said. A love beyond all rhyme and reason. Without it, she was just going through the motions and it felt like she'd been doing that, stuck in a bad-boy holding pattern, *waiting* for years.

'Well, Noah is great, so please don't hurt him,' Posy implored. 'He doesn't deserve to have his heart broken and also, Sebastian would be very cross. He thinks of Noah as an honorary younger brother.' Posy sighed and then went all melty and misty-eyed. 'You know, Sebastian is a lot more sensitive than most people give him credit for. And yes, he is very passionate and overly dramatic, but not all the time, thank goodness. Passion and drama can get very old very fast, Nina.'

'Maybe what you think you want and what you actually need are two very different things,' Verity said with all the calm logic that usually Nina valued. 'I really like Noah, except when he's eavesdropping on my private conversations or manhandling Strumpet. He might not be big with the passion and the drama but he could be so good for you.'

And that was the one problem with Noah – which was odd because usually when Nina was seeing someone they came with at least ninety-nine problems – who wanted to go out with someone that everyone liked? Who wasn't a misunderstood renegade?

Even if Nina and Noah did have a proper relationship, it would still implode like all Nina's relationships did. Not in a dramatic, passionate, china-smashing way because that wasn't Noah's style, which was why their break-up would be inevitable because they were absolutely incompatible. And, if Nina was really honest with herself, it wasn't just his lack of drama and passion that was the issue.

The secret truth that Nina had been shying away from since that train journey back from Worcester Park was that Noah, for all his talk of compartmentalisation and being a cold fish, had risked life and limb on all sorts of hair-raising adventures. He never stayed in one place for too long and had been all around the world and was planning a road trip across America. Nina, on the other hand, for all her talk of living life to the full, hadn't ventured further than the fifteen or so miles that separated Bloomsbury from Worcester Park. If you took away the vintage clothes and make-up and the extra four stone she'd put on since then, Nina suspected that she was still the same girl who nearly got married at twenty. Clinging on to the twin pillars of drama and passion was the only way Nina knew to rid herself of that girl.

As soon as Nina remembered the girl she'd been, inevitably she thought about the boy Noah had been. Creeping and cringing down the school corridors as people chanted 'Know It All' at him or tried to shove him headfirst into lockers or down toilets. And more often than not, it was her brother who was doing the shoving.

And when Nina remembered their school days, she was also reminded of the terrible secret she was keeping from him, which meant that she and Noah could never be anything.

It was probably best to end things now. Two non-dates in, before there was too much collateral damage and especially before Noah realised that Nina was the very last woman on earth that he wanted to have feelings for.

Verity and Posy were both looking at her, eyes wide with hope and expectation that all Nina needed were a few dates with a good man to see the error of her ways. So that she'd settle down like they had. She hated to disappoint them because she really did love them both but . . .

'Let's not get ahead of ourselves here!' she declared in her most careless voice. 'Noah and I have been on two dates. We're not even exclusive, so stop getting ideas. Yes, he's a lovely bloke but he could never be my Heathcliff.'

CHAPTER

19

'You know that I could as soon forget you as my existence!'

Normally, Nina wasn't the kind of woman to dither. She was a ripper-off of plasters, a plunger into cold swimming pools, but instead of immediately breaking things off with Noah, she decided to sleep on it.

Then Noah gave her the perfect opportunity the next day when he texted Nina to tell her that he had to fly to Glasgow to sort out a crisis at a packaging plant.

'Posy and Verity know about us,' she texted back, reasoning that it was only fair to have the difficult conversation face to face. Binning people by text message was so ten years ago . . . 'Apparently, we weren't very stealthy.'

'I know they know. Sebastian is worried that you'll be a bad influence and I'll end up with all sorts of body parts pierced and tattooed.'

What Sebastian had probably said was more along the lines of 'You could do better than Tattoo Girl: she's been around the block more times than the milkman.' Nina also didn't want to think about Noah's body parts or his lovely freckly skin covered up with tattoos.

She couldn't remember the last time she'd had so many conflicting thoughts about a man. Probably not since Orlando Bloom (her teen crush) had married Miranda Kerr.

She texted back a perfunctory: 'I guess I'll see you when you get back' and in the meantime, set about trying to forget Noah, which meant firing up HookUpp and up-swiping on a graphic designer who worked just round the corner. In his profile pic he was dark and smouldering and his bio was one line: 'Let me paint you like one of those French girls.'

When Nina turned up to meet him in The Thornton Arms, Wilhelm was even more smouldering in the flesh. Smirky too and Nina was a sucker for a smirk as much as she was for guys in skinny jeans, Ramones T-shirts (did they give out Ramones T-shirts on the first day at art college along with an orientation pack?) and designer stubble.

Nina hadn't even had three sips of her vodka tonic before he said that he'd like to draw Nina naked.

'Yeah, what*ever*,' Nina heard herself drawl in a world-weary tone when usually that was just the kind of

ANNIE DARLING

suggestion that had her firing back with some flirty repartee of her own but honestly, she was so done with the frogs who were only interested in getting her knickers off. The date only lasted that one drink.

Noah had ruined her for all other men and for the rest of the week, Nina lived like a nun. Well, a very progressive, liberal nun who still went to the pub with her friends, but Nina was determined not to get chatted up or picked up so she kept her eyes to herself.

'Are you ill?' Verity asked Nina one night in The Midnight Bell when Nina turned down the offer of a drink from a scruffy-haired Australian with tribal tattoos. 'He's just your type.'

'Sickening for Noah, maybe?' Posy suggested with a sly smile while Tom, who hadn't been privy to the latest intel on Nina's love life said, 'Why would you say that? Noah and Nina? Don't be ridiculous.'

Even Tom knew that Nina and Noah were two people who didn't fit together, like oil and water, or spots and stripes.

'We were quite surprised when you rocked up with Noah,' Marianne told Nina when they met for their monthly 'nana night out' which involved a big sesh at the Mecca bingo hall in Camden then spending their winnings on a bowl of pasta and a bottle of wine at the old-fashioned ristorante across the road.

'Yeah yeah, he's not my type,' Nina murmured as they waited for the bingo to start. 'I got that memo.'

'He might not *look* your type, but that doesn't mean a

thing. You've been out with some absolute pigs simply because they did look your type,' Marianne pointed out, which wasn't very helpful. She waved at an elderly lady sitting across the aisle from them. 'Hello Lily, how are your knees?'

'I wouldn't wish them on my worst enemy,' Lily said, as she always did, and then she started listing her other ailments, of which there were many, and for the rest of the evening, Nina made sure that Noah's name didn't come up.

She did such a great job of forgetting about him that when she came downstairs on Friday morning, ten days after Noah had flown to Glasgow, to see him coming through the shop door, she felt rocked where she stood. Her heart thumped giddily, her body jerked in joyful recognition and she had to tell herself sternly not to smile too much, not to run over to him.

She was going to play it cool.

Then Noah looked up, caught sight of Nina hovering uncertainly in the no-man's-land between shop and counter and he smiled broadly and brilliantly as if just the sight of her was enough to make everything right in his world.

Forgetting all about her resolutions to end things before they'd started, Nina felt her heart and her spirits perk up like nobody's business.

'You're back!' she noted and her powers of observation weren't going to give Sherlock Holmes any sleepless nights.

'I am back,' Noah agreed. 'You've changed your hair.'

Nina put a hand up to her hair, which was platinum once more. 'Well, you know what they say about blondes having more fun,' she said in a breathy voice as if she were seconds away from an asthma attack.

'Talking of fun, you have the rest of the week off,' said a voice behind her, which made Nina jump before she turned round to see Posy standing there. Two minutes with Noah and, once again, the rest of the world ceased to exist.

'What do you mean, I have the rest of the week off?' she asked, because Nina was pretty sure that if she'd booked Friday and Saturday off she'd have remembered it.

'I hope you don't mind, I asked Posy . . . it's a surprise,' Noah said a little hesitantly. 'Do you like surprises?'

'Depends,' Nina said, because often when a man asked her if she liked surprises, it usually involved him whipping down his trousers. Plus, she was supposed to be breaking them up at the earliest opportunity. 'What kind of surprise?'

'Well, it's a road-trip kind of surprise,' Noah revealed with a hopeful smile. 'How does that sound?'

Nina clasped her hands to her chest. 'Oh my God, that sounds thrilling!'

'We'll be gone overnight,' Noah explained. 'I did ask Verity to pack a bag for you to add to the surprise element but she said that she didn't feel comfortable doing that.'

'The make-up alone,' Verity called out from the kitchen. 'I wouldn't know where to start.'

Nina was very grateful that Verity had recognised her limitations and hadn't attempted to send her off without any liquid eyeliner or night cream. 'I'll go and pack, shall

I?' she asked, a little dazed that Noah was here and whisking her off to some place that wasn't here.

'You'll need sensible walking shoes and a thick coat,' Noah said, which, truthfully, sounded a lot less thrilling.

It took Nina twenty minutes (a personal best) to pack two bags (one just for her make-up, skincare and hair products) and then Noah was escorting her to the hire car parked in the mews, with a food parcel from Mattie and coffee from Paloma.

'Don't worry about the time off!' Posy called out kindly as she waved them off. 'You can make it up when we start our extended summer opening hours.'

Nina was quite beside herself. This was all so unexpected. She'd convinced herself that for his own emotional well-being she needed to end things with Noah as soon as he got back from Glasgow and yet he'd suddenly reappeared to rescue her from two days of retail drudgery and whisk her away on an adventure.

A proper adventure.

'Where are we going?' she asked as Regent's Park came into view. 'Is it in London?'

'It wouldn't be a surprise if I told you,' Noah said firmly, like he was one of those annoying people who wouldn't crack under interrogation.

Soon they joined the M1, past a sign that said 'To The North', which made Nina think of polar bears and ice caps and igloos. Then Noah started telling her about the packaging-plant emergency in Glasgow and how he'd had to spend most of his time in a factory in the middle of a huge industrial estate. 'I had lots to say about staff morale,' he said. 'They didn't even have a staff canteen. Just a whole wall of vending machines, half of which were broken, and the other half sold over-priced protein bars.'

'It sounds like you've been to a very dark place,' Nina noted, catching Noah's eye. There was a lot of eye-catching going on.

'The very darkest,' he said mournfully.

There was a quick stop at Watford Gap services for coffee and then back in the car and heading to the Midlands as Nina bragged about her success on social media.

'Nearly two thousand followers on Instagram,' she was proud to report. 'Just over a thousand on Twitter and I got Sam to give me a tutorial on how to update the website, though I didn't understand a word of it.'

'I'll help you with that,' Noah offered immediately. Then he tried to explain how to game the Google rankings but Nina only understood every other word. Still, it was so good to see Noah again, to have his hand brush against her leg when he changed gears, to think greedily of all the time they were going to spend with each other.

Past Derby and Nottingham, past signs to the Peak National Park and Nina couldn't imagine where Noah might be taking her. 'We're not going to Glasgow, are we?' she asked with a hint of genuine suspicion. 'Do you have unfinished business at that packaging plant?'

'You've found me out.' Noah smiled and shook his head. 'Guess again.'

They came off the motorway to stop for an early lunch

of toasted-cheese sandwiches in a pretty village pub on the outskirts of Chesterfield and talked about how Noah had missed pretty village pubs when he'd been in the States. Also *Coronation Street* (which he had a secret fondness for, even though his parents were very against commercial television) and 'a decent cup of tea'.

'Isn't it a bit of a cliché to complain that you can't get a decent cup of tea once you leave British shipping waters?' Nina asked teasingly.

'It's a cliché only because it's true,' Noah replied. 'You have to pay a fortune for a proper brand of tea bags from an import shop and their water tastes funny and they don't even do proper milk. They have this stuff called half and half. It's half milk and half I don't even know what.'

'This is why I only drink coffee,' Nina said and Noah's eyes widened even further.

'That's it. I'm dropping you at the nearest station to make your own way home,' he said, putting his hand over the bill as Nina reached for the saucer. 'No, it's my treat.'

'There's no point in treating me if you plan to drop me off like an unwanted parcel,' Nina told him and Noah smiled.

'I suppose if we've come this far we might as well continue.'

They were deep in the darkest North now. Past Barnsley, past Wakefield, past little towns and villages whose names sounded clunky when Nina tried to say them out loud. Cleckheaton. Scholes. Hipperholme. Northowram. Dark-green fields were a blur out of the car window until they gave way to a grey stone sprawl as they drove through Bradford.

Queensbury.

Denholme.

Nina's heart was pounding because she knew they were now deep into Brontë country before she even saw the first sign to Haworth, the village where the Brontës had lived for most of their lives, but she didn't want to ruin Noah's surprise. The lovely, kind surprise he'd devised as he spent his days trapped in a packaging plant on an industrial estate on the outskirts of Glasgow and thought about her, about where she might like to go for their third date.

'Are we . . . We are, aren't we?' Nina blurted out because they were now driving through Haworth and she had to twist around in her seat to take it all in. 'Oh, Noah, I can't believe we're here! You . . . you . . .'

'You what?' Noah asked but Nina shook her head, words beyond her, which was a first. Instead she put her hand over Noah's hand, which was resting lightly on the gearshift, and tried to convey her gratitude, that giddiness he made her feel, through her fingertips.

Haworth was as charming a village as she'd ever seen. Maybe not as chocolate-box pretty as its Devonian or Cornish counterparts: its little shops were hewn from rugged, weatherbeaten stone, its church imposing. All the more so for it being a grey, damp March day, not quite raining, but not quite *not* raining.

'Mizzle,' Noah said, as he switched on the windscreen wipers. 'A misty drizzle or a drizzly mist, one of the two.'

Nina stared out of the window at an old-fashioned apothecary shop that reminded her of the one across the mews that had been boarded up and closed for decades.

As they followed the signs to the Parsonage, the village seemed strangely familiar. 'I feel like I've been here before,' she remarked, peering out at a small row of shops. 'I wouldn't be at all surprised to see Emily, Charlotte and Anne suddenly materialise in front of me.'

'Anne? I didn't know there was a third Brontë sister,' Noah said, as he pulled into a car park.

'She wrote *The Tenant Of Wildfell Hall*.' Nina rolled her eyes. 'I struggled to finish it though and I didn't even attempt *Agnes Grey*, her other book. Beyond my GCSE English, I'm afraid,' she added in what she hoped was a breezy manner. Noah could probably polish off *The Tenant Of Wildfell Hall* in a couple of hours and then give a presentation on it, complete with graphics and charts and gifs.

'Oh, please. You've read more books than almost anyone I know,' Noah said, switching off the engine. 'Apart from Posy and I think her love of books is verging on pathology.'

It was very disloyal to let Noah speak about her dear friend and employer in that way except . . . 'Posy reads so fast that her eyes do this rapid flicker thing from side to side and Verity and I worry that she's going to have a stroke,' Nina shared with a grin and then because they were no longer in a moving vehicle and she'd regained the power of speech, she took Noah's hand again.

'Thank you,' she said. 'Thank you so much for bringing me here.' Holding Noah's hand, her fingers entwined with his, felt quite different to touching his hand when they were in motion. As if now, the hand-holding could be a prelude to . . . well, anything. 'I've always dreamed of coming here. Not just because it's where *Wuthering Heights* is set but because I wanted to get inside Emily Brontë's head for a little while; see what she saw, that kind of thing. It sounds silly, doesn't it?'

Nina ducked her head and she would have tugged her hand free too but Noah wouldn't let her. 'It doesn't sound silly,' he said. He gestured out of the misty windscreen with his free hand. 'Well, now that we've seen it, shall we head back to London in time to beat the rush hour?'

Nina's mouth hung open for just one very unflattering second before she did succeed in tugging her hand free so she could lightly smack Noah on the shoulder. 'Say that you're joking.'

He pretended to cower away from her. 'I'm joking. We're actually due at the Parsonage at four. It's not even half past one now. Is it too drizzly for you to want to walk on the moors?'

If they were in London, Nina would have insisted on arming herself with her huge, flamingo-printed golf umbrella in case a drop of rain went anywhere near her. But she'd wanted to come to Haworth for ten years and she wasn't going to let a little rain get in her way.

'I'm pretty sure I won't melt,' she said stoutly. 'I have sensible walking shoes, a thick coat and a burning desire to see the Brontë Waterfalls.'

CHAPTER 20

*'I have fled my country
and gone to the heather.'*

'You know,' said Noah reflectively two minutes into their walk. 'I'm not sure that motorcycle boots and a leopard-print fun fur constitute sensible walking shoes and a thick coat.'

'They do in my world,' Nina said, panting slightly. Her boots were fine for the job in hand. Her coat, not so much.

Noah, of course, was wearing a navy windcheater cum anorak-type affair (Nina didn't know what the technical name for it was), which was no doubt made of some space-age, weather-proof, anti-sweat wicking. He had also not been idle during his downtime in Glasgow.

Armed with his trusty iPad, which was also clad in a weather-proof case, Noah was the font of all things Brontë.

As they walked back along Main Street, it was to a running commentary.

'And that gift shop used to be the post office, which was where the Brontës mailed off their manuscripts,' he said. Then, as they walked a narrow path through the old churchyard, Noah made Nina stop at 'the iron kissing gate'. Her heart began to beat faster than was strictly necessary. How romantic, she thought, and she raised her face, pursed her lips ever so slightly in anticipation of a . . .

'And the oldest part of the church dates back to the fifteenth century.'

. . . a lecture on how many times the church had been knocked down and rebuilt and could Nina spot the Ordnance Survey mark on the south-west corner of the church tower to mark the fact that they were seven hundred and ninety-six feet above sea level?

When they came to a rustic wooden sign informing them that they had two and a half miles to go until they reached the waterfall, Nina thought that she might cry. Not just because she didn't think she'd ever walked two and a half miles in her life, but the anticipation of Noah commenting on every fence-post and large rock they passed was too awful to contemplate.

'So, Penistone Hill, don't worry, it's quite a gentle incline, means we're now in an official country park and this area used to be a quarry.'

It looked quarryish. There were big lumps of rock scattered about as Noah walked and Nina trudged along. They crossed over a main road, not a car in sight unfortunately because Nina wouldn't have thought twice about flagging one down and demanding that the driver take her back to civilisation. Noah was banging on about the reservoir they could see in the distance and that there should be a cattle grid coming up.

'And now we're on open moorland,' Noah said, squinting down at his iPad and trying to wipe the screen as the drizzle was starting to upgrade to proper rain. 'This is an area of special scientific interest, especially if you're a bird-watcher . . .'

'Stop! Just stop!' Nina demanded, holding out her hands like she was trying to beat back a flock of scientifically interesting birds. 'Please . . .'

'I was trying to make the walk interesting,' Noah protested. 'I know you're a city girl and I thought if I pointed out significant features, it would make the walk less . . . *walky*.'

'And I appreciate that, I really do,' Nina said, because she did, even if Noah pointing out significant features was making her want to scream. 'I appreciate all the trouble you've gone to and how much time you must have spent in your hotel room in Glasgow putting this all together, but I don't need to know about reservoirs or starlings and sparrows or whatever these scientifically interesting birds are.'

'Curlews and peregrines actually,' Noah said with a little sniff.

'I went on a date with a guy called Peregrine once,' Nina recalled. 'He was so posh that what came out of his mouth didn't even sound like English.'

Noah sniffed again as Nina slowly turned a full circle. 'Do you want to go back then?' he asked in the same huffy voice.

Nina turned again. 'No,' she said. 'But look. Just *look*.'

No wonder they described Yorkshire as God's own country. The moors weren't like the neatly clipped lawns and manicured paths of the parks that Nina was used to. Here, up this high, the sky, dark and grey, hung heavy and looked bigger, mightier than sky normally did. It was the perfect dramatic backdrop for the lush green below; every shade of green that Nina had names for, from sludgy khaki to rich emerald, moss and fern, to palest seafoam.

But the scenery stretching out before her from every side wasn't pretty. There was a savage beauty to the land, deep seams riven through it, teetering, haphazard rock formations looming at every turn.

It was wild, untethered, elemental. And over the light patter of the rain on the unflinching stones from the old quarry, Nina could hear the wind wrapping around them.

'Noah! Listen!'

'I thought I was meant to be looking,' he grumbled.

'The wind . . . I think it's wuthering.'

'What even is wuthering?'

Nina put a hand to her ear. 'It sounds like the wind's calling us.' She shivered and not just because she was bloody freezing. 'This is the same wuthering that Emily Brontë wrote about and if you forget about the reservoirs and the quarry and Ordnance Survey marks, and just look around us, this, *this*, is what the Brontës saw. We might even be standing where they stood. Charlotte wrote about the water-fall so all three of them must have walked these paths two hundred years ago. That just blows my mind.'

'It's blowing mine too. Or that might just be the wind. Wuthering,' Noah said and he wasn't looking quite so cross now. 'Shall we take a moment?'

'Let's.'

They stood side by side to appreciate again the rugged moors, the untamed landscape, how insignificant they both were compared to the vastness of nature.

'OK, I'm done taking a moment,' Nina decided. 'How about you?'

Noah nodded. His face was quite raw from being so rigorously scrubbed by the wind. 'Moment taken.'

They set off again and though Noah couldn't resist a few informed remarks about the terrain or the occasional derelict cottage they came across, he kept them brief. Nina's head was full of images of Cathy and Heathcliff. Now that she'd been here, she couldn't wait to reread *Wuthering Heights*.

The last part of their journey to the waterfall involved clambering over stone steps slick with rain and unevenly dispersed like they'd been thrown down by an angry god.

Noah raised an eyebrow when Nina told him this. 'OK, if you say so.'

'I'm really big on the symbolism of *Wuthering Heights* right now,' she explained. 'How the moors represent Heathcliff; all savage and unpredictable. Luckily, no one is going to make me write an essay on the use of nature as metaphor.'

'Oh, that's what I had planned for this evening – among other things,' Noah said and then he smiled in a way that made Nina feel quite hot even though she was still bloody freezing.

They were joined for the last few metres of their journey by a small group of ramblers and then, at last! They were at Brontë Falls.

It had rained heavily the day before according to the man who was leading the ramble, which was why the waterfall was such an impressive sight as it gushed down a series of stone shelves that had been carved into the hill over thousands of years. There was a stone bridge at the bottom of the falls, though apparently the original bridge had been swept away in a flash flood in 1989, according to a small plaque.

'Do you think it's safe?' Nina asked Noah before she stepped on to it. 'I really want a selfie but I don't want to be swept away by the current.'

Noah cast what looked like a professional eye over the water descending down from above. 'Well, it is a pretty small waterfall as waterfalls go. I reckon you'll be safe.'

It wasn't the ideal conditions for a selfie. The lighting was *terrible*. And even with it pinned up and mostly hidden under a polka-dot scarf, Nina's hair looked awful and the wind and the mizzle seemed to have removed quite a lot of her make-up so that her . . .

'Come on, you know you always look good,' Noah said though Nina knew no such thing.

'My eyeliner is but a distant memory,' she groused as she

held her phone up, sucked in her cheeks, pouted then shot off ten quick frames, angling her head in a different position in each one.

If there was one thing that Nina knew how to do, it was taking a selfie, though the ramblers were looking at her like she'd suddenly started spewing ectoplasm out of her ears.

Noah was watching her too, with amusement that quickly turned to horror when Nina beckoned him closer. 'You don't want me cluttering up your selfies.'

''Course I do!' Nina insisted. She'd dreamed of coming here, well maybe not to a waterfall, across open moorland in damp, cold weather, but of coming to Haworth and Noah was the person who'd made it happen. And they'd been on two dates or non-dates, hung out an awful lot and they hadn't even taken a selfie together. 'Get your arse over here!'

Noah was taller and with longer arms so he held up his phone and patiently (though there did seem to be some teeth grinding) listened to Nina's instructions to 'move your hand a fraction to the left, no, too far, back, back, back!' and suffered her deleting most of the photos as they didn't come up to the high standards she expected from her selfies.

'Much as I hate to rush you, we're due at Haworth Parsonage at four and it's quarter to three now,' he said at last. 'We really should turn back.'

'Oh, you'll be wanting to go at a brisk pace,' a lady rambler swathed in a purple cagoule told them. 'Forecast is for rain.'

'Isn't it already raining?' Nina ventured.

'Pfffttt! You call this rain? It's barely even spitting,' the woman said with a derisory snort, though actually the mizzle was far more like a very determined drizzle now. 'Come on, you can walk back with us and I'll make sure you don't start to dawdle.'

'So kind,' Noah murmured, giving Nina a little warning nudge when she giggled a little hysterically at the thought of having to yomp back the way they came with Mrs Purple Cagoule yelling at them if they dared to lollygag.

Maureen, as Mrs Purple Cagoule had been christened, 'though you can call me Mo,' was a small, sprightly woman of very strong opinions. 'I don't think much of the soles on your boots,' she said, eyeing Nina's motorcycle boots with distaste. 'And as for that coat. Well, you'll catch your death,' she added.

'Here's hoping,' Nina muttered because the brisk pace that Maureen had promised felt like a very close cousin to jogging and Maureen's hectoring tone was very similar to her mother's. In fact, it was a pity that the FitBit that Alison had bought her for Christmas last year (her mother excelled in the buying of passive-aggressive gifts) was languishing in a drawer, because Nina was sure that she'd smashed ten thousand steps today and they weren't even halfway back to Haworth.

Noah, who'd been walking on ahead with the other ramblers, stopped to wait for Nina. 'How you doing?' he asked.

'I've decided that it's best that you leave me here on the moors,' Nina panted. 'It's too late for me and I'll only slow you down but you can still make it back to civilisation. Christ, I'm unfit.'

'You're doing fine,' Noah said encouragingly even though Nina was doing the very opposite of fine. Even though she was cold and yes, her sodding coat was sodden through, she was also hot and sweaty from the enforced exercise. 'We haven't got that far to go.'

'Oh, it's at least another mile,' Mo said cheerfully as if she was actually enjoying this. Yes, she must definitely share DNA with Alison O'Kelly.

'But just think, it won't be long before you're standing in Haworth Parsonage,' Noah reminded her. 'Where Emily and her sisters and that wastrel brother of theirs, what's his name again, lived.'

'Branwell,' Nina said, although she wanted to use what breath she had left for walking not talking. 'He was a wrong 'un if ever there was one. Ran up huge debts gambling and drinking – it was one of the reasons why the sisters turned to writing. Branwell ploughed through what little money they had.'

'Are these relatives of yours?' Mo asked with a little gleam in her eye as if she suspected that Nina came from a whole family of wrong 'uns.

'No, we're talking about the Brontës,' Noah said politely. 'It's why we came to Haworth. Nina loves *Wuthering Heights*.'

If Noah could make an effort then so could Nina. 'It's my favourite book,' she explained. 'And I've always wanted to come here to see where Emily Brontë lived. Have you read it?'

'I don't have time to read,' Mo said, a censorious expression on her weather-beaten face.

Usually those six smug words were a red rag to a bull but now Nina merely grunted as they were retracing their steps over the site of the old quarry, the slabs slick and wet, and she didn't want to go arse over tit.

'Careful.' Noah took her arm without commenting on the non-grippiness of her boots. 'Broken bones didn't feature too highly in my plans for the day.'

'I'm glad to hear that,' Nina panted then decided she needed all of her energy for walking and not talking because the ramblers, despite the fact that they were all much, much older than her, were still cracking on at a punishing pace.

But the journey was much easier with Noah to lean on and soon the church spire came into view and not long after that, they were passing through the kissing gate again and saying goodbye to their companions.

'Mark my words, you'll be coughing and sneezing before the day's out,' was mighty Mo's parting shot.

Nina waved her off, though her instinct was to flip her off instead.

'I'm fine,' she insisted when she saw the concerned look on Noah's face. 'Honestly, I'm not about to do an Emily Brontë.'

'How does one do an Emily Brontë?' Noah asked as they headed back to where he'd parked the car.

'She caught a bad cold at Branwell's funeral, which turned into TB and she refused all medical treatment until it was too late, and then she died. In Haworth Parsonage,' Nina added and a little chill did run through her at the thought of poor headstrong Emily finally asking Charlotte to send for the doctor, then dying a couple of hours after that. 'But I'm not about to keel over during our tour. I'll take off my coat though, because it smells like wet dog, and anyway since the mid-nineteenth century they've invented Lemsip and Day Nurse and all sorts of over-the-counter medicines for cold and flu.'

'Are you sure?' Noah took one of Nina's hands, which made her shiver again, but not because she was thinking of untimely death. 'You're freezing.'

'I'm going to swap my damp coat for a jumper,' Nina said. They were at the car now. 'Um, do you have a jumper I can borrow?'

There was no way that Nina and her breasts could fit into one of Noah's navy-blue jumpers – unlike Emily Brontë and her infamous coffin that had measured only sixteen inches wide – so she had to make do with a zip-up fleece that didn't go with her black fifties dress with its novelty print of sleek white pussycats.

'You should never go out with a man skinnier, shorter or younger than you,' had been one of Alison's life lessons when Nina had hit her teens and her words came back to taunt Nina as she tried, and failed, to heave up the zip on the fleece.

'That fleece looks much better on you than it does on me,' Noah said appreciatively even if Nina was sure that he was lying.

Then he took her hand again and not because he was

helping her over wet quarry slabs or checking that she hadn't developed tuberculosis. Just taking her hand for the pleasure of taking her hand. Like he enjoyed touching her.

Nina squeezed Noah's fingers gently and he instantly returned the pressure. The fleece smelt faintly of the clean, zesty scent of his aftershave so it felt a lot like she was wrapped up in him. She shivered for the third time, glanced up to see Noah looking at her with that thoughtful expression on his face as if he wished he had his iPad on him so he could make some detailed notes.

Finally, she looked away and then her breath caught in her throat and she gasped as she saw the neat garden in front of them and the neat house beyond them.

The Brontë Parsonage.

CHAPTER

21

'Any relic of the dead is precious,
if they were valued living.'

Stepping through the white door into the parsonage, a
journey that Emily Brontë and her sisters had made
hundreds, even thousands of times, was quite something.

Nina paused to look around her at the dove-grey walls,
to soak it all in, but was interrupted by a small group of
middle-aged ladies who were coming down the stairs in
front of them and chattering loudly.

'So much cleaner than I thought it would be,' one of
them announced in a soft American accent. 'And much
smaller too.'

'Well, people were smaller back then. What with the
poor sanitation and the lack of fresh vegetables,' another
lady commented and they all hmm'ed in agreement.

'I would have thought that one thing they weren't lacking were fresh vegetables,' Noah murmured in her ear, but Nina was still standing rooted to the spot and could hardly concentrate on anything but where she was. Emily Brontë wasn't just a figure from history, an entry on Wikipedia, but had been made of flesh and blood and living within these four walls.

Nina looked through the open doorway to her left into a small room with a small table next to the fireplace, four chairs arranged around it, papers and pens and an inkwell on its polished surface. She stood there with a moony expression on her face, hardly noticing that she'd created a bottleneck for the American ladies who wanted to leave.

'Sorry,' Nina said and moved closer to the red rope that barred her from entering the dining room to rub her hands over every available surface. 'Noah.' She reached behind her to tug him closer. 'This . . . this is the room where the Brontës wrote their novels. Can you even imagine it? Emily writing *Wuthering Heights* while Charlotte worked on *Jane Eyre* and Anne wrote *The Tenant Of Wildfell Hall*. It would be like Posy, Verity and I all writing novels at the shop that went on to become bestsellers.' Nina shook her head. 'What would the odds of that be?'

'Worth putting a tenner on each way,' Noah decided and he stood there patiently while Nina strained against the rope, desperate not to miss any small detail of the room where so much bookish greatness had occurred.

They wandered the house, peering in at Mr Brontë's

study and the kitchen with its old-fashioned range, then up the stairs to look in at the children's study and Charlotte's room. Emily and Anne didn't seem to have had their own rooms but as the information cards explained, a Reverend Wade, who'd moved in after the Brontës were dead and gone, had added a new wing to the house and some of the old rooms had been converted into a corridor.

'Not only did their mother, Maria, die in this room, so did Charlotte herself,' Nina said in shocked but quiet tones as they peered into Charlotte's room. It wasn't the kind of information you said at a normal volume. In the middle of the room was a glass display case with one of Charlotte's dresses in it. Despite its voluminous skirts and huge sleeves, it was obvious that its original wearer had been tiny. 'God, I couldn't even get one of my legs in it,' Nina exclaimed. 'Also when I die, I hope no one displays my stockings for public viewing.'

She turned her head to see what Noah thought but he wasn't looking at Charlotte Brontë's white stockings pinned up behind her dress but at his watch. He'd been quite restless all the way through their tour, though Nina could hardly blame him. It had to be a quite dull way to spend an hour if you weren't a mad Brontë fangirl.

'I'm sorry,' Nina said. 'I don't think there's much more to see. I thought, and this isn't a criticism, that it would be much bigger. It seemed bigger when I looked at it on the internet. Is this very boring for you?'

'Oh no, it's great. Very interesting,' Noah said without much conviction.

''Cause I don't think there can be that much more to see, then we can visit the gift shop.' Nina cracked her knuckles in anticipation. 'I *love* a gift shop.'

'Who doesn't?' Noah agreed rather vaguely and then, as if he couldn't help himself, he checked his watch again. 'Sorry. Are you mad at me?'

'Not at all,' Nina decided, because it would be weird if Noah were as obsessed with *Wuthering Heights* and Emily Brontë as she was. He didn't expect Nina to embrace kayaking through white-water rapids or ziplining, thank God. 'And I can't be mad at you when you've arranged this amazing surprise for me. You've set the bar pretty high for all other dates.'

It felt presumptuous to assume that there might be other dates but this third date was so spectacular that Nina wanted a fourth date, a fifth date, maybe so many subsequent dates that it stopped being dating and became a relationship, and it had been so long since she'd had one of them, that the idea of it made her insides flutter like a lorry load of butter-flies had taken up residence in her stomach. Perhaps if she explained about Paul, about the accident and how it had changed him, Noah would be all right with it. Maybe . . .

'Talking of surprises,' he was saying, so Nina was forced to stop imagining what might be and focus on what was. 'It's why I keep looking at my watch. I have you booked in at quarter past four.'

'Booked in for what?' Nina wondered. She cast a doubtful eye at Charlotte's dress. 'Am I going to get kitted out in old-timey gear and have my picture taken?'

'Are you *what*? No! It's, well, I hope it's more amazing than that,' Noah said hesitantly as if he wasn't sure how Nina would react to this latest surprise.

She was definitely intrigued and yes, a little nervous, as they headed back down the stairs.

Then Noah led her through to the back of the parsonage and into an exhibition room. Like everywhere else in the Parsonage, at this time on a damp, grey Friday afternoon off-season, it was empty apart from one member of staff who smiled as they entered the room.

'Noah Harewood?' she asked with a friendly smile. 'And Noah's friend?'

'This is Nina,' Noah said, pulling Nina forward. 'We're not too late, are we?'

'And I'm Moira. You're just in time. We're closing in fifteen minutes.' The woman gestured at the table in front of her, then at Nina. 'Would you like to take a seat?'

Nina was desperate to sit down, mostly because she'd been on her feet for *hours*. Her curiosity was like a restless beast that couldn't be caged. 'What is going on?' she asked, her voice quite squeaky with suspense.

'Next year is the bicentennial of Emily Brontë's birth and to commemorate it, we're asking visitors to the museum to each write a line from *Wuthering Heights* in a specially commissioned hand-written book,' the woman explained.

'And you get a special pencil to keep,' Noah added as if Nina might need an incentive, which she didn't. Her bottom was already in the chair.

'I'll do it!' she yelped, hands in the air, fingers outstretched. 'Look! I'm limbering up!'

'Let's create a little ambience, shall we?' Moira suggested. She switched off the main lights so that the room was almost in darkness, apart from the desk lamp in front of Nina which cast a warm glow.

Now that she'd calmed down a fraction, Nina could see a huge but neat pile of paper to her left, an old copy of *Wuthering Heights* open about two thirds of the way through with an old-fashioned slide rule marking the page, and an open wooden box with curved corners filled with black pencils.

Nina dipped her head so she could see that each one was inscribed, *Wuthering Heights – A Manuscript.*

'You'll be needing one of them,' Moira said, and with great care Nina chose a pencil, even though they were all identical. 'Now, here's the manuscript and this is your line: *I put on my bonnet and sullied out, thinking nothing more of the matter.*'

Never in her life had Nina concentrated so hard on her penmanship as she copied the words in her best, her nicest, joined-up writing. All her muscles were tensed until she was done and found that, oddly, she felt close to tears.

'It's quite emotional,' she said in a husky voice. 'To sit here, in this house, and write the very same words that Emily Brontë wrote in this same house nearly two hundred years ago. Never knowing that the story she was telling would be read and loved two centuries later. God, it's doing my head in!'

'Lots of people have had a similar reaction,' Moira noted. She looked at Noah. 'Now, your turn.'

'Oh yes! Noah! You should!' Nina exclaimed, but he was backing away, hands held up.

'No, I don't want to rain on your parade,' he said firmly. 'This is your thing.'

'But I want to share it with you,' Nina said just as firmly, pushing the chair back and standing up. 'This is a once-in-a-lifetime kind of deal. He can write a line too, can't he?'

'Of course you can.' Moira smiled a little at the deter-mined expression on Nina's face as she tugged at Noah's arm.

'Sit!' she demanded. 'Go on, sit!'

'I'm not a dog,' Noah grumbled, but he was sitting. 'You know, I have terrible handwriting. I'll have to write in block capitals, otherwise it will be completely illegible.'

'No judgement,' Moira assured him. 'Take a pencil and this is the line you need to copy out: *She bounded before me, and returned to my side, and was off again like a young grey-hound.*'

Nina wanted to keep a respectful distance while he worked but she was distracted by the way Noah laboured with pencil and paper. He held the pencil as if he were expecting it to suddenly make a break for freedom and he came at the paper like it was a mortal enemy.

'Oh my God! I'd forgotten about the time you sent me that note and I could barely read it. You really weren't joking about your handwriting,' Nina blurted out, then cursed her lack of tact. Even Noah's block capitals looked like they were having a nervous breakdown across the page.

'Now, now, Nina. I can't be good at *everything*,' Noah said and Nina waited until he'd finished his last letter, though it looked more like an insect had just died on the page, and dug him in the shoulder.

'I was going to tell you that you're amazing at arranging surprise road trips but it would only go to your head,' she said, as Noah got up from the chair. She turned to Moira. 'Thank you so much for letting us do this.'

'Well, you really have your young man to thank but I think that would go to his head too,' Moira said. She ushered them towards the door, a regretful smile on her face as if she'd have liked nothing more than to stay there and watch them banter back and forth. 'I'm sorry but we close at five and you'll be wanting to visit the shop before you go.'

'Yes!' they both said in unison and Nina took hold of Noah's hand and hustled them away. God, she'd packed more exercise into one day than she had in a whole year.

'We only have fifteen minutes to shop!' she told Noah with genuine alarm as they reached the shop. 'Talk about pressure!'

Nina was a very focused shopper. She put it down to all the years of riffling through charity-shop and jumble-sale rails looking for good vintage. Now, she immediately homed in on a pretty print of the Parsonage in autumn, then grabbed a handful of postcards and added Brontë-branded chocolate bars to take into work on Monday (a milk chocolate Charlotte bar for Posy, a milk orange chocolate Branwell for Tom and though Verity was always saying that she was an Austenite and that the Brontës were too dour and histrionic for her liking, she could have an Anne bar and count herself lucky). Nina snatched up five Emily dark chocolate bars for herself. She really wanted to get Noah a gift too. Some small, entirely inadequate way of saying thank you for the day out he'd given her. He seemed to have looked deep inside her soul to plan out the most perfect set of experiences – even that hellish march across the moors to the waterfall had had its highlights – and she'd like to look deep into his soul to decide on the perfect thank-you gift. Though her options were limited, what with being in a gift shop in the Brontë Parsonage. Perhaps she could get him an iPad or mobile-phone case? Nina looked around for inspiration and then came to a halt by a display of gifts featuring quotations from some of the Brontë novels.

She couldn't help the snort that exploded out of her nostrils at the sight of a 'Reader, I Married Him' mug. She'd suggested the famous quote from *Jane Eyre* as a possible new name for the shop, which had been shot down in flames though Posy had commissioned a 'Reader, I Married Him' tote bag and rashly ordered five hundred of them.

'Oh God, Posy must never find out about all this branded merchandise,' said Noah, coming up behind her. 'Verity told me about the tote bags.'

'We have "Reader, I Married Him" T-shirts too,' Nina said. 'They do surprisingly well as gifts for brides-to-be. But we can't tell Posy about these,' she added, pointing at oven mitts and an apron both with the quote 'I Am Heathcliff' printed on them.

'You tempted?'

'Not really, they don't go with my aesthetic and making toast or heating up a ready meal, which is all I do in the kitchen, doesn't really need accessories,' Nina explained. 'But I will have a mug and you're having one too! I mean, everyone needs a mug.'

The Emily Brontë mug had the quote 'No Coward Soul Is Mine' which seemed appropriate for someone like Noah who had such a love of death-defying activities. A mug that cost seven pounds fifty was a very poor way of saying thank you but it would do for now.

'Everyone does need a mug,' Noah solemnly agreed and Nina saw that he'd been doing his fair share of shopping.

'Nice scarf,' she said, nodding at the grey-and-lilac scarf adorned with pale-blue dots, which Noah was holding.

'For my mother, for Mother's Day,' Noah said. He frowned. 'We're not meant to spend more than ten pounds on gifts and I don't know if the lamb's wool comes from ethically sourced, free-range lambs who spend their days happily gambolling about the moors.'

'I'm sure she'll love it.' Nina was sure of no such thing. Noah's mother, like her own, seemed like a tough crowd. He was also holding several boxes of Bron-Tea. 'Is the tea for her too?'

'The Emily, er, Bron-Tea is for my father. He's on this detox diet since he was diagnosed with MS and this has wild nettles and berries in it, and I got the Branwell one too, which has yerba maté and spice, for my younger brother. He prides himself on being able to drink the most foul-tasting concoctions.'

'Like green juice? Ugh!' Nina, Posy and Verity had been on a collective health kick last year that had lasted two days and had involved one yoga class and a green juice that had cost ten pounds and had tasted like pond scum.

'Green juice is the work of the devil.' Noah shuddered. 'When I lived in San Francisco, everyone was on green juice. If you ordered a fully caffeinated coffee, they'd look at you like you'd just asked them to chuck in a couple of rocks of crack and hold the foam.'

'But isn't caffeine one of the five major food groups?' Nina mused as they walked towards the till where a woman was staring at them with the desperate look of someone who wanted to close up the shop and go home.

They paid for their purchases and left the Parsonage. It was quite dark as they walked back to the car park and suddenly, despite her legs aching, actually all of her aching due to all the enforced activity, and being ravenously hungry, Nina felt quite skittish with nerves.

Noah had told her to pack an overnight bag so he obviously wasn't planning to drive them back to London. They'd be staying somewhere.

Maybe sharing a room. And a bed.

It was their third date and they both knew *exactly* what that meant.

The shivers were back because Nina wasn't at all adverse to the idea of finally getting down to some serious funny business. Quite the contrary, especially when he took her hand and asked, 'Are you cold?'

Nina paused to consider the question. Actually, she *was* cold, to add to the general achiness and the hunger. 'A little bit, but I have a few ideas on how I might warm up,' she said huskily and squeezed Noah's hand just before he let her go because they were at the car now.

'A pot of tea and a round of toast?' he suggested primly. 'Then an early night with an improving book.'

'Well, maybe one out of those four,' Nina agreed.

CHAPTER

22

'Make the world stop right here. Make everything stop and stand still and never move again. Make the moors never change and you and I never change.'

I t was a short drive to their next destination. They hadn't even been in the car ten minutes with the lady on the satnav purring directions before they were turning into a drive at the end of which was a long, low, slate-grey house. The lights were on in the windows and as they pulled up the front door opened.

'This looks nice,' Nina said. 'Cosy and welcoming.'

'That's not all it is,' Noah said, a little smugly, which wasn't that becoming but indicated that he had more surprises in store for her. 'I'll grab our bags.'

'Come inside!' called the woman who stood in the doorway. 'You must be freezing!'

It wasn't long after that that Nina and Noah were side by side on a gloriously squashy sofa, with a mug of tea and a huge slice of cake each as the owners of the bed and breakfast explained how the Brontës had been frequent visitors and that it was generally regarded as the inspiration for *Wuthering Heights* itself. Nina didn't think her eyes could get much wider – it felt like they might pop out of their sockets altogether – when they also revealed that Nina would be staying in the Earnshaw Room with its 'Cathy window' where Cathy's ghost had struggled to get in.

It sounded magical. Nina could only stare at Noah who ducked his head modestly. Hands down, this was the best date Nina had ever been on. The best date, in fact, since records had begun.

Also, best road trip. Best mini-break. Best foreplay because, oh yes, they were definitely going to do IT tonight.

'We did wonder if you were still wanting a second room. It's just we've had a phone call from an American couple who were hoping we might still have a room free for tonight,' their host, who was extremely genial in both face and character, asked apologetically.

'We only need the one room,' Nina said firmly and a little forcefully. 'Right?' She patted Noah's knee with heavy emphasis. No one could, or ever had, accused Nina of being subtle.

'In case you get scared that you hear something tapping

at the window?' Noah enquired with just a little bit of arched eyebrow. 'Or someone?'

'Exactly, you know what a vivid imagination I have,' Nina said and she winked so theatrically that she practically dislocated her eyelid.

There was a moment's silence, *awkward*, then the landlady coughed quietly. 'Well, you'll be wanting to see your room and get straightened up.'

'That would be great,' Nina agreed. She was still wearing damp clothes and she would have paid vast sums of money for a hot bath.

Their room was something to behold. If you stripped away the fripperies of twenty-first-century living – the sofas, the velvet throws, the retro-looking but actually very modern wood-burning stove, which lit the room with a warm, cosy glow – then little had changed from when the Brontës had been visitors to the house. There were rough brick walls and thick wooden beams, like tree trunks, supporting the sloping ceiling, smaller beams bisecting them.

And there was what their hosts called 'a box bed', just like the one that Emily Brontë described in *Wuthering Heights*. A bed hidden in an oak cabinet: 'I slid back the panelled sides, got in with my light, pulled them together again, and felt secure against the vigilance of Heathcliff, and every one else.'

Nina felt as if she had stepped into the pages of *Wuthering Heights*.

Noah was asking about local places to eat and what time breakfast was in the morning as Nina wandered the room, hands running over each piece of furniture, eyes trying to take in every detail. In its little cubbyhole, the bed looked so inviting, so soft and comfortable, piled with pillows, that Nina wasn't even thinking about what a suitable venue it would be for their third-date activities but how she'd like to fall face down on it and sleep for a hundred days.

'Nina? So, does that sound like a plan?' Noah asked and she turned to him with a fixed but bright smile on her face.

'Sorry, didn't catch that. What is the plan?'

The plan was that Nina would spend a 'not ridiculous amount of time' freshening up, then their hosts would very kindly drive her and Noah to a local pub for dinner and pick them up when they were ready to call it a night.

Nina had never got this treatment in any of the hotels she'd stayed in before, though admittedly the hotels she'd stayed in before tended to be nana-ish B&Bs or Premier Inns.

She was even promised the loan of a coat as her bedraggled leopard-print faux fur was carried away to be dried, Noah going with it, so Nina was alone.

When she'd woken up that morning, it seemed like weeks ago, she'd expected nothing more than a hard day of bookselling, maybe a trip to The Midnight Bell for after-work drinks. She certainly hadn't expected, well, any of this or that their first night together was imminent.

Her heart sank when she saw that the en suite only had a shower and not the bath she was hoping for but it was probably just as well. She'd definitely fall asleep in a hot bath. As it was, even a hot shower made her want to sink to the floor of the shower cubicle and have a nap.

But there was no time for napping. Not when Nina needed to do her whole third-date-night getting-ready regime in half an hour. Washing, conditioning, depilating, exfoliating, moisturising and then trying to quickly blow-dry her hair so she'd have time to get to work with the curling tongs after.

When Noah tapped on the door thirty-seven minutes after he'd left, Nina was ready. She opened the door and his eyes widened, his mouth fell open, which was all the validation she needed. But his awestruck 'Nina, you look absolutely gorgeous!' was the cherry on top of the validation cake.

It was their third date, after all, and most of the time Noah had seen Nina in her hated Happy Ever After T-shirt. He'd seen her in her Land Girl dungarees. He'd seen her in a laser-tag-friendly ensemble but he'd never seen Nina in all her full glory before.

Noah's eyes didn't know where to focus first. At her glossy, platinum Veronica Lake-style waves or her face with brows perfectly arched and HD ready, a sweep of liquid eyeliner, false eyelashes, and matt-red lips. Many other products had happened and the finished effect was siren of the silver screen, which was further emphasised by the black satin wiggle dress that plunged in the right places and clung lovingly like a sailor on shore leave in all the other places.

'I'm meant to be serving Old Hollywood realness,' Nina said and finished with a giggle because she hadn't realised how nervous she was. Or maybe it was just the way that

Noah was still looking at her fishnet-clad legs, toes curling in perilously high black suede heels.

'Mission accomplished,' Noah said hoarsely and he took hold of Nina by the wrists, his eyes all pupil, so she wondered if they might just skip going out to dinner and move straight on to pudding but . . . no. He was moving her gently but firmly out of the way.

'Give me ten minutes,' he said, pushing her out the door. 'That's all the time I need to shower and put on *my* warpaint,' and Nina was laughing as she snatched up her leopard-print clutch bag from the sideboard by the door.

Their fellow guests were a young American couple, Rachel and Ford, who were touring around Europe and slightly dismayed to find themselves in Britain in a March that was mostly grey and damp.

'We're from Austin, Texas,' Rachel explained as they all squashed into a car to be driven to the pub for dinner. 'No one told us that it would be this cold.'

'Or wet,' Ford added glumly.

When they got to the pub, which was as charming and old-looking as any pub in Brontë country should be, Nina realised that there was no chance of ditching Rachel and Ford for a table for two.

Well, Nina would have been happy to dump them, but Noah had far better manners and said with convincing enthusiasm that it would be lovely to all eat together but Nina saw the way he swallowed to hide his disappointment and as he took her borrowed puffa anorak, he whispered 'sorry' in her ear.

As it was, dinner passed in a mellow blur for Nina. What with the heat from the obligatory roaring fire and the brandy in her glass and the hearty steak pie in front of her, she was feeling no pain. Rachel and Ford, despite their scrubbed, wholesome appearance, like they should be advertising wholegrain cereal or paraben-free cleaning products, were good company. Before touring Europe, they'd sold all their worldly possessions, bought a camper van and had road-tripped across the States so they were full of stories about the time they went to the Grand Canyon or the Utah salt flats and how Rachel had got locked in a bathroom at Graceland.

Noah was full of questions about road-tripping that they were only too happy to answer and Nina was content to sip her brandy and murmur the odd comment as she and Noah played footsie under the table. They were exchanging so many heated looks that they hardly needed to be seated so close to the inglenook fireplace.

The only thing that slightly killed the mood was that every person in the pub found a reason to pass their table so they could gawp at Nina. Normally, Nina wouldn't have minded the attention (on the contrary, she usually loved it) but tonight she'd dressed solely for Noah to gawp at.

In fact, she'd have been quite happy to skip pudding and head back to their B&B and their box bed, but Rachel and Ford had walked over 25,000 steps that day so they did want pudding. They were both really nice, super nice, but Nina wanted to punch them.

'You all right?' Noah asked when they'd given their

pudding orders and Rachel and Ford left the table to take photos of the rustic, rural charms of the pub and post them on Instagram. 'Shall I come and sit next to you?'

'Yes, please,' Nina said and when Noah was seated in the chair that Ford had just vacated, he slipped his arm around her shoulders. She almost wanted to shrug it off because she was too hot after spending most of the day being too cold, but then he pulled her even closer to kiss her cheek. Nina leaned into Noah's touch and his lips were moving down, just glancing the corner of her mouth, when something occurred to her. 'I can't believe this is the first time we've kissed today!'

'Yes we have!' Noah frowned. 'No, we haven't. We should probably rectify the non-kissing situation quite soon.'

'Very soon,' Nina agreed. She pulled away. 'But not here, especially not when those two girls have walked past our table twice already and think that I don't know that they're trying to take a sneaky picture of me.' She raised her voice and the two girls backed away, phone still pointed in Nina's direction. 'But yeah, more kissing needs to happen as soon as humanly possible.'

'Sooner than that,' Noah said, his gaze fixed on Nina's mouth. 'Really wish we hadn't ordered pudding now.'

'Talk of the devil . . .'

Their pudding was in sight as were Rachel and Ford, who were loudly enthusing about the history of the pub now that one of the bar staff had told them it was haunted by several different ghosts.

For perhaps the first time in ten years, Nina hadn't

ordered dessert but Noah stayed seated next to her and fed her delicious morsels of his sticky-toffee pudding, though she had no appetite for them.

It all got a bit hazy after that. There was definitely another brandy. And nuzzling. Quite a lot of nuzzling. Especially in the car on the way back.

Nina supposed they must have made small talk with Rachel and Ford and their hosts. Possibly refused a nightcap because the next thing she was aware of was climbing the stairs to their room, the wooden banister rail smooth under her fingers, Noah walking behind her and pausing to nuzzle the back of her neck again when she stopped on the landing to get her bearings.

Then finally they were in their room. The fire had been stoked while they were out and it was toasty warm and Nina was coming to boiling point just from all that nuzzling.

The door shut behind Noah with a heavy thud that matched the beat of Nina's heart.

'So,' she said hoarsely. 'About that kiss . . .'

'Yes, that kiss,' Noah said prowling towards her and Nina didn't think she'd ever wanted to be kissed quite so badly as she did at that moment . . .

Then the wait was over because Noah had closed the small gap between them, closed his arms around her and Nina was dragging his head down, her fingers clutched in his hair and they were kissing.

At last!

There was no point in being polite about it. No time for hesitant, closed-mouth pecks but greedy, grabby, hungry, hot-mouthed kisses, both of them clutching at each other. Nina found herself swooning, actually swooning, in Noah's arms and God, he tasted divine. Like brandy and caramel and coffee.

Eventually Nina had to push him away so she could drag some air into her lungs. They stood, only centimetres apart, fighting for breath, unable to tear their eyes away from each other.

'We don't have to do anything,' Noah managed to say. 'I don't *expect* you to do anything because you feel you have to.'

'I know that,' Nina was quick to assure him. 'I *don't* feel like I have to.'

'Oh.' Noah's shoulders fell, as did the corners of his mouth as he tried not to look too crestfallen but failed.

'I don't *have* to,' Nina said in case Noah hadn't heard her the first time, 'but my God, I really *want* to.'

'You do?' Noah asked hopefully.

'Yes! Of course, yes! Why are we even talking about it when we could be doing it instead?' Nina had barely got to the end of her sentence before Noah's mouth was on hers again and then it was an ungainly scramble over to the cabinet and Nina banged her elbow and Noah knocked his head as they tried to slide back the wooden panel that hid the bed from view.

Noah threw himself down on the pile of cushions and pillows. 'Come here,' he said in a very commanding, very unNoah-like way, which played havoc with Nina's nerve endings.

'Hang on,' she said because she was wearing a genuine nineteen-forties vintage dress which was hard to get into but even harder to get out of. This one had a hidden side zip and Nina sometimes wondered if they were called wiggle dresses because the only way in or out of them was with a lot of wiggling.

She was wiggling now as she eased the dress up over her hips, Noah's eyes wide as a kid looking at all the presents under the tree on Christmas morning. Then she was pulling the dress over her head, carefully disentangling her arms from the tight sleeves and no matter how much she loved her curves, she felt a moment of sheer terror that Noah's awestruck look would be replaced by one of disgust, but when she was finally free of all the black satin and could see again, Noah was staring at her like he hadn't just had a three-course dinner but was starving. Ravenous.

'Wow!' he breathed. 'Nina. Wow. I must have done something very good in a previous life to be here with you and you . . . looking like . . . *that*.'

Nina put her hands on her hips, all the better to display the black lace bra and panties and suspender belt and garters which held up her stockings, because if something was worth doing, it was worth doing properly. 'Oh, these old things!' she said mockingly.

'I'm almost scared to touch you.' Noah held up a hand hesitantly as if he couldn't believe that soon they might be on Nina's skin.

'Well, we're not going to get very far then.' Nina was back to being nervous. Because it was one thing to pose prettily while Noah stared at her in awe but now she was waiting for the green light and he seemed to be stuck on red.

'Almost, I said I was *almost* scared to touch you,' Noah said with a wicked little smile and then he was moving quickly, reaching forward, to pull Nina up and onto the bed so she was in his arms again as he slammed the panel closed so the world outside ceased to exist and it was just the two of them.

It was dark inside their little cubbyhole so Nina couldn't see Noah, but then his hands, his mouth, were on her and she didn't need to see him, because she could feel him. On her. In her. All around her.

The first time was hot and hard and frantic, but oh so good.

Nina didn't even care that afterwards she was a sweaty, clammy mess. They lay on their backs in the dark, little fingers entwined, breathing the same rhythm.

The second time was slow and sensual, as they took long moments to learn each other's secrets, murmur promises against each other's skin and finish the long climb together, and it was just as good, if not better.

There was a chill to the air when they slipped under the covers at last and normally Nina wasn't a snuggler, snuggling was not cool, but it was lovely to have Noah's arms around her, big spoon to her little spoon.

She thought he was asleep. His breathing was deep, even, but then he said quietly, 'This isn't just some fling is it, Nina? I don't want just a fling.'

It was half question, half confession, as if he were worried that Nina had had her night of passion and was now going to bail. Which was ridiculous. She'd known Noah for just over a month but it wasn't enough. She knew with a rare certainty that Noah was the kind of man that she could be with for a year, ten years, a lifetime and he'd still find new ways to surprise her, to make her laugh, to make her feel safe.

Suddenly Nina got it. What a fool she'd been! Passion was one thing, there had been plenty of passion tonight, but when it was accompanied by something softer, sweeter, deeper, then maybe passion could have real staying power.

A man who could make you come undone then hold you while you slept, might just be a keeper.

Or at least Nina hoped so.

CHAPTER 23

*'I have not broken your heart –
you have broken it; and in breaking it,
you have broken mine.'*

When Nina woke up the next morning, she was groggy and disorientated. Couldn't think where she was or why it was so dark and why she seemed to be snuggled up to a hot water bottle.

She lay there willing her brain to work until slowly the events of yesterday came back into focus. No wonder she was so achy and sore, slightly hungover too, and that was no hot water bottle; that was a hot naked Noah.

'Nina? Are you awake?' hot naked Noah whispered in her ear and she tried to say yes, but it came out as more of a grunt.

'I think I am,' she croaked out and it took all the effort

in the world but she managed to find the energy to roll over so they were facing each other. 'Hi!'

'Hello. I missed you. Let's never go to sleep again,' Noah said and he kissed the tip of her nose and Nina had experienced enough awkward morning-afters to know that this wasn't one of them. Noah wasn't the type of man to get his goodies then exit stage left; he'd meant what he said last night about this not being a fling.

And Nina? Despite the aches and pains and the suspicion that some small woodland creature had crawled into her mouth during the night and died, she'd rarely felt more content. 'Or we could have another sleep right now?' she suggested, because she was still tired.

'When you say sleep, do you mean sleep or do you mean something else?' Noah asked, nudging Nina in a way that should have ignited all sorts of fires, but as it was all she could manage was a feeble smoulder and when he leaned in to kiss her, she had to shift her face away.

'I did actually mean sleep,' she said huskily. 'You've worn me out and also, I have the worst morning mouth ever so stop trying to kiss me.'

'Poor Nina.' Noah didn't seem to care that there was a small animal corpse in Nina's mouth because he did steal one swift but tender kiss, then laughed and let her go. 'Because you're my current favourite person in the world, I'll let you have a lie-in while I grab the first shower, but it's gone nine already. I think we've probably missed breakfast.'

Usually Nina loved a hotel breakfast. No continental option for her, but full fry-up every time, but even the thought of bacon, eggs and a couple of rounds of toast couldn't stir her from her recumbent position. She felt Noah shift off the bed and took the opportunity to burrow deeper under the covers. She could sleep for a week.

Her phone started ringing from across the room where it had been charging since before they went to dinner last night. 'Shall I grab that for you?' Noah asked.

'No, leave it.'

'Too late, lazybones,' Noah said and Nina opened one eye to see him staring down at her ringing phone.

'Please . . . it can't be that important,' she grumbled, keen to get back to dozing.

'What?' Noah asked sharply, sharp enough that Nina managed to prop herself up on one elbow, but then the phone stopped ringing and he shook his head and walked to the bathroom with such an unsteady gait that he cannoned off the wall.

It seemed like she wasn't the only one who was tired, Nina thought as her phone beeped to let her know she had a voicemail. Then it started ringing again. Stop. Snuggle. Beep.

Lather, rinse, repeat.

The fourth time it rang, Nina flung back the covers with a growl of pure frustration. There was obviously some kind of emergency and someone needed to contact her urgently, or there had better be, otherwise Nina was going to hunt down her caller and hurt him or her terribly.

Her legs were very wobbly as she wrapped herself mummy-style in a sheet and teetered over to the sideboard and her phone.

It started to ring again, with Paul's name and a picture of Ellie and Rosie flashing on the screen. Nina reached for it with fumbling fingers.

'What's up? Is it an emergency? Is it Gran? Oh God, it *is* Gran! Has she had another funny turn?'

'It's not Gran, she's fine,' Paul said cheerfully so there obviously wasn't any urgent reason for him to bombard her with phone calls this early on a Saturday morning. 'But you, you don't sound fine. You sound rougher than a badger's arse. Big night last night, was it?'

Nina blushed. Why she was blushing, she didn't exactly know. And she also didn't know how she was going to break it to Noah that she was the sister of his adolescent tormentor. That she, in fact, had gone to Orange Hill too and had witnessed her brother's crimes first-hand.

It was a very complicated situation, which would need to be handled with a lot of finesse. But she was getting way ahead of herself. The most pressing thing was to come clean: it was not going to be pleasant but what they had was so special, so rare, that surely it could overcome a few obstacles? She'd tell him when they got back to London.

'Just a medium-sized night,' she rasped, her voice scratchy. 'I'm actually out of town for the weekend . . .'

'Yeah, that's nice, can we talk about me now?' Paul obviously wasn't calling to exchange social pleasantries. 'You have to help me! It's our ninth wedding anniversary and it will be my last if I don't get Chloe an amazing present.'

Nina's legs really didn't want to keep her upright any

longer so she collapsed onto one of the armchairs on either side of the fire. 'Why have you left it to the last minute?'

'Because we said that we weren't going to make a fuss about our anniversary. We agreed! And now she's got a right cob on because I haven't got her anything,' Paul said in an aggrieved voice. 'Says that she still hasn't forgiven me for her birthday present.'

'You got her a vacuum cleaner,' Nina reminded him. 'You're a monster.'

'It was a top-of-the-range model . . .' Paul tailed off because there was no way he was winning this argument. 'You're a woman. What do I get her?'

Nina tipped her head back. She couldn't decide if she was hot or cold. She felt like she was burning up under the sheet but her legs, exposed to the air, were freezing. And her brain really didn't want to work. 'Do you want my help?' Nina barked, which made her throat feel even scratchier. 'Because if you do, you can lose the tone, mate.'

'Yeah, sorry about that,' Paul struggled to find a more genial manner. 'It's just she's already pretty mad. I've already been shouted at for not putting my cereal bowl in the dishwasher. So, have you got any bright ideas about what to get Chloe?'

This conversation was giving Nina the mother of all headaches. 'Isn't there a gift assigned to each year you've been married. Like, silver for twenty-five years, gold for fifty . . . Hang on, I'll Google what nine years stands for.'

She was busy Googling when there was a polite cough. Nina looked up from her phone screen to see Noah standing there, a towel tucked round his waist. 'Sorry,' she mouthed.

'Family crisis.' And then she had to look away because last night she couldn't see a thing and this morning, she could see everything. Or she could see that Noah was lean but muscly like all that kayaking and ziplining was quite the workout and yes, he was covered in freckles and next time, she was going to kiss every single one of them.

Which was probably why Noah was frowning because Nina was staring at him the way Strumpet stared at the fridge when it was still *hours* before his dinnertime.

'So . . . you Googled it then? What's nine years?' demanded Paul who she'd put on speaker while she was searching and Noah seemed to flinch, then gathered up clean clothes and whisked himself back into the bathroom.

'It's pottery and willow,' Nina told Paul distractedly.

'Ah, that's why Clo got me a cricket bat. Clever girl. What other stuff is made out of willow?'

'Nothing that I can think of.'

By the time Noah came back into the room, fully dressed in jeans and ubiquitous navy jumper, the same frowny look on his face, Paul was under strict instructions to go to the nearest John Lewis ('but that's Kingston!') to get a limited edition Diptyque candle in a beautiful, hand-made porcelain jar.

'Fifty-five quid for a bloody candle!' Paul shouted down the phone.

'And get her some perfume while you're there,' Nina snapped back. 'She's the mother of your children. She spent two whole days in labour with Rosie so you can pony up on the anniversary present.'

'I suppose,' Paul grumbled but Nina knew that he'd do as he was told. He adored Chloe; she was the best thing that had ever happened to him and he didn't really deserve her.

'I mean, no one else but Chloe would put up with you,' she reminded him sweetly. 'Have I mentioned that lately?'

'Maybe. Only about fifty times or so because you're the most annoying sister ever,' Paul said and Noah was packing his bag, still with the same grim expression on his face and Nina didn't know why he looked so *angry* . . .

Oh!

Oh God!

No!

Surely there was no way he could know. Not yet!

Because Nina needed time to explain this properly, oh so carefully, and once she had done so and reintroduced them, then Noah would see how Paul had changed, was a completely different person from the hateful boy he'd been at school. It would be all right. It had to be all right.

But that was in the future. Not too long in the future but he couldn't know yet. Could he? Nina said a quick goodbye to Paul and turned her attention back to Noah. 'Sorry,' she said, blood rushing in her ears. 'Boring family drama.'

'It's fine,' Noah said, putting his phone charger into one of the pockets of his holdall. 'Look, I hate to rush you but you should probably have a shower and I'll go and see if breakfast is still an option.'

Nina wasn't that hungry but she flashed Noah what she

hoped was a brilliant smile. 'Lifesaver,' she said, but he didn't smile back, just nodded his head and maybe she was reading too much into the taut lines of his face. Maybe he was just one of those people who were really grumpy in the morning until they'd had at least one caffeinated beverage.

There was still so much to discover about each other, Nina mused, as she stepped into the shower. Noah hadn't even seen her without make-up as she hadn't had a chance to take yesterday's slap off. She was tempted to angle her face away from the stream of water and just retouch what she already had on but when she eventually left the en suite she was showered, dressed and fresh-faced.

'I'm not a natural beauty, all right?' she thought she'd better clarify to Noah who was sitting stiff-backed in one of the armchairs. She'd obviously taken much longer than she intended. 'Sorry, was I ages? Were you about to scrounge up some breakfast? Even a couple of pieces of toast would do. I'm not even that hungry, which is weird because normally . . .'

'This isn't going to work,' Noah said abruptly, one hand held up to cut through Nina's ponderings on her lack of appetite.

'Oh, it's all right,' Nina assured him. 'We can easily go out for breakfast. Though I suppose it would really be brunch by now. Have I got time to do a light daytime make-up?'

Noah sighed. 'I'm talking about us. We're not going to work,' he said heavily and with such an air of finality that it was like a door slamming shut in Nina's make-up-free face.

'What are you talking about?' She'd felt heavy and achy ever since she'd woken up, but now there was a leaden weight inside her so it seemed as if all of Nina's organs were hurtling towards the ground. 'We're fine! Last night was great. Better than great and this morning you said . . .' It was hard to remember what Noah had said . . . Then she remembered the nudge of his hips and . . . 'You said that you'd missed me while I slept. You wanted to go again!'

He shut his eyes as if the memory of those delicious moments caught between sleep and waking was painful. Nina could hardly look at him. She had this crazy notion that if she did, she might turn to stone like in the Greek legends, but when she did steel herself to look at Noah, her eyes blazing, it was he who looked as if he'd been turned to stone. 'There's too much baggage for this to work.'

Nina's lips twisted. It wasn't the first time she'd had this conversation with a man the morning after. 'It's not like I'm a virgin. I'm nearly thirty,' she said bitterly. 'But I haven't slept with as many men as people think I have. And anyway, even if I'd had sex with a thousand men, that shouldn't matter. It should only matter that I'm having sex with you.'

'I'm not talking about that kind of baggage.' It would have been easier, better, if Noah were red in the face and raising his voice. That was familiar territory for Nina; stand-up rows. But Noah's face was as dull as the flat tone in which he spoke. 'I saw his picture flash up when I went to get your phone. It's been a while, but I'd recognise him anywhere. Paul O'Kelly. He's your brother.'

It wasn't a question. Just an absolutely unequivocal statement that Nina couldn't deny. Couldn't fudge. Couldn't
come back to at a later date. 'Yes,' she answered in a broken
whisper. 'He is and I wanted to . . .'

Noah held up a hand to silence her. 'You know, I did
wonder if he was your brother. I mean, you do have the
same surname and I was sure I saw him outside the soft-
play centre when I picked you up the other week, but I
told myself I was being silly. If he had been your brother,
you'd have mentioned it, but you didn't so I thought it was
just an unhappy coincidence.'

'I wanted to tell you,' Nina offered weakly, all of her
cold and clammy now that the awful truth had come out
when everything had been so perfect. 'I meant to tell you.'

'And my grandmother, you remember her, a regular
visitor at your aunt's salon? She was insistent that the girl
who used to work there who did her colour was Paul
O'Kelly's sister but I decided that couldn't be true because
she's always getting things muddled and anyway, Nina would
have told me. Just like she would have told me that she'd
gone to Orange Hill,' Noah said. 'Because you did, didn't
you? You knew me back then.' His eyes bored into her and
Nina dropped her gaze to her feet. 'When did you figure
it out?'

There was an edge to his voice now too: the dullness
starting to crack under the sheer weight of Noah's anger.
Not just anger; when she dared a fleeting glance up at
Noah's face she could see hurt, betrayal, confusion all play
across his features. 'After the quiz, when you were walking

me to the bus stop,' she admitted and she shivered because she felt as if she'd been entombed in ice. 'But . . . but . . .'

'But you never thought to mention it? It just slipped your mind, did it?'

'I didn't want to drag up the past, when I knew it was so painful for you.' Nina held her hand out towards Noah but he took a step back. 'You don't know how I've tortured myself over this . . .' Nina began and Noah smiled. It wasn't a nice smile.

'*Torture?* Like the way your *brother*,' he spat the word out like it tasted rotten in his mouth, 'would punch me, hit me, throw things at me, spit at me, the names he would call me . . . God, I think his words hurt the most.'

'Don't!' Nina clapped her hands over her ears because she couldn't bear to listen to the catalogue of Paul's crimes and then she closed her eyes so she wouldn't have to see the ugly expression on Noah's face.

'Oh, I'm sorry, Nina, am I upsetting you?' Noah snapped and when Nina forced herself to open her eyes, his expression was grim, resolute, uncompromising. 'He's a monster.'

'He's my brother,' Nina said helplessly. 'That doesn't mean that he gets a free pass for what he did to you, and he and I weren't close then, God, we barely tolerated each other, but it was *years* ago. He was the person in the accident that I told you about and he nearly died, and it made him take stock of everything, of who he was and how he'd behaved. And now he has Chloe and the niecelets.' The tears were prickling, soon they'd be streaming down her face.

This was meant to be different. Noah *was* different to

all her others. And last night, she'd even imagined that he was the one; that rare mix of passion and staying power. Not even imagined, but had been sure of it in a way that Nina was rarely sure about anything.

And now?

Everything, them, the us they could have been was dust and ashes and it was all her fault, but there had to be a way, something she could say, to turn this round. To make Noah see that the past was nothing to do with their future. 'He's not the same person he was when we were at school. He's changed and only for the good and he knows that what he did was wrong. He wants the opportunity to say sorry, to make it up to you,' she said, her words distorted by the sob that was rising up in her throat.

'There is nothing he could say or do to make it up to me. Nothing,' Noah said. He put his hand to his temples. 'You should have told me! Instead you've deceived me. Lied to me. So many lies! You even brushed away the very simple fact that we were at school together.'

'I never meant to lie,' Nina cried. 'How was I to know that you and I were going to become something? That I'd have feelings for you?'

She broke off so Noah could say that he had feelings for her too but he didn't and judging from the tight cast to his face, any feelings that he did have for her weren't good ones. Still, she was determined to soldier on.

'I've felt terrible about not telling you, felt so guilty and ashamed about what Paul did to you when we were at school . . . it was why I agreed to go on that first non-date.

Because I felt so sorry for you and I wanted, in some small way, to make it up to you.' It wasn't what she meant to say but Nina could hardly think. Her head seemed to be stuffed with cotton wool.

'You felt sorry for me?'

'Not sorry, guilty,' Nina amended as if that made it any better.

It didn't.

'So, it was a pity date. Not even a date, but a non-date?' Noah queried, but he still wasn't shouting or swearing at her so that had to be good.

'Well, *yeah*. I mean, you're hardly my type or me yours, but that was before . . .'

'Actually, now that I think about it, it's obvious that you're *his* sister. Cruelty apparently runs in the family,' Noah said.

Nina gasped. It was a low blow, the lowest, and she deserved it – though that didn't mean that she was going to take it either.

She opened her mouth and was all set to point out that it hadn't just been Paul; he alone couldn't be held responsible for the bullying – and then she realised how that sounded. She would be diminishing Noah's pain, the fear and loathing that had characterised his adolescence, and the fact that her brother had been the chief architect of Noah's destruction.

What was that saying? *Love the sinner, hate the sin.*

'I'm sorry,' she said and she tried to make those two words count, to mean something and everything. Noah was sitting there, his limbs arranged awkwardly, his head hanging low, as if he was broken. 'Going on a date with you out of guilt was before I got to know you. And now . . .'

'Now, I wish I'd never got to know you. In fact, I realise I didn't know the real you until I saw your brother's face on your phone.' Noah gave a short, humourless chuckle. 'You're still the same mean-spirited girl like all the other girls at that school were. The ones who would jeer as they watched your brother beat the hell out of me.'

'I never jeered. Not once,' Nina protested, though the picture Noah was painting of his school days was familiar. She never jeered, but she'd definitely hurried past with her head down. 'I'm not mean-spirited. I'm not like that at all. I was just as pleased to leave Worcester Park as you.'

'All the evidence indicates otherwise.' Noah's face was ashen white. 'I think it's pretty mean-spirited to have been lying to me this entire time.'

'I didn't set out to lie to you. I didn't lie *lie*, I just lied by omission. If you'd asked me if Paul was my brother, then I'd have told you the truth but you never did,' Nina said and again, it wasn't what she meant to say and she shook her head to try and clear the fug where her brain should be, but it just made everything throb.

'So it's my fault for not having better deductive reasoning? Honestly, Nina, how did you think this was going to play out?' Noah demanded.

Nina rested the tips of her fingers on her aching forehead. '*You* were the one who asked me out,' she mumbled.

'You didn't have to say yes . . . OK! I get it!' Noah nodded. 'This is exactly what you wanted, isn't it?'

'How can you think that *this* is what I wanted?'

'As you don't seem to be at all familiar with the concept of honesty, allow me to give you a few home truths. The reason that you want passion and drama is because you haven't got what it takes to make a real relationship work. A relationship is about loving someone, it's about kindness, being selfless sometimes − all qualities that you're lacking.' Noah threw his words at her as if they were poisoned darts, each one aimed straight at Nina's heart.

For someone who insisted that he was a cold fish, in this moment, Noah was more passionate than Nina had ever seen him − apart from the night before. And yes, this was the drama and passion that Nina craved, but it was destructive and corrosive and suddenly Nina didn't want anything to do with drama and passion ever again.

Because Noah was half right. There was something lacking in her and she tried to disguise it with hair dye and tattoos and leopard print, but underneath it all, there wasn't much substance, hardly any depth. Nina knew that she could be hard and abrasive, but surely she was never spiteful? There was a softer side to her and now Noah would never see it. See her. See a woman that he might fall in love with.

'I'm sorry,' she said yet again but she'd never meant the words as much as she meant them now.

Noah's gaze flickered over her dismissively. 'It wasn't even as if last night could make up for this. It wasn't *that* good,' he said as he hammered the final nails into the coffin of what they could have been. 'Get your bags packed, we're going back to London. I had a whole day planned for us, but not now, not with you.'

Then he got up and walked out of the room as if he couldn't bear to look at her, which was fine with Nina because she couldn't bear for him to see her cry.

CHAPTER 24

'He shall never know I love him:
and that, not because he's handsome,
but because he's more myself than I am.'

The journey home was five long, awkward hours, maybe the most awkward hours of Nina's life. Noah had said only nine words to her during the entire journey. 'Do you want to stop at the next services?' he'd asked somewhere around Leicester and though Nina could have done with a visit to the Ladies, she said only two words to him, 'No, thanks,' because she didn't want to prolong the agony. She'd just have to clench her pelvic floor muscles the rest of the way to London.

Her head pounded with all the thoughts crowding her mind.

Her throat ached with all the words she wanted to say.

Nina went from hot to cold as she thought about the night before, tangled up in each other, and then the bitter morning after.

She felt terrible and from the tense lines of Noah's face in profile, when she dared to steal a glance at him, he wasn't feeling much better himself.

However awful the trip home, Nina was aware that this was the last time that she'd spend with Noah and already, even though he was sitting next to her and changing gears very aggressively, she missed him.

And then, though it seemed like no time at all and also as if several decades had passed, Noah pulled into Rochester Street.

'No need to turn into the mews,' Nina insisted in a voice so croaky from unshed tears and not speaking that it sounded as if she had a forty-a-day fag habit. 'You'll never be able to turn the car around again.'

Noah unclipped his seatbelt. 'I'll get your bag,' he offered tersely.

'It's all right. I can manage,' Nina rasped brightly, reaching round to grab the bag off the back seat and nearly decapitating Noah in the process. 'Sorry! And thanks for yesterday. I'll see you around, OK?'

For a second, not even a second, their eyes met and immediately, Nina could feel the hot sting of tears. Noah opened his mouth to say something but she couldn't take hearing another cruel but well deserved jibe from the lips that had kissed her so sweetly. She quickly slammed the door and scurried for the mews, for the sanctuary that was

Happy Ever After though it was hard to scurry when her legs felt as heavy as sand bags.

It was Saturday afternoon and the sun was shining so the shop was heaving with customers. The queue to pay snaked all the way across the main room so Nina had to fight her way through a crowd of book-lovers to get to the door that led to the stairs without being spotted by . . .

'Nina! What are you doing here? I didn't expect to see you until Monday,' Posy shouted from behind the till. 'What's wrong? You look very puffy-faced. Have you been crying? Don't tell me that you and Noah have broken up already. Oh, Nina! I was hoping this wouldn't happen.'

Everyone waiting in the queue swivelled round to eyeball Nina with expressions that were sympathetic, curious, kind.

But Nina didn't want their kindness. If anyone were even a little bit nice to her, she'd start sobbing. So she shrugged. 'You know me, Posy,' she croaked. 'Breaking men's hearts is my speciality.'

'Poor Noah,' Posy said sadly. 'Sebastian is going to be so cross with you.'

Sebastian Thorndyke would rue the day he was ever born if he decided to give Nina ANY grief at all about what she'd done to poor Noah.

Verity, who was bagging up books and had obviously been drafted in to help in the shop against her will, from the woebegone look on her face, shook her head sorrowfully. 'Poor Noah,' she added her voice to the chorus, then gave Nina a swift and assessing once over. 'I don't think

Noah is the only one suffering. You look awful. Are you sure you're OK?'

Nina was not OK. Nina didn't think she was going to be OK ever again. 'I'm fine,' she assured Verity. 'Hate to break it you, Very, but this is what I look like without make-up on.'

Verity narrowed her eyes. 'I've seen you without make-up on and you didn't look like you'd been to hell and back like you do right now.'

'Way to make a girl feel special,' Nina said in the same carefree tone that took every ounce of acting ability that she possessed. 'Now, I don't know what you're doing serving on the till but would you like me to take over, Very? Your left eyelid is twitching.'

Verity's left eyelid was indeed twitching, which meant she was a couple of customers away from a meltdown. 'Oh, would you? It's just that Tom's at lunch and Little Sophie had to go to Sainsbury's to get some things for Mattie.'

It was the very last thing Nina wanted to do: having to put her gameface on and be sociable. But then the very, *very* last thing she wanted to do was go upstairs to be on her own with her tangled, head-hurting thoughts.

'Sure, yeah, I wouldn't have offered otherwise,' she said, coming forward to relieve Verity of her customer-serving duties.

And for the next three hours, Nina smiled and commented on people's book selections and generally acted as if she didn't have a care in the world.

Eventually it was seven o'clock. The door shut behind

the last customer. Then it was seven thirty and the cashing up had been done, the floor had been swept, books left higgledy-piggledy on tables and sofas and counters had been reshelved and Tom, Posy and Little Sophie were heading out the door too.

'I'm staying over at Johnny's tonight,' Verity informed Nina as they trooped up the stairs to their flat. 'I'm so sorry that your weekend with Noah ended so badly. Have you got any other plans for tonight?'

Nina had made a tentative arrangement earlier in the week to go to a rockabilly rave in Kings Cross with Marianne and Claude but earlier in the week was a millenium ago.

'Of course you've got plans,' Verity said without waiting for Nina to confirm. 'You, Nina, stay in on a Saturday night? It would be like the ravens leaving the Tower. England would fall!'

It took ages for Verity to be gone. First she had to have her half-hour decompression lie-down, then she had to pack her overnight bag and ponder where she and Johnny might go for dinner, which depended on where they might go for brunch tomorrow and did Nina want to meet up with them and though Verity was an introvert, God, the girl could talk, Nina thought as she grunted in the places where Verity expected a response.

Then, at last, *at last*, Verity was running down the stairs because she was late and a minute later the shop door closed behind her and Nina was alone.

★

All those years Nina had spent wondering what love really felt like and now she knew. It felt like hell. It felt like the worst thing on earth. It felt much, much worse than anything she'd read about in *Wuthering Heights*. Compared to what she was experiencing on a lonely Saturday night, Cathy and Heathcliff had simply been a pair of idiots who'd needed their heads knocking together.

Nina lay in bed unable to sleep. It wasn't even all the pain and regret she'd been bottling up since Noah had told her 'This isn't going to work' that kept her awake. Her torment was less emotional and more physical. She was either so hot that it felt as if she was being roasted alive, sweat stinging her eyes and making her kick off the covers, or she felt so cold that her body would suddenly rattle with shudders that were a pretty close cousin to convulsions and she barely had enough energy to pull the duvet tighter around her.

Come Sunday morning, sleep deprivation was the least of her ailments. Nina had a skull-crushing headache, made worse by the coughs that wrenched her inside out. Her limbs had been stuffed with sawdust and getting from bed to hall to kitchen was as arduous as her walk across the moors two days before. Making a cup of coffee took what was left of her depleted strength so she barely had enough energy to drink it. Then the shivers started again and Nina all but crawled to the sofa because the living room was nearer than her bedroom.

Then she must have fallen asleep because she was plagued by dreams where she was lost on the moors. She could hear Noah's voice calling her, but each time she tried to stumble towards him, she realised it was just the wind wuthering at her and that Noah was nowhere to be found. Or she'd see him in the distance but when she got closer, it wouldn't be Noah but an old gnarled log or a slab of stone.

'Where are you?' dream Nina cried. 'Don't leave me. My heart's broken.'

'What is she going on about?' asked a piercing, familiar voice.

'I never thought that a broken heart would feel like this,' Nina whispered to the cruel, uncaring wind.

'It's not a broken heart, it's the flu,' said the same voice and when Nina forced her eyes open, there was a face staring down at her, which was mostly obscured by a surgical mask. 'Open your mouth!'

Nina opened her mouth, only to have a thermometer rammed in it.

'Your bedside manner sucks,' said a voice from the doorway and Nina turned her head, groaning around the thermometer because her neck ached, to see a cluster of people standing there. Posy, who'd just spoken, Verity and behind them, a tall, dark figure . . .

'Heathcliff,' Nina mumbled.

'No, not Heathcliff, it's me, Merry!' and a hand on Nina's chin turned her head back to the person standing over her. Nina blinked sleep-encrusted, swollen eyes as she stared up at Merry, or Mercy as she'd been christened, one of Verity's many sisters. Mercy was a medical researcher at nearby

University College Hospital and their go-to person whenever they were feeling poorly. 'Let's be having this.' The thermometer was yanked out of Nina's mouth. 'Just nudging thirty-nine degrees. Are you achy?'

'So achy. Hot. Then cold. Everything hurts,' Nina realised. 'Oh God, this is just like when Emily Brontë caught a chill, which turned into tuberculosis and then she died.'

'It's not TB. I keep telling you, you have the flu. You're not going to die,' Merry said comfortingly. 'Although actually, flu isn't to be taken lightly, people can die from the flu,' she added not so comfortingly.

'Morland, I absolutely forbid you from entering this disease-ridden hovel. Go downstairs this instant,' commanded the tall, dark figure at the living-room door, who wasn't Heathcliff, but Sebastian Thorndyke. 'I'm not having you dying on me.'

'For God's sakes, Sebastian,' Posy hissed, but she took a couple of cautious steps back. 'I wish you'd think before you speak.'

'Well, of course Tattoo Girl isn't going to die,' Sebastian said witheringly. 'You're far too robust to be snuffed out by the flu. Though, quite frankly, a light dose of the flu is just desserts for what you've done to poor Noah. He's trying to put a brave face on it, but he's *devastated*.'

Nina hadn't thought it was possible to feel any more rotten but her visitors were doing a good job of proving her wrong. Tears leaked from the corners of her eyes. She wanted to ask after Noah, demand to know what he'd said about her, though it couldn't be anything good, but the effort was too much and all she could manage was a feeble cough that hurt like hell.

'Well, Nina is devastated too and she absolutely isn't going to die,' Verity said firmly, but she didn't move from the door so she could take Nina's hand or mop her exceedingly sweaty brow. 'And I'm sure people who die of the flu have underlying medical conditions or are very old. Do you think she should see a doctor, Merry?'

'Nothing a doctor can do for her,' Merry said cheerfully and in an odd sort of way, it was also quite comforting to have everyone talk about Nina as if she wasn't a very present, hot and sweaty lump on the sofa. 'Flu's a virus so she can't take antibiotics. Just paracetamol or ibuprofen to lower her temperature and plenty of liquids to stop her from getting dehydrated.'

'Poor Nina,' Posy cooed from the door. 'We'll make sure you have plenty of Lemsip. And I'm sure we can scrounge up some chicken soup from somewhere for you.'

'Such a pity that you and Noah only lasted three dates,' Verity noted sorrowfully. 'I bet he'd be the kind of boyfriend you'd really want around you when you had the flu.'

'He thinks I'm a horrible person.' Nina couldn't raise her voice above a creaky whisper. 'Because I am. No one will ever love me.'

'Oh, Nina! That's not true,' Posy gasped. 'We all love you.'

There was a rousing chorus of agreement from Verity and Mercy though Sebastian protested that 'love is pushing it, especially as you've just broken Noah's heart, *ooof*,' this from an elbow in the side from Posy, 'however, generally I think you're a cracking girl.' Then Tom's distant voice called up the stairs, 'Is anyone but me going to do any work today? Posy! There's a delivery.'

'All right, all right,' Posy snapped. 'I'd better go. You too, Very. Text us if you need anything, Nina.'

'Yes, feel better soon,' Verity said earnestly but she was already backing away and Sebastian was long gone, which left only Mercy who proudly produced a battered box of ibuprofen from her handbag.

'Two of these bad boys, every six hours.' She frowned. 'You should try and eat. It's not a good idea to take tablets on an empty stomach.'

But Nina didn't want to eat, which was a first. She could barely force down the glasses of water and Lemsip that Posy and Verity brought her at regular intervals, both of them wearing latex gloves and surgical masks courtesy of Mercy, so they didn't catch flu too.

Normally, Nina quite liked having a minor illness. She could lie on the sofa watching boxed sets and eating food without any nutritional value. But this was a major illness and all Nina could do was vacillate between too hot and too cold on sheets that were starting to stink a little bit.

She hardly slept and hardly stayed awake either but existed in a delirious dream state where Noah and Heathcliff had morphed into one distant, disdainful ex-lover.

Nina couldn't even say how long she was out of action because day and night, hours and minutes, had ceased to have any meaning. She'd later find out that it was Thursday morning, the fifth day of her confinement, when she struggled her way to wakefulness only to wonder if she was still asleep because this had to be a nightmare.

Staring down at her with a pained expression was her mother.

CHAPTER

25

*'Time brought resignation and
a melancholy sweeter than common joy.'*

'Look at you,' Alison O'Kelly said and Nina was
surprised that she didn't whip out a mirror so Nina
could see for herself how dreadful she looked. 'I'm not
surprised you got ill when you never do your coat up and
I doubt you can even remember the last time you had your
five a day.' Her mother pursed her lips. 'Actually, it should
really be ten a day.'

'Just kill me now,' Nina moaned and she really did wish
for a sudden death because her mother was brandishing a
plastic cup full of a virulent green juice at her.

'Stop being so melodramatic and get this down you,' her
mother said. 'It's full of antioxidants. And I have chicken
soup. I was going to heat it up in your microwave but I'll

need to clean it first. It's filthy. Talking of which, you'll feel much better once you've had a shower.'

'I haven't got the energy,' Nina insisted weakly, though if she was being entirely honest, she did feel a little bit better than she had done. She mentally downgraded herself from critical to stable and responding to treatment. But she certainly didn't want to respond to her mother's treatment. 'You should go, I don't want to make you ill.'

'I doubt you're infectious any more and besides, last time I had the flu, you and Paul were both under five and your father was working every hour God sent and I just had to soldier on.'

Alison carried on in that vein for the time it took to choke down the disgusting green juice, which tasted like bong water.

Then on shaky legs and mainly to get away from her mother (who was now loudly questioning Nina's taste in home décor as a thinly veiled attack of Nina's lifestyle choices. 'My goodness, how much do you drink exactly if you need a home bar?'), Nina made it to the bathroom. They didn't actually have a shower but a rubber hose attachment that fitted rather ineptly to the bath taps. Nina was grateful to sit down in the tub as she washed her hair for the first time in a week. It took three shampoos to get all the sweat and dirt out and she didn't have enough oomph to shave her legs, which were so bristly that if she brushed against any manmade fibres she'd set herself on fire.

By the time she emerged from the bathroom in clean

pyjamas – a black-and-pink, satin, polka-dot set gifted to her by Marianne – her mother had her Marigolds on and was headfirst in the microwave.

'Don't even think about going back to bed,' Alison said, her voice muffled. 'I've stripped your sheets but that room needs to air before I make the bed again. I opened the windows but I had half a mind to call in a fumigator.'

'What are you doing here, Mum?' Nina asked in a voice that was creaky both from disuse and a ravaged throat. 'Not that I'm not grateful,' she added, which was a bare-faced lie.

'Your friend Posy called me. Said you'd been delirious for the last few days and that she was worried about you.' Alison's head emerged from the microwave to fix Nina with a hurt look. 'If you'd have called me, I'd have come round immediately. You know I would.'

'You just told me that when you had flu you kept calm and carried on so even if I had called you, you'd have probably accused me of malingering.'

Alison puffed like an angry dragon. 'Well . . .' she said once she could form words again. 'Well, I like that. Go and sit on the sofa and I'll bring you in some soup and then I'll go.'

It was Nina's turn to puff. 'Mum . . .'

'I know when I'm not welcome,' Alison said with a martyred air. Her mother had been saying things with a martyred air for as long as Nina could remember so she didn't feel at all guilty. In fact, she couldn't wait for her mother to leave. Now that her flu had transitioned into a heavy cold and she was able to shuffle from one room to the next, she might as well make the most of being ill. That would involve taking to the sofa for a Netflix binge and texting down to Verity or Posy whenever she needed more coffee or cake. Nina sank gratefully on to the sofa because actually she was quite exhausted from so much activity.

She could hear Alison still banging things about and muttering under her breath in the kitchen. Nina rolled her eyes and it was then that she saw it. Placed neatly by one of the armchairs was her mother's overnight case and Nina's heart sank to the floor, which admittedly could do with a good vacuum.

'Do you want toast with your soup?' Alison called out. 'Is it starve a cold and feed a fever or is it the other way round? I can never remember.'

'Just the soup would be great, thanks,' Nina called back, her voice cracking as she attempted an upper register. Her heart was plummeting again, from guilt and shame this time. Noah really had sussed her out – she was completely lacking in decency and kindness.

She felt even worse when Alison came into the room with the soup and toast, which she'd cut into triangles.

'You know how I feel about carbs,' she said thinly, as she placed the laden tray on the coffee table. 'But you do need to keep your strength up.'

'Mum, your case . . .'

'Try a spoonful. It might need more seasoning,' Alison said, not sitting down but hovering so she could whisk the soup away as soon as Nina gave her the word that it tasted a bit bland.

In fact, it smelt wonderful. The aroma found its way past Nina's blocked sinuses although her taste buds could only tell her that the soup was hot and savoury. 'It tastes great,' she said enthusiastically because she hadn't realised how hungry she was.

Alison perched on the very edge of an armchair and watched while Nina managed to eat half a bowl of the soup and a couple of toast triangles before she had to admit defeat. 'I just don't have much of an appetite,' Nina said sadly. 'That *never* happens.'

'Best thing about being ill.' Alison allowed a tiny smile in Nina's direction. 'You get to lose weight without even trying.'

'Well, it beats having to go to the gym,' Nina said and before her mother could extol the virtues of her regular Zumba classes, she ploughed on. 'Your case . . . you were going to stay the night? Why would you want to do that?'

'Because you were ill,' Alison spelt out. Again. 'That Posy wouldn't have rung me if it wasn't serious and she said your flatmate – Very, what kind of name is Very?'

'It's short for Verity . . .'

'That she'd been on high alert for three nights on the trot and the poor girl was exhausted.'

Nina had a very vague memory of a cool, damp cloth on her hot, sweaty forehead and also of opening bleary eyes after a particularly savage coughing fit to see a shadowy figure standing by her bed with a glass of water and a bottle of Benylin.

'I've been so out of it that it's been hard to know what was real and what was a dream,' Nina said with a pang because now that she was feeling better she remembered what had happened with Noah with painful accuracy. What they'd had together was real. Yes, it had only been three dates and a lot of hanging out and one night spent in wild, sexual abandon (that Nina would still remember when she was on her deathbed), but they meant more to her than all the other dates, all the other relationships, that had fizzled out. Even more than the five years she'd spent with Dan.

Noah had got under her skin, had found his way right to her heart and even though he was gone, he'd left his possessions strewn about her ventricle chambers. His smile, the way he said her name, the half-indulgent, half-exasperated look he'd give her when she was being a brat . . .

'Nina! Nina! You're not listening to a word I'm saying!' Nina was forced to turn her attention back to her mother, who was giving her a look that was all exasperation.

'Sorry, still finding it quite hard to focus,' Nina mumbled.

'I was just saying that this Verity girl is going to spend the night with her boyfriend. Apparently, he's an architect and Posy is with some techy billionaire. You never told me she got married!' Alison finished on an aggrieved note, even though there was no reason why Nina should have told Alison that her boss at 'that bookshop', that her mother had never expressed any interest in, was getting married.

'Yeah, bit of a whirlwind romance. Took everyone by surprise, Posy included,' Nina said and she expected her mother to follow up with some negative observation ('marry in haste, repent at leisure' being an obvious contender) but her mother was too busy digesting this news.

'I hope you're not getting similar notions about that Noah,' was what she did say, rather unbelievably. 'I would not want *that* woman as an in-law.'

'What are you talking about?' Nina demanded and she winced because her headache was back with a pounding vengeance. She doubted it had much to do with the flu and everything to do with her mother who leapt to her feet to put a cool hand on Nina's sweaty forehead.

'Back to bed with you,' Alison decided. 'I'll just go and make it up with fresh bedding. You should have said you were feeling poorly again.'

Even when she was being kind, Alison O'Kelly still found a way to sound like everything was Nina's fault. But ten minutes later when Nina was sliding into bed, the covers cool and crisp, rather than bedraggled and damp with sweat, and Alison stood over her with a glass of water and two more ibuprofen, she was actually relieved that her mother had come round.

She had to be having a relapse, which had addled her brain again. There was no other explanation for it – because Nina couldn't remember the last time she was glad to see her mother.

It was the sound of the door to the flat slamming shut that woke Nina a couple of hours later. She looked at the time on her phone, which was charging on her nightstand. It was gone seven. The shop would be closed now and Verity must have come upstairs.

This time when Nina got out of bed, the covers weren't clammy and her legs did a pretty good job of holding her up as she walked towards the living room. 'Very! I had no idea I'd been so ill. Thanks for being such a Florence Nightingale,' she called out. 'Was I very annoying?'

'Quite annoying, from what I hear,' said her mother and Nina poked her head around the living-room door to confirm that yes, Alison was still on the premises. 'That Verity's gone to spend the night at her boyfriend's.'

'And you're still here,' Nina pointed out in a neutral voice but it was still enough to make her mother's lips tighten.

'Well, I can go . . . I was just going. I'm not one to outstay my welcome,' she said with that well-worn martyred air and there was nothing that Nina wanted more than for her mother to go. Then she'd be on her own. Well enough and lucid enough that all her thoughts would be of Noah and how desperately unhappy she was now that she didn't feel like death.

'You don't have to go,' she found herself saying. 'We could have a sleepover.'

'We're not five, but I can stay, if you want me to. Your father can fend for himself for one night.'

'Great,' Nina said and she tried to sound enthusiastic but she wasn't sure that she succeeded because Alison's lips tightened again. 'Is there any more of that soup going?'

Instead of eating dinner on their laps in the front room

like any normal person, Alison set the tiny table in the kitchen, where Nina and Verity usually dumped their post, keys and stray books. It was really too tiny for two people to sit around it, at right angles, bumping knees and knocking elbows.

Nina found that, again, she could hardly manage a bowl of soup and a piece of toast. Her mother was making tense conversation about her next-door neighbour, Mrs Cortes, who was well into her nineties and had met a younger man at a tea dance at the local community centre ('He's eighty, if he's a day!') and had moved him in and now Mrs Cortes's sons were up in arms at their mother's toy-boy lover.

To be fair, it was quite a riveting topic. 'Do you think they're doing it?' Nina asked.

Her mother's eyes widened. 'Oh, Nina, don't! What if she breaks a hip?'

'Or her fancy man might have an attack of sciatica at a pivotal moment?' Nina suggested and they both giggled.

'Tell you what, I'll get dinner cleared away and then I'll give you a mani-pedi if you like,' Alison offered. Then she paused and Nina braced herself for an implied insult or passive-aggressive dig. 'It's just that I don't have any of my nail kit with me.'

Relief made Nina quite light-headed although that might have been because she'd just stood up far too quickly. 'I've got everything that you could possibly need to do a mani-pedi. Even a fancy foot spa! Come and have a look.'

There were few things that Nina could do right in her

mother's eyes but Alison's hands clasped together in sheer, wordless joy when Nina wheeled her three-tier beauty trolley into the front room. 'All my nail supplies are on the bottom level,' she said. 'I'll go and sort out the foot spa.'

'You'll do no such thing,' Alison exclaimed. 'You're convalescing. I'll do it.'

Fifteen minutes later, Nina's feet were soaking as her fingernails were being buffed and filed and the only criticism that Alison had made was that when she went into the bathroom to retrieve the foot spa from the cupboard under the sink, she couldn't help but notice that the bathroom tiles could do with being regrouted.

Nina quickly steered the conversation to the new gel polishes she'd picked up from the big beauty supply store on Shaftesbury Avenue and this was one thing that she and her mother still had in common. They discussed the new Chanel palettes, that no one had warned Alison that her eyelids would be the first thing to sag as she got older and how much primer she had to use to get her eye make-up to stay on, and if the Olaplex hair conditioning in-salon treatment was really all that it was cracked up to be.

It was a conversation that nourished Nina's soul. Not just because she and Alison hadn't exchanged a single cross word or sniped at each other once. It was also one of the few things that Nina missed about working in a salon; being surrounded by other women who were obsessed with products in the same way that Posy and Verity were obsessed with books.

Nina liked books as much as the next person. More than

the next person, in fact, but she'd come late to a love of reading. She didn't have much to contribute when Posy and Verity were really going for it on the book talk; exchanging titles of much-loved stories from their childhoods or reminiscing about their A-level texts or how they both spent their teen years reading Nancy Mitford and early Jilly Cooper novels.

So to be able to discuss the benefits of a tinted moisturiser over a BB cream or even a CC cream with her mother was, well . . . 'This is really lovely. I can't remember the last time that we got together and managed not to have an argument.'

Nina inwardly cursed herself as soon as she said it because it seemed guaranteed to lead to an argument, but Alison nodded her head in agreement.

'I know,' she said softly as she applied a second coat of deep-red polish to the nails on Nina's right hand. 'Don't take this the wrong way, Nina, but sometimes I think you hate me.'

Maybe it was because she was still weak from the flu and didn't have the energy for a ruckus, but Nina decided not to tense all her muscles and go into fight mode. 'Of course I don't hate you,' she said and she raised her head so she could look her mother in the eye. 'But there are quite a lot of times that I think *you* hate *me*.'

'Don't be silly,' Alison snapped, twisting the top of the nail-varnish bottle shut so violently that Nina was amazed that the bottle didn't shatter. 'I love you very much but you've made it clear what you think of me and my life and that you want no part of it.'

'Well, no, I don't want your life,' Nina said very carefully. 'I want my own life.' Exasperation took over. 'But come on, Mum, the way you brought me up meant that it was hard to see that there was another life out there. That I had options, choices . . .'

Alison had pursed her lips, chin tipped forward. 'There's nothing wrong with wanting to get married and have children.'

'I'm not saying that there is anything wrong with wanting those things but not at twenty! I hadn't done anything, been anywhere.' Nina shook her head. She still hadn't done anything but been on at least a thousand first dates. Still hadn't gone anywhere but on a few mini-breaks and hen weekends.

'But all the women in our family marry young. Have children young. It's tradition,' Alison insisted, even if it was a pretty rubbish tradition that should have been phased out fifty years ago.

It was time for Nina to blow her mother's mind. 'You do realise that the only reason why both Granny and Great-Granny got married so young is because they were knocked up,' she blurted.

'No! Nina!' Alison shook her head, her mouth falling open.

'Of course they were. Haven't you ever done the maths?' Nina watched as her mother narrowed her eyes and did the maths.

'No! Oh my goodness!'

Nina took advantage of her mother's shock to press on.

'I didn't reject *you*, but I have been angry with you. You were so determined that my life should follow one path, your path, when actually I could have stayed on to do A-levels, maybe gone to university. But you wanted me to be exactly the same as you.'

'I wanted you with me, is that so terrible?' Alison asked, patting Nina's knee. 'We used to be best friends but now I feel like I don't know you at all. You don't want me to know you.'

'Oh God, if you knew the real me, you'd be horrified,' Nina exclaimed, Noah's words echoing in her head as they had done ever since he'd thrown them at her.

Alison reached out to brush the back of her hand against her daughter's cheek.

'You look so sad, darling. Not just today. When I see you, I think that you don't look that happy for someone who's meant to be living her best life.'

'But it's not my best life,' Nina said and she was near to tears, determined to blame it on the flu or on the gentleness of Alison's unaccustomed touch. 'I feel like I'm lost. That for all my wanting to be wild and free, I'm as trapped as I ever was. My life feels so small, so dull.'

'It's not dull at all! You've got an interesting job with lovely friends and you live in central London.' If Alison continued to list all of Nina's achievements then this wasn't going to take very long. 'And you're brave, Nina. You look the way you want, you live the way you want and I might not say it very often, but I am proud of you and I love you very much.'

Nina was full-on big ugly crying by now. 'I love you too,' she sobbed.

'You are a silly girl,' Alison said in a voice that was suddenly hoarse as if the tears might be contagious. 'Come here!'

Her mother was far too bony to be a good cuddler but Nina was still happy to snuggle into her shoulder so what Alison said next sounded muffled: 'I have to tell you, Nina, I was always a bit envious of your freedom. And I never thought I'd enjoy having a job, but I do! I bloody love it!'

Nina struggled to free herself. 'If you love having a job, then can you even imagine how good it's going to feel when you let yourself eat carbs again?'

'That's never going to happen!' Alison pretended to cuff her. Nina was starting to wonder if her real mother had been abducted by aliens and replaced with a new and improved model. Or was she taking HRT or Prozac or some other tablet that had chilled her out in ways that she'd never been chilled out before?

But then Alison's smile disappeared and she gave Nina a look. It was a look that Nina knew only too well. A look that asked, 'How did I manage to spawn a creature like you?' and was unable to come up with a satisfactory answer.

'What?' Nina asked defensively. 'What have I done *now*?'

'You tell me,' Alison replied. She shook her head as if she were trying to rid herself of an unpleasant mental image. 'What on *earth* is going on with you and that Harewood boy?'

'What? Who? How? I mean – I don't know what you mean,' she finished lamely.

'I've had years of practice and I can tell when you're lying,' her mother said though Nina was sure she hadn't twitched or scratched her nose or displayed any other tells. 'Besides, Paul said that he was sure it was the Harewood boy—'

'His name is Noah—'

'—who picked you up from little Ellie's birthday party,' her mother continued. 'And then Posy was telling me that you'd been seeing that Hare . . . Noah or whatever his name is, that he took you away, *overnight*, and when you got back the two of you were broken up and you were at death's door!'

'He didn't make me ill. Not really,' Nina tried to explain though a small part of her maintained that she'd have probably got away with a bad cold if the pain of having her heart broken hadn't upgraded it to flu. 'We went for a walk on open moorland and I wasn't wearing a proper waterproof coat.'

'Who goes for a walk on open moorland?' Alison was horrified. 'Honestly, that family! I expect he's a vegan like that mother of his.'

'He's not a vegan, he's actually really lovely,' Nina said then burst into tears again.

CHAPTER

26

*'If you ever looked at me once with what
I know is in you, I would be your slave.'*

O n Monday morning, Nina decided that she was well
enough to leave her quarters and re-enter the world
of work.

She'd managed to wolf down a huge curry the night
before so she was obviously on the mend, even if she still
felt terrible. But now it was only an emotional kind of
terrible. She was mourning the loss of Noah and also the
fact that she'd gone down two whole cup sizes.

'No, I'm not wearing that horrible grey T-shirt,' Nina
announced to Posy as she barrelled down the stairs from the
flat to find Posy standing in the hall sorting through the post.
'I currently don't have the boobs to fill it out. But on the
bright side, I haven't been able to get in this dress for *years*.'

Nina was wearing a tightly fitted black crepe dress with a black velvet Peter Pan collar – sombre to match her mood – though she was trying to put a brave face on things.

Posy squinched up all her features in distress. Nina came to a halt on the third step from the bottom with her hands on her hips.

'Honestly, Posy, the Happy Ever After T-shirt is *hanging* off me,' she said plaintively.

'It's not that.' Posy peered up at Nina, still looking mighty uncomfortable. 'I really think you should still be convalescing.' She made shooing motions with her hands. 'Back to bed with you.'

Nina carried on down the stairs. 'I'm going stir crazy up there. You don't even want to know how many old episodes of *Masterchef* I've watched this weekend.'

'We can absolutely manage without you,' Verity interrupted, poking her head round the office door. 'I told you not to bother coming downstairs if you didn't feel up to it.'

'But I do feel up to it and you could hardly manage without me this weekend,' Nina reminded them, because her back-to-back watching of *Masterchef* had been constantly interrupted by people texting Nina to ask about books that she'd put to one side for certain customers or to complain that the till drawer was sticking again and what was the special trick for hitting Bertha and countless other enquiries. 'I'm not going to do any heavy lifting, but I can sit behind the till and take money. It's not exactly brain surgery, is it? Posy! Get out of my way!'

Nina had to squeeze past a motionless Posy, who seemed

to be doing her best to block Nina's passage through to the shop. 'We're not even opening this morning!' Posy squeaked, grabbing hold of Nina's sleeve. 'So you might as well go upstairs and put your feet up.'

'Posy! Don't manhandle the vintage,' Nina said crossly. She'd never had to work so hard to actually *work* before. 'Why aren't you opening this morning? Are you doing a stock-take? Why? We've never done one of those before, so why bother now?'

'It's not a stock-take,' Verity said. 'It's a er, staff meeting.'

'Shut up!' Posy hissed at her and if Nina had been a dog her hackles would have risen. As it was, a little shiver raced its way down her spine.

'A staff meeting?' she queried suspiciously. 'A staff meeting that I'm not invited to? Oh my God, you're all going to discuss sacking me!'

'Who's sacking you? That would be madness. No one knew how anything in the shop worked while you were on your sickbed.' Now it was Tom's turn to stick his head around the door. 'Are we starting anytime soon? Noah's here now and I've finished my breakfast panini so we really should get on with it.'

At the mention of Noah, Nina's stomach lurched so violently that for a moment she wondered if she was relapsing and also if last night's curry was about to put in an encore performance.

'Noah . . .' Nina echoed tremulously, one hand to her heart, which had started beating erratically, even though it was meant to be out of order for the foreseeable future.

During her confinement, Nina had come to realise that the tragic, passionate love she'd always craved wasn't everything it was cracked up to be. In reality, it was exhausting (as everyone had warned her) and added to that, it was soul-destroying and heart-breaking and what good was a heart that didn't work?

More than that, she'd *ached* for Noah and had played back his every smile, every kind, sweet and funny thing he'd said to her, every kiss, until the memories were worn thin. But the memory of the fight they'd had, of how Noah had ripped away the mask Nina wore to expose the miserable, mean-spirited girl behind it, still shone bright. And yet, here he was, just a few metres away when Nina had been half tormented/half comforted by the fact that she'd never have to see him again.

'Yes, Noah,' Posy whispered. 'Why do you think I've been trying to persuade you back upstairs? Also, I did tell him that you'd be a no-show.'

'He doesn't want to see me?' Nina queried in a hurt voice. She couldn't blame Noah for never wanting to clap eyes on her again, but that didn't mean she had to be happy about it.

'He didn't say that he *didn't* want to see you, but he's been so *sad* since he got back from taking you on that disastrous road trip.' Posy shrugged helplessly. 'And actually now that you are feeling better, what did happen with you and Noah? Did you really break his heart? He has the look of a man whose world has crumbled.'

'What happened is between me and Noah,' Nina said

because she was ashamed enough of her behaviour without having Posy on her case.

No, she wouldn't hide. She was going to style it out, so she brushed past Posy, her nose in the air, sweeping into the shop with a haughty expression. Noah's heart was no concern of hers because she was a badass bitch who ate men for breakfast. Then she came stumbling to a halt.

Noah was standing by the rolling ladder, his attention fixed on the screen of his iPad. He was wearing the navy-blue suit that he'd worn on his first day at Happy Ever After, a white shirt and navy-blue tie. He looked so corporate, so smart – even his unruly cowlick of hair that would never lie flat had been tamed into submission – that Nina wondered what he'd ever seen in her.

Then Noah looked up to look at Nina looking at him and his face seemed to draw in on itself, eyebrows pulling together, mouth puckering into an awkward shape, his body shrinking back as if the sight of her was a very unexpected, unpleasant surprise.

Nina wanted to beg for forgiveness but instead found a reserve of strength from deep, deep within and plonked herself down on one of the sofas with what she hoped was a nonchalant grace. 'Oh, hi Noah,' she trilled, like them seeing each other again was absolutely not a big deal at all.

Noah muttered something that might have been 'Hi.' Or could just as easily have been 'I hate you,' but then Posy bustled in with Verity bringing up the rear.

'OK, we're going to keep this civilised and on a purely

business footing, aren't we?' Posy asked anxiously as she perched on the arm of the sofa that Nina was determinedly lounging on.

'Of course,' Nina scoffed, though actually she didn't know what Noah was doing here, all suited and booted, and looking like he wished he were anywhere else, even if it involved being waterboarded.

'This is strictly professional,' Noah said huffily and Nina had missed his huffy voice, but she masked that by rolling her eyes at Tom sitting on the sofa opposite, who gave Nina one of his stern looks.

'Let's just get this over with,' Tom mouthed at Nina as Verity asked Noah if he needed 'a flipchart? We've found flipcharts very effective in the past.'

'I don't need a flipchart,' Noah said gravely. 'And I'll be emailing my report to you all afterwards on your new Happy Ever After email addresses as part of Happy Ever After's new digital network. I've also set you up with a shop WhatsUpp account. It's much more efficient than Post-it notes and writing things on the backs of envelopes.'

Posy gave a low-level grumble. 'Post-it notes are quite efficient.'

'Yes, but a group email and WhatsUpp account are *more* efficient,' Noah said and he was in full proper grown-up mode this morning; not prepared to take any nonsense. Much like the time he'd stood up to the awful Peter at Ye Olde Medieval Laser Tag, Nina remembered with grudging fondness, as Noah gave a short speech about how interesting it had been to spend time at Happy Ever After. Also, that he had lots of suggestions on how they could work smarter and grow the business.

'They are just suggestions,' he concluded with a tiny smile that didn't reach his eyes. 'For instance, you'd have a much better flow to the shop if you knocked through . . .'

'No! Not another word,' Posy yelped, jumping up so she could form a one-woman human shield against the new-releases shelves as if she suspected that Noah had a bulldozer waiting in the mews. 'I'm not knocking through. End of.'

'I suspected as much, but even you have to agree that you can't continue with only one till, especially one that you have to thump at least once every ten minutes,' Noah pointed out.

'You *have* to agree, Posy,' Verity chimed in. 'When we're really busy, Bertha has a meltdown so the queue ends up stretching all the way back to the door and then new customers can't even come in.'

'But Bertha has been here forever,' Posy cried. Nina and Tom exchanged looks. It was hard to understand why Posy had agreed to Noah analysing her business if she was going to have conniptions at each one of his suggestions.

'Which is why you can keep Bertha for cash transactions, though she really needs to be serviced, and you can take card payments, even PayPal or Apple Pay, on the shop floor if you give the staff iPads,' Noah said smoothly, as if he was more sure of himself now that it really was strictly profes-sional. 'Then you can email the customer their receipt and add them to the mailing list at the same time.'

'But . . . bagging up . . . complimentary bookmarks . . .' Posy moaned.

'All the new display cabinets have drawers in them, we could stash bags and bookmarks in there,' Tom supplied in a weary voice like this was all too boring for words.

Although it wasn't boring. Not exactly. 'Will we really be getting iPads?' Nina asked and everyone glared at her for the interruption. Everyone, but especially Noah – his glare was like the sharpest knife cutting Nina to the quick.

'Once you're digitised then ordering stock, taking care of inventory and even doing the accounts will be so much easier. Posy and Verity will be freed up to work on promotions and events as you talked about doing when you were planning the relaunch.'

Nina couldn't help but feel slighted because hadn't she been the one who'd kept badgering Posy about doing more events? Then along comes Noah with his navy-blue suits and his business analytics and now Posy was nodding her head eagerly and even Verity wasn't looking unduly alarmed at the prospect of having to leave the back office on occasion.

Nina sighed and looked to Tom for solidarity but Noah had now reached the Tom part of his report and Tom was hanging onto his every word. Big whoop. They all knew that Tom was one of the main reasons why they had so many repeat lady customers of a certain age.

'So Tom will take over the shop Twitter account from today,' intoned Noah. Say *what*?!

It was hard not to flail her limbs at the sheer unfairness

of it all. Hadn't Nina taken control of the shop's social media? Grown their Instagram followers? Asked Sam repeatedly to show her how to update the shop website? She had! Now Tom was going to take the Twitter from her just because he'd apparently posted a couple of amusing tweets while Nina had been upstairs hovering between life and death.

'Judas,' she mouthed at Tom, who shrugged. 'I hate you.'

'And then we come to Nina,' Noah said thinly and she'd been trying to avoid looking at Noah but now he had her full attention. It was hard to believe that this cold, remote man in bespoke navy-blue suiting had held her while she slept. 'Where to even start? Maybe with her lack of professional boundaries.'

It turned out that all of Nina's fears about what Noah had been tapping into his iPad were entirely founded. He had noted every single time that she'd given Posy and Verity backchat, or talked about their sex lives or her own sex life, read out the dirty bits in books when there was a queue waiting to pay, eaten food while she was handling the books or serving customers. The list went on and on.

Obviously, Nina was biased in her own favour but even she would have given herself the sack. She was a *terrible* employee.

Nina hoped he was getting to the end of his long list of her moral and professional failings. Then they could move swiftly on to Posy sacking her and Nina going upstairs to clear her stuff out of the flat – oh God, being sacked meant being evicted too. She'd never dreamed that he would get his revenge in such a petty way though.

'And she behaves like this because . . . she's bored,' Noah said. 'You don't use her talents enough. She takes it upon herself to create the most wonderful window displays,' Noah continued and Nina looked around the room to see if he was talking about some other Nina, because he couldn't be talking about her. 'She's so creative that she even designed the Happy Ever After logo but she told you her friend Claude had done it. She didn't think you'd take the design seriously if you'd known that it was her own work.'

'Oh, Nina!' Posy said, sounding much crosser than when Noah had been extolling the virtues of knocking through. 'Why didn't you say?'

For precisely the reason that Noah had given. And Nina hadn't even told Noah about the logo; the only person who could have mentioned it was Marianne when she'd been left alone with Noah while Nina was getting tattooed.

'There was never a good time,' Nina said weakly.

'And look what Nina's done with the shop Instagram.' Noah held up his iPad. 'She added two thousand followers in less than two weeks. Send her on a course so she can build on her skills, learn to code and use CMS, then she can take sole responsibility for the Happy Ever After website. You really need to start focusing on your web revenue stream anyway.'

Once again, Nina hardly knew where to look. How could it be that Noah was saying these things about her when he hated her, and with good reason too?

'So, you're saying that Nina shouldn't work in the shop any more because she behaves in a completely unprofessional manner?' Verity clarified. 'Well, no! That doesn't work for me. Happy Ever After would be so dull without Nina. No offence, Posy.'

'None taken,' Posy said. She'd been lolling back against the counter but now she hurried back to Nina's sofa. 'A day without Nina making completely unacceptable personal remarks is like a day without sunshine.'

'I couldn't get through a working day without Nina providing a bit of light relief and saving me from some of the more handsy customers,' Tom added. 'You can't hide her away in the back office doing boring techy stuff.'

All this support was quite unexpected and Nina felt the tell-tale throbbing of her tear ducts because she was off her game and still getting over flu and her workmates loved her. They really loved her. And Noah . . .

'I agree. The shop would descend into chaos without Nina,' he said and now Nina noticed that he'd lost the puckered, frigid cast to his face. That he was looking at her now but would then quickly avert his eyes as if he didn't have the courage to gaze at her for longer than a few seconds. 'Nina has the back-cover blurb for pretty much every book in the shop memorised, along with the reading preferences for all your regular customers. She's the only person who knows exactly the right spot to thump Bertha when she's playing up and she can charm a queue of grumpy customers waiting to pay into actually apologising for being grumpy. Nina is the heart and soul of Happy Ever After.'

'Oh,' Nina said. She couldn't say much more than that so she said it again. 'Oh . . .'

'I know this because it's my job to analyse businesses,' Noah said. He blinked. Then put down his iPad on the shelf behind him. There was silence, expectant, almost pregnant with promise. Noah smiled. It was a crooked, broken smile, which was a match for Nina's crooked, broken heart. 'It's my job, you see, to find solutions to problems and I've realised that loving you is only a problem if I make it into one.'

'What?' Posy said. 'What is he going on about?'

'Shut up,' Verity hissed at her.

'You will never know how many times I was all set to tell you about Paul,' Nina said with a throat that suddenly felt like she'd swallowed an elephant. Just saying her brother's name punctured the sweet joy that had swelled inside her when Noah had said that he loved her. 'But when we were together, it was so special that I didn't want to do anything to break the spell. Then the longer I kept it secret, the harder it became to tell you because I knew that once the truth was out, it would ruin everything. I handled the situation terribly but it wasn't meant maliciously. You have to believe me.'

'I do believe you,' Noah said and surely he wouldn't be looking at her like that, softly and tenderly, if he still thought she was a cruel, mean-spirited witch.

'And for what it's worth, Paul is truly sorry, sickened even, by what he did to you at school.'

'Well. That's something. Look, I can't see your brother becoming my best friend, but I'll never be able to let go of the past, if I don't let go of my resentment,' Noah said.

'I mean, there are parents who manage to forgive the people who've killed their children, even when they haven't shown any remorse. And it's not like Paul's murdered anyone, has he?'

'He really hasn't and honestly, if you play it right I reckon you'll get free plumbing for the rest of your life,' Nina said, then her expression sobered. 'But I don't expect you to act like nothing had ever gone down between you two, because it did and it's important not to brush that aside. All I'm asking is that you let him take you out for one really hideously awkward drink so he can apologise in person.'

Noah nodded. 'I could do that,' he said and his face, which had unscrunched itself, scrunched up again. 'I didn't mean it when I said you were incapable of love.'

'But you were right in a way,' she said with a sob. 'I think I've always been afraid of falling in love because I'm afraid of being trapped again, but when I'm with you, I don't feel trapped at all.' Nina leant forwards. 'After you found out what I'd done, all the deceit, all the lying which, again, I really am so very sorry about, I was convinced that you hated me. And the worst thing was that I couldn't blame you for hating me. I hated me! If I'd thought I could change your mind, I would have given it my all. Actually, what did change your mind?'

'I don't like to resort to cliché, but my God, could you two get a room?' Tom sniped even though no one was asking him to stay and watch.

'Shut up!' Posy and Verity snapped in unison but Nina

hardly heard them, she only had ears and eyes for Noah, who took a step forward.

'Well, I've spent a week reading up all the many, many notes I'd written about you, and incidentally, you made the two weeks I spent analysing Happy Ever After the most entertaining two weeks of my career. So even though I was very angry with you, I began to miss you.' Noah let out a shaky breath.

'I missed you too,' Nina admitted. 'I missed you so much that it hurt.'

'You made me realise that actually I'm not the king of compartmentalisation. In fact, since we met, I haven't stopped thinking about you, looking forward to spending time together, and then I had to spend nine days without you. Knowing that you had flu, which was all my fault because I dragged you on an enforced march across open moorland.' Noah's eyes had never looked so green and fathomless. 'People can die from the flu, you know.'

'It was my fault though for not having a sensible all-weather coat,' was a sentence that Nina had never imagined that she'd utter. 'All that time that I wanted passion and drama and a love that knew no bounds, but that wasn't real. Cathy and Heathcliff aren't real. But we are, we *were* real.'

'And we could be again, couldn't we?' Noah asked, hope putting colour in his cheeks and a hitch in his voice.

Over the last few weeks, Nina had had lots of time to contemplate just how lacking in bravery she was. She hadn't ziplined or kayaked. She couldn't go more than three rungs on the rolling ladder without someone standing underneath to cushion her if she fell. She might want adventure, but there was plenty of evidence to suggest that she was allergic to adrenalin. And for all her longing for a *coup de foudre*, she'd dated a succession of losers, safe in the knowledge that none of them would ever steal her heart.

She was a coward.

'Nina . . .' Noah faltered. He took a step back. 'Do you think we could start again?'

'No,' she said. 'I don't want to start again.'

There was a shocked intake of collective breath from their audience. 'Harsh,' Posy muttered. 'So harsh.'

'Fine,' Noah said. He turned away as if he couldn't bear to look at her and picked up his iPad. 'Well, at least I know where I stand now.'

No, Nina would never jump from aeroplanes or hurl herself off bridges attached to a rubber rope. And she was never going for another walk across open moorland, because she wasn't that kind of brave.

She was another kind of brave.

'I don't want to start again . . .'

Noah shut his eyes. 'You already said that.'

'. . . I want to pick up right where we left off,' Nina said and she stood up and the eight steps that she took to Noah were the bravest steps that anyone had ever taken, even people who liked to walk on hot coals. 'Whatever our souls are made of, yours and mine are the same.'

Then she kissed him or maybe Noah kissed her. Either way, they were kissing and Nina's arms no longer ached because they were holding him and her lips were no longer dull because Noah's mouth had brought them back to life. And Nina's heart . . . Oh, her heart! It was no longer broken and empty but full of love.

Eventually, when lack of oxygen started to become an issue, they broke apart to the sound of applause from Posy and Verity, and Tom saying in scandalised tones, 'I'm writing you up in the sexual harassment book, Nina, for flagrant and public displays of affection.'

'That was so romantic,' Posy said rapturously.

'And I loved it when you quoted *Wuthering Heights*,' Verity added. She stood up. 'Now are we done here because it's gone eleven and we really should open up the shop?'

'Stick a fork in me, I'm done,' Nina declared and she swooned a little but it was wasted on Noah because he'd already picked up his precious iPad again.

'Almost done,' he said, looking at his screen and Nina didn't know how she could go from wanting to kiss him to wanting to hit him. 'Just one more suggestion. Or more of an order really, Posy. You'll have to give Nina a six-month sabbatical starting in May because we're going to road trip across the States.'

It was perfect, even down to the gobsmacked look on Posy's face. It just needed one more act of bravery from Nina.

She took the iPad out of Noah's hands. Had a good mind to throw it a great distance, but instead she placed it carefully on the nearest flat surface. Then she took a deep breath, took Noah's hands, and her heart was pounding but when she looked up and saw the tender look on his face that she thought she'd never see again, she no longer needed to be brave. It was actually the easiest thing in the world.

'I absolutely love you,' Nina said. 'And when I'm in, I'm all in. Is that going to be a problem?'

'If it is a problem then I don't want to find a solution to it,' Noah said and he took Nina in his arms again.

By now, Verity had flipped the shop sign to open and the first customers were streaming in. Posy was muttering about the threat of knocking through like she wasn't going to get over it any time soon, Tom was tutting furiously as he stepped around Nina and Noah and Verity was wondering aloud if anyone planned to do any work that morning.

But neither Nina nor Noah took any notice. They only had eyes for each other.

'We're going to end up getting matching tattoos, aren't we?' Noah asked in a good-humoured but resigned voice between kisses. 'Some appropriate quote from *Wuthering Heights*?'

'You can count on it,' Nina assured him. 'I've already got it narrowed down to three possible contenders. But you have to be certain. I mean, tattoos are forever.'

'Forever isn't nearly long enough,' Noah said and even though all three of Nina's colleagues were now moaning at her to do some work, she ignored them and, reaching up on her tiptoes, pressed a heartfelt kiss to Noah's lips.

After all, what better place to pledge undying love to each other than in a shop called Happy Ever After?

Acknowledgements

Thanks to my wonderful agent, Rebecca Ritchie, though the word 'wonderful' doesn't really do her justice, and Hélène Ferey, Jennifer Custer and all at AM Heath.

Also, many slightly awkward hugs to Martha Ashby, my editor, for always knowing what I'm trying to do with a book even if I haven't realised it myself and thanks to Jaime Frost, Emma Pickard and all the team at HarperCollins.

Look out for Annie's
next book

UNDER
the MISTLETOE
at the
LONELY HEARTS
BOOKSHOP

Coming
autumn 2018

BECOME A
VINTAGE QUEEN

Get Nina's retro glam look from these five websites.

www.collectif.co.uk
Reproduction vintage inspired fashion from
perfect little black dresses to leopard print cardigans
and all things Hollywood glam.

www.freddiesofpinewood.co.uk
Purveyors of vintage-style denim and casualwear
and the place where Nina got her Land Girl-style dungarees.

www.scarletragevintage.com
There are many places online to buy good quality
(and not so good quality) vintage, but my favourite
is Scarlet Rage with lovingly sourced vintage fashion
from the 1920s through to the 1960s.

www.rocketoriginals.co.uk
While Nina might prefer her shoes skyscraper high, other
vintage girls head for Rocket Original for shoes reproduced
from genuine vintage designs, including saddle shoes and the
most wonderful wedge sandals you ever did see.

www.whatkatiedid.com
Even the most dedicated vintage shopper might baulk
at buying second hand undies but there's no need
thanks to What Katie Did and its beautiful vintage-
inspired lingerie and hosiery. From bullet bras
to seamed stockings, they have it all.

TOXIC ROMANTIC HEROES

Passionate on the page,
you'd block them in real life...

1. Heathcliff from *Wuthering Heights*

Yes, he can brood like no other but he's the kind
of emotionally manipulative charmer that would have
your friends calling an intervention.

2. Darcy from *Pride & Prejudice*

'I must tell you how ardently I love and admire...'
Yeah, yeah, jog on, Haughty McHaughtyface.

3. Rupert Campbell-Black from *Riders*

Kind of loses his brash appeal when you do a google search
to find out the real-life inspiration behind Jilly Cooper's
politically incorrect shagger extraordinaire.
(Google at your peril!)

4. Mr Rochester from *Jane Eyre*

Reader, I didn't marry him because, ugh, issues much?

5. James Bond

In real-life the super sleuth would be
up on sexual harassment charges faster than
he could shake a martini.

If you enjoyed this,
why not read the first
two books from

ANNIE DARLING

HAPPY EVER AFTER –

where true love is only

a page away...